SOPHIE

JURASSIC BARK

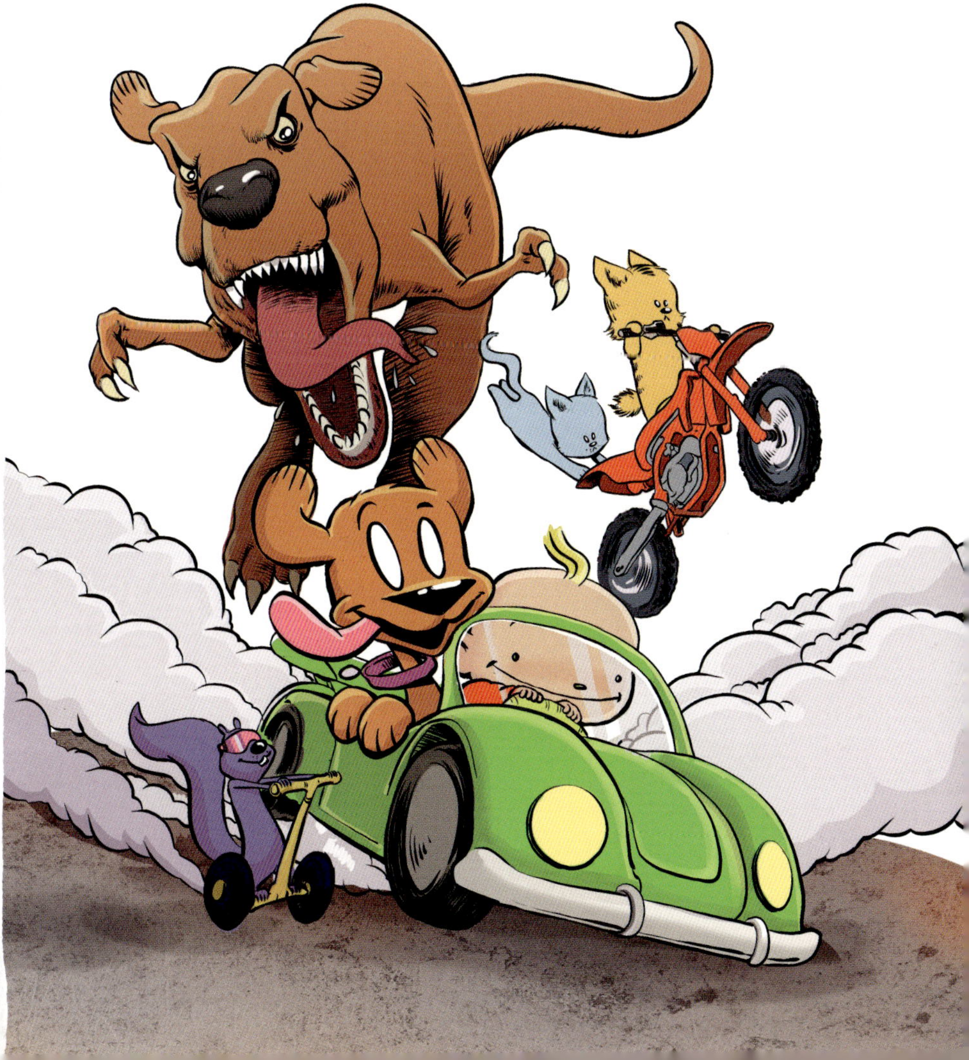

Text and art copyright © 2024 by Brian Anderson

All rights reserved. No part of this book may be reproduced, distributed, or transmitted in any form or by any means, mechanical or electronic, including scanning, photocopying, recording, uploading, or downloading, without written permission of the publisher, except by a reviewer who may quote brief passages in a review.
Permission requests should be directed to the publisher at the address below.
Marble Press LLC, 2260 Hanover Street, Palo Alto, CA 94306
www.MarblePress.com

MARBLE PRESS

The Marble Press name and logo are trademarks of Marble Press LLC.

ISBN: 978-1-958325-29-2 (hardcover)
ISBN: 978-1-958325-14-8 (paperback)
ISBN: 978-1-958325-27-8 (ebook)

Library of Congress Control Number: 2024934902

Any references to historical events, real people, or real places are used fictitiously. Names, characters, and places are products of the author's imagination.

First Edition: October 2024
Edited by Michael Green
Color by Roland Pilcz
Art direction and design by Susan Szecsi

Printed in China
10 9 8 7 6 5 4 3 2 1

SOPHIE

JURASSIC BARK

Do we have time for the drive-thru?

BRIAN ANDERSON

MARBLE PRESS

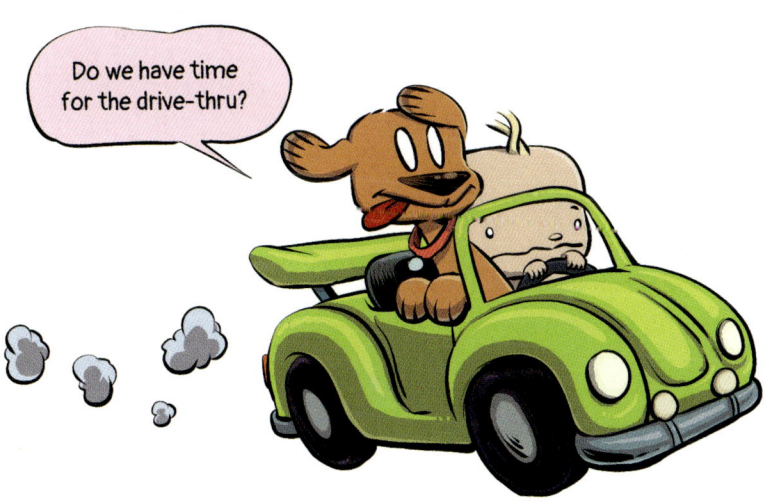

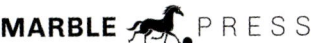

For Sophie, who proved angels have paws.

— B. A.

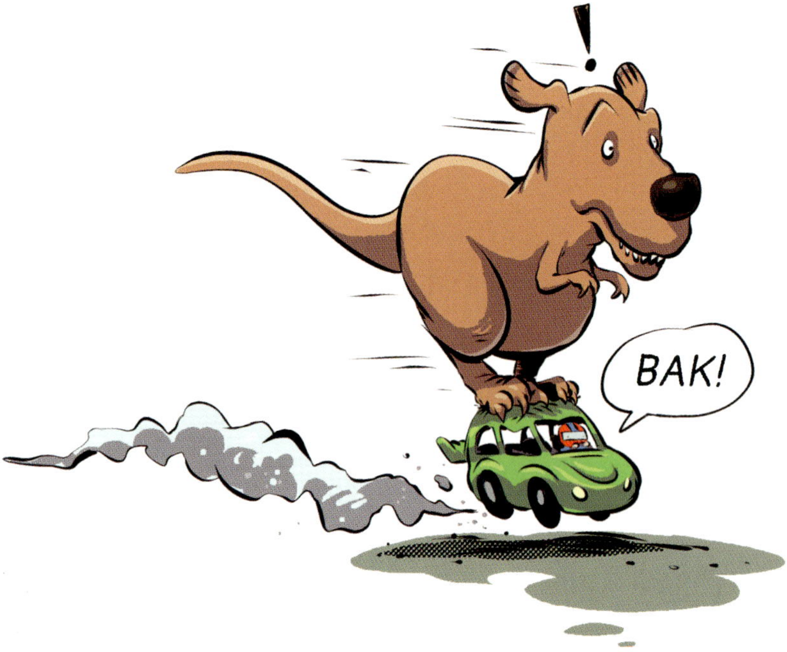
!
BAK!

CONTENTS

Introduction
-6-

1. The End of the World
-9-

2. The Temple of the Lost Cookie
-33-

3. Strange Crib Fellows
-53-

4. Time-Traveling Cats
-81-

5. Commander Doug vs. the Labradorian
-93-

6. Jurassic Bark
-105-

7. The Binky Bandit
-121-

8. The Canine Crusader
-143-

9. The Adorable Doom
-157-

10. Claws Encounters
-175-

Meet the Characters
-214-

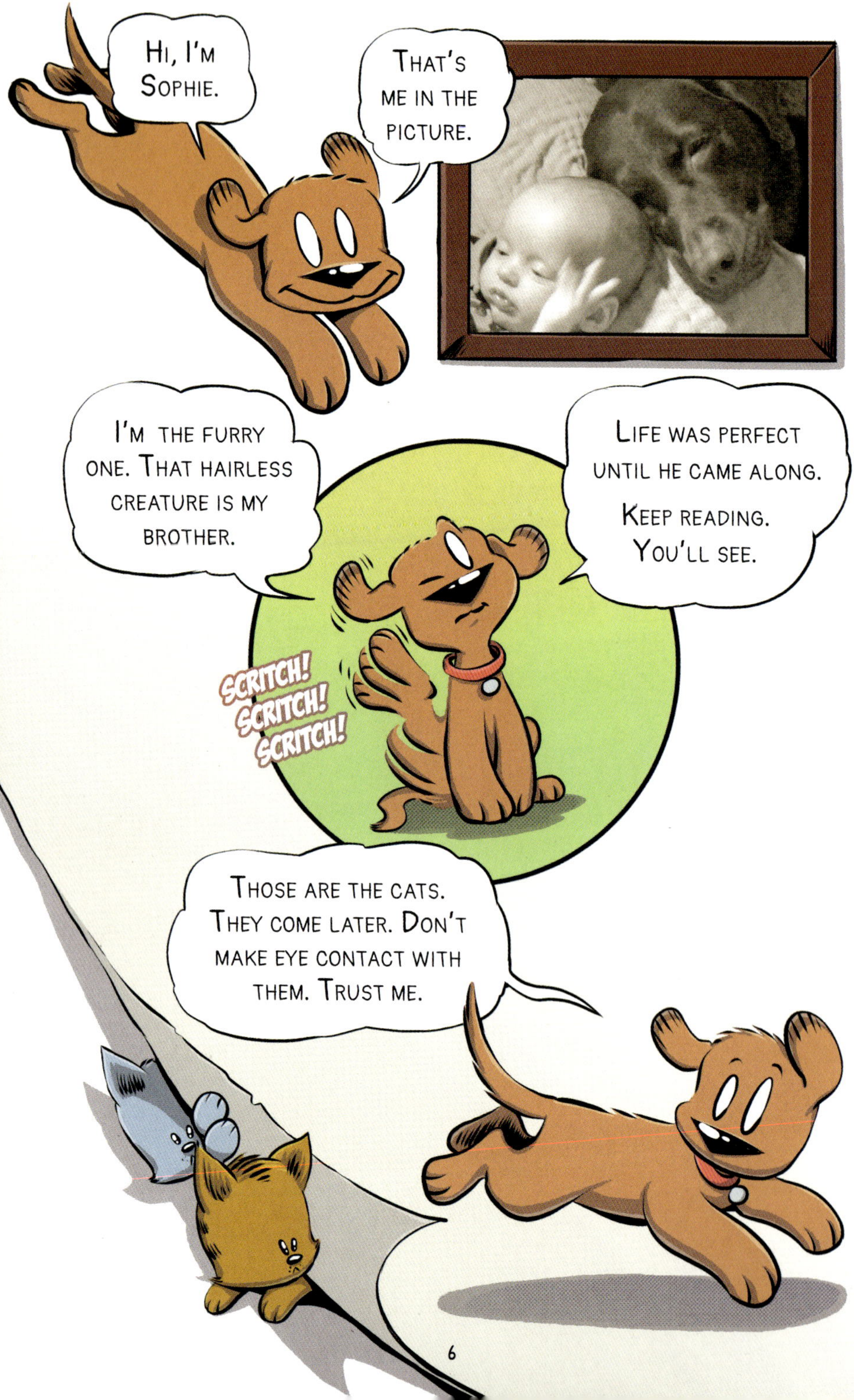
HI, I'M SOPHIE.
THAT'S ME IN THE PICTURE.
I'M THE FURRY ONE. THAT HAIRLESS CREATURE IS MY BROTHER.
LIFE WAS PERFECT UNTIL HE CAME ALONG.
KEEP READING. YOU'LL SEE.
SCRITCH! SCRITCH! SCRITCH!
THOSE ARE THE CATS. THEY COME LATER. DON'T MAKE EYE CONTACT WITH THEM. TRUST ME.

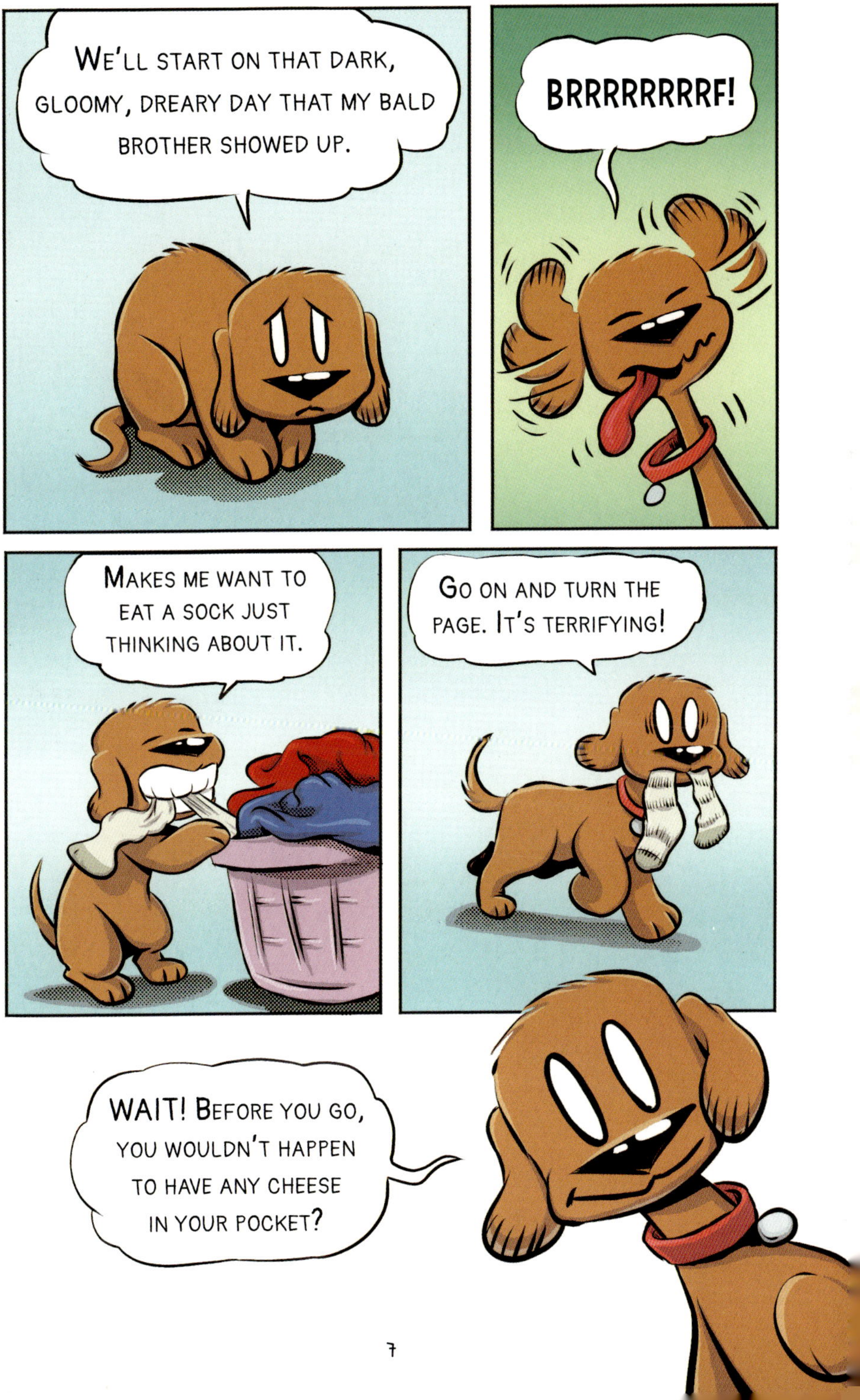
WE'LL START ON THAT DARK, GLOOMY, DREARY DAY THAT MY BALD BROTHER SHOWED UP.
BRRRRRRRRF!
MAKES ME WANT TO EAT A SOCK JUST THINKING ABOUT IT.
GO ON AND TURN THE PAGE. IT'S TERRIFYING!
WAIT! BEFORE YOU GO, YOU WOULDN'T HAPPEN TO HAVE ANY CHEESE IN YOUR POCKET?

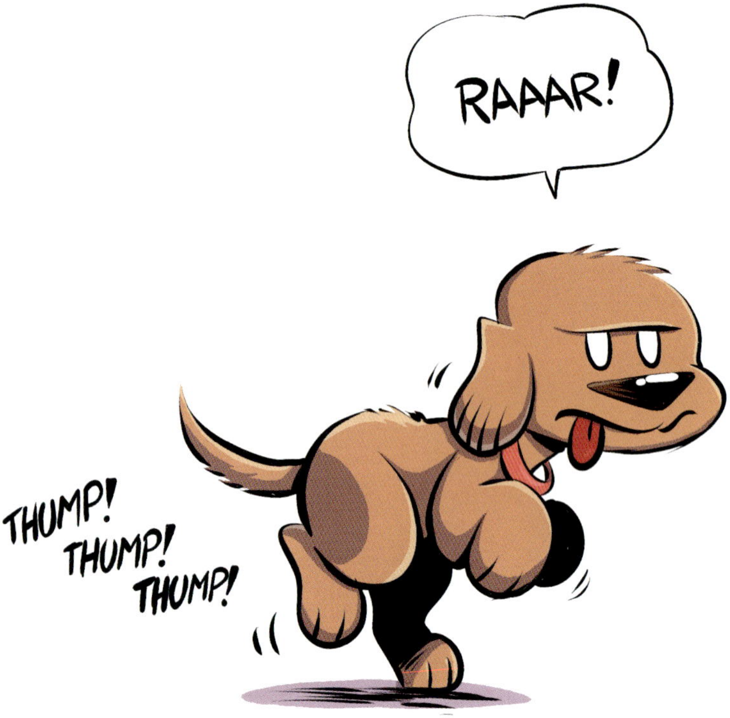
RAAAR!
THUMP! THUMP! THUMP!

CHAPTER 1

THE END OF THE WORLD

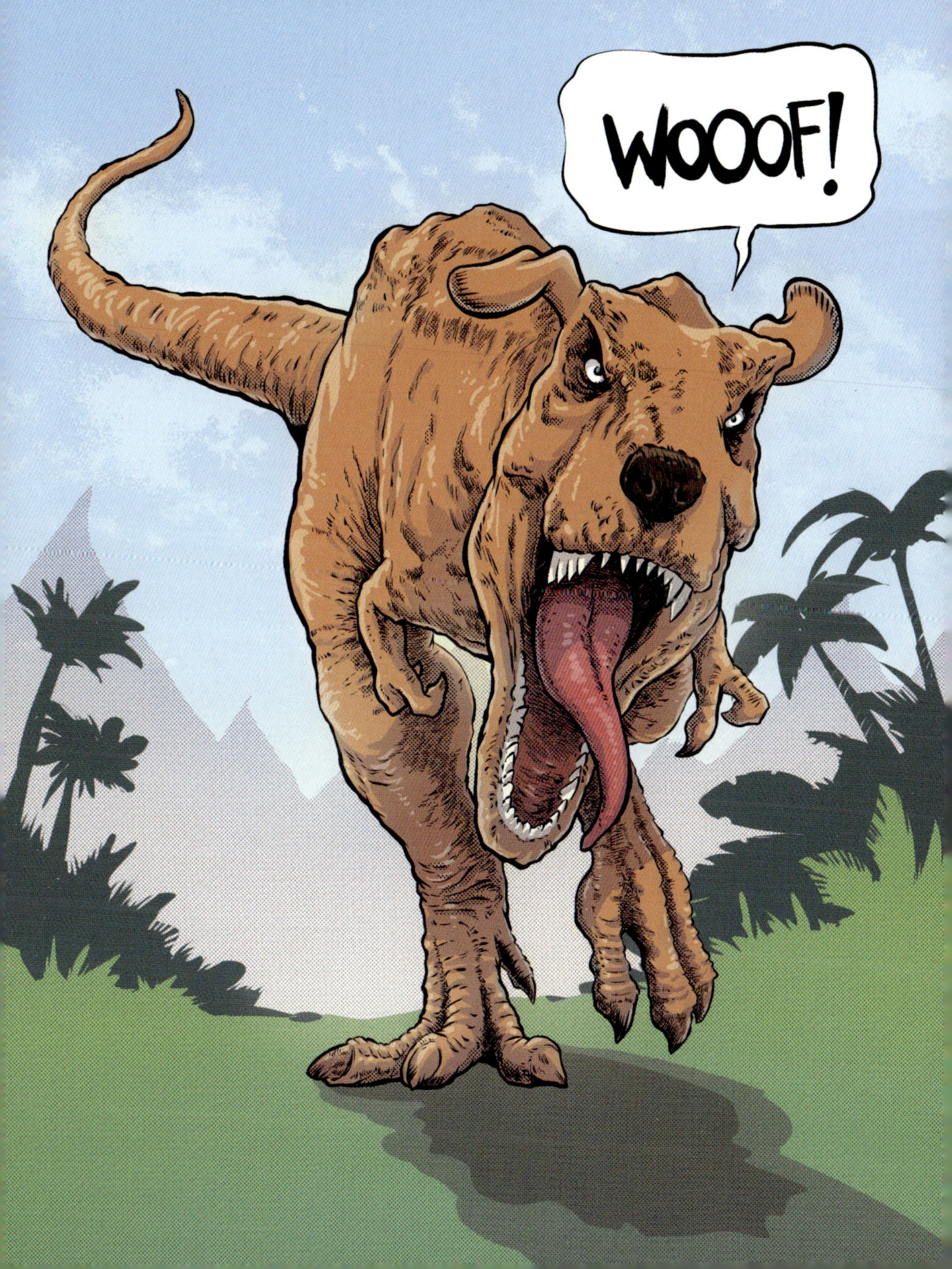
WOOOF!

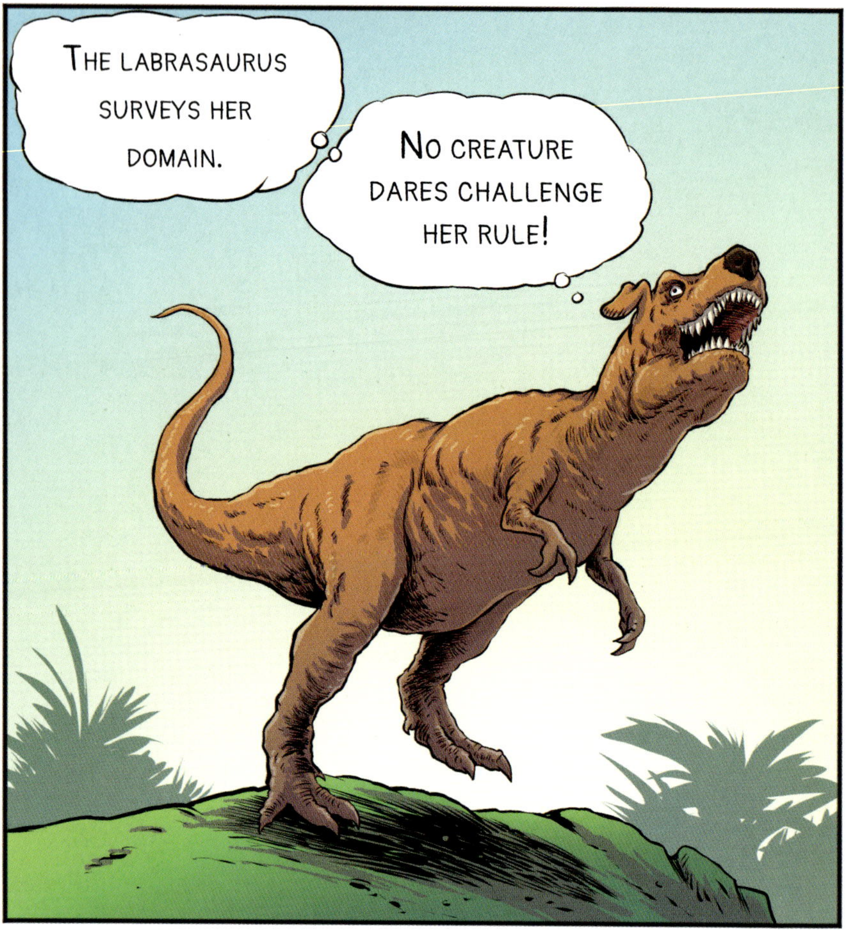
THE LABRASAURUS SURVEYS HER DOMAIN.
NO CREATURE DARES CHALLENGE HER RULE!

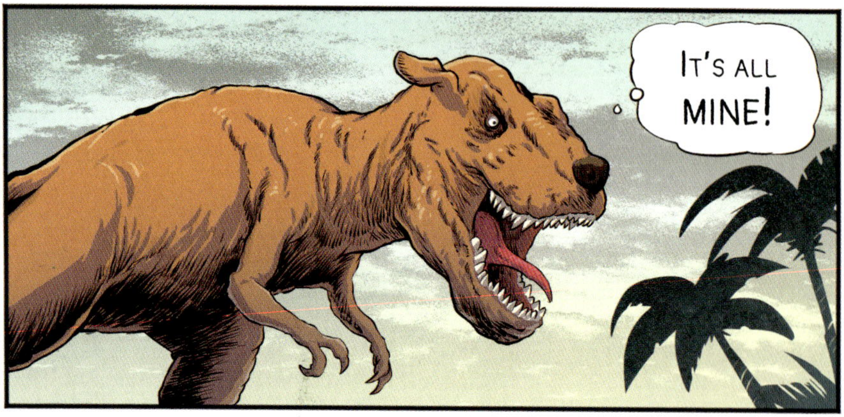
IT'S ALL MINE!

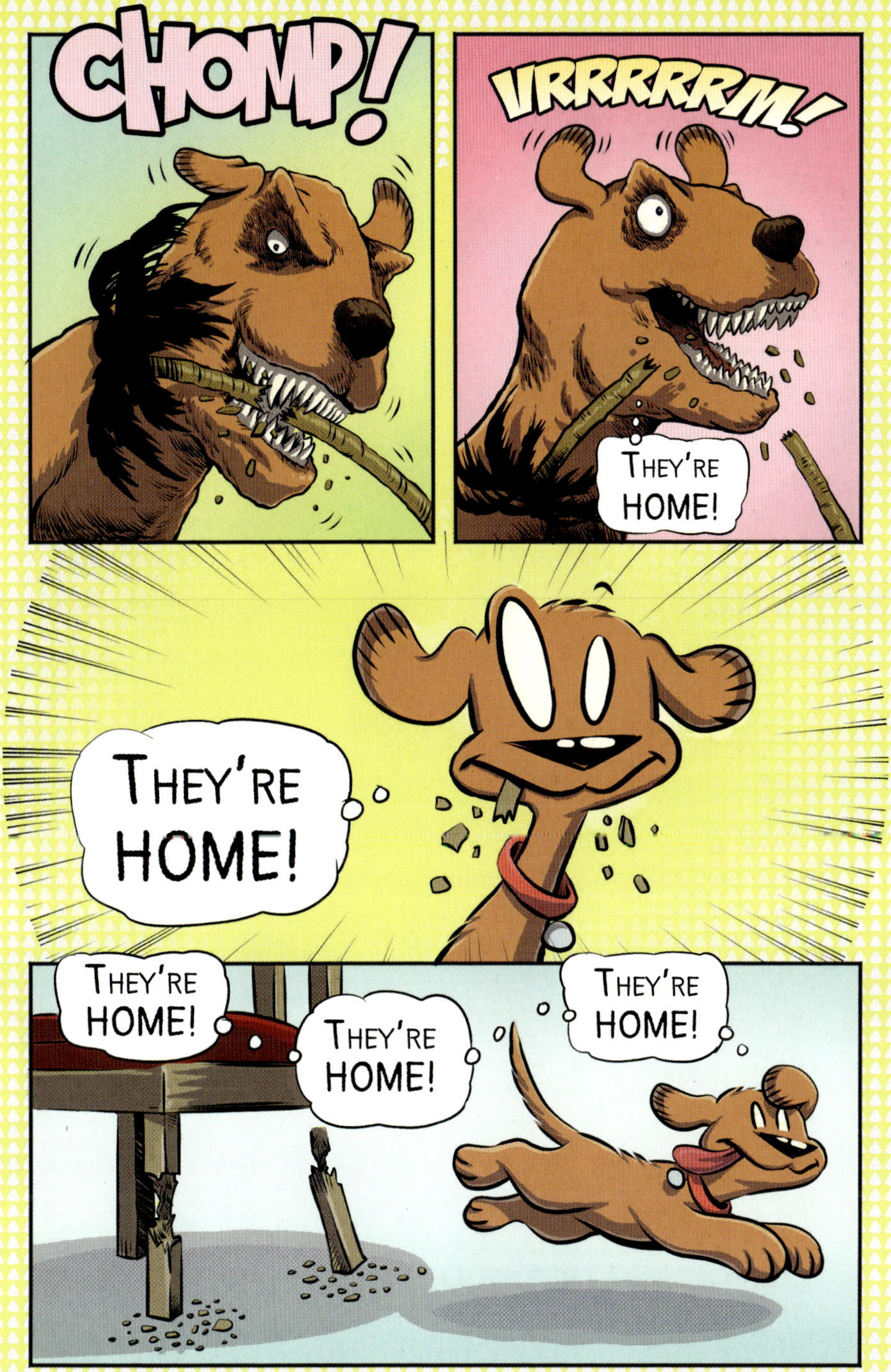
CHOMP!
VRRRRRRM!
THEY'RE HOME!
THEY'RE HOME!
THEY'RE HOME!
THEY'RE HOME!
THEY'RE HOME!

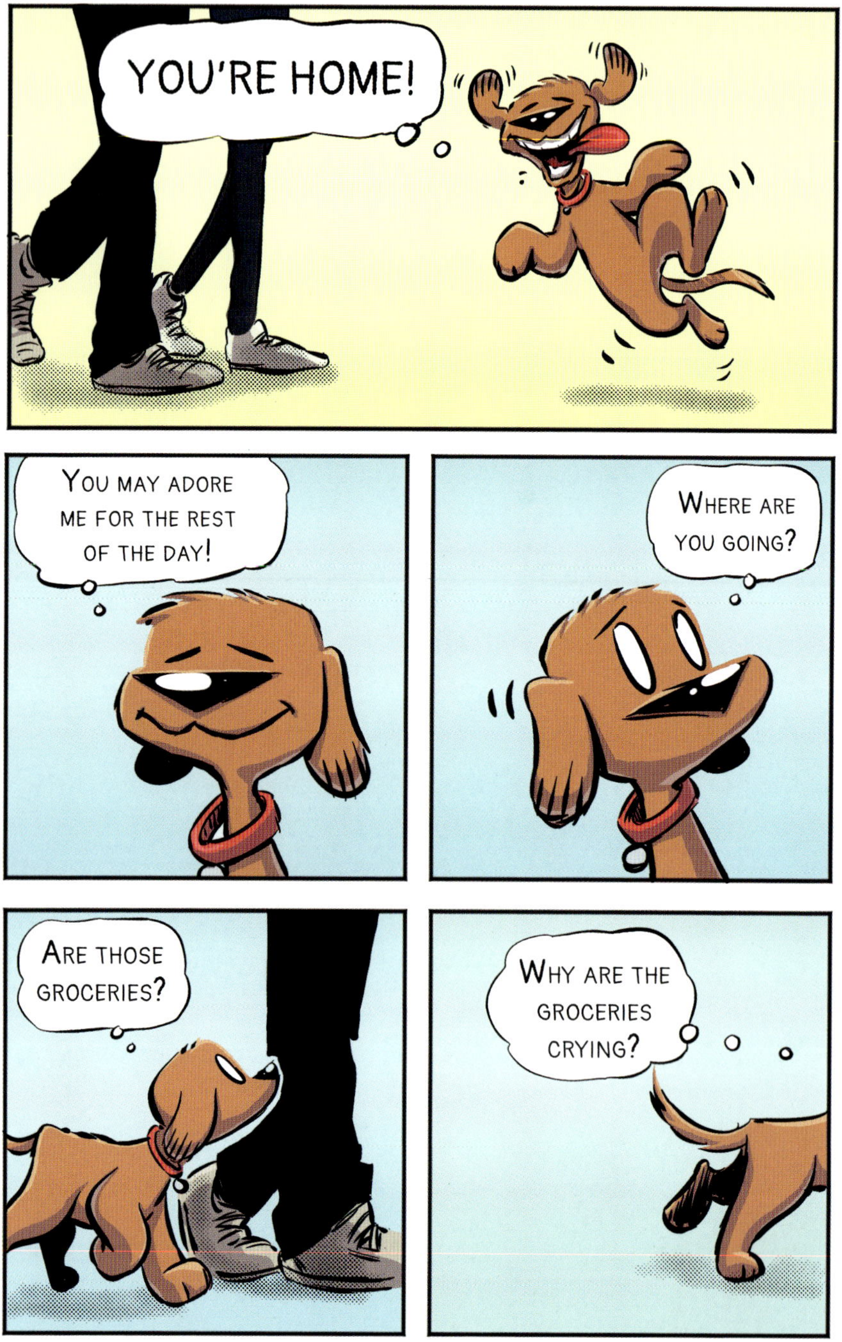
YOU'RE HOME!
YOU MAY ADORE ME FOR THE REST OF THE DAY!
WHERE ARE YOU GOING?
ARE THOSE GROCERIES?
WHY ARE THE GROCERIES CRYING?

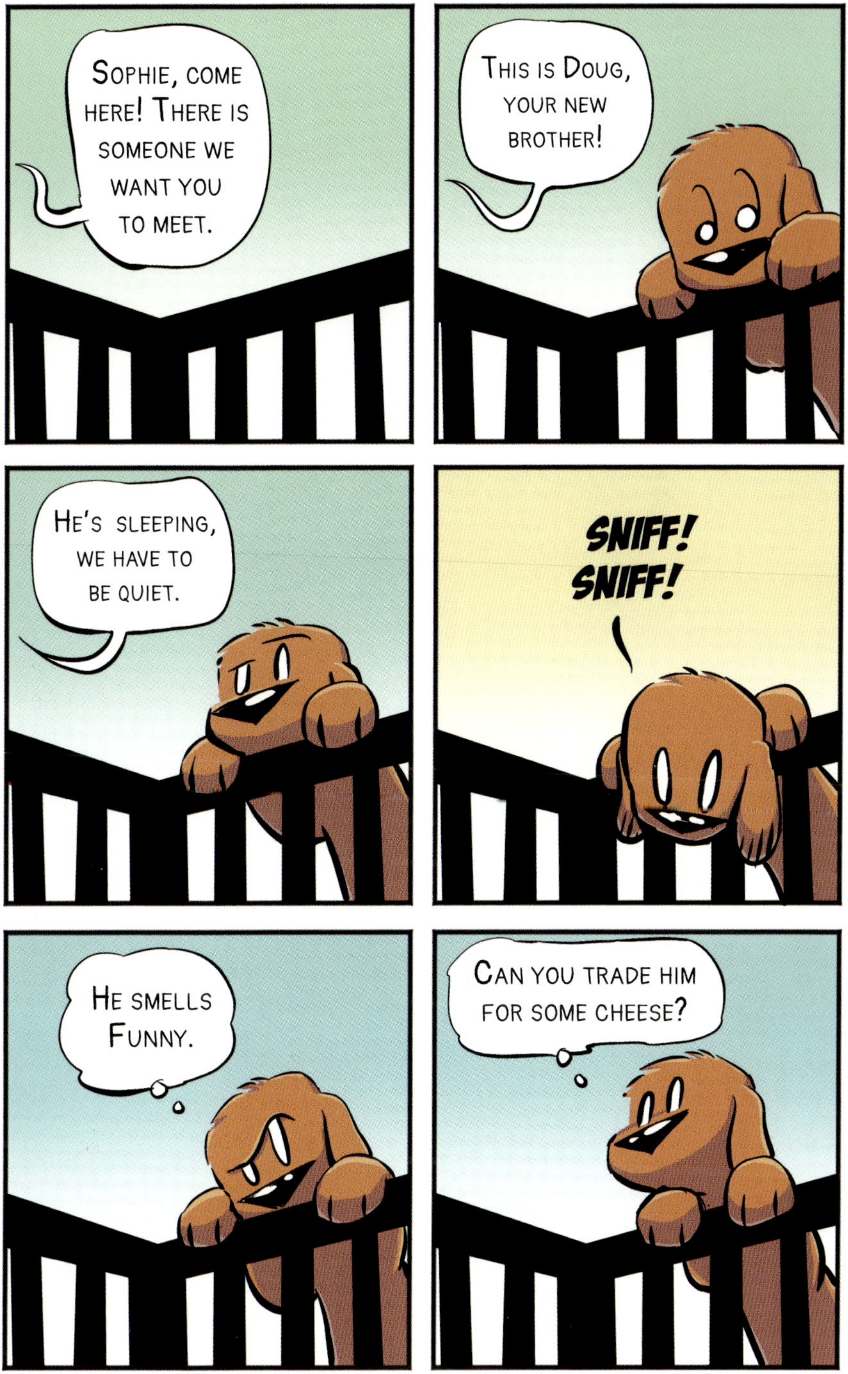
SOPHIE, COME HERE! THERE IS SOMEONE WE WANT YOU TO MEET.
THIS IS DOUG, YOUR NEW BROTHER!
HE'S SLEEPING, WE HAVE TO BE QUIET.
SNIFF! SNIFF!
HE SMELLS FUNNY.
CAN YOU TRADE HIM FOR SOME CHEESE?

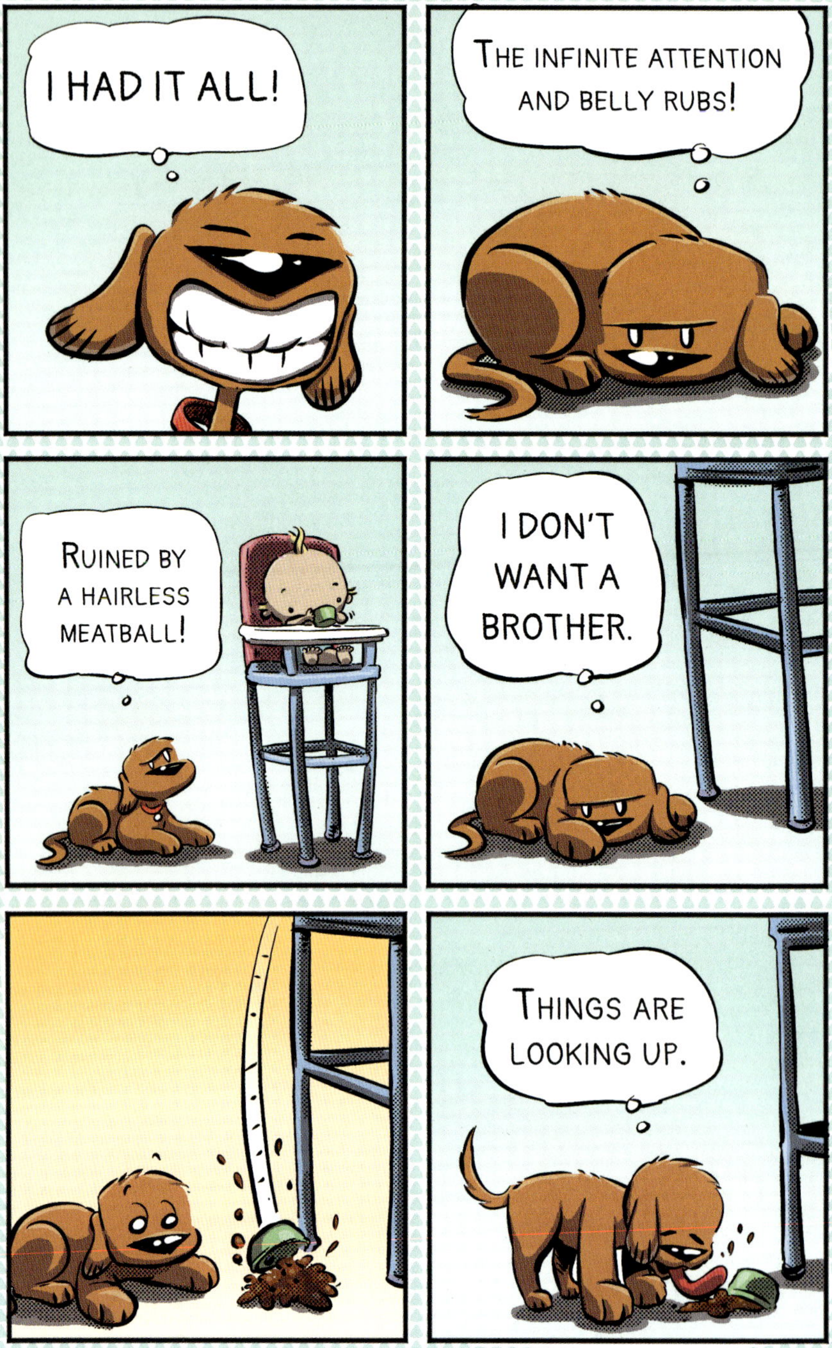
I HAD IT ALL!
THE INFINITE ATTENTION AND BELLY RUBS!
RUINED BY A HAIRLESS MEATBALL!
I DON'T WANT A BROTHER.
THINGS ARE LOOKING UP.

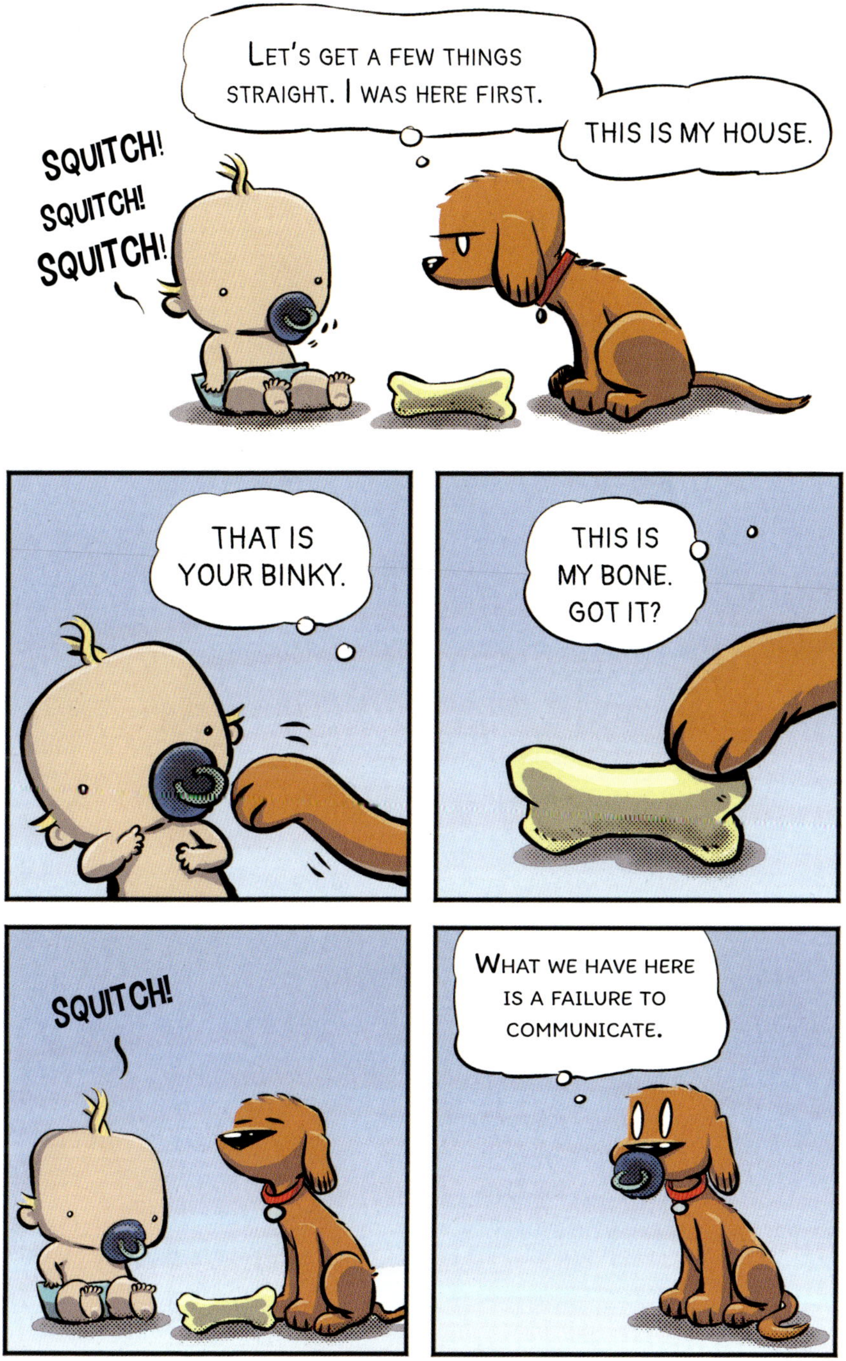
LET'S GET A FEW THINGS STRAIGHT. I WAS HERE FIRST.
THIS IS MY HOUSE.
SQUITCH! SQUITCH! SQUITCH!
THAT IS YOUR BINKY.
THIS IS MY BONE. GOT IT?
SQUITCH!
WHAT WE HAVE HERE IS A FAILURE TO COMMUNICATE.

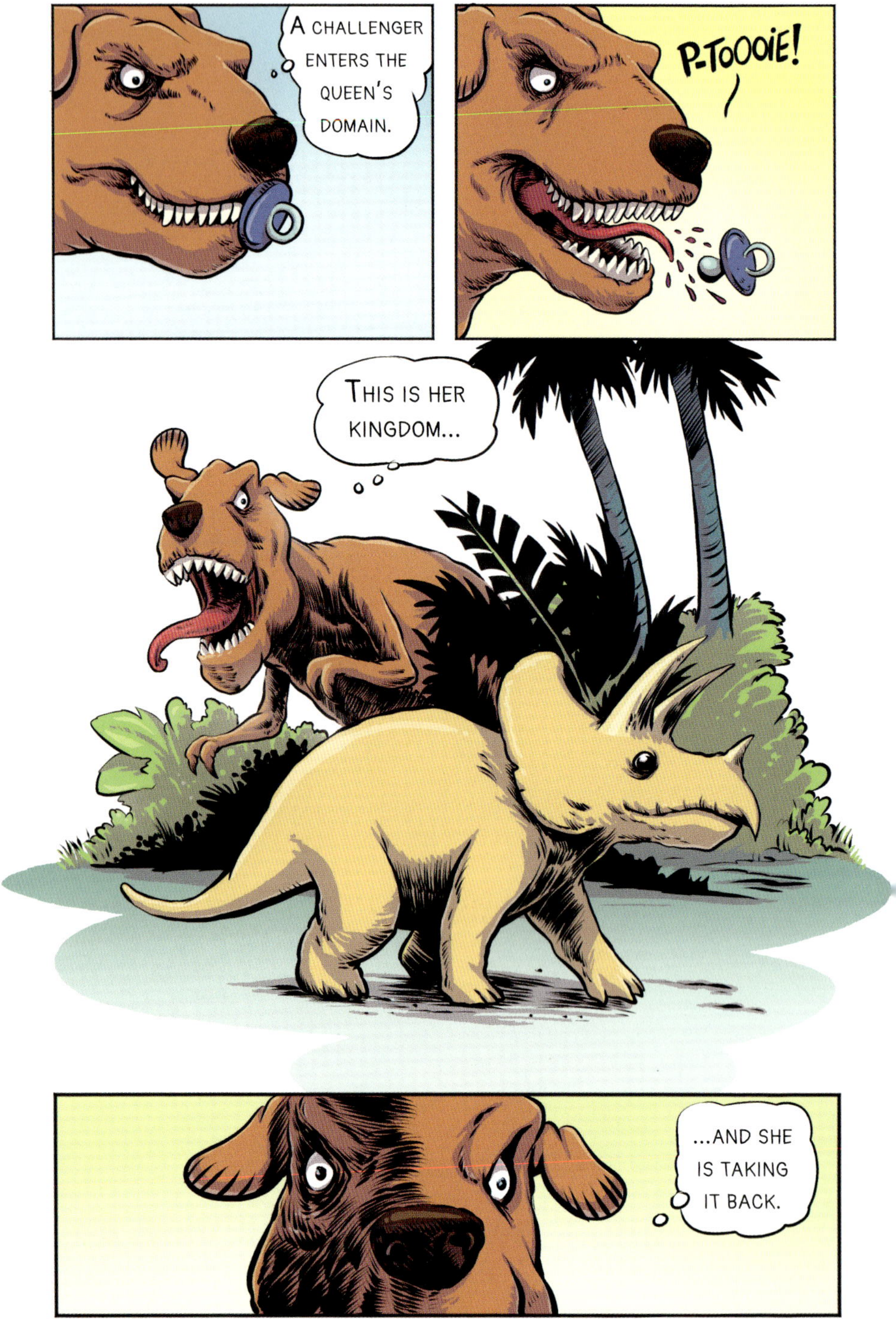
A CHALLENGER ENTERS THE QUEEN'S DOMAIN.
P-TOOOIE!
THIS IS HER KINGDOM...
...AND SHE IS TAKING IT BACK.

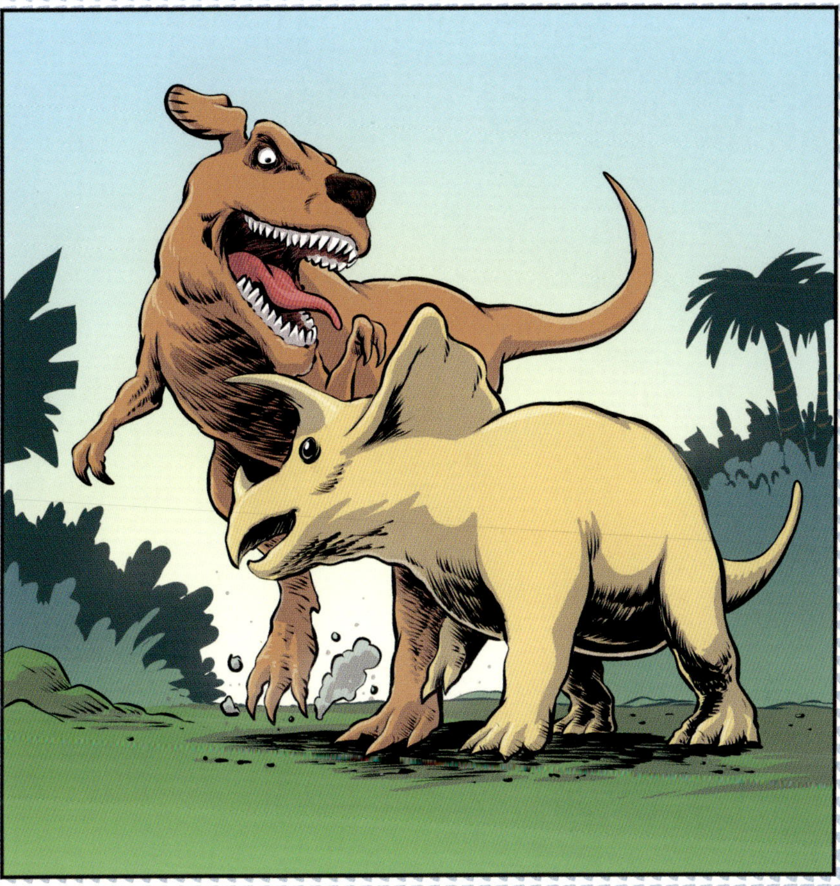

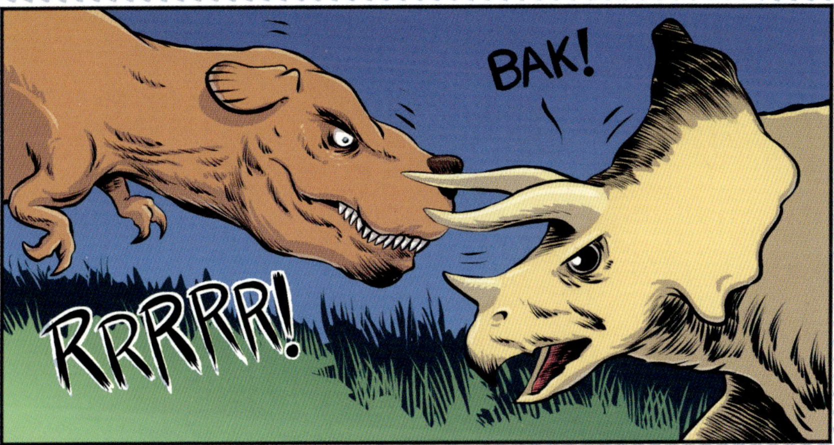
BAK!
RRRRR!

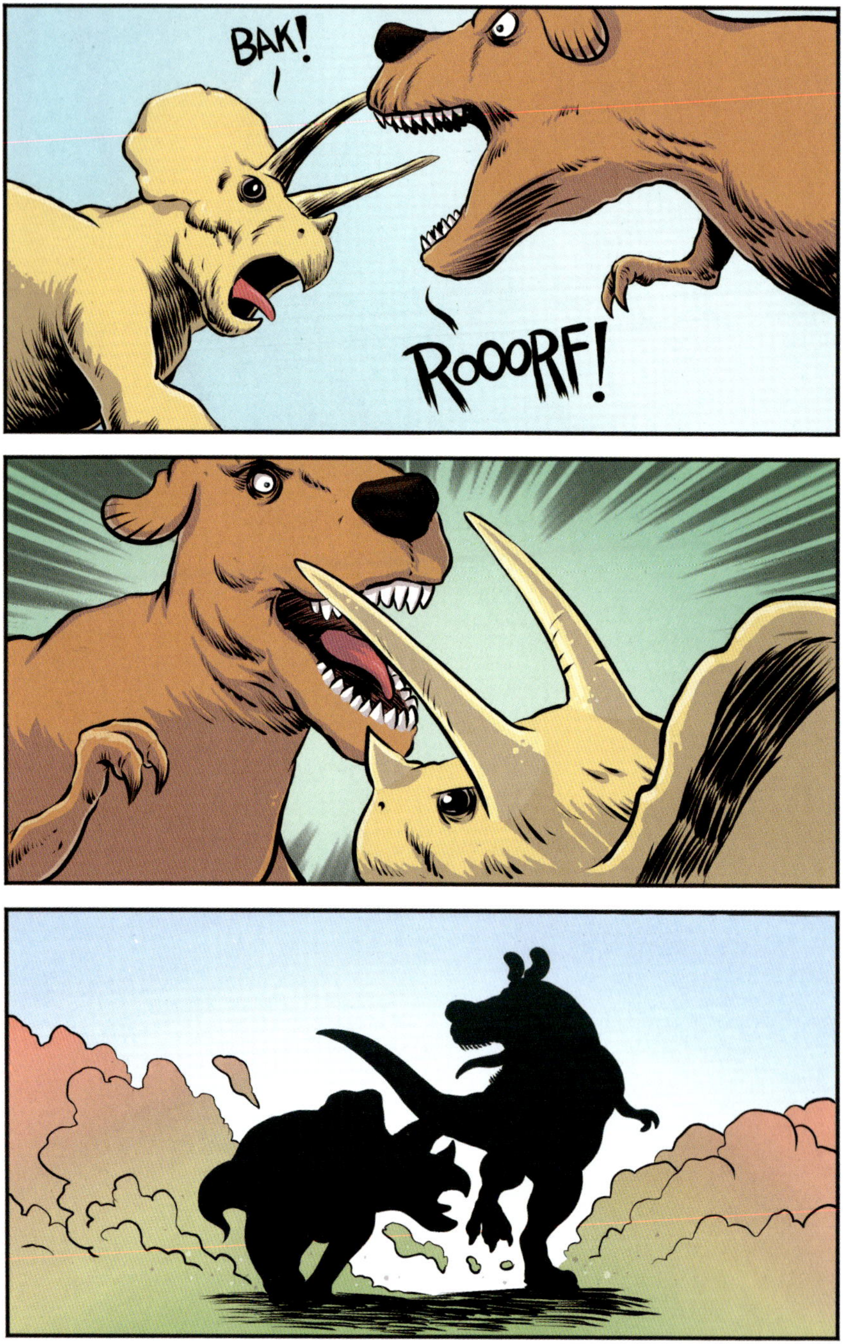
BAK!
ROOORF!

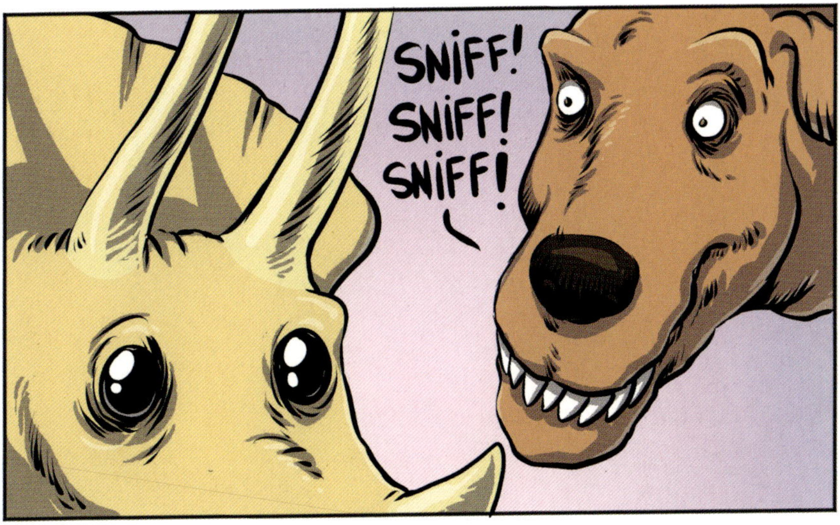
SNIFF!
SNIFF!
SNIFF!

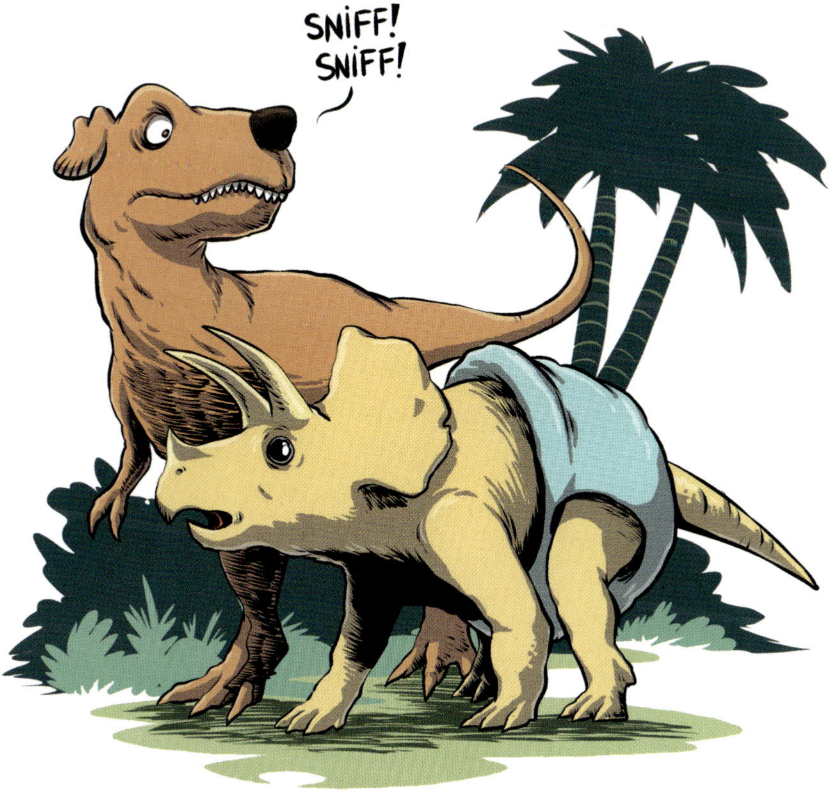
SNIFF!
SNIFF!

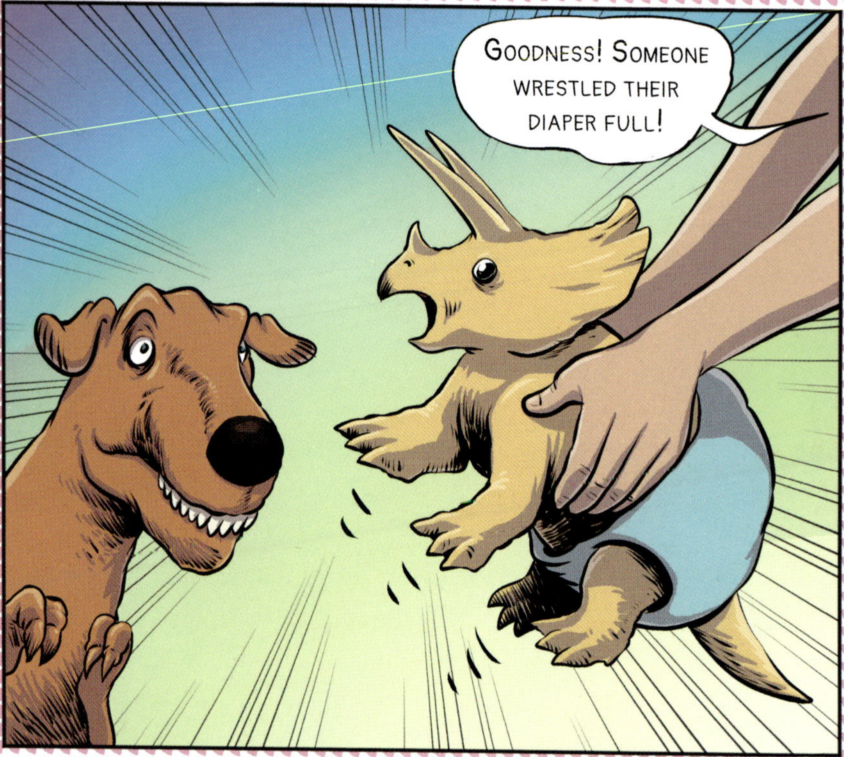
GOODNESS! SOMEONE WRESTLED THEIR DIAPER FULL!

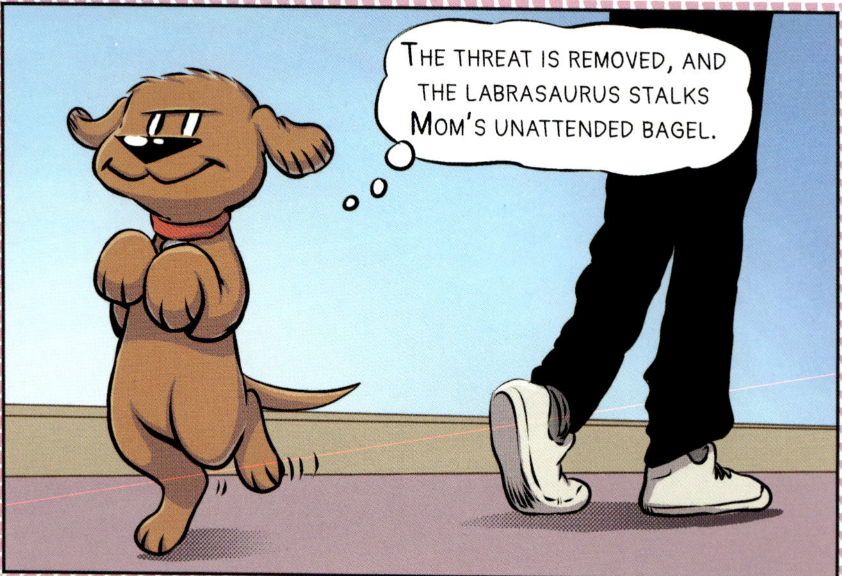
THE THREAT IS REMOVED, AND THE LABRASAURUS STALKS MOM'S UNATTENDED BAGEL.

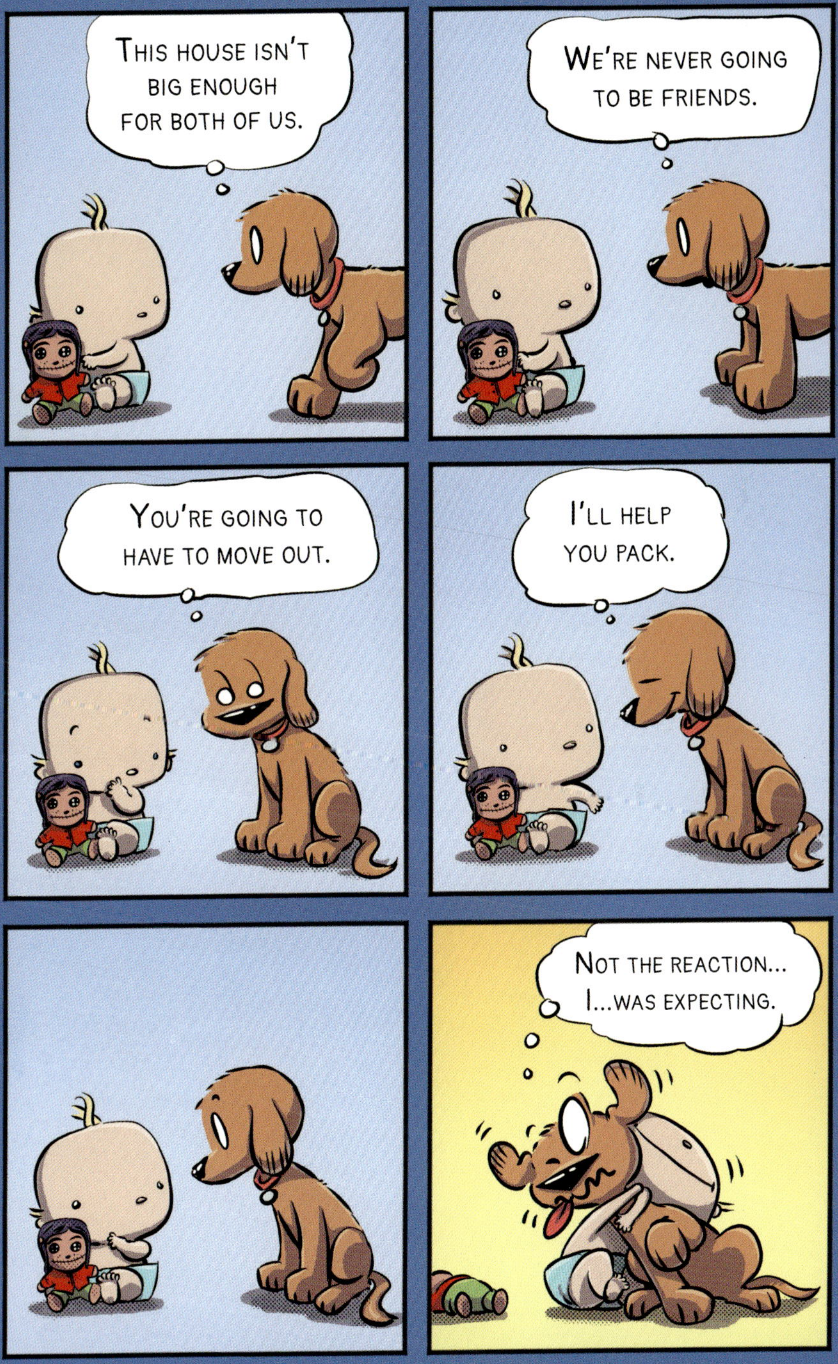
THIS HOUSE ISN'T BIG ENOUGH FOR BOTH OF US.
WE'RE NEVER GOING TO BE FRIENDS.
YOU'RE GOING TO HAVE TO MOVE OUT.
I'LL HELP YOU PACK.
NOT THE REACTION... I...WAS EXPECTING.

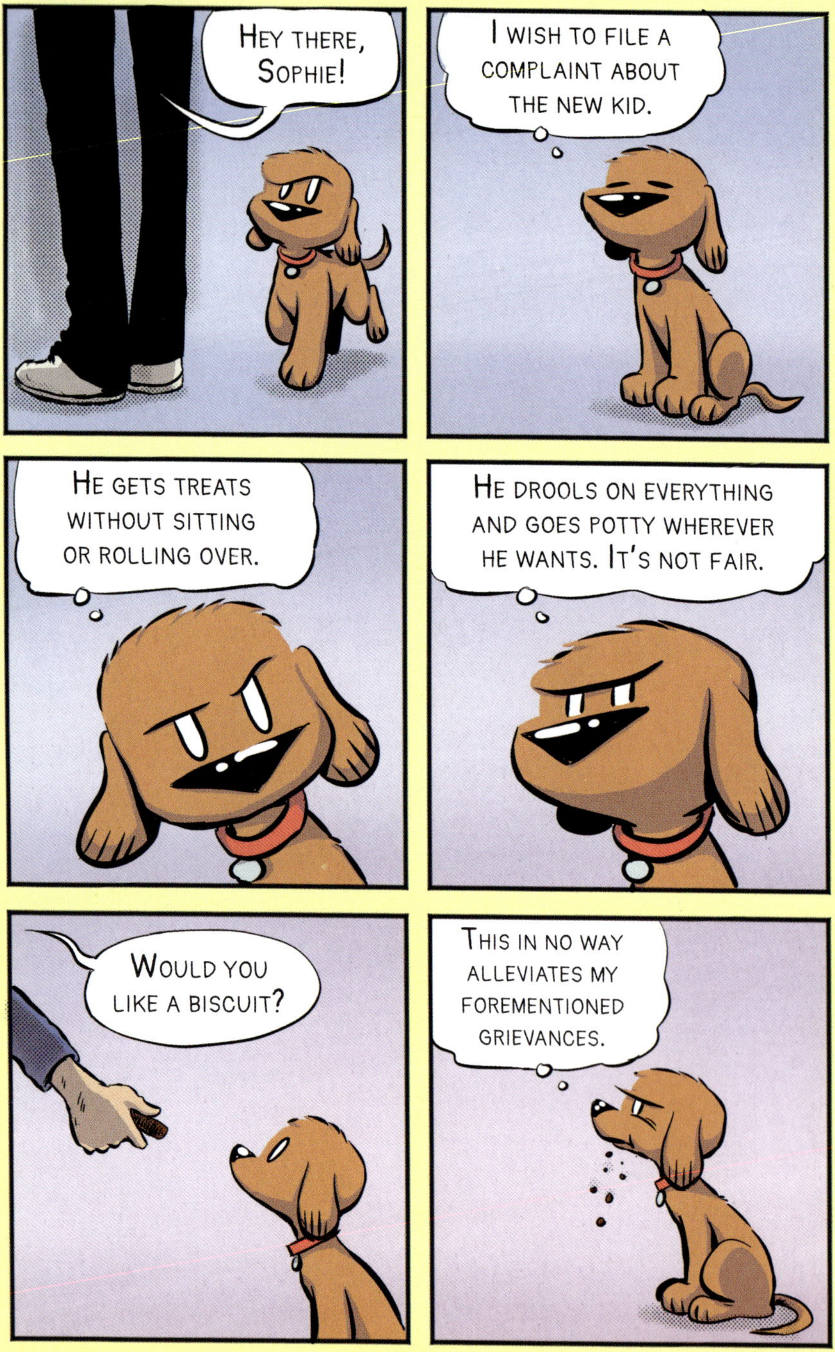
HEY THERE, SOPHIE!
I WISH TO FILE A COMPLAINT ABOUT THE NEW KID.
HE GETS TREATS WITHOUT SITTING OR ROLLING OVER.
HE DROOLS ON EVERYTHING AND GOES POTTY WHEREVER HE WANTS. IT'S NOT FAIR.
WOULD YOU LIKE A BISCUIT?
THIS IN NO WAY ALLEVIATES MY FOREMENTIONED GRIEVANCES.

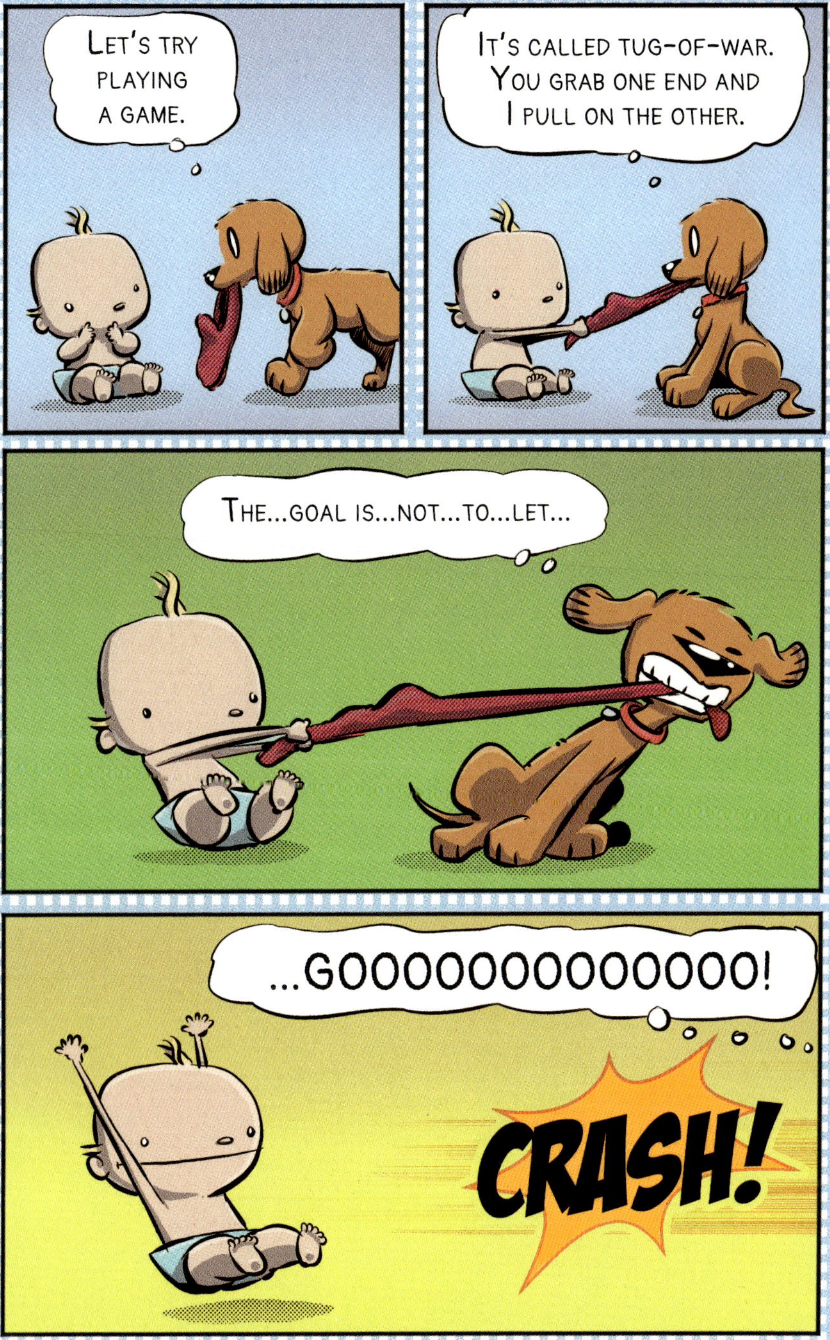
LET'S TRY PLAYING A GAME.
IT'S CALLED TUG-OF-WAR. YOU GRAB ONE END AND I PULL ON THE OTHER.
THE...GOAL IS...NOT...TO...LET...
...GOOOOOOOOOOOOO!
CRASH!

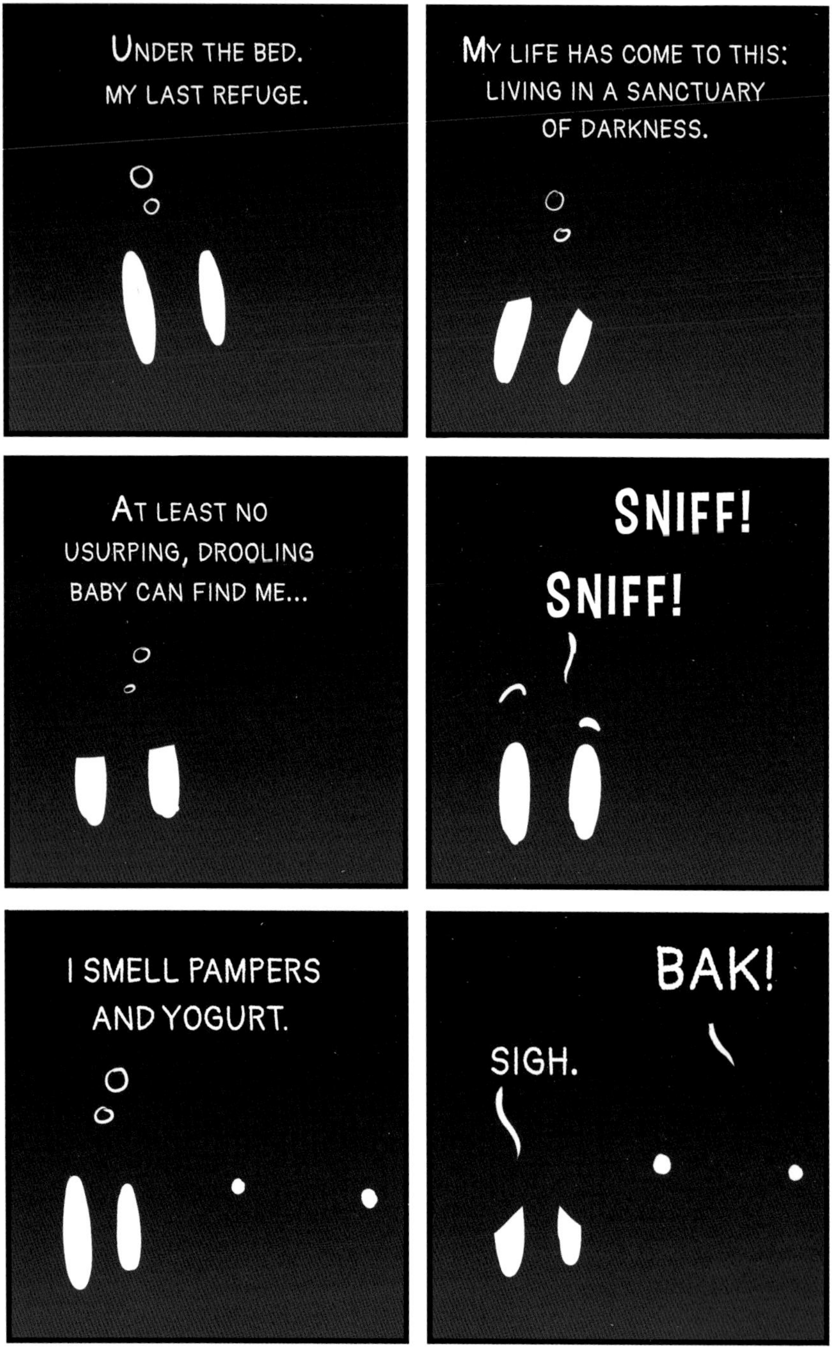
UNDER THE BED.
MY LAST REFUGE.
MY LIFE HAS COME TO THIS: LIVING IN A SANCTUARY OF DARKNESS.
AT LEAST NO USURPING, DROOLING BABY CAN FIND ME...
SNIFF!
SNIFF!
I SMELL PAMPERS AND YOGURT.
BAK!
SIGH.

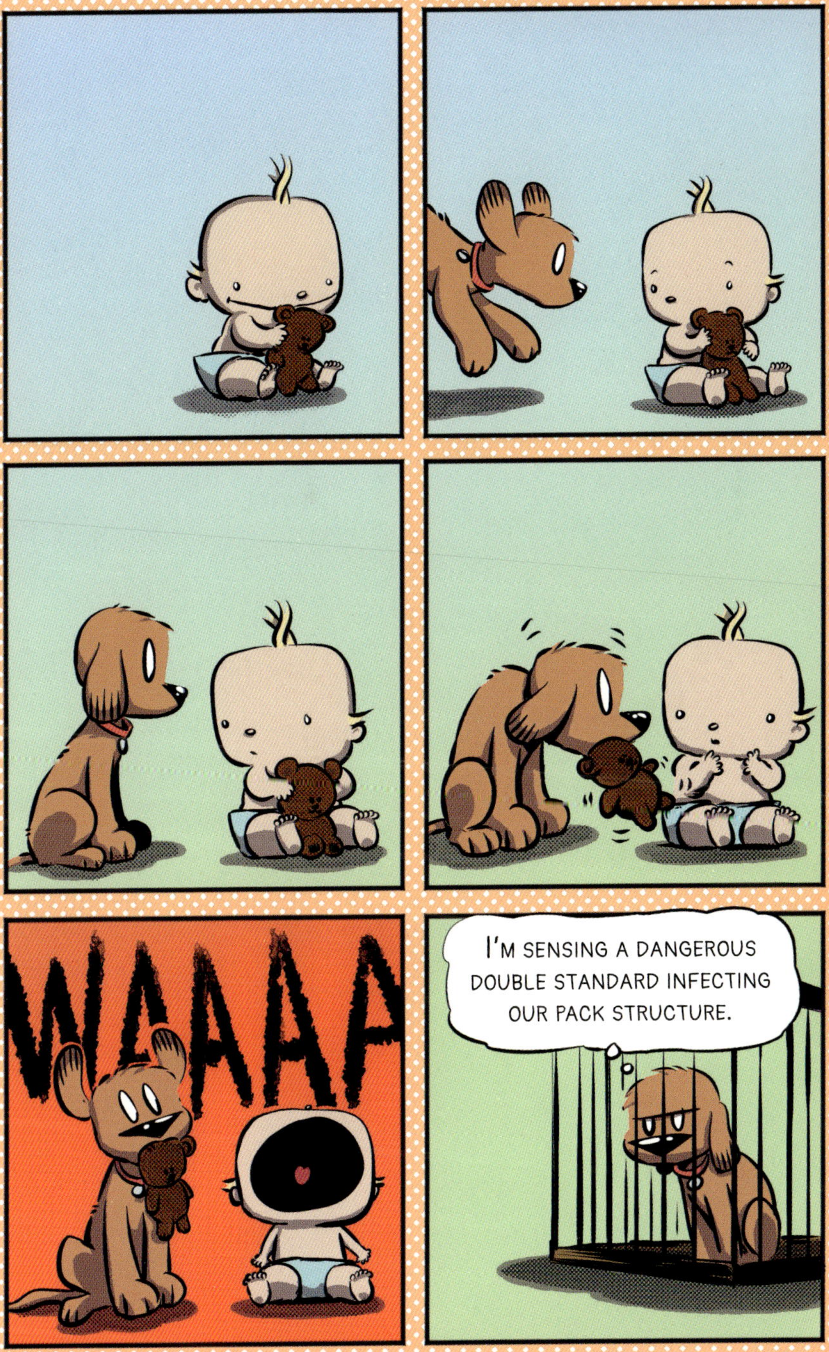
WAAAA
I'M SENSING A DANGEROUS DOUBLE STANDARD INFECTING OUR PACK STRUCTURE.

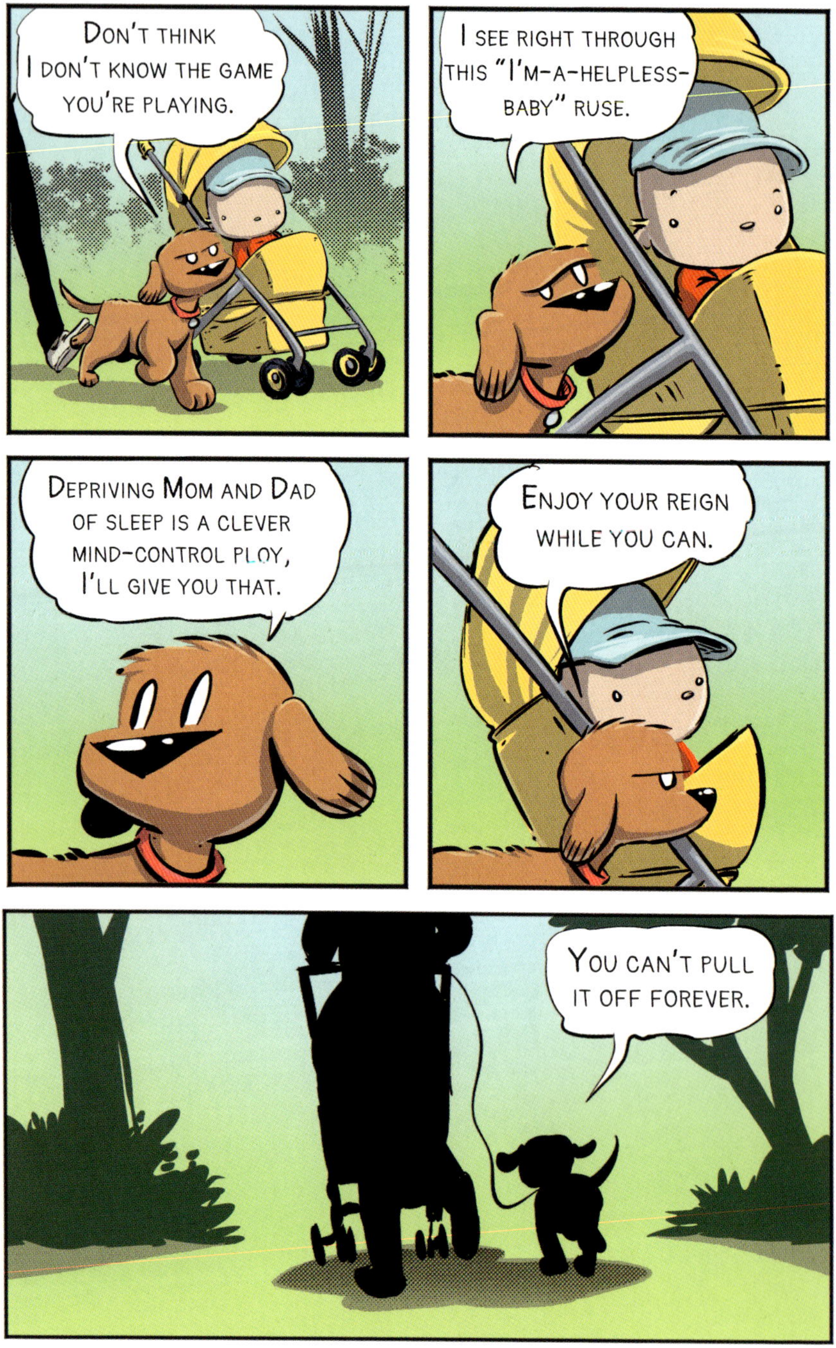
DON'T THINK I DON'T KNOW THE GAME YOU'RE PLAYING.
I SEE RIGHT THROUGH THIS "I'M-A-HELPLESS-BABY" RUSE.
DEPRIVING MOM AND DAD OF SLEEP IS A CLEVER MIND-CONTROL PLOY, I'LL GIVE YOU THAT.
ENJOY YOUR REIGN WHILE YOU CAN.
YOU CAN'T PULL IT OFF FOREVER.

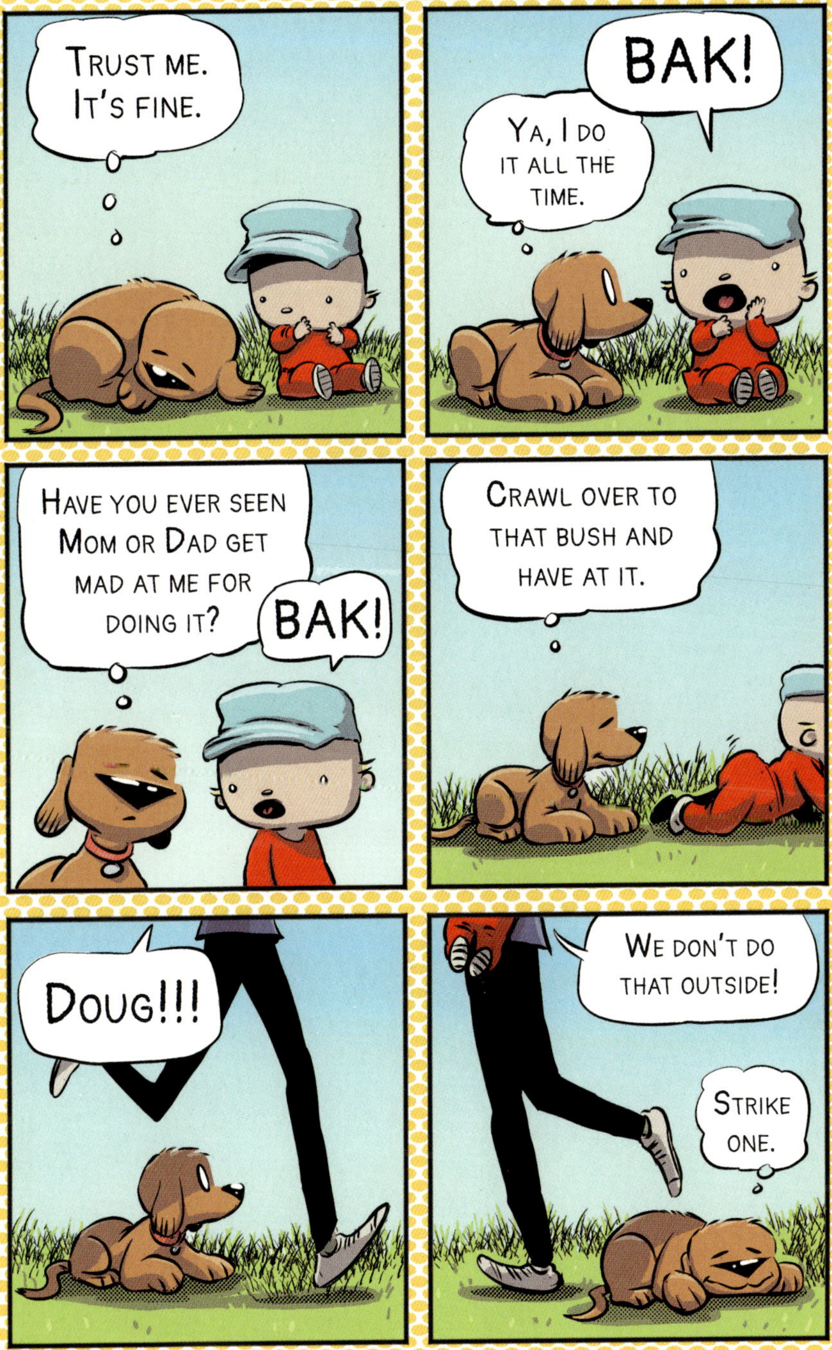
TRUST ME.
IT'S FINE.
BAK!
YA, I DO IT ALL THE TIME.
HAVE YOU EVER SEEN MOM OR DAD GET MAD AT ME FOR DOING IT?
BAK!
CRAWL OVER TO THAT BUSH AND HAVE AT IT.
DOUG!!!
WE DON'T DO THAT OUTSIDE!
STRIKE ONE.

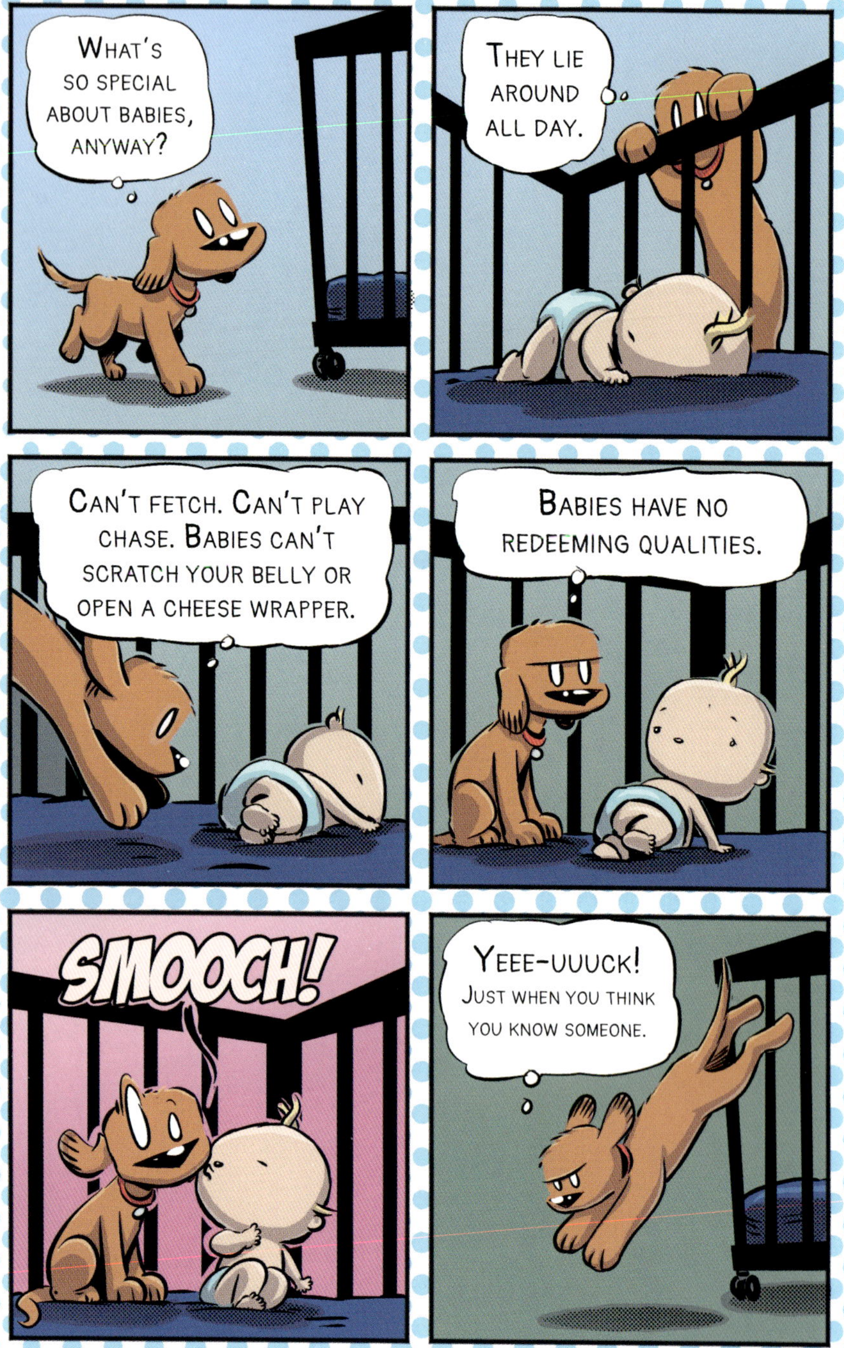
WHAT'S SO SPECIAL ABOUT BABIES, ANYWAY?
THEY LIE AROUND ALL DAY.
CAN'T FETCH. CAN'T PLAY CHASE. BABIES CAN'T SCRATCH YOUR BELLY OR OPEN A CHEESE WRAPPER.
BABIES HAVE NO REDEEMING QUALITIES.
SMOOCH!
YEEE-UUUCK!
JUST WHEN YOU THINK YOU KNOW SOMEONE.

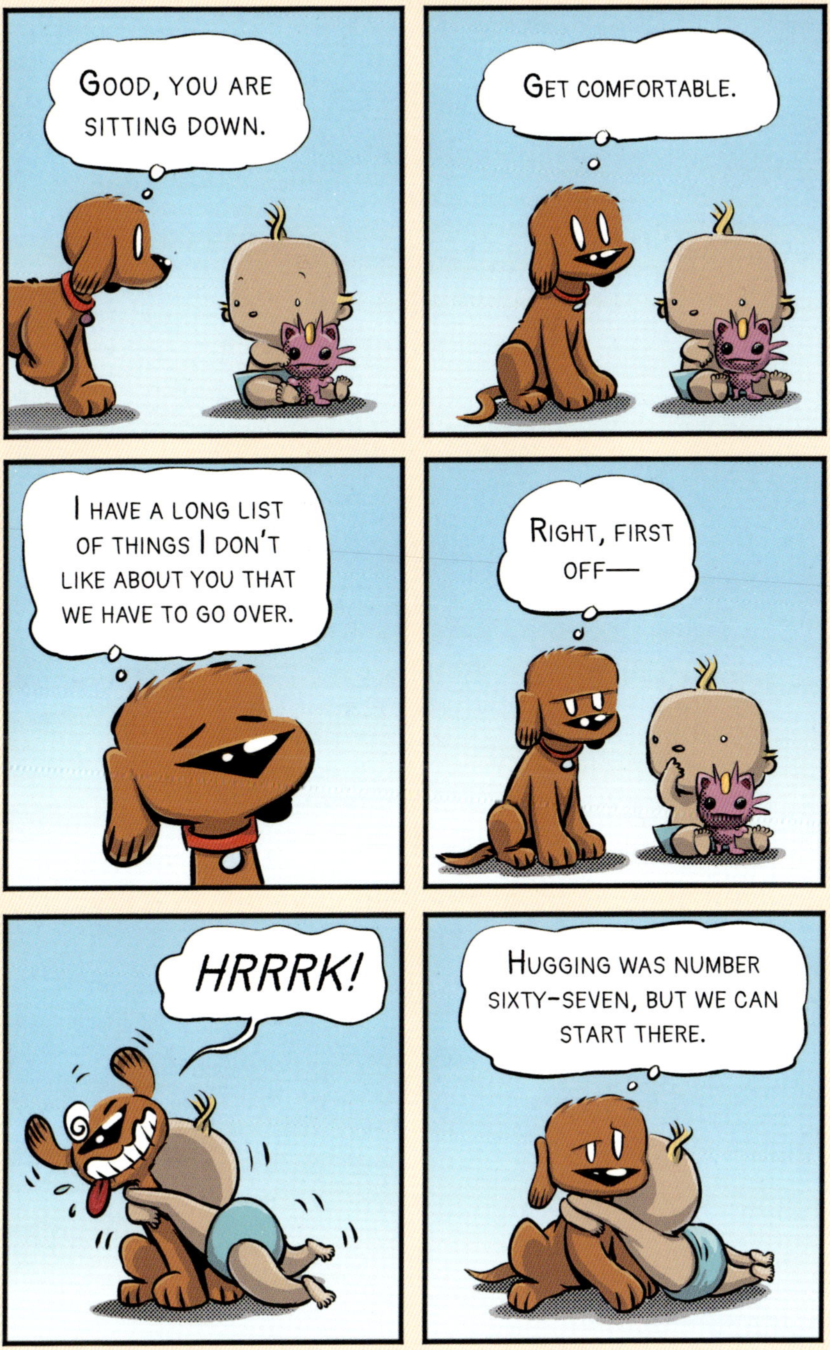
GOOD, YOU ARE SITTING DOWN.
GET COMFORTABLE.
I HAVE A LONG LIST OF THINGS I DON'T LIKE ABOUT YOU THAT WE HAVE TO GO OVER.
RIGHT, FIRST OFF—
HRRRK!
HUGGING WAS NUMBER SIXTY-SEVEN, BUT WE CAN START THERE.

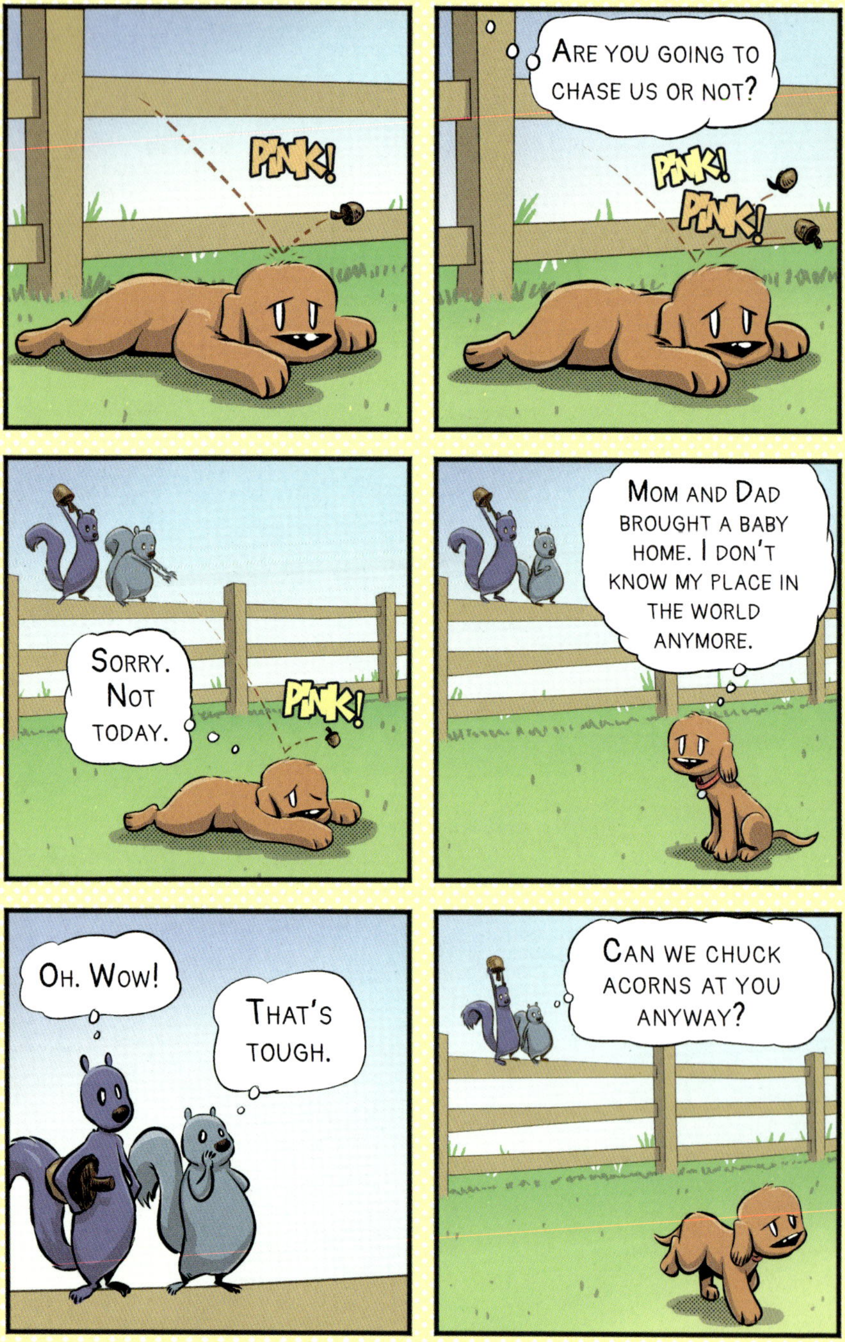
PINK!
ARE YOU GOING TO CHASE US OR NOT?
PINK!
PINK!
SORRY. NOT TODAY.
PINK!
MOM AND DAD BROUGHT A BABY HOME. I DON'T KNOW MY PLACE IN THE WORLD ANYMORE.
OH. WOW!
THAT'S TOUGH.
CAN WE CHUCK ACORNS AT YOU ANYWAY?

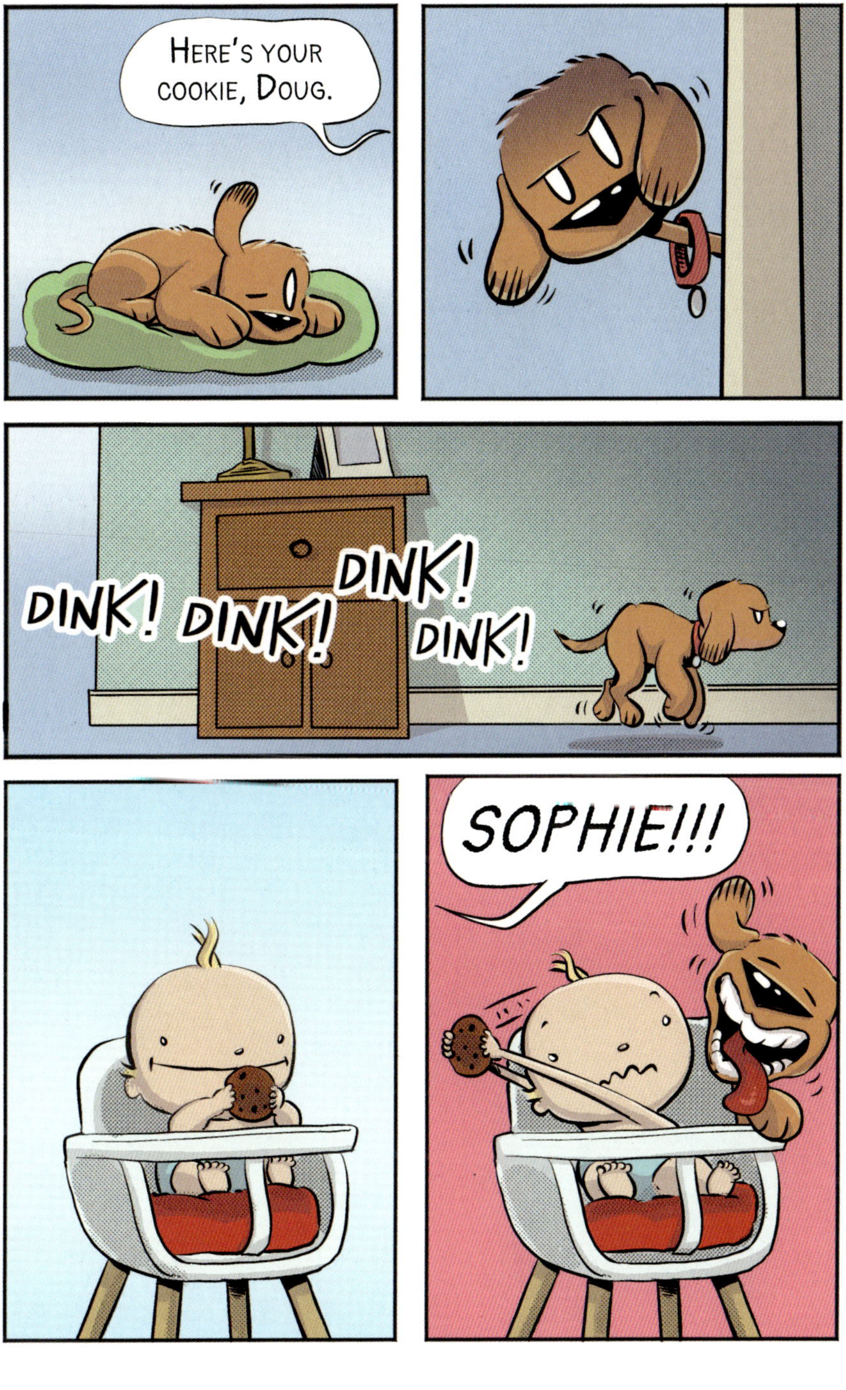
HERE'S YOUR COOKIE, DOUG.
DINK! DINK! DINK! DINK!
SOPHIE!!!

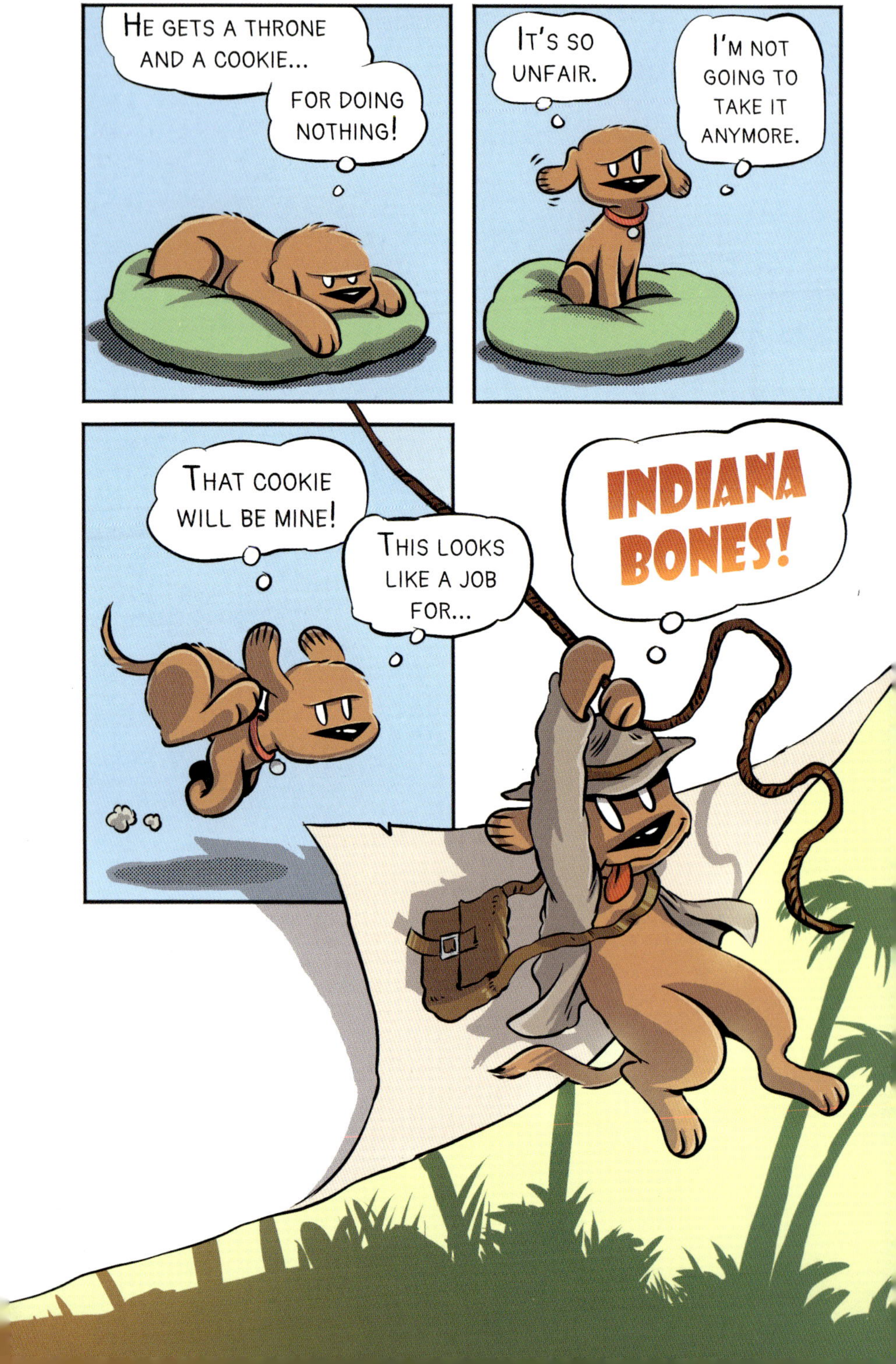

HE GETS A THRONE AND A COOKIE...
FOR DOING NOTHING!
IT'S SO UNFAIR.
I'M NOT GOING TO TAKE IT ANYMORE.
THAT COOKIE WILL BE MINE!
THIS LOOKS LIKE A JOB FOR...
INDIANA BONES!

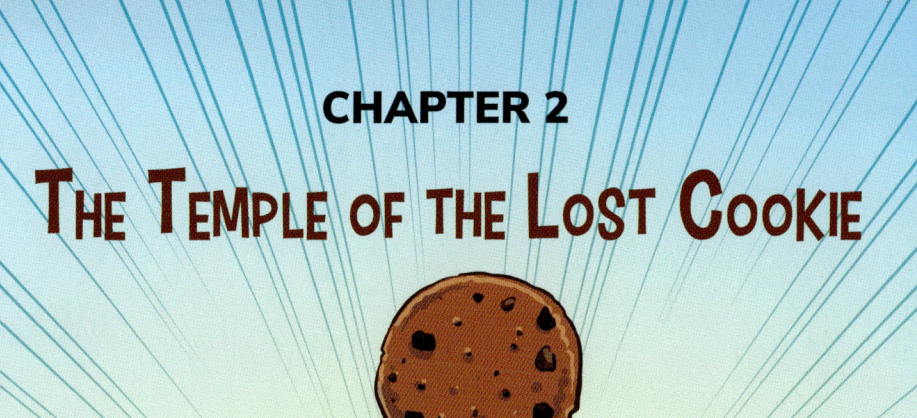

CHAPTER 2

The Temple of the Lost Cookie

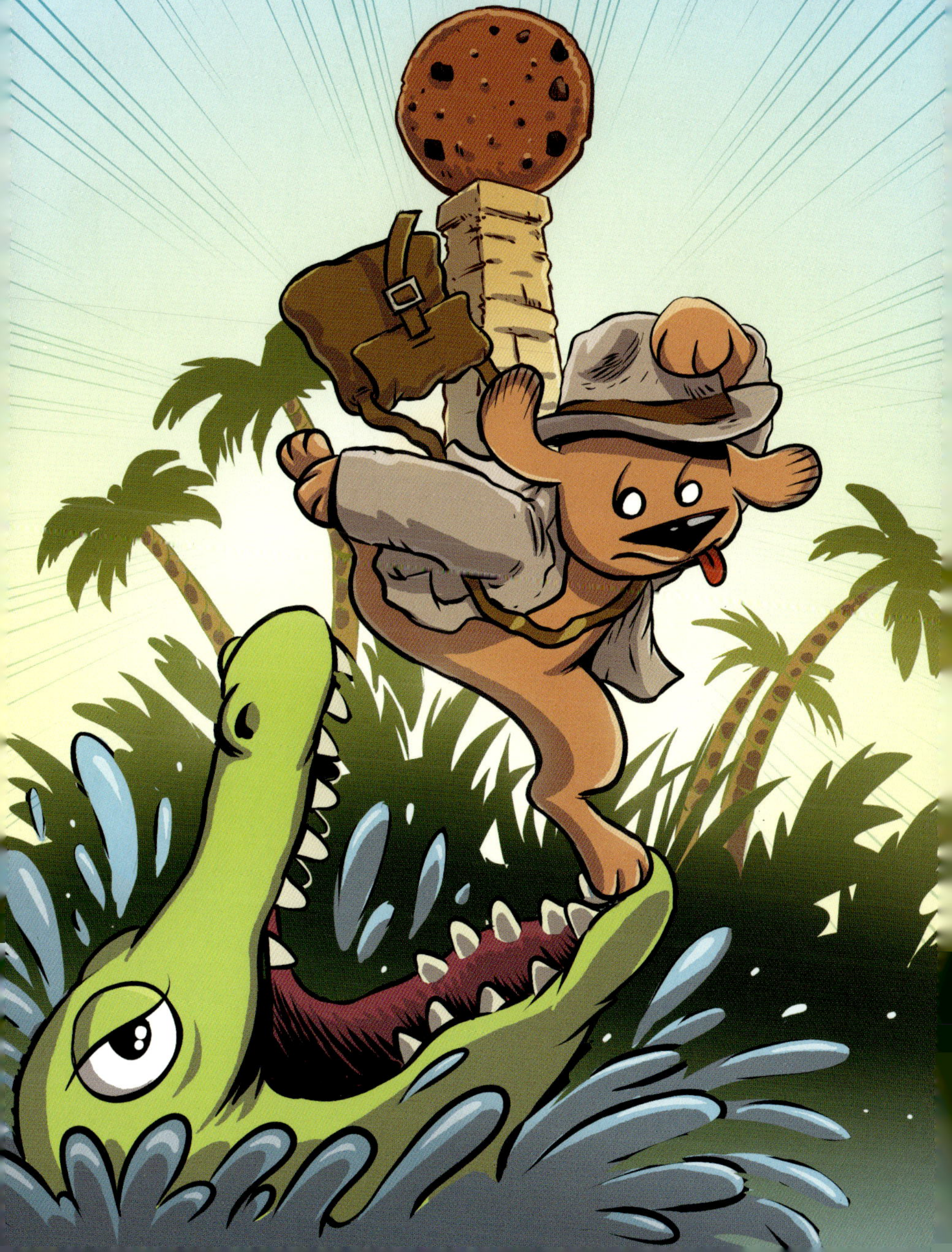

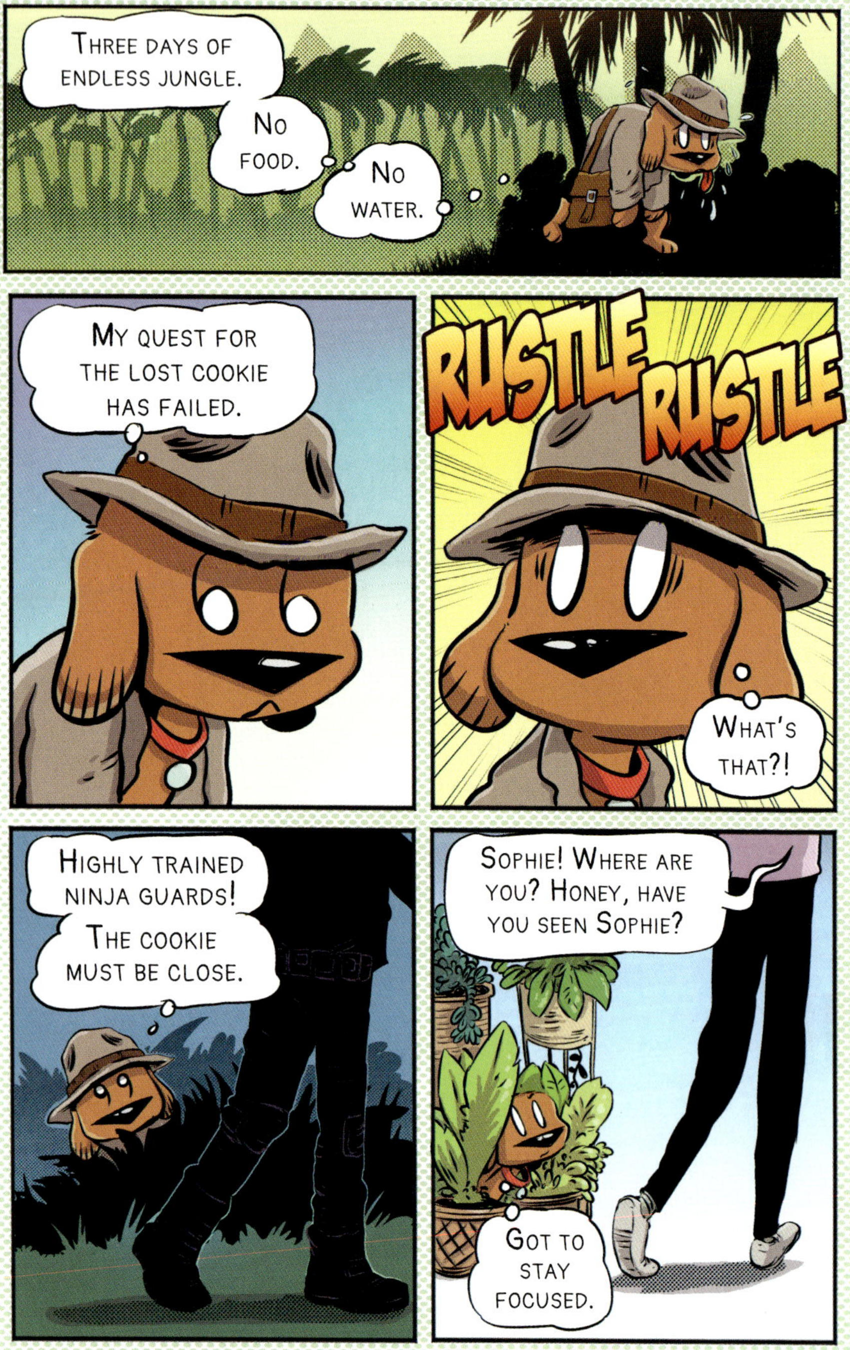
THREE DAYS OF ENDLESS JUNGLE.
NO FOOD.
NO WATER.
MY QUEST FOR THE LOST COOKIE HAS FAILED.
RUSTLE RUSTLE
WHAT'S THAT?!
HIGHLY TRAINED NINJA GUARDS!
THE COOKIE MUST BE CLOSE.
SOPHIE! WHERE ARE YOU? HONEY, HAVE YOU SEEN SOPHIE?
GOT TO STAY FOCUSED.

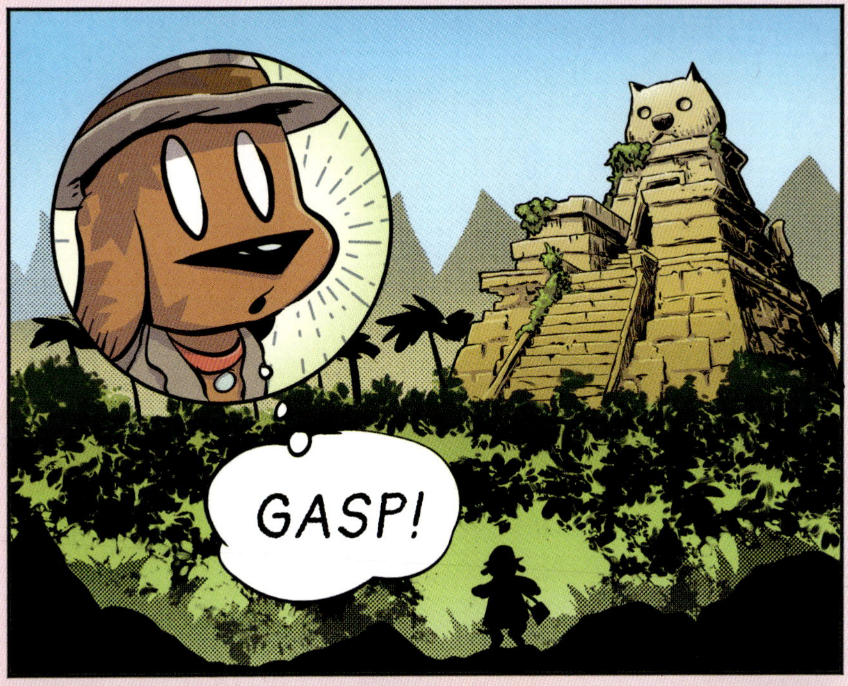
GASP!

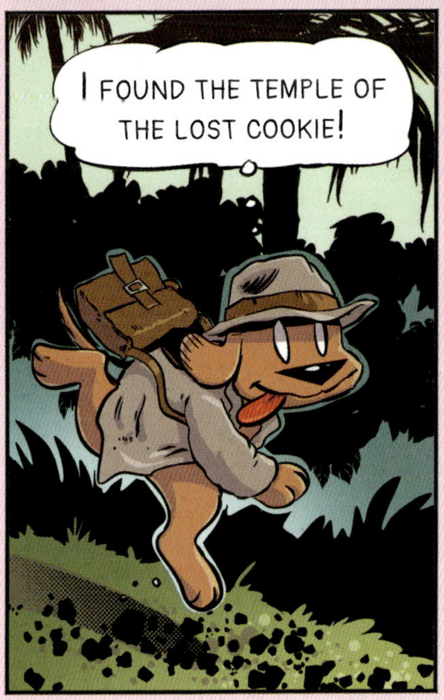
I FOUND THE TEMPLE OF THE LOST COOKIE!

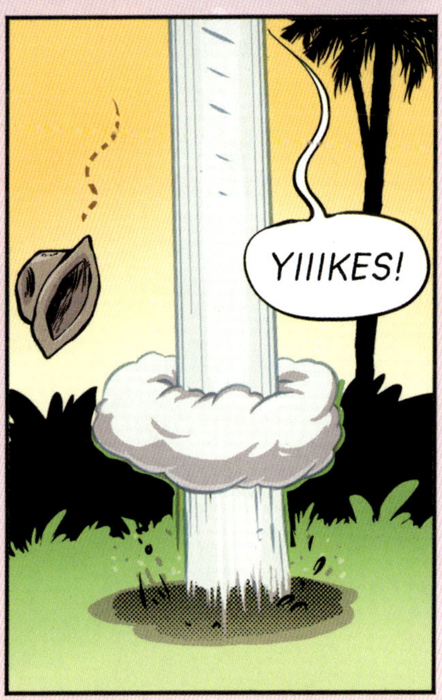
YIIIKES!

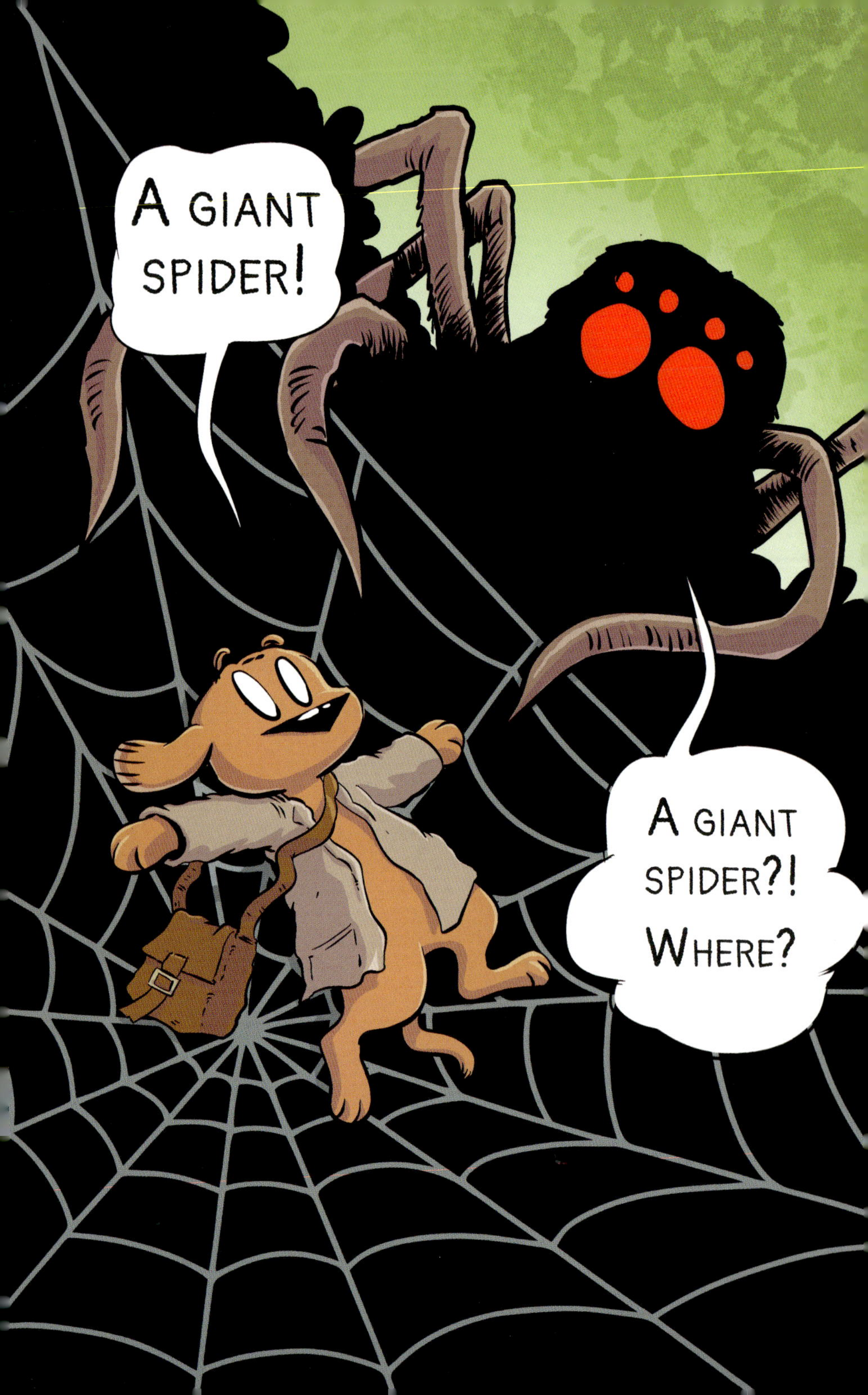
A GIANT SPIDER!
A GIANT SPIDER?! WHERE?

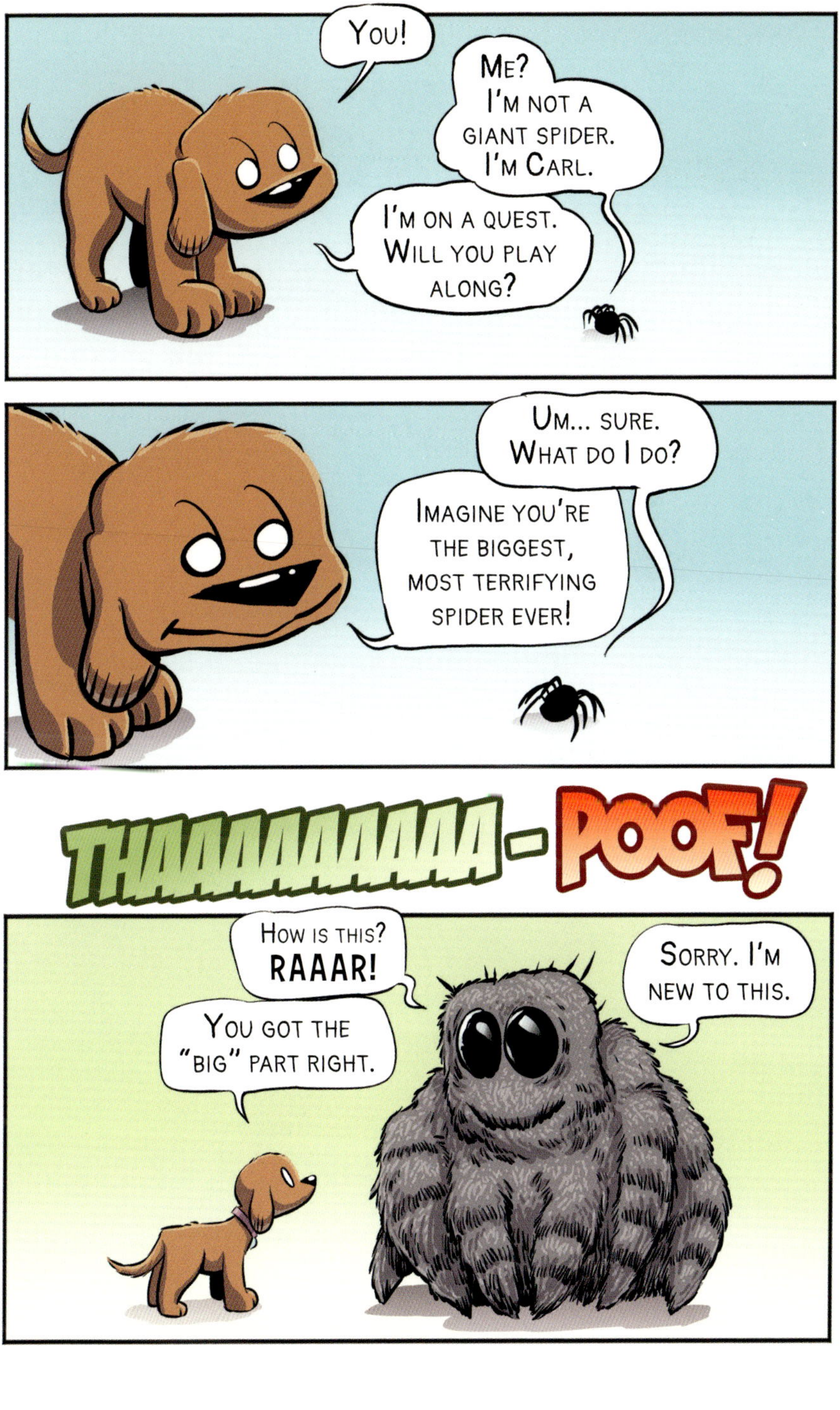
YOU!
ME? I'M NOT A GIANT SPIDER. I'M CARL.
I'M ON A QUEST. WILL YOU PLAY ALONG?
UM... SURE. WHAT DO I DO?
IMAGINE YOU'RE THE BIGGEST, MOST TERRIFYING SPIDER EVER!
THAAAAAAAAAA-POOF!
HOW IS THIS? RAAAR!
YOU GOT THE "BIG" PART RIGHT.
SORRY. I'M NEW TO THIS.

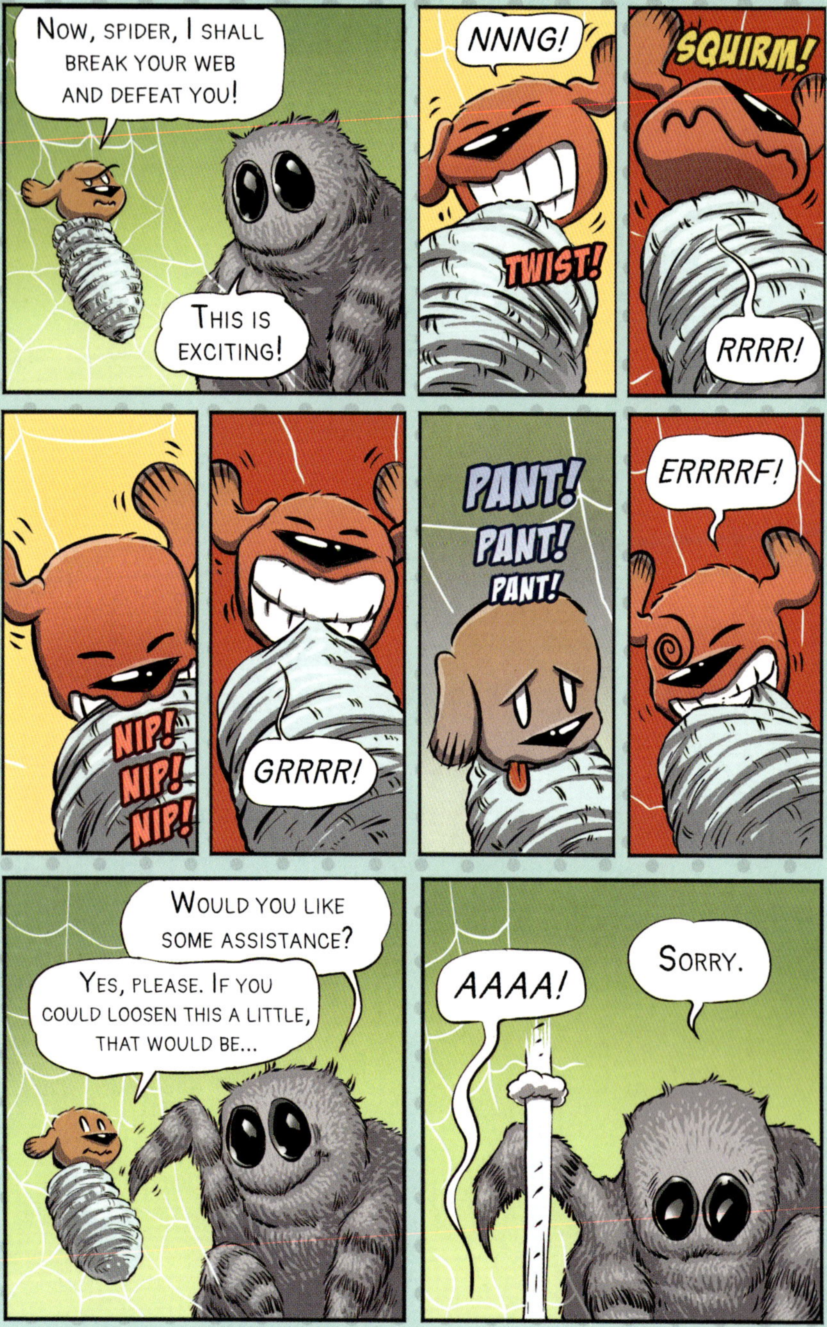
Now, spider, I shall break your web and defeat you!
This is exciting!
NNNG!
TWIST!
SQUIRM!
RRRR!
NIP! NIP! NIP!
GRRRR!
PANT! PANT! PANT!
ERRRRF!
Would you like some assistance?
Yes, please. If you could loosen this a little, that would be...
AAAA!
Sorry.

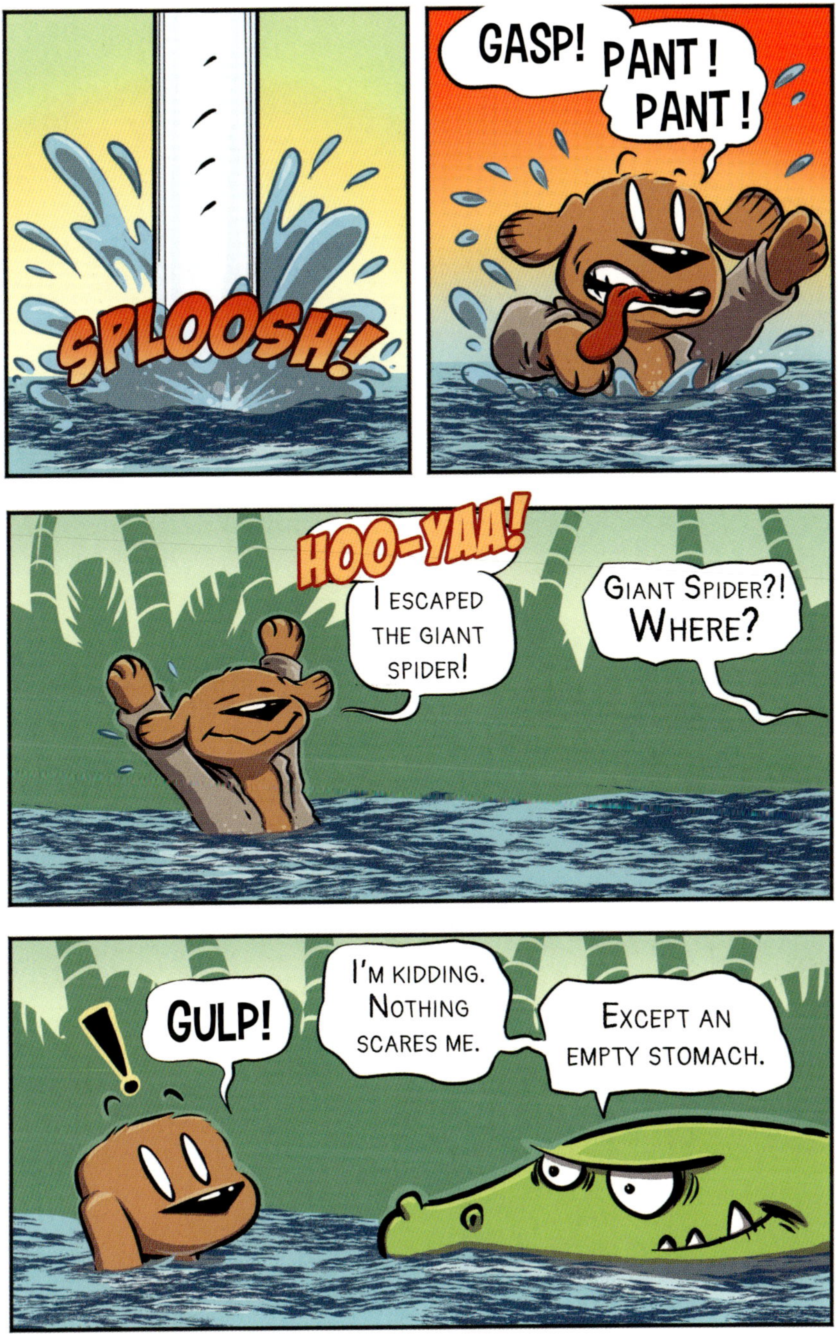
SPLOOSH!
GASP!
PANT! PANT!
HOO-YAA!
I ESCAPED THE GIANT SPIDER!
GIANT SPIDER?! WHERE?
GULP!
I'M KIDDING. NOTHING SCARES ME.
EXCEPT AN EMPTY STOMACH.

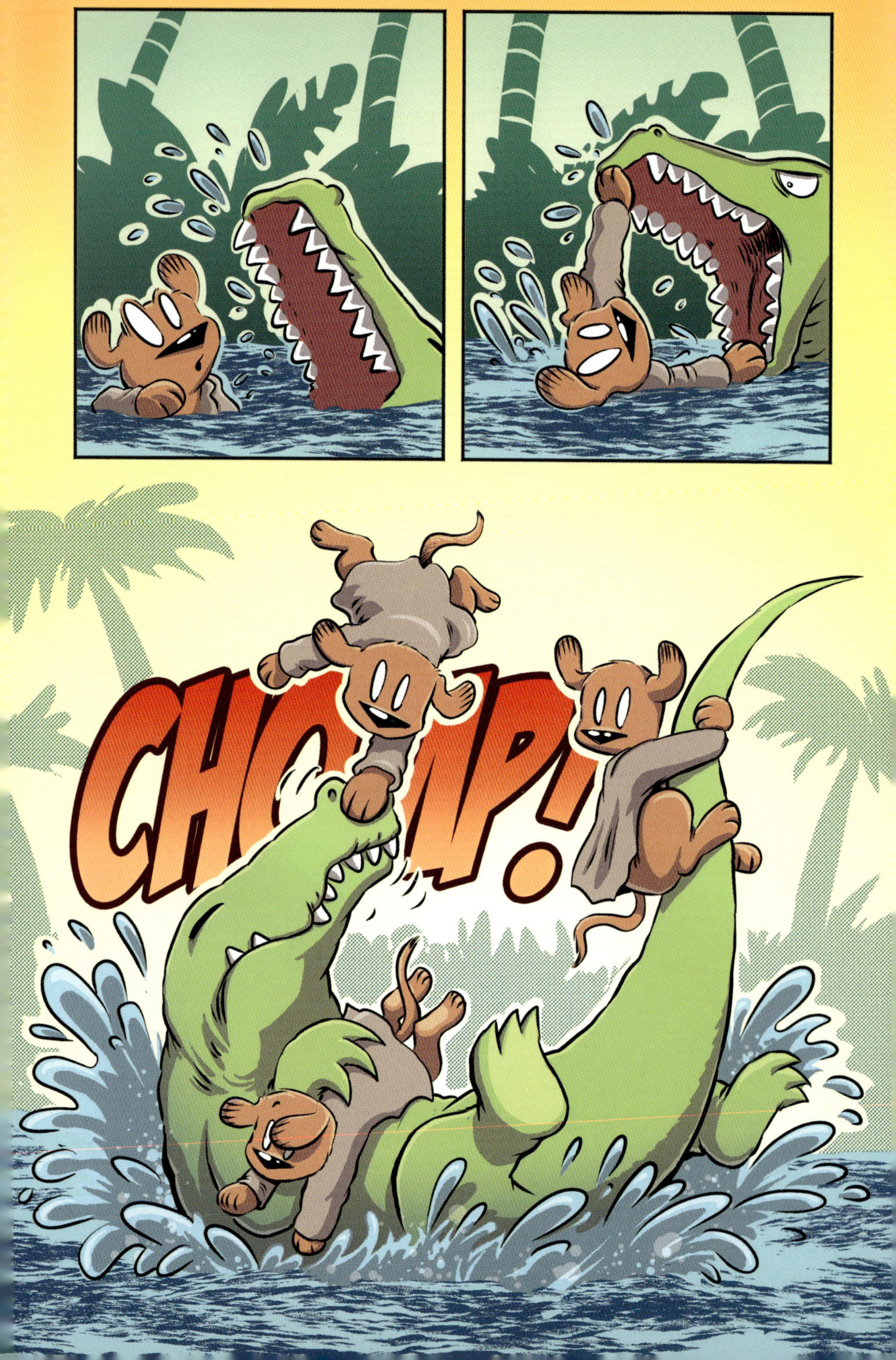
CHOMP!

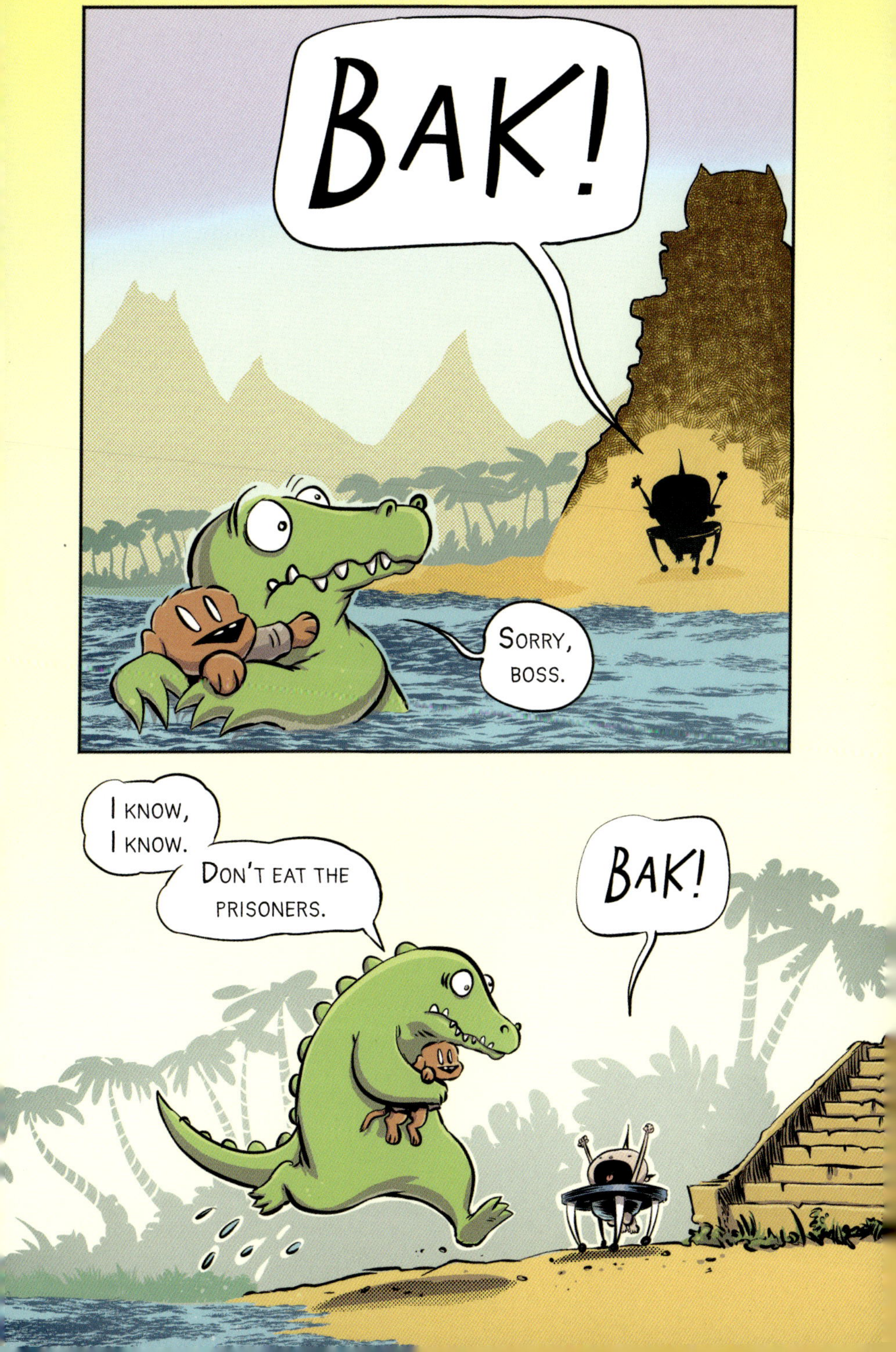
BAK!
SORRY, BOSS.
I KNOW, I KNOW.
DON'T EAT THE PRISONERS.
BAK!

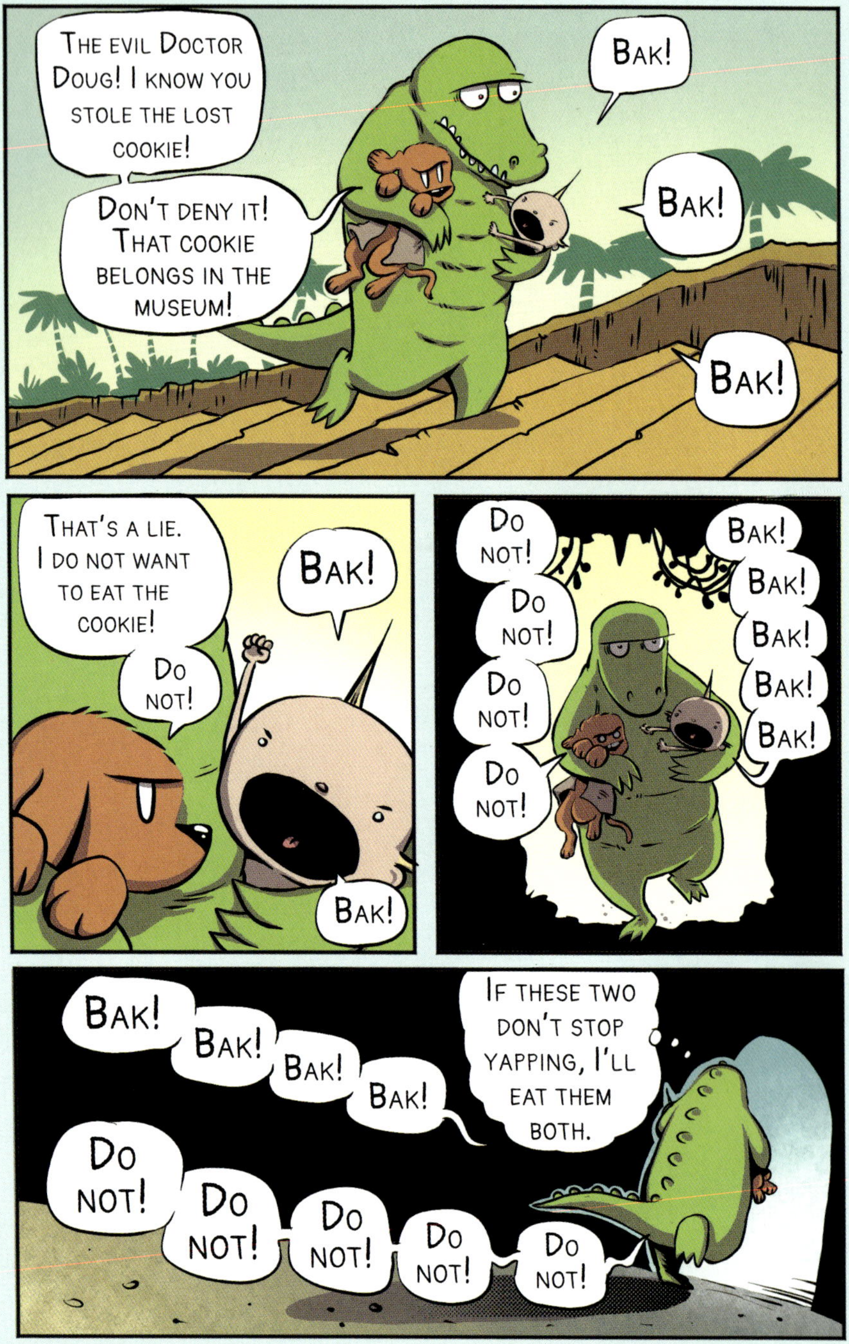
THE EVIL DOCTOR DOUG! I KNOW YOU STOLE THE LOST COOKIE!
BAK!
DON'T DENY IT! THAT COOKIE BELONGS IN THE MUSEUM!
BAK!
BAK!
THAT'S A LIE. I DO NOT WANT TO EAT THE COOKIE!
BAK!
DO NOT!
BAK!
DO NOT!
BAK!
DO NOT!
BAK!
DO NOT!
BAK!
DO NOT!
BAK!
BAK!
BAK!
BAK!
BAK!
BAK!
IF THESE TWO DON'T STOP YAPPING, I'LL EAT THEM BOTH.
DO NOT!
DO NOT!
DO NOT!
DO NOT!
DO NOT!

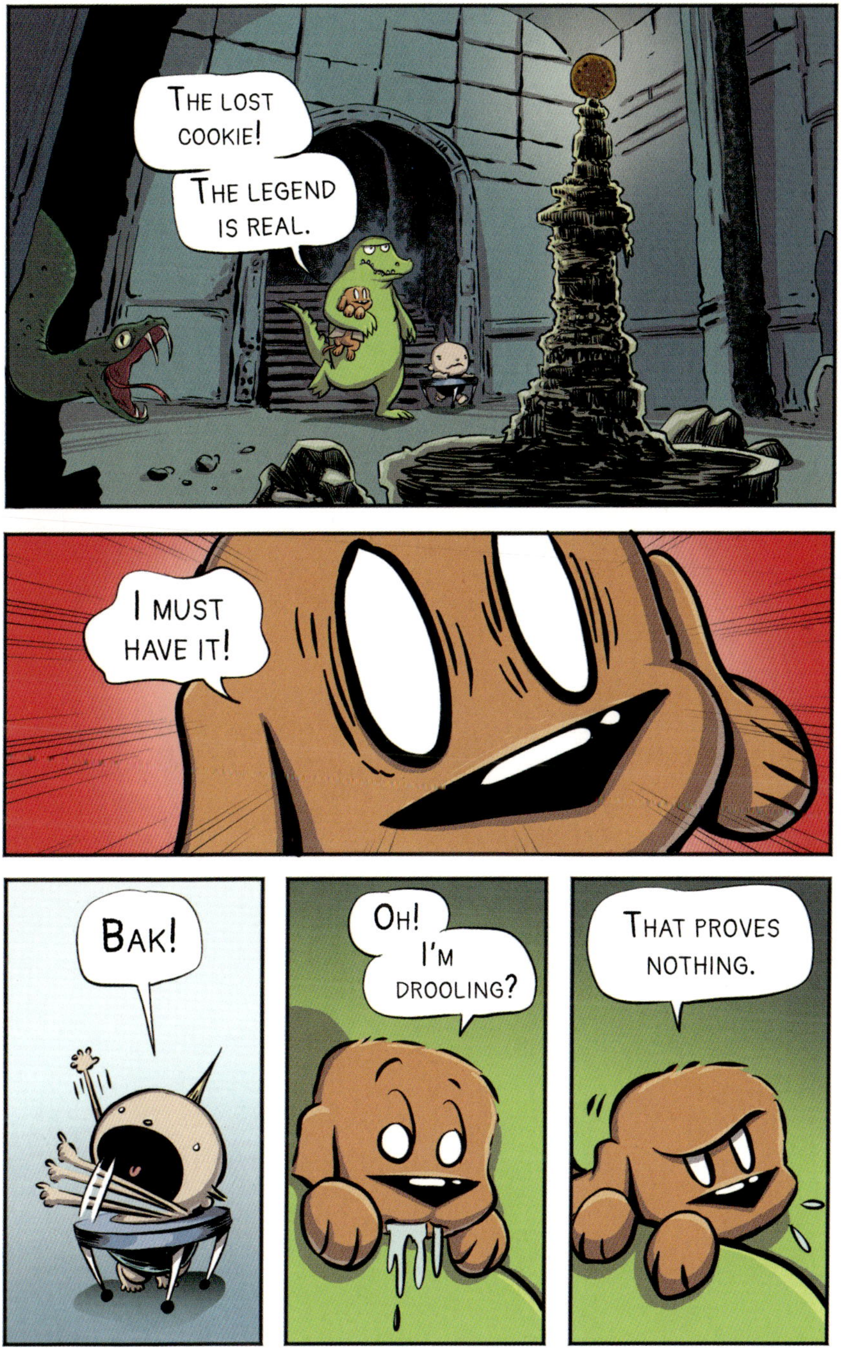
THE LOST COOKIE!
THE LEGEND IS REAL.
I MUST HAVE IT!
BAK!
OH! I'M DROOLING?
THAT PROVES NOTHING.

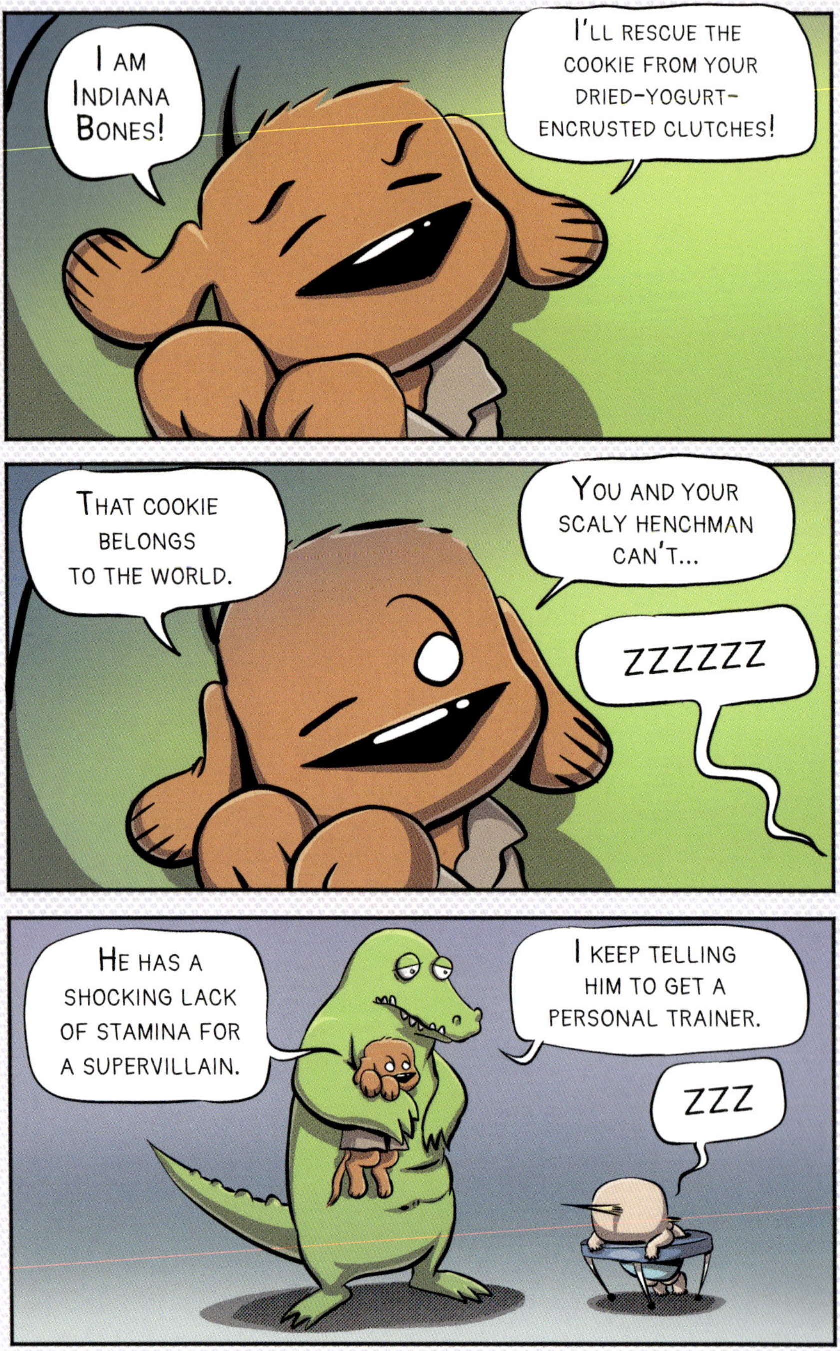
I AM INDIANA BONES!
I'LL RESCUE THE COOKIE FROM YOUR DRIED-YOGURT-ENCRUSTED CLUTCHES!
THAT COOKIE BELONGS TO THE WORLD.
YOU AND YOUR SCALY HENCHMAN CAN'T...
ZZZZZZ
HE HAS A SHOCKING LACK OF STAMINA FOR A SUPERVILLAIN.
I KEEP TELLING HIM TO GET A PERSONAL TRAINER.
ZZZ

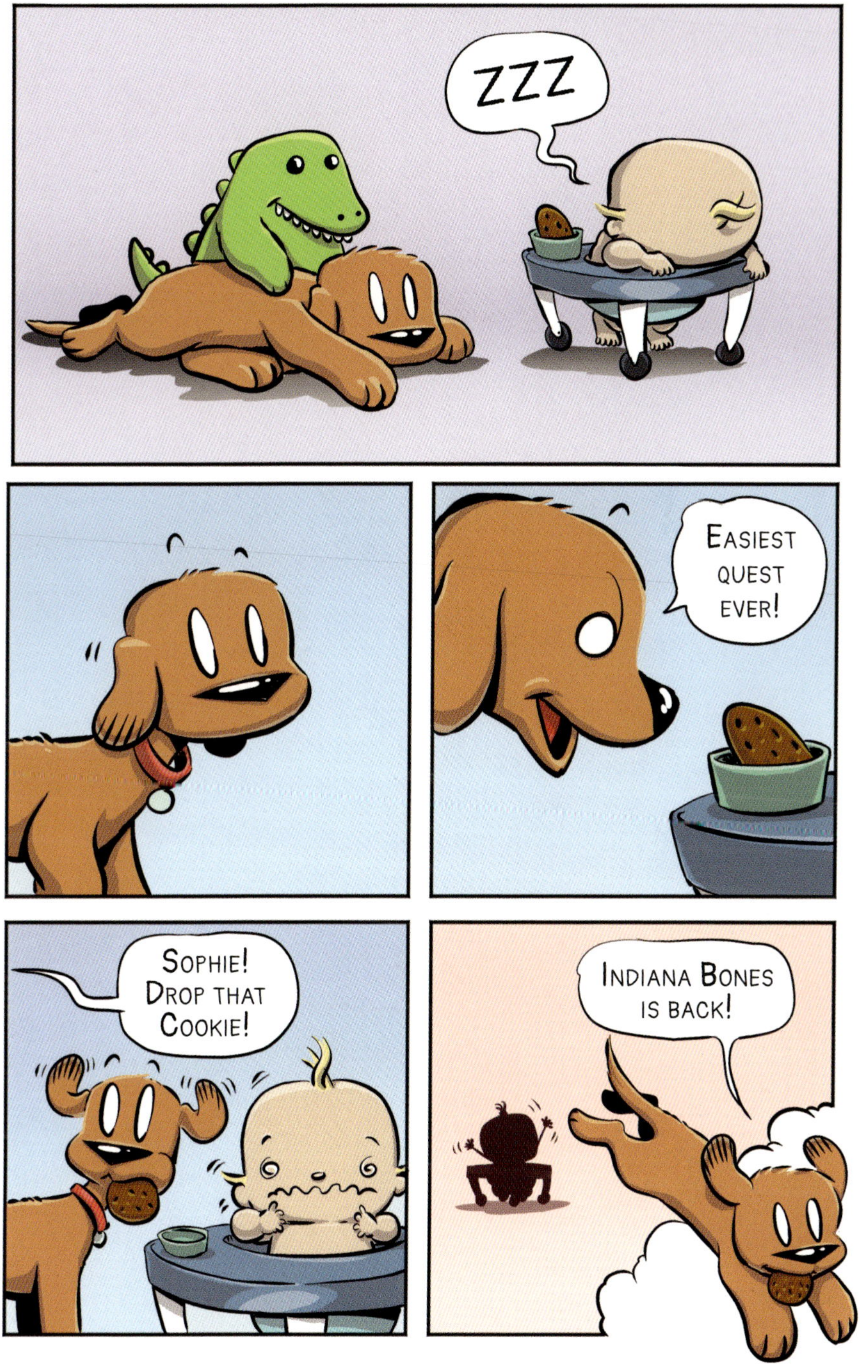
ZZZ
EASIEST QUEST EVER!
SOPHIE! DROP THAT COOKIE!
INDIANA BONES IS BACK!

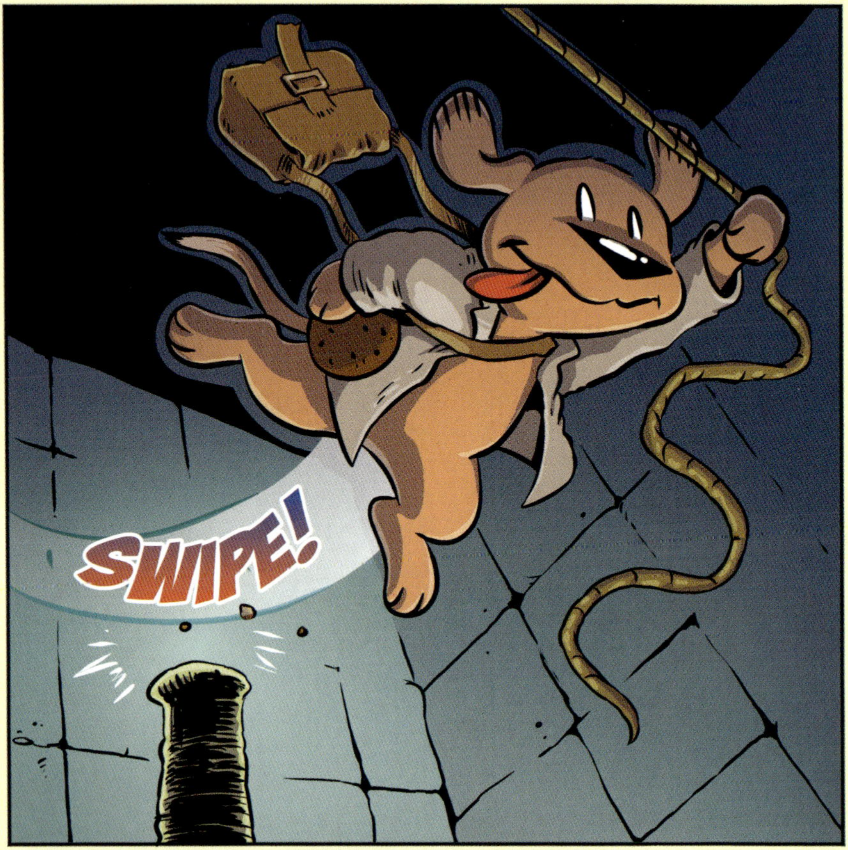
SWIPE!

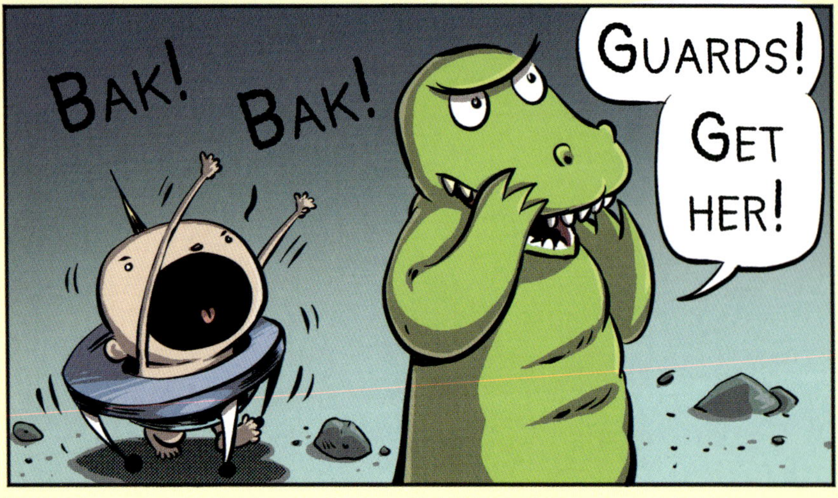
BAK!
BAK!
GUARDS!
GET HER!

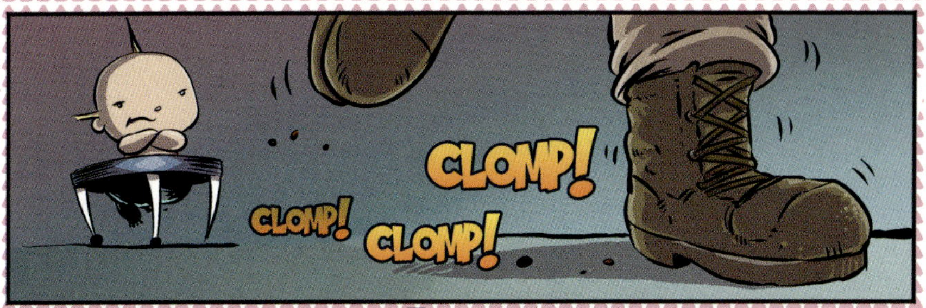
CLOMP!
CLOMP!
CLOMP!

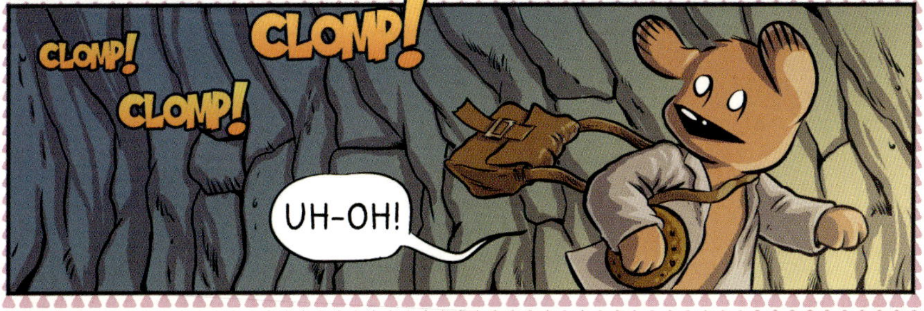
CLOMP!
CLOMP!
CLOMP!
UH-OH!

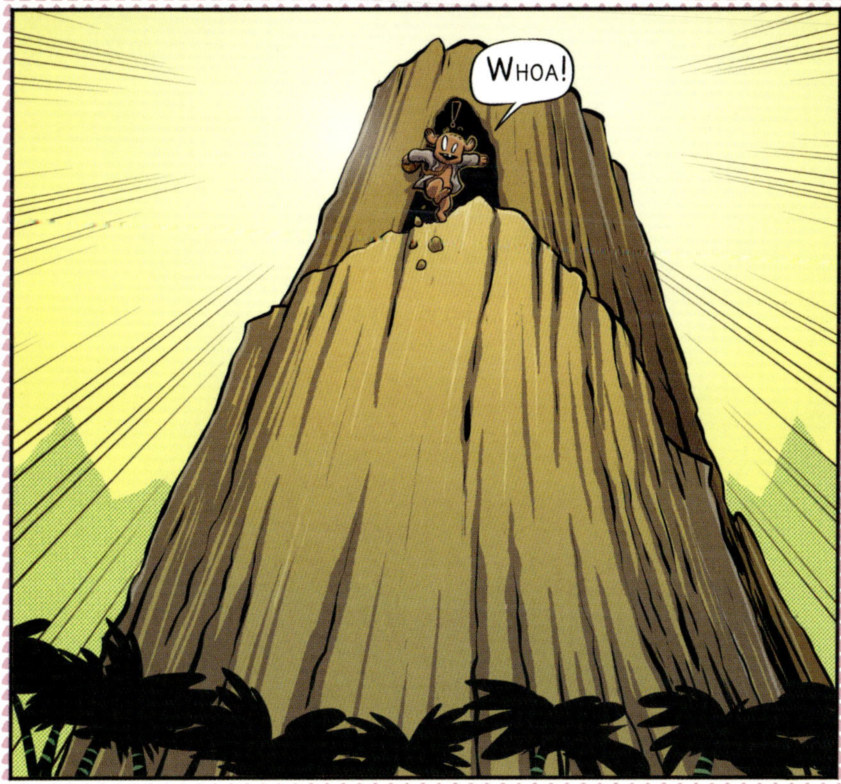
WHOA!

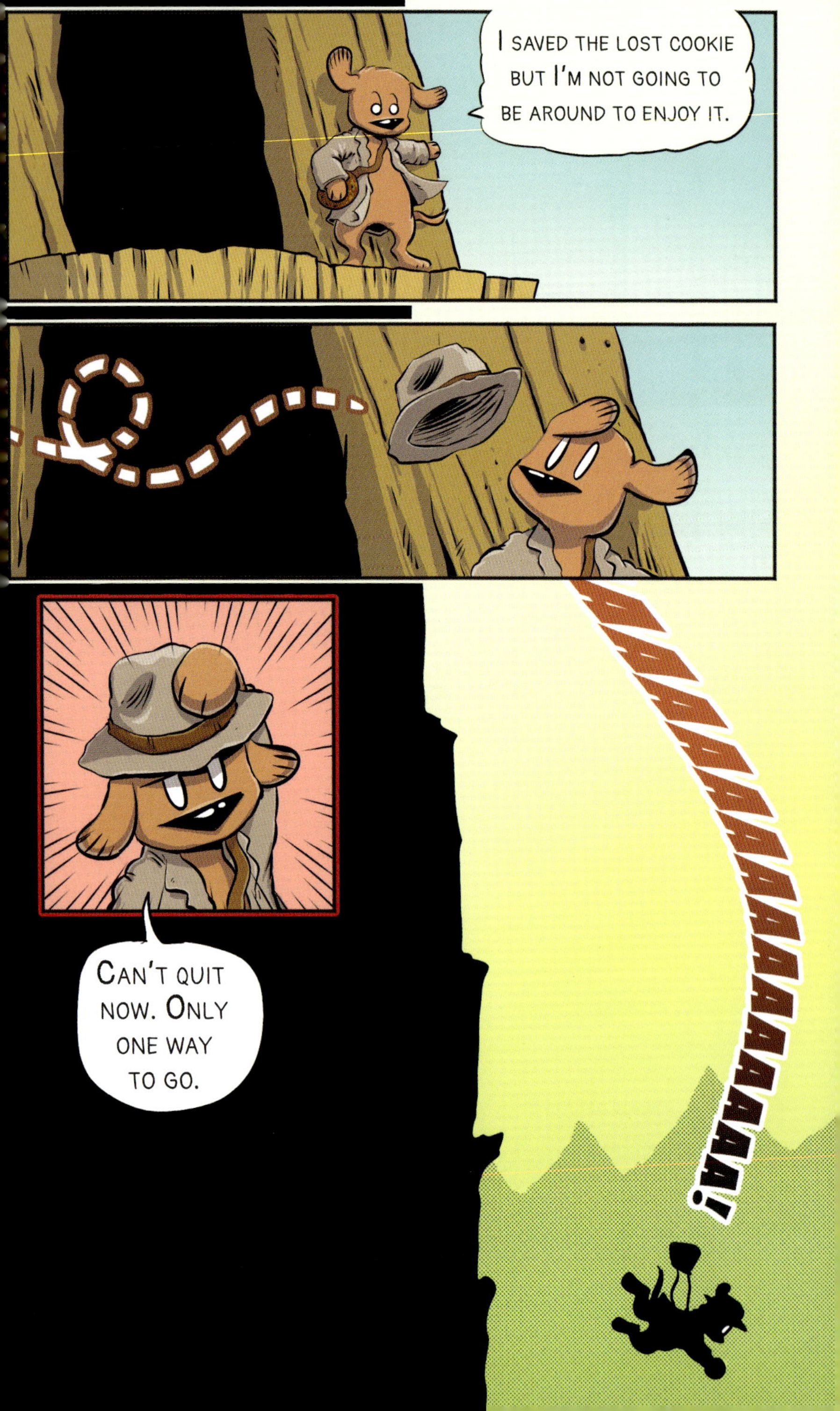
I SAVED THE LOST COOKIE BUT I'M NOT GOING TO BE AROUND TO ENJOY IT.
CAN'T QUIT NOW. ONLY ONE WAY TO GO.
AAAAAAAAAAAAAAAAAAAA!

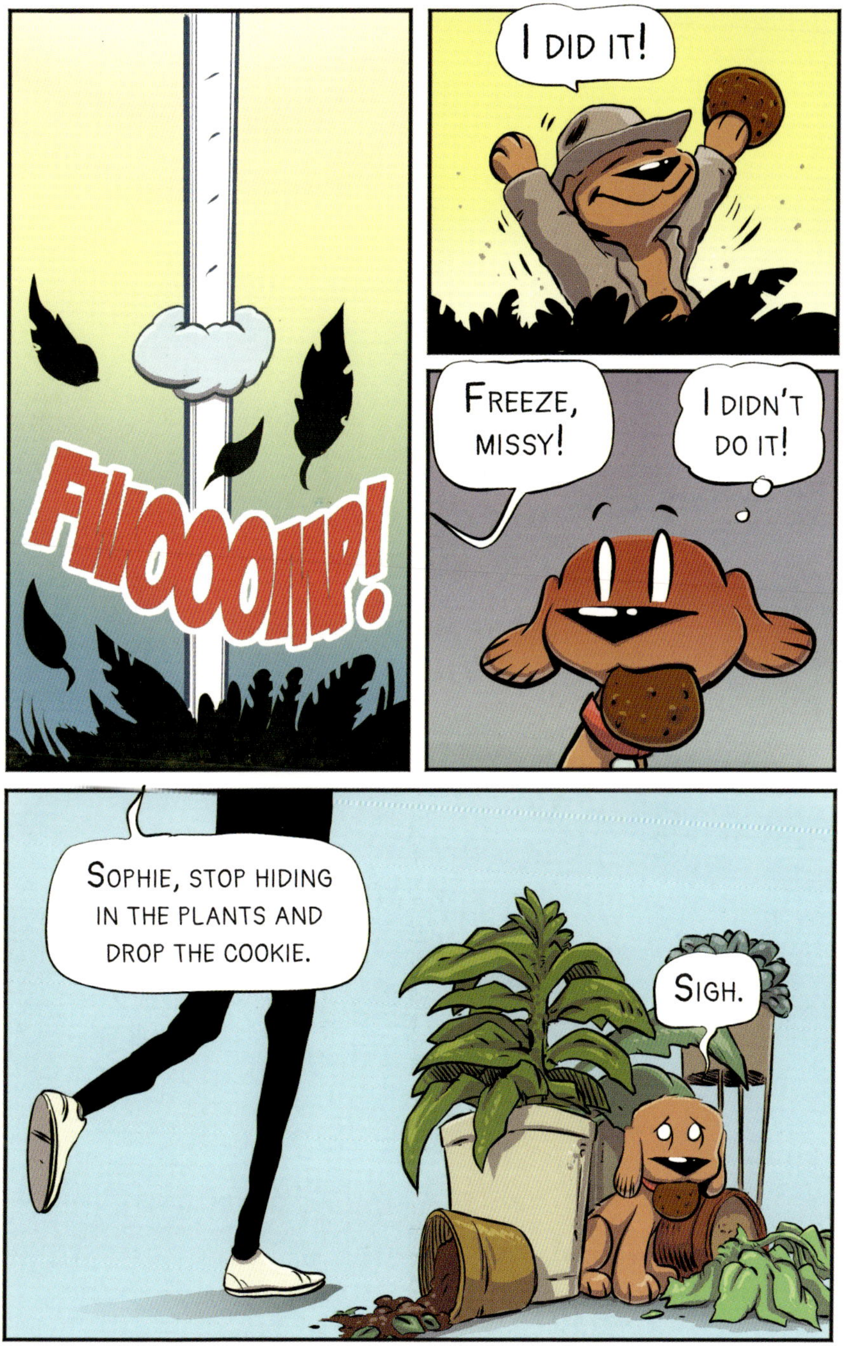
FWOOOOMP!
I DID IT!
FREEZE, MISSY!
I DIDN'T DO IT!
SOPHIE, STOP HIDING IN THE PLANTS AND DROP THE COOKIE.
SIGH.

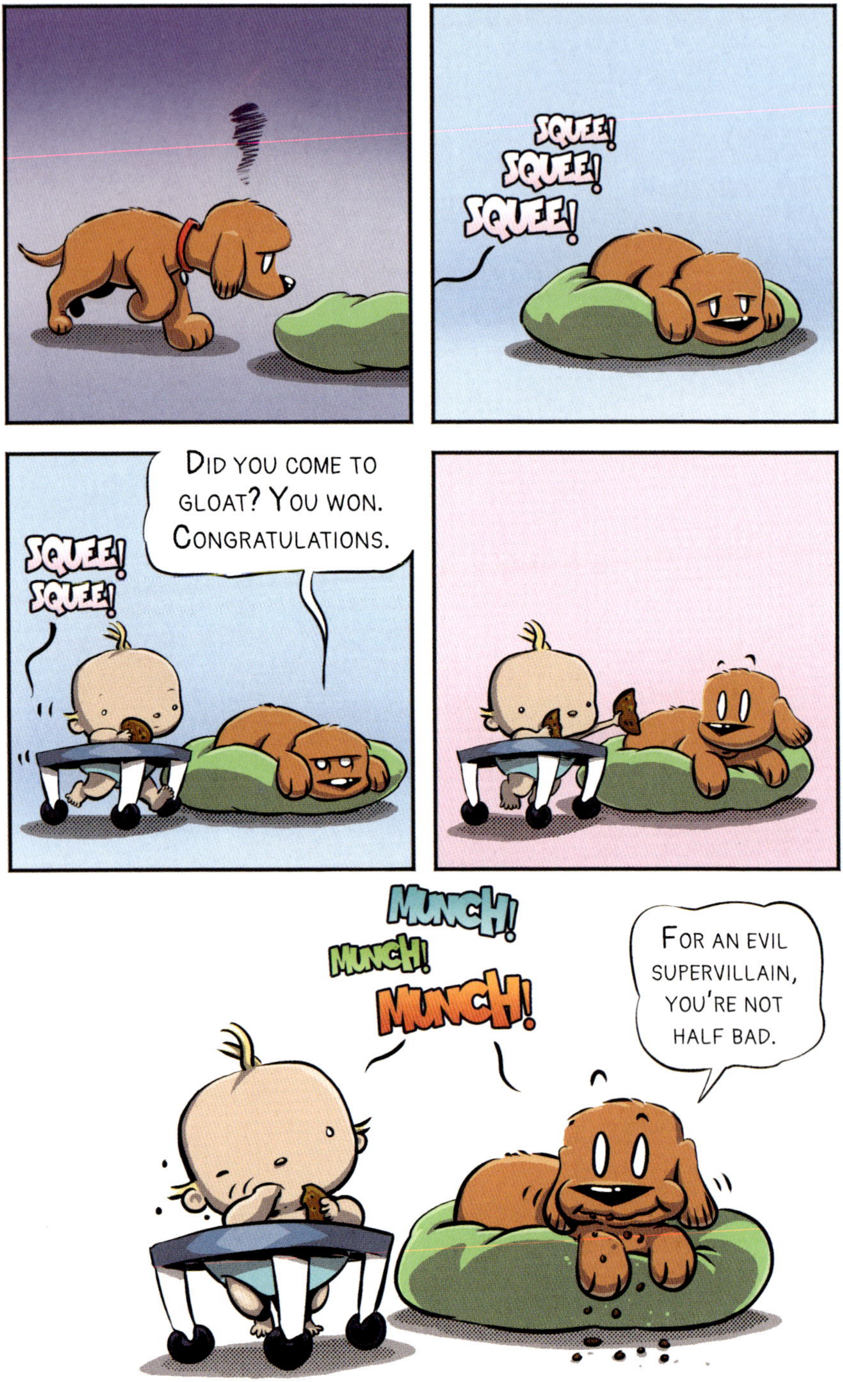
SQUEE!
SQUEE!
SQUEE!
SQUEE!
SQUEE!
DID YOU COME TO GLOAT? YOU WON. CONGRATULATIONS.
MUNCH!
MUNCH!
MUNCH!
FOR AN EVIL SUPERVILLAIN, YOU'RE NOT HALF BAD.

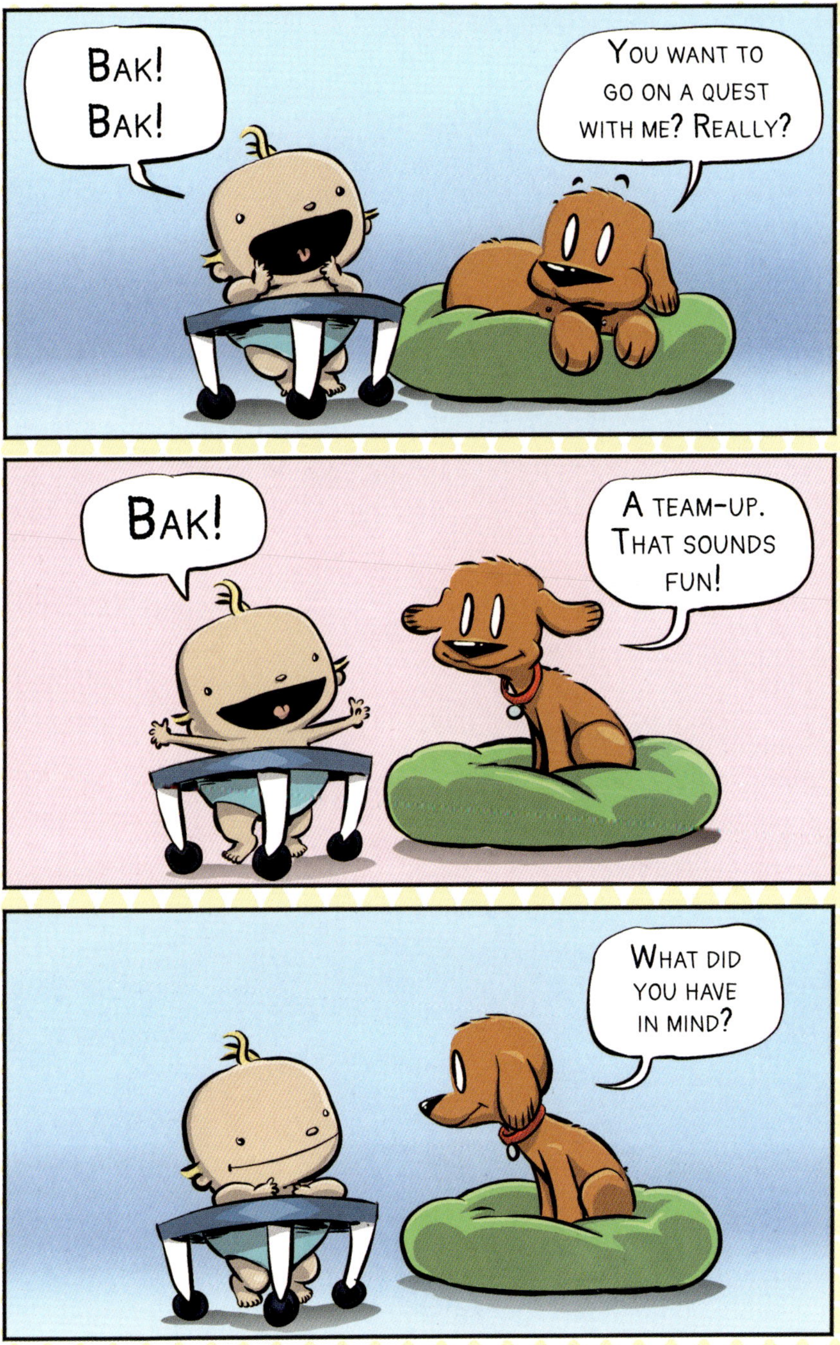
BAK!
BAK!
YOU WANT TO GO ON A QUEST WITH ME? REALLY?
BAK!
A TEAM-UP. THAT SOUNDS FUN!
WHAT DID YOU HAVE IN MIND?

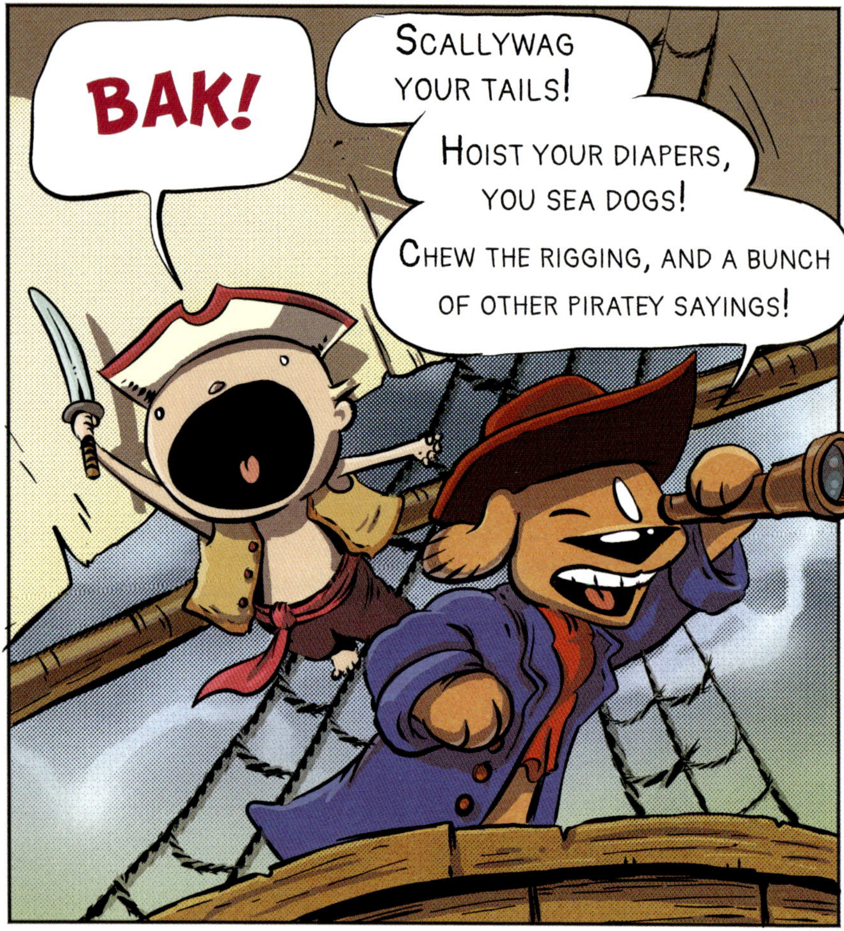
BAK!
SCALLYWAG YOUR TAILS!
HOIST YOUR DIAPERS, YOU SEA DOGS!
CHEW THE RIGGING, AND A BUNCH OF OTHER PIRATEY SAYINGS!

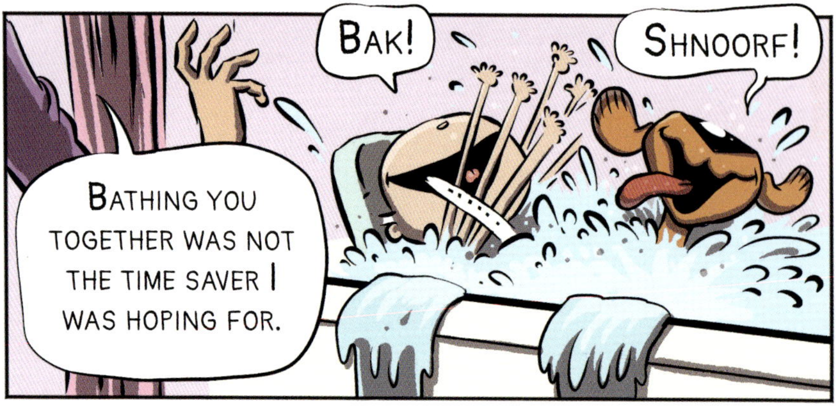
BATHING YOU TOGETHER WAS NOT THE TIME SAVER I WAS HOPING FOR.
BAK!
SHNOORF!

CHAPTER 3

Strange Crib Fellows

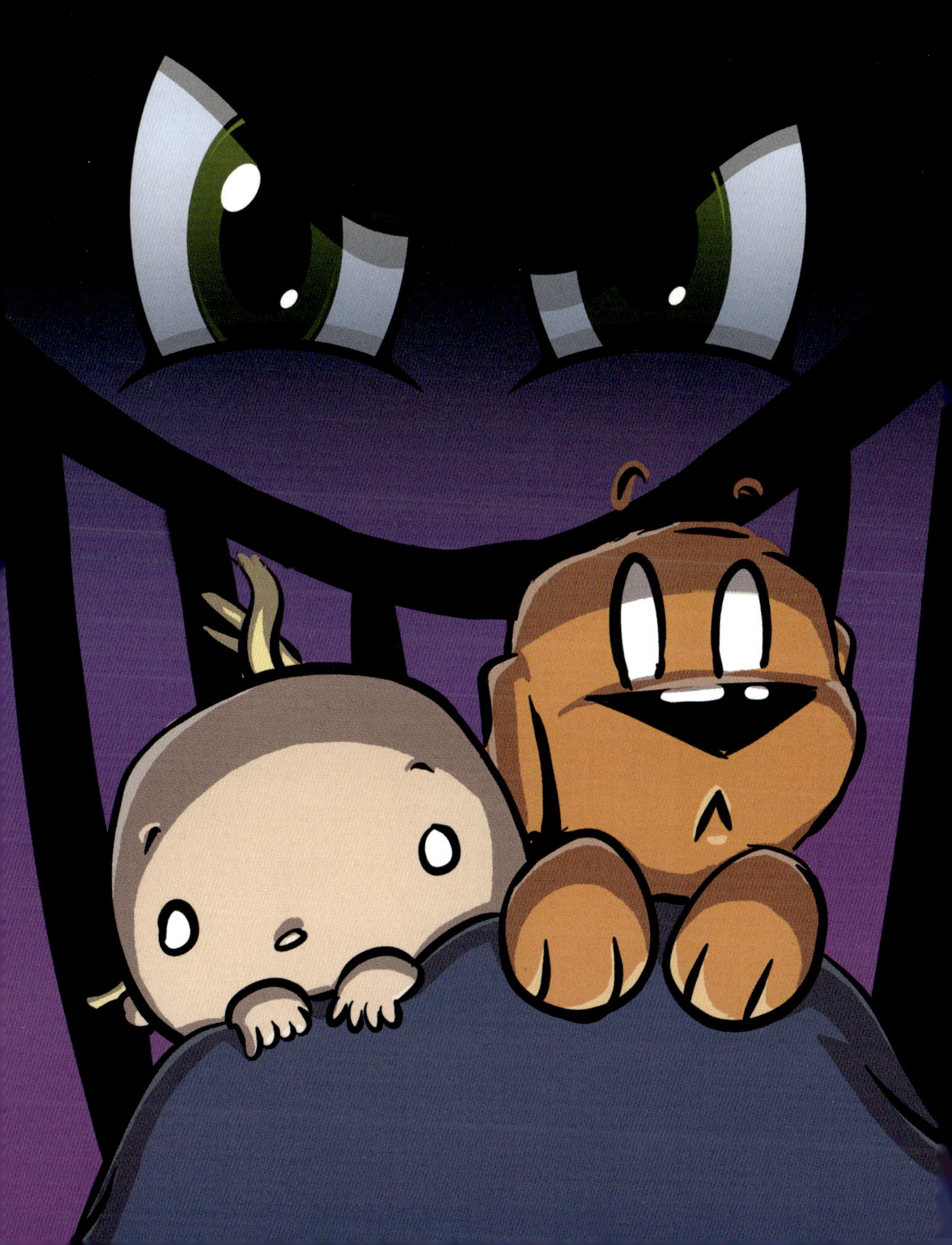

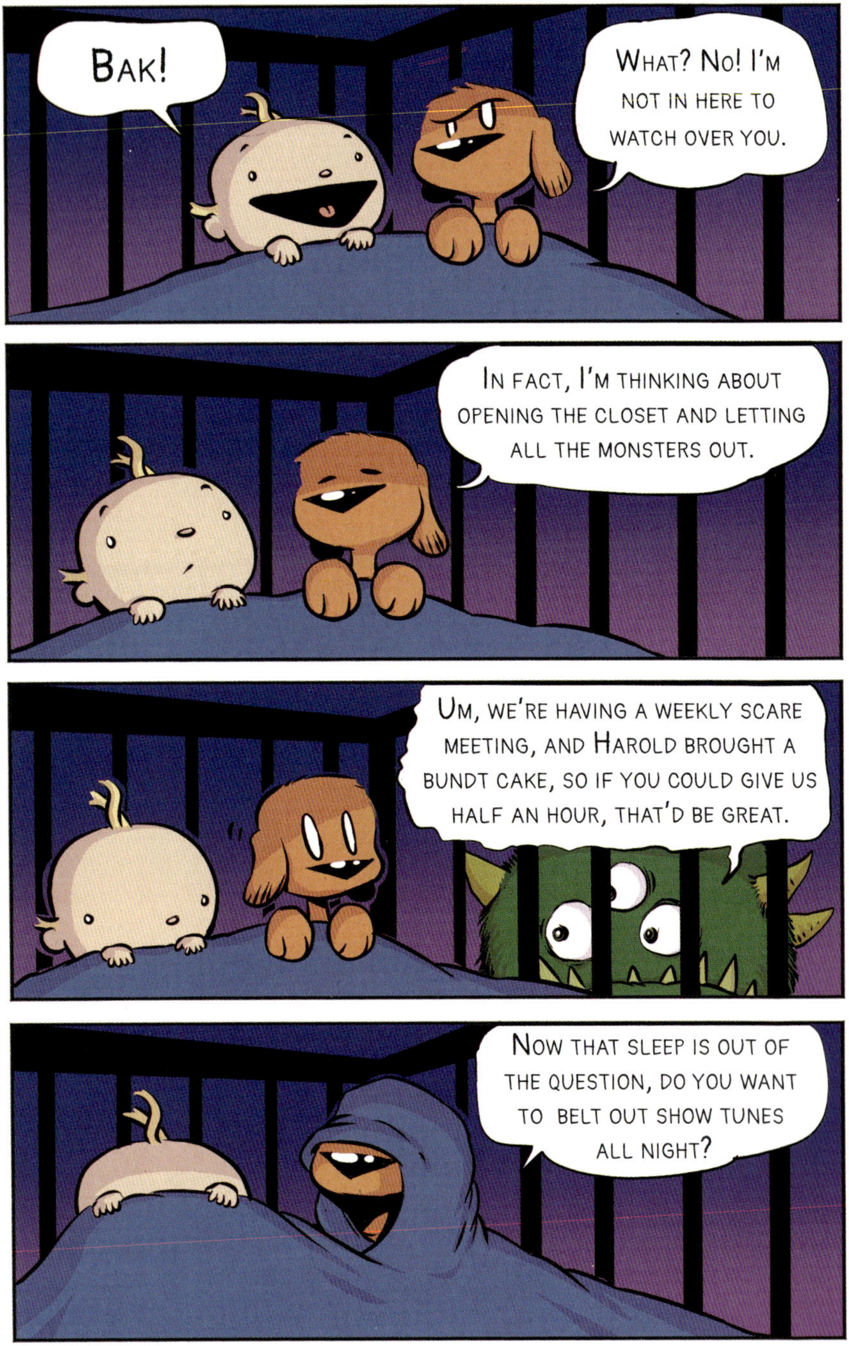
BAK!
WHAT? NO! I'M NOT IN HERE TO WATCH OVER YOU.
IN FACT, I'M THINKING ABOUT OPENING THE CLOSET AND LETTING ALL THE MONSTERS OUT.
UM, WE'RE HAVING A WEEKLY SCARE MEETING, AND HAROLD BROUGHT A BUNDT CAKE, SO IF YOU COULD GIVE US HALF AN HOUR, THAT'D BE GREAT.
NOW THAT SLEEP IS OUT OF THE QUESTION, DO YOU WANT TO BELT OUT SHOW TUNES ALL NIGHT?

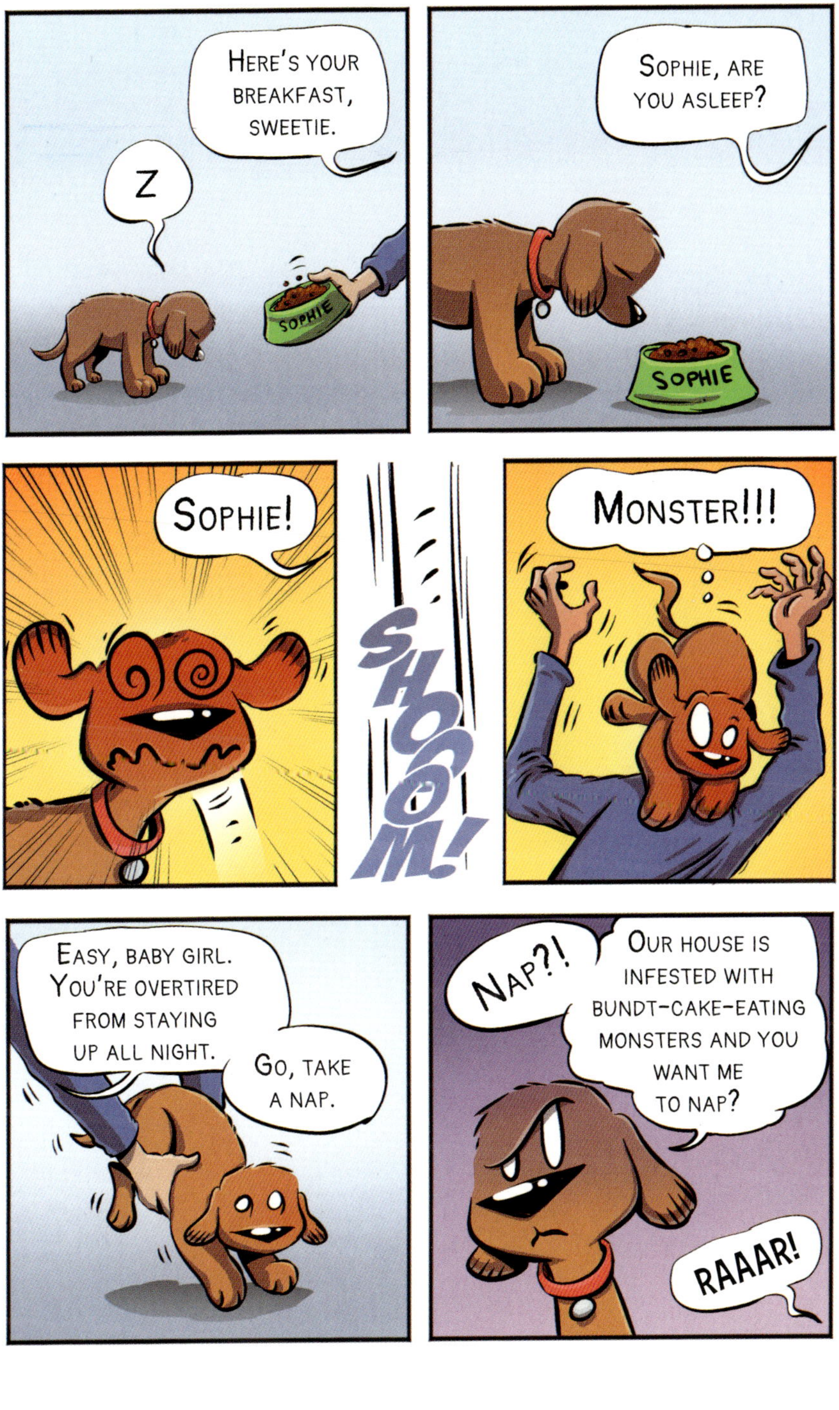
HERE'S YOUR BREAKFAST, SWEETIE.
Z
SOPHIE
SOPHIE, ARE YOU ASLEEP?
SOPHIE
SOPHIE!
SHOOOOM!
MONSTER!!!
EASY, BABY GIRL. YOU'RE OVERTIRED FROM STAYING UP ALL NIGHT.
GO, TAKE A NAP.
NAP?!
OUR HOUSE IS INFESTED WITH BUNDT-CAKE-EATING MONSTERS AND YOU WANT ME TO NAP?
RAAAR!

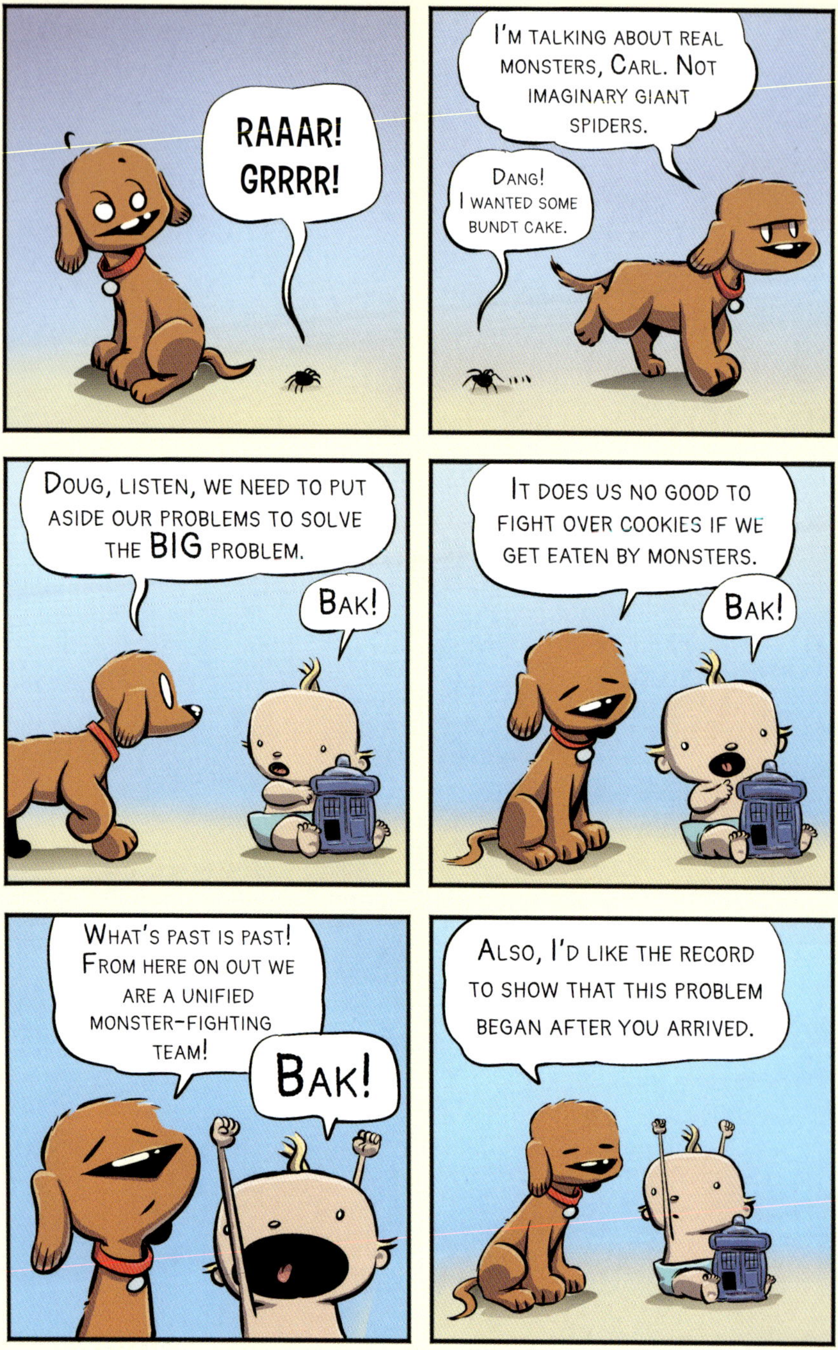
RAAAR! GRRRR!
I'M TALKING ABOUT REAL MONSTERS, CARL. NOT IMAGINARY GIANT SPIDERS.
DANG! I WANTED SOME BUNDT CAKE.
DOUG, LISTEN, WE NEED TO PUT ASIDE OUR PROBLEMS TO SOLVE THE BIG PROBLEM.
BAK!
IT DOES US NO GOOD TO FIGHT OVER COOKIES IF WE GET EATEN BY MONSTERS.
BAK!
WHAT'S PAST IS PAST! FROM HERE ON OUT WE ARE A UNIFIED MONSTER-FIGHTING TEAM!
BAK!
ALSO, I'D LIKE THE RECORD TO SHOW THAT THIS PROBLEM BEGAN AFTER YOU ARRIVED.

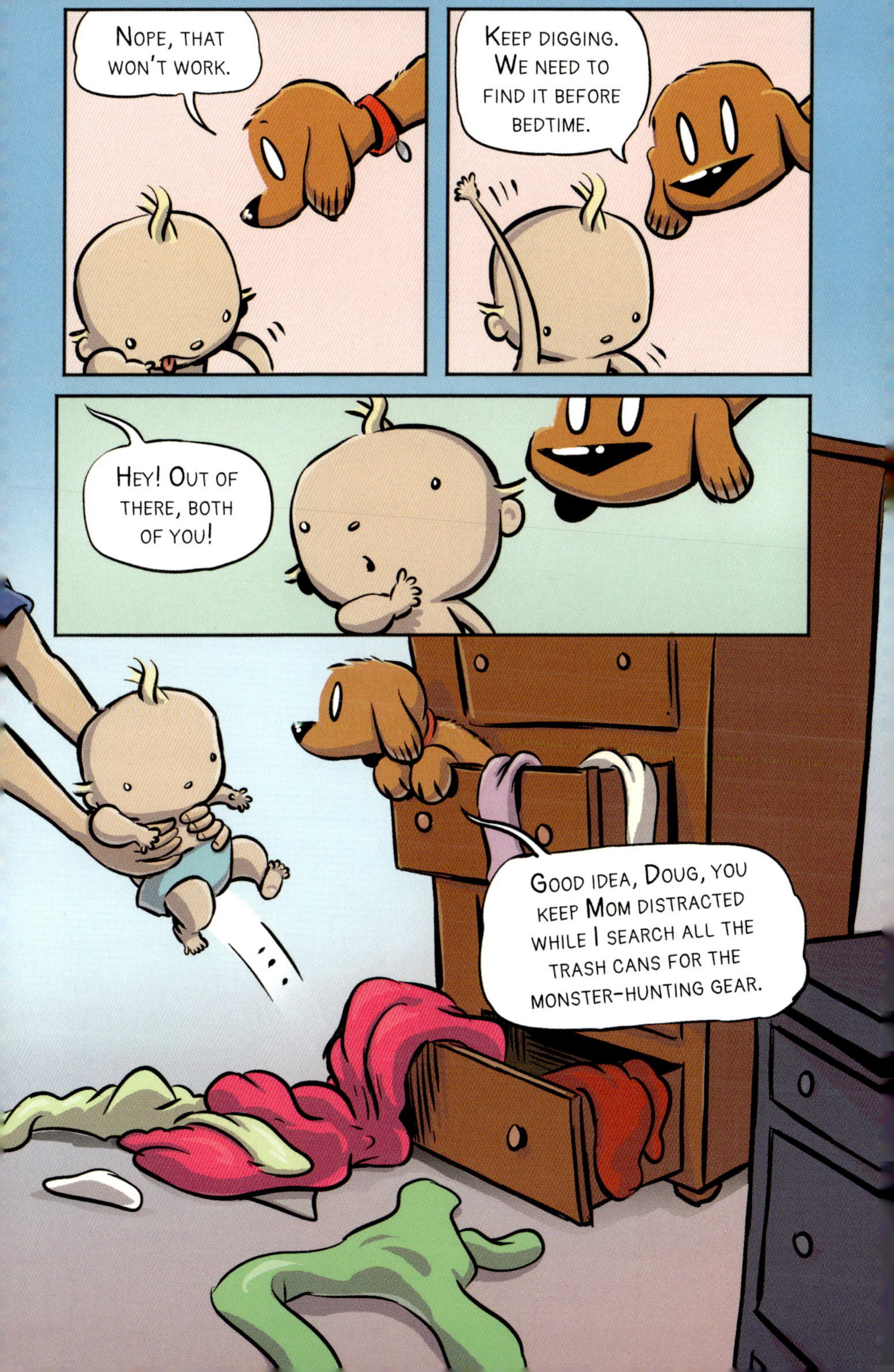
NOPE, THAT WON'T WORK.
KEEP DIGGING. WE NEED TO FIND IT BEFORE BEDTIME.
HEY! OUT OF THERE, BOTH OF YOU!
GOOD IDEA, DOUG, YOU KEEP MOM DISTRACTED WHILE I SEARCH ALL THE TRASH CANS FOR THE MONSTER-HUNTING GEAR.

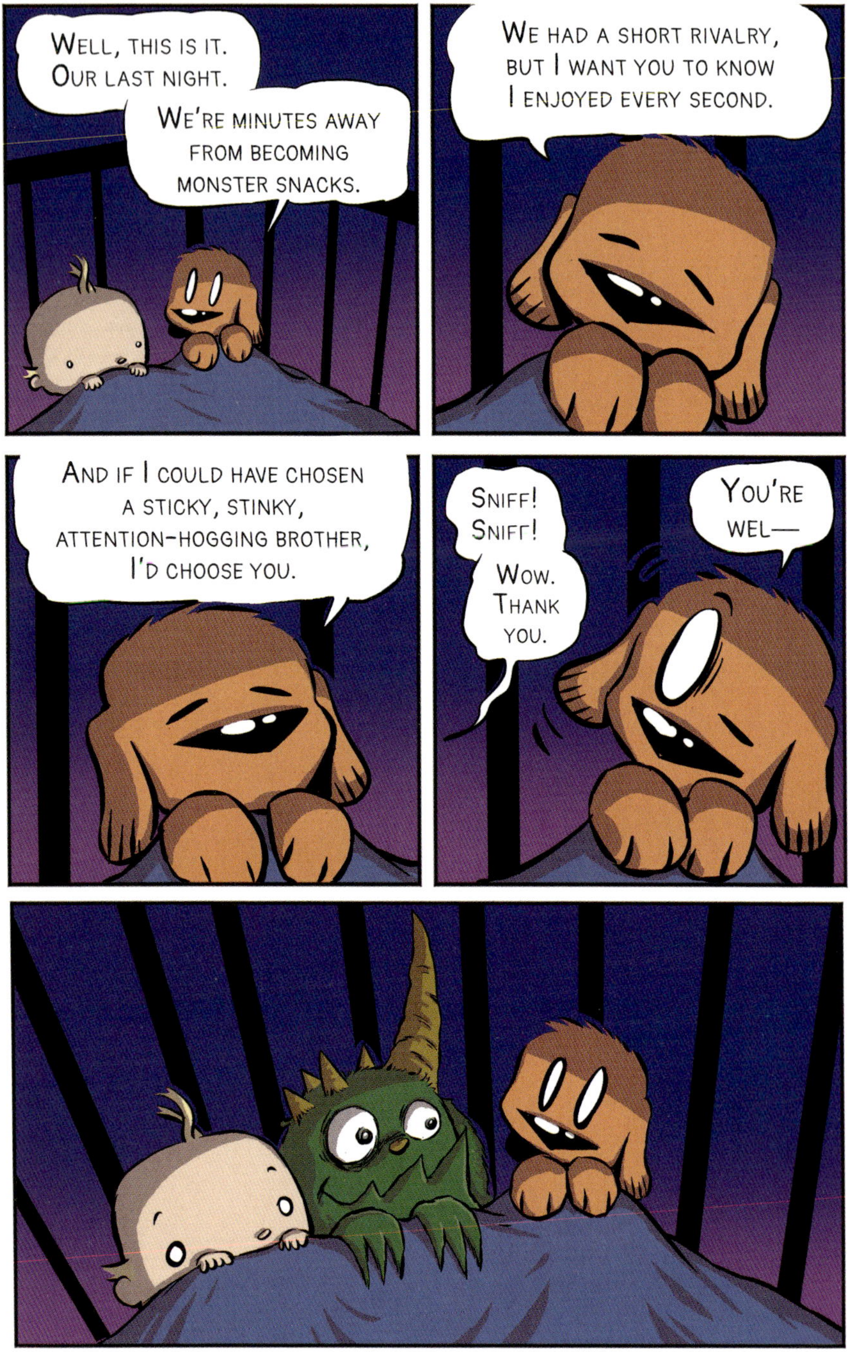
WELL, THIS IS IT.
OUR LAST NIGHT.
WE'RE MINUTES AWAY FROM BECOMING MONSTER SNACKS.
WE HAD A SHORT RIVALRY, BUT I WANT YOU TO KNOW I ENJOYED EVERY SECOND.
AND IF I COULD HAVE CHOSEN A STICKY, STINKY, ATTENTION-HOGGING BROTHER, I'D CHOOSE YOU.
SNIFF! SNIFF!
WOW. THANK YOU.
YOU'RE WEL—

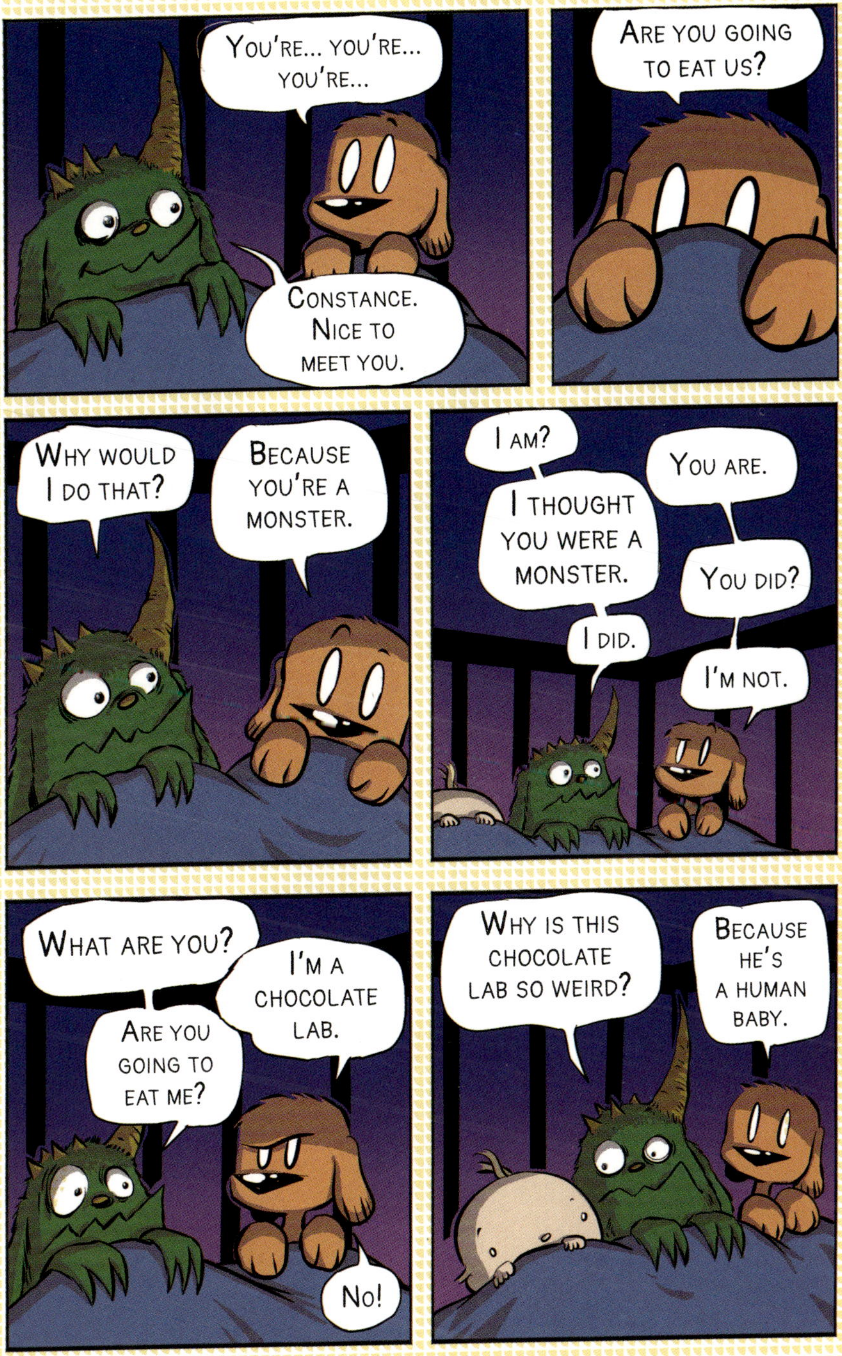
You're... you're... you're...
Constance. Nice to meet you.
Are you going to eat us?
Why would I do that?
Because you're a monster.
I am?
I thought you were a monster.
I did.
You are.
You did?
I'm not.
What are you?
Are you going to eat me?
I'm a chocolate lab.
No!
Why is this chocolate lab so weird?
Because he's a human baby.

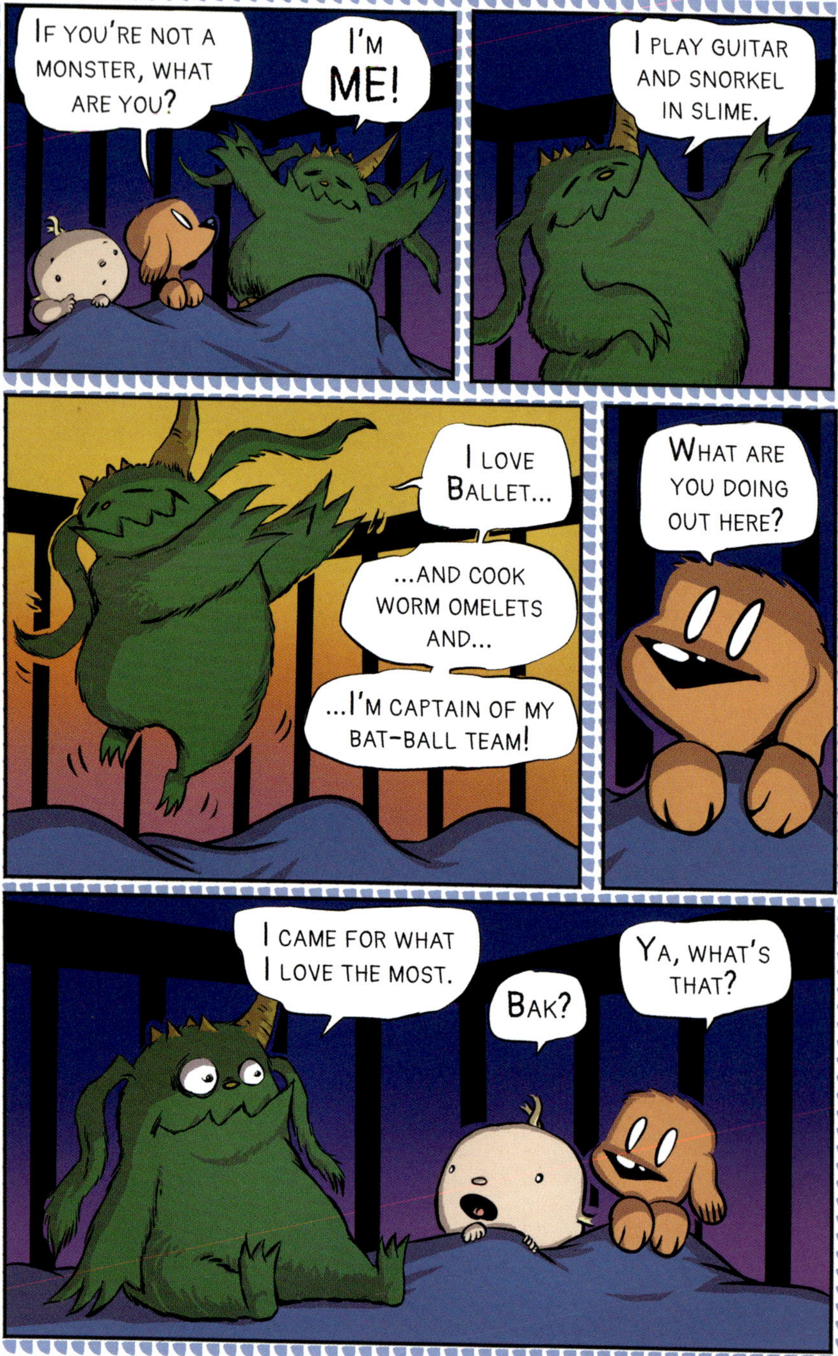

IF YOU'RE NOT A MONSTER, WHAT ARE YOU?
I'M ME!
I PLAY GUITAR AND SNORKEL IN SLIME.
I LOVE BALLET...
...AND COOK WORM OMELETS AND...
...I'M CAPTAIN OF MY BAT-BALL TEAM!
WHAT ARE YOU DOING OUT HERE?
I CAME FOR WHAT I LOVE THE MOST.
BAK?
YA, WHAT'S THAT?

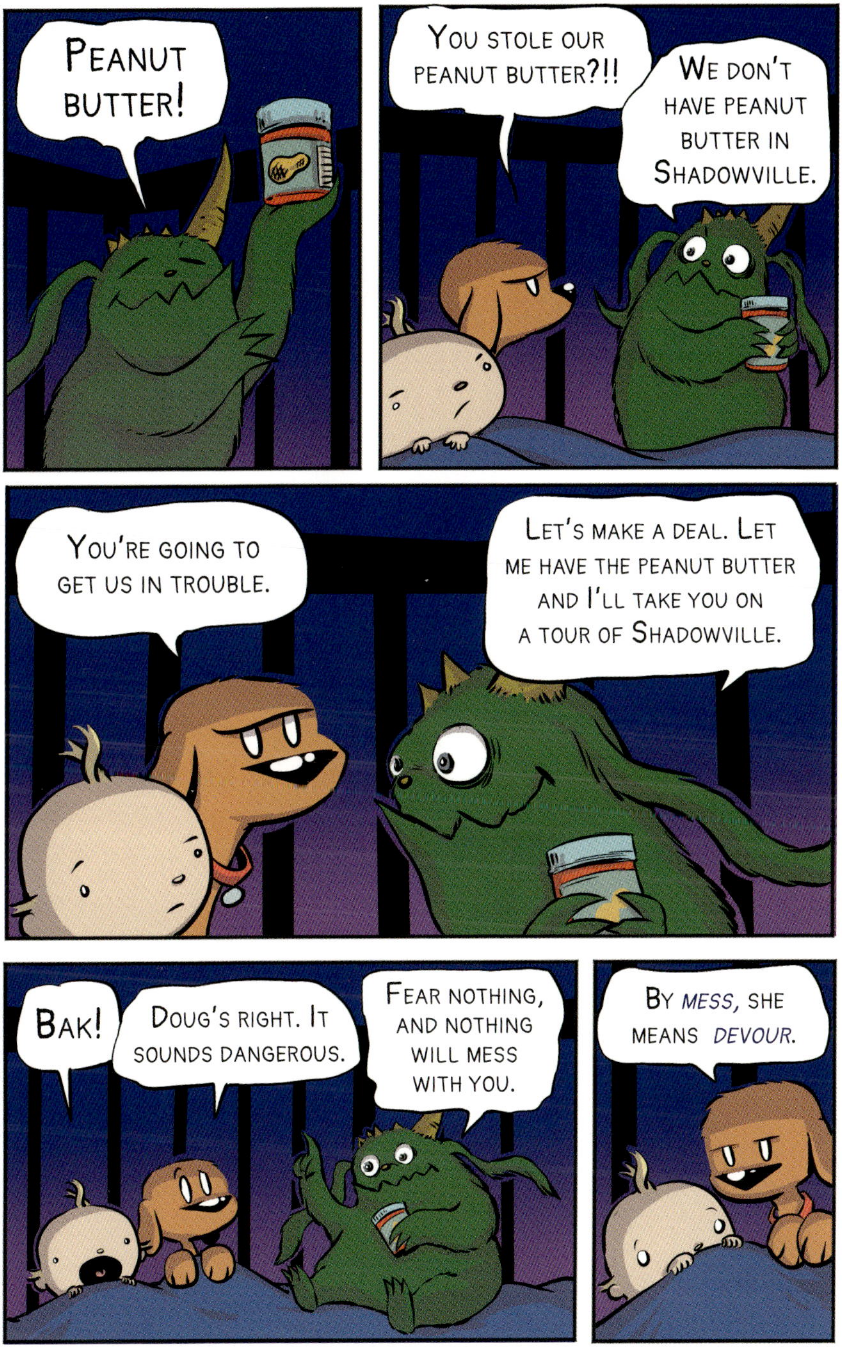
PEANUT BUTTER!
YOU STOLE OUR PEANUT BUTTER?!!
WE DON'T HAVE PEANUT BUTTER IN SHADOWVILLE.
YOU'RE GOING TO GET US IN TROUBLE.
LET'S MAKE A DEAL. LET ME HAVE THE PEANUT BUTTER AND I'LL TAKE YOU ON A TOUR OF SHADOWVILLE.
BAK!
DOUG'S RIGHT. IT SOUNDS DANGEROUS.
FEAR NOTHING, AND NOTHING WILL MESS WITH YOU.
BY *MESS,* SHE MEANS *DEVOUR*.

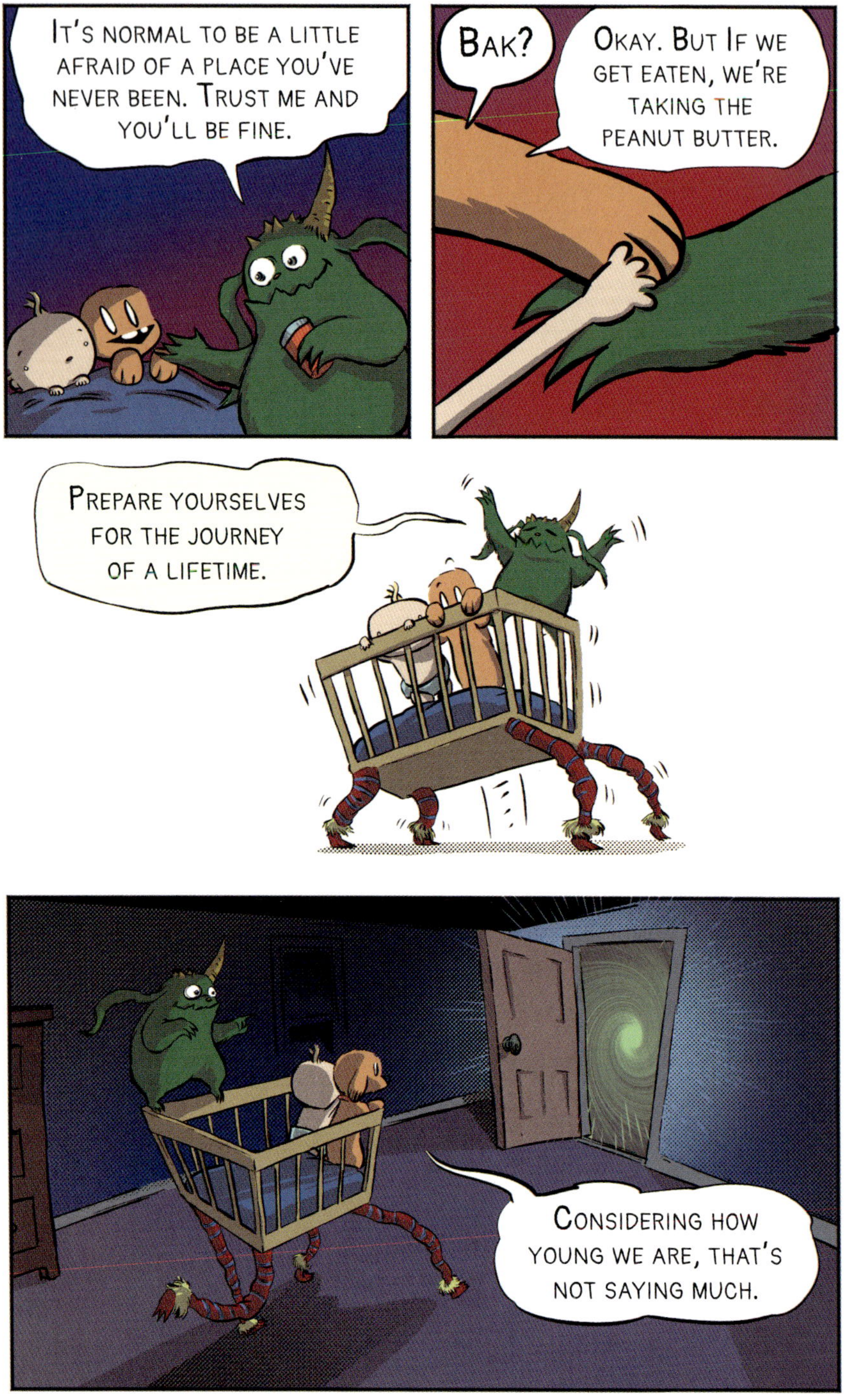
It's normal to be a little afraid of a place you've never been. Trust me and you'll be fine.
Bak?
Okay. But if we get eaten, we're taking the peanut butter.
Prepare yourselves for the journey of a lifetime.
Considering how young we are, that's not saying much.

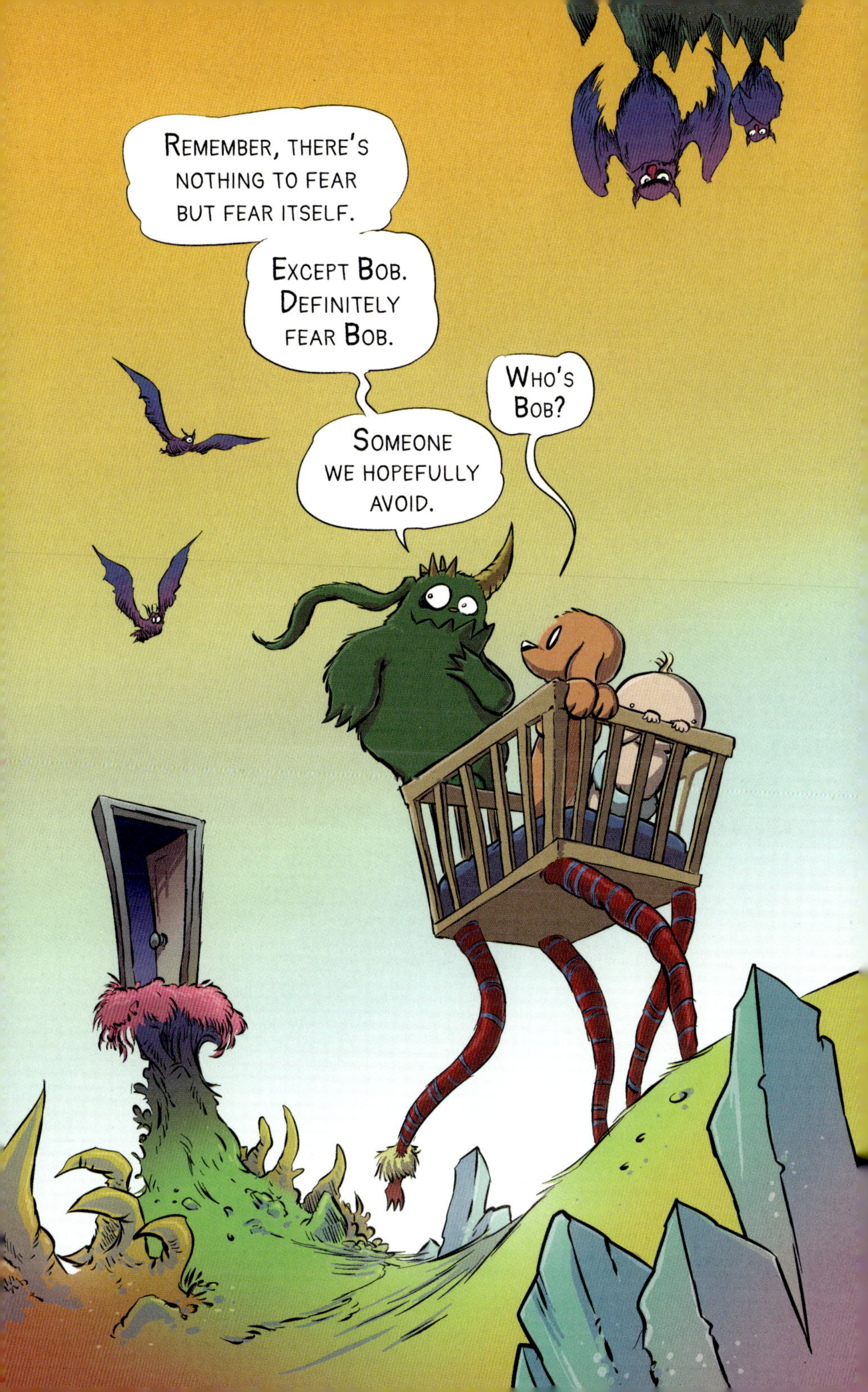
REMEMBER, THERE'S NOTHING TO FEAR BUT FEAR ITSELF.
EXCEPT BOB. DEFINITELY FEAR BOB.
WHO'S BOB?
SOMEONE WE HOPEFULLY AVOID.

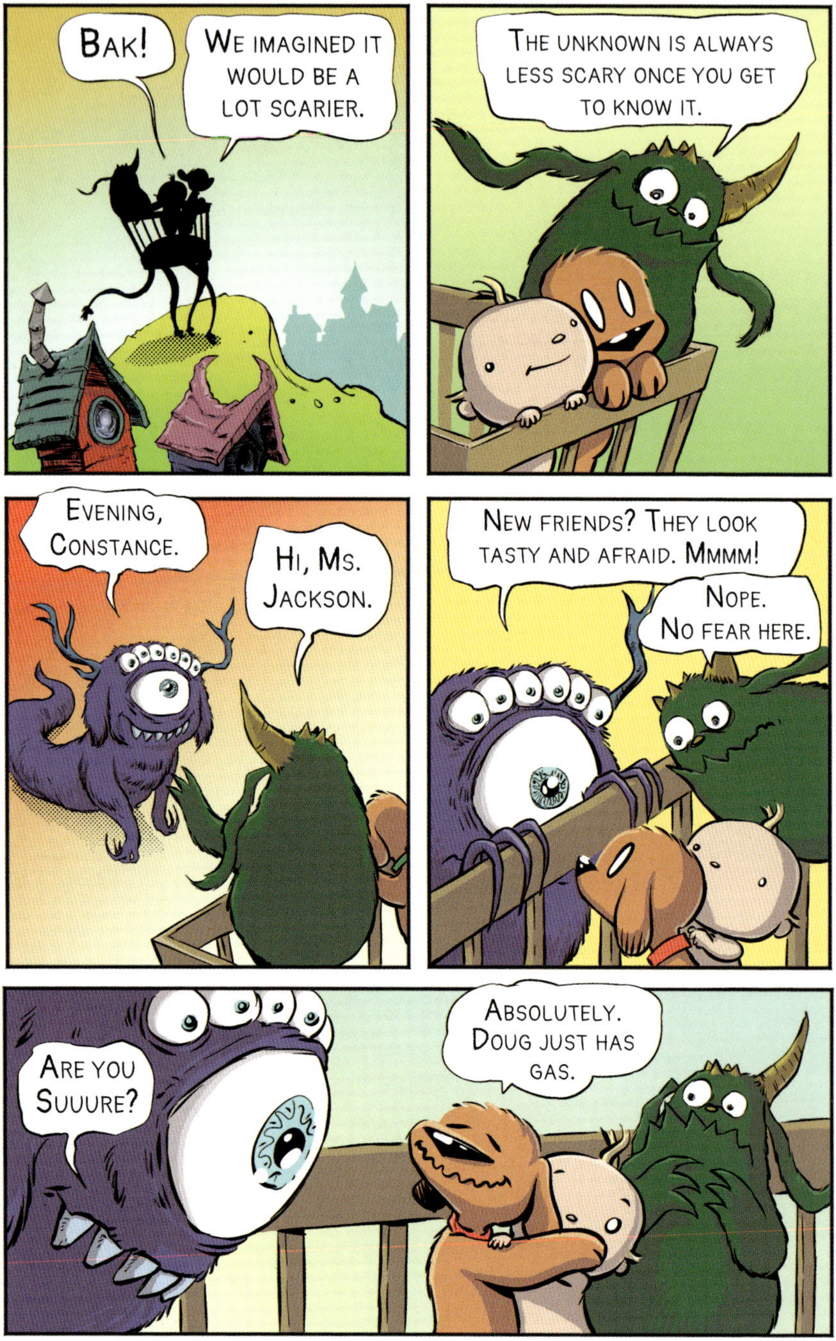
BAK!
WE IMAGINED IT WOULD BE A LOT SCARIER.
THE UNKNOWN IS ALWAYS LESS SCARY ONCE YOU GET TO KNOW IT.
EVENING, CONSTANCE.
HI, MS. JACKSON.
NEW FRIENDS? THEY LOOK TASTY AND AFRAID. MMMM!
NOPE. NO FEAR HERE.
ARE YOU SUUURE?
ABSOLUTELY. DOUG JUST HAS GAS.

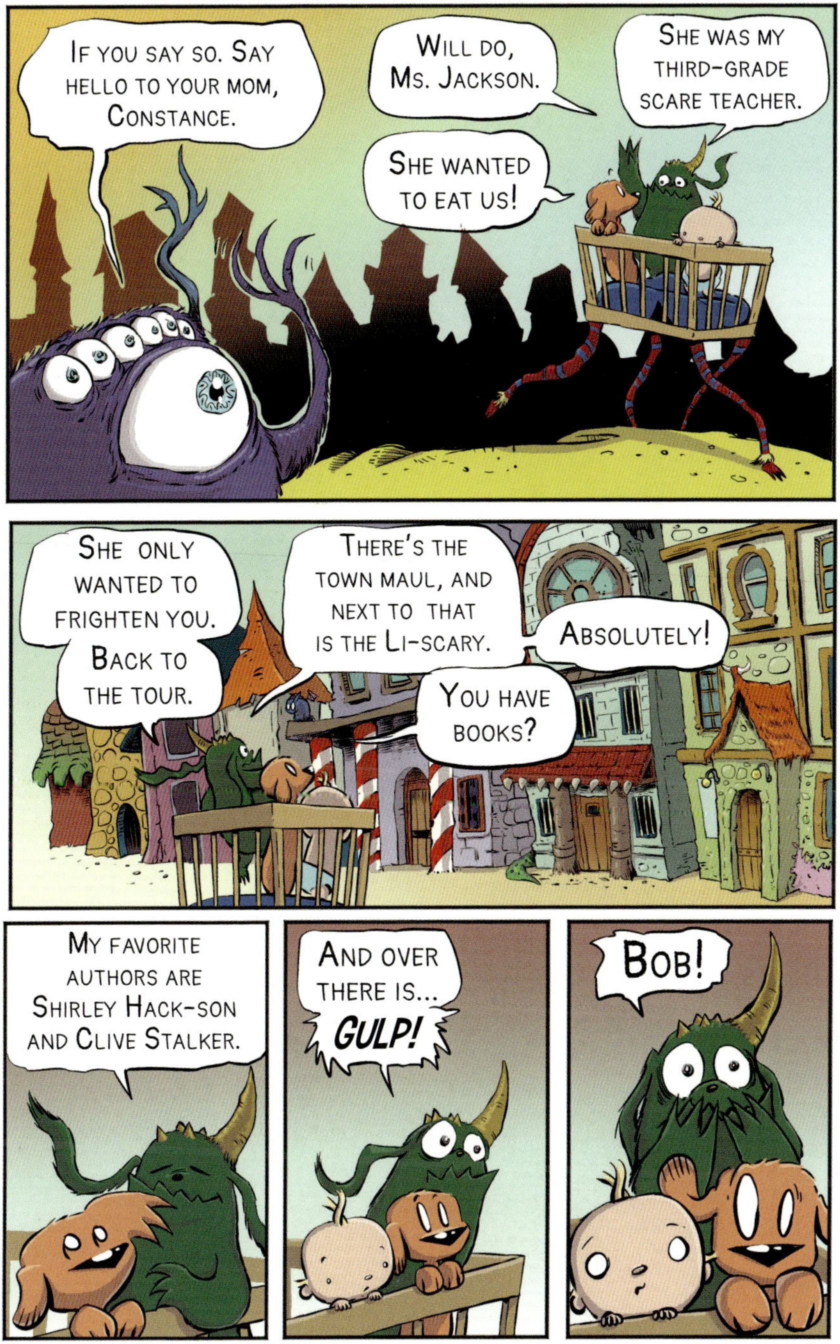
If you say so. Say hello to your mom, Constance.
Will do, Ms. Jackson.
She was my third-grade scare teacher.
She wanted to eat us!
She only wanted to frighten you.
Back to the tour.
There's the town maul, and next to that is the Li-scary.
Absolutely!
You have books?
My favorite authors are Shirley Hack-son and Clive Stalker.
And over there is...
GULP!
Bob!

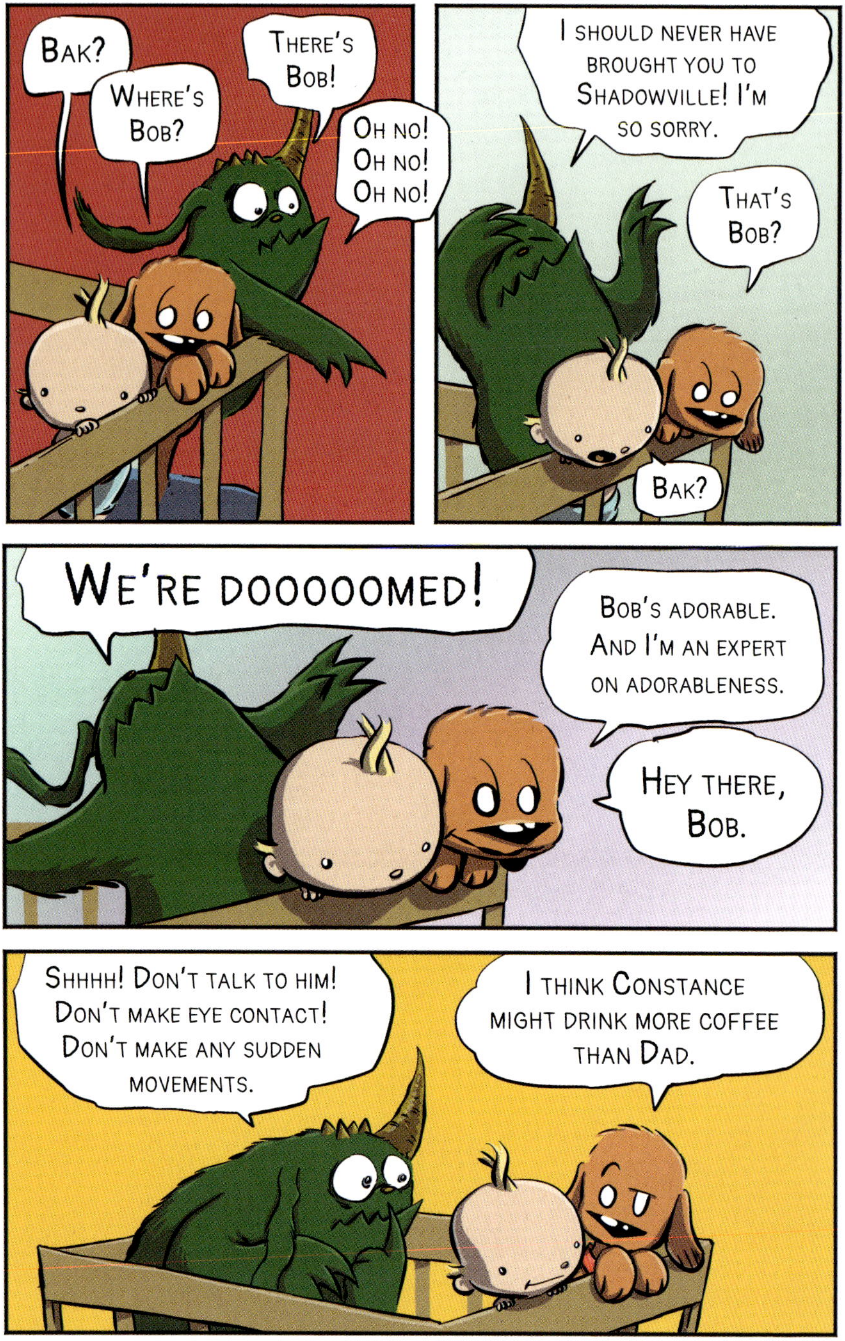
BAK?
WHERE'S BOB?
THERE'S BOB!
OH NO! OH NO! OH NO!
I SHOULD NEVER HAVE BROUGHT YOU TO SHADOWVILLE! I'M SO SORRY.
THAT'S BOB?
BAK?
WE'RE DOOOOOMED!
BOB'S ADORABLE. AND I'M AN EXPERT ON ADORABLENESS.
HEY THERE, BOB.
SHHHH! DON'T TALK TO HIM! DON'T MAKE EYE CONTACT! DON'T MAKE ANY SUDDEN MOVEMENTS.
I THINK CONSTANCE MIGHT DRINK MORE COFFEE THAN DAD.

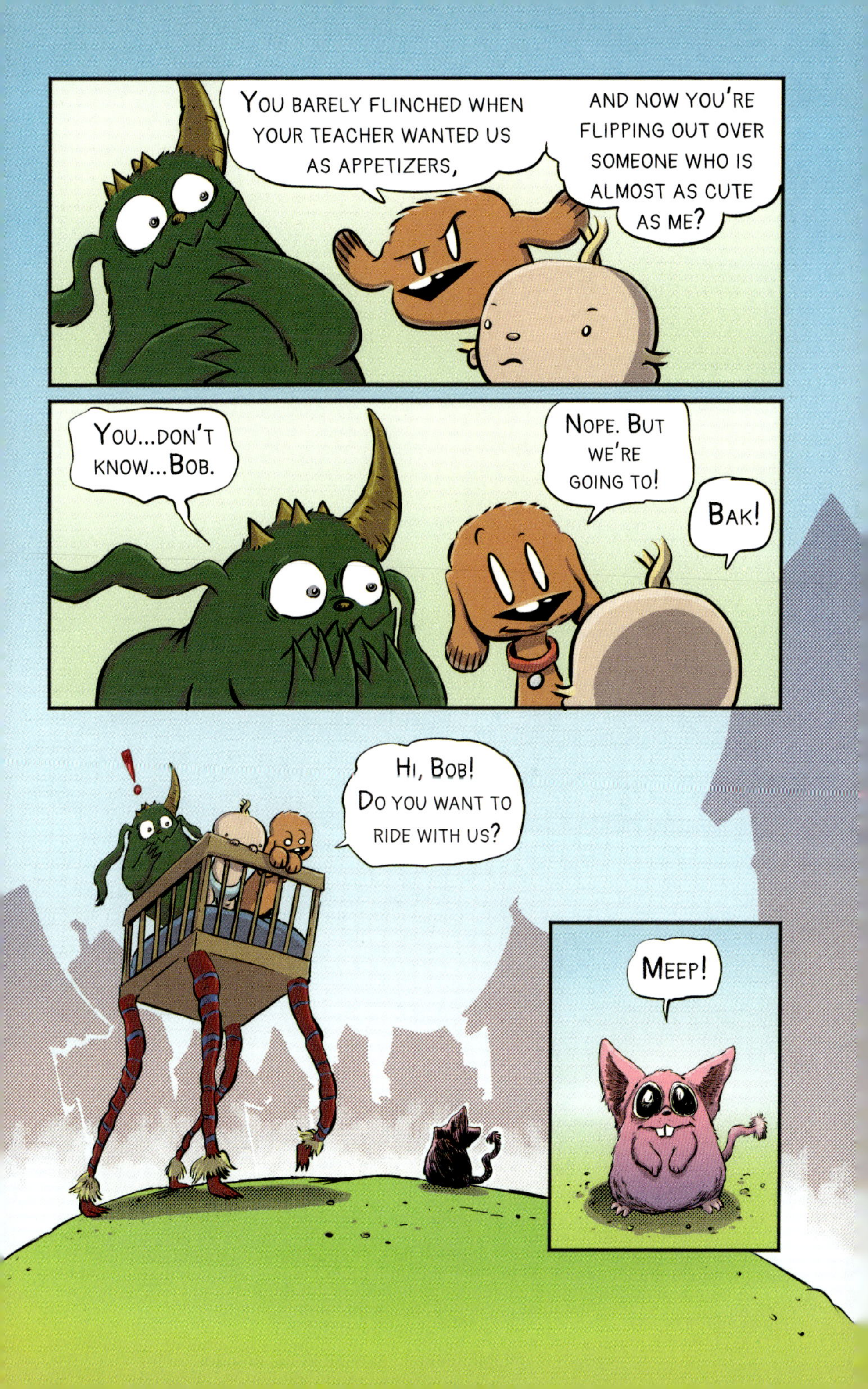
YOU BARELY FLINCHED WHEN YOUR TEACHER WANTED US AS APPETIZERS,
AND NOW YOU'RE FLIPPING OUT OVER SOMEONE WHO IS ALMOST AS CUTE AS ME?
YOU...DON'T KNOW...BOB.
NOPE. BUT WE'RE GOING TO!
BAK!
!
HI, BOB! DO YOU WANT TO RIDE WITH US?
MEEP!

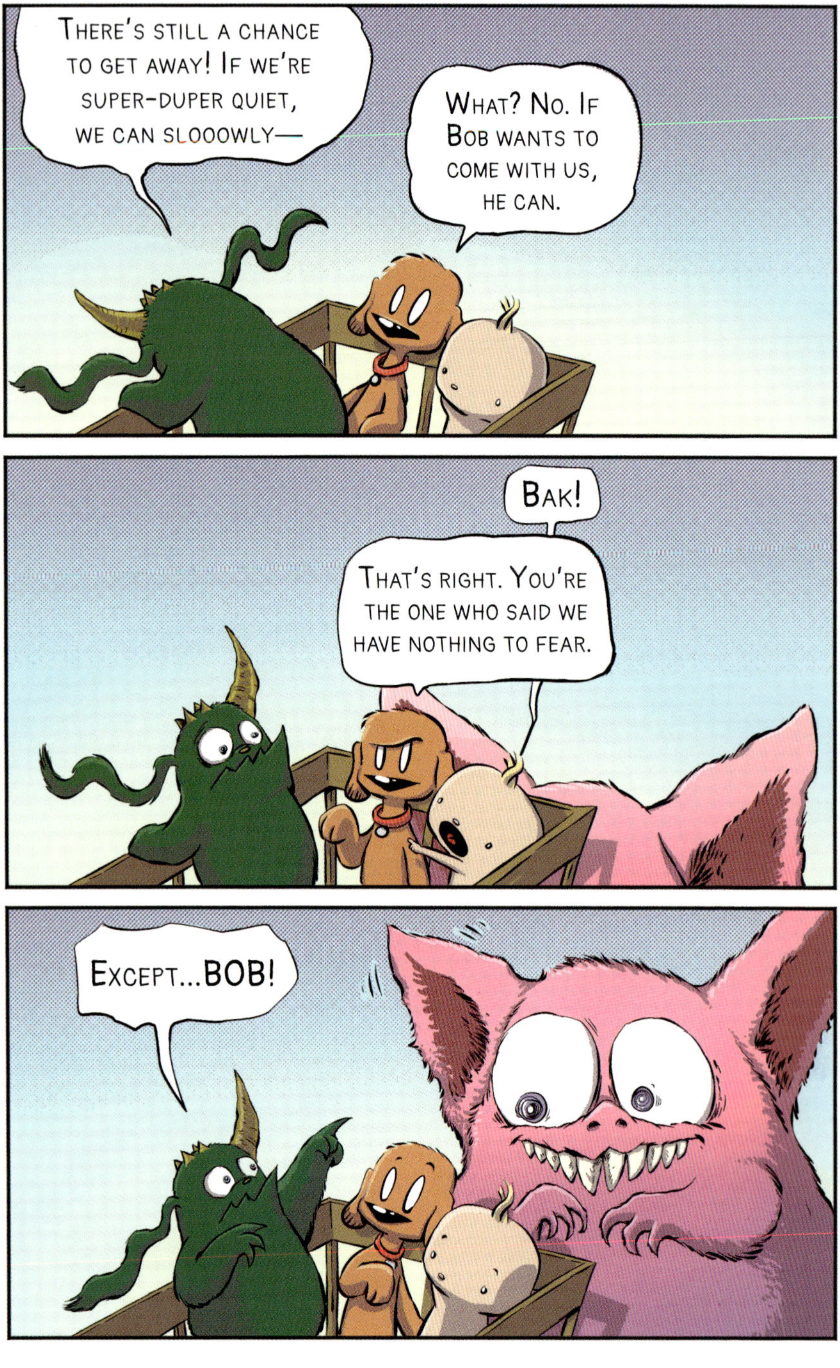
There's still a chance to get away! If we're super-duper quiet, we can slooowly—
What? No. If Bob wants to come with us, he can.
Bak!
That's right. You're the one who said we have nothing to fear.
Except...BOB!

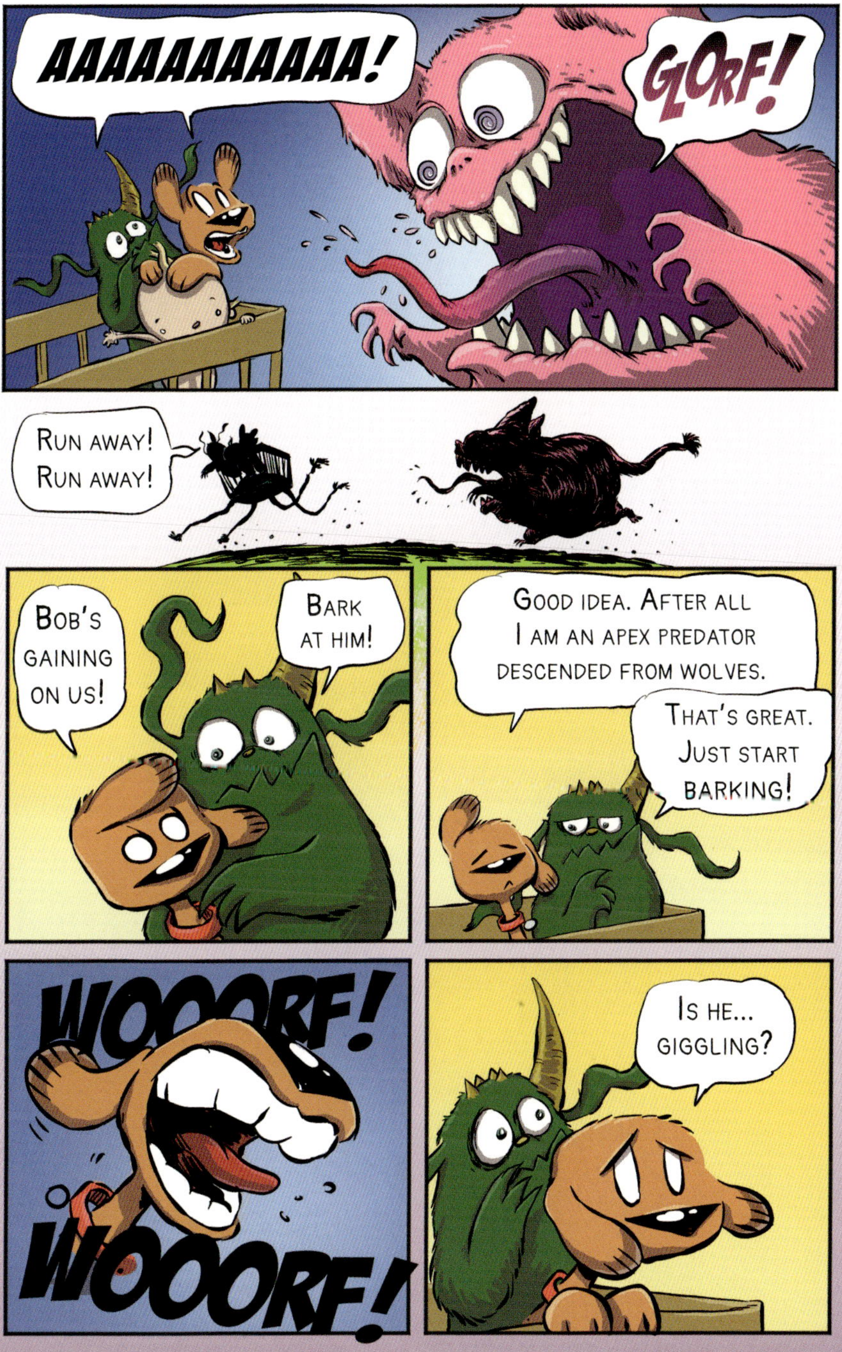
AAAAAAAAAAA!
GLORF!
RUN AWAY! RUN AWAY!
BOB'S GAINING ON US!
BARK AT HIM!
GOOD IDEA. AFTER ALL I AM AN APEX PREDATOR DESCENDED FROM WOLVES.
THAT'S GREAT. JUST START BARKING!
WOOORF!
WOOORF!
IS HE... GIGGLING?

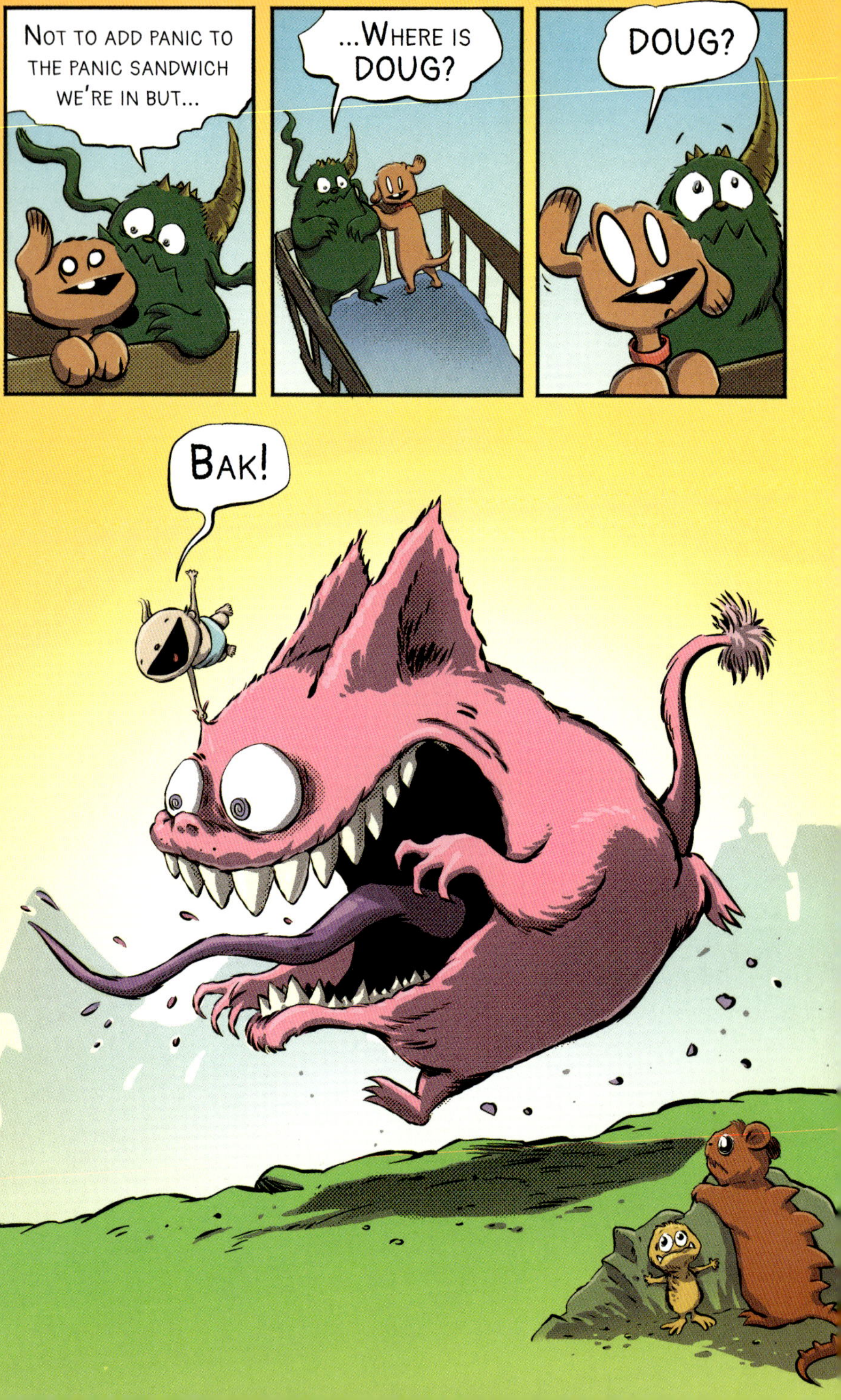
NOT TO ADD PANIC TO THE PANIC SANDWICH WE'RE IN BUT...
...WHERE IS DOUG?
DOUG?
BAK!

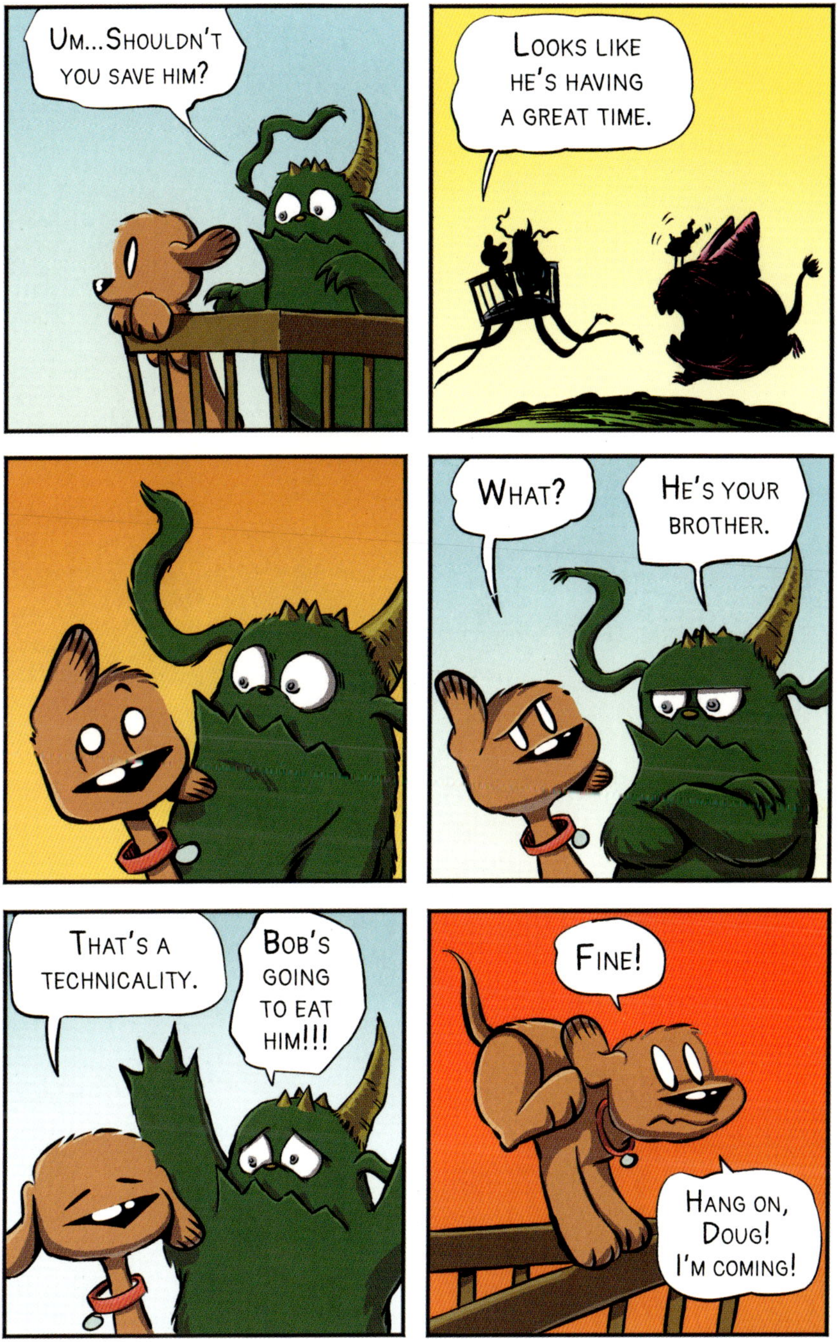
UM...SHOULDN'T YOU SAVE HIM?
LOOKS LIKE HE'S HAVING A GREAT TIME.
WHAT?
HE'S YOUR BROTHER.
THAT'S A TECHNICALITY.
BOB'S GOING TO EAT HIM!!!
FINE!
HANG ON, DOUG! I'M COMING!

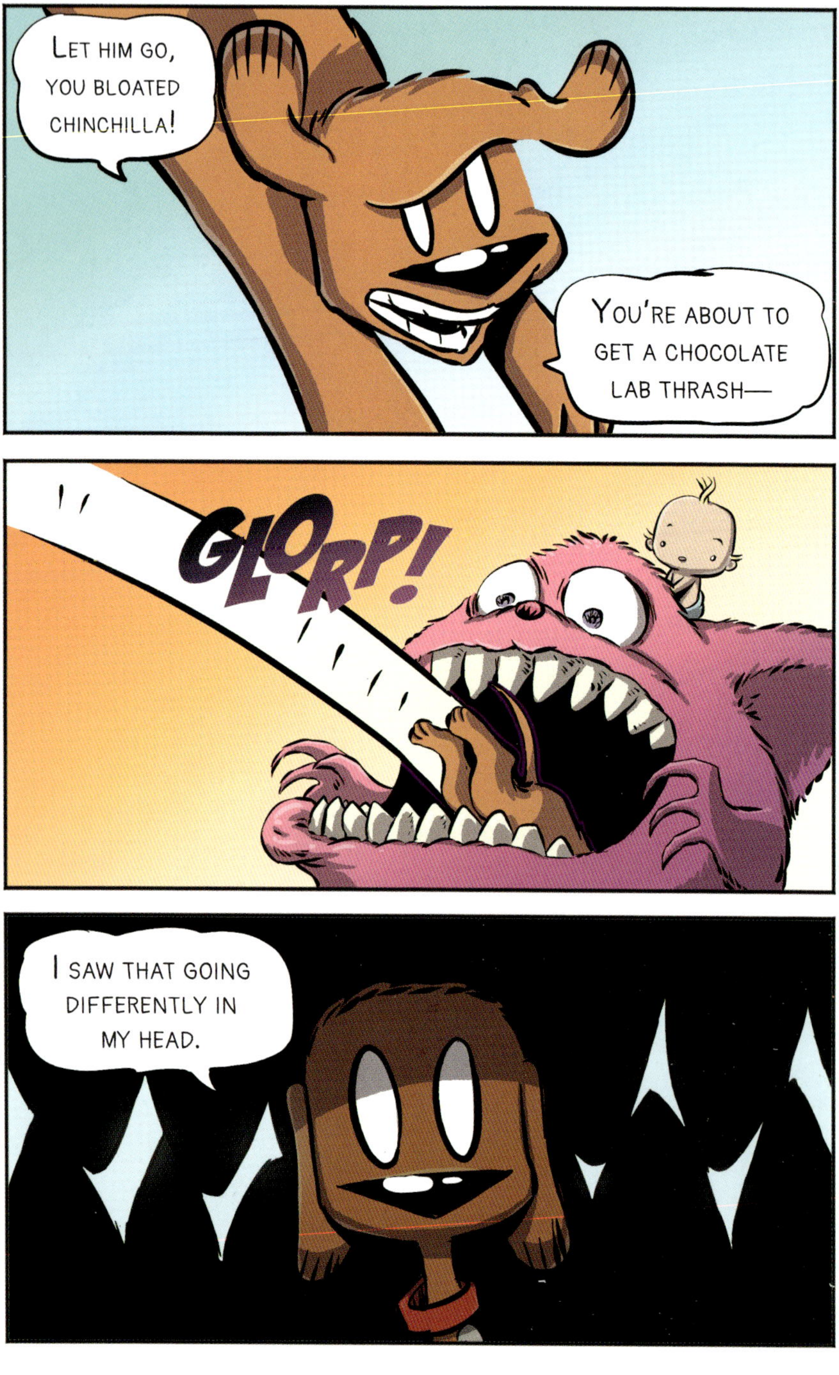
LET HIM GO, YOU BLOATED CHINCHILLA!
YOU'RE ABOUT TO GET A CHOCOLATE LAB THRASH—
GLORP!
I SAW THAT GOING DIFFERENTLY IN MY HEAD.

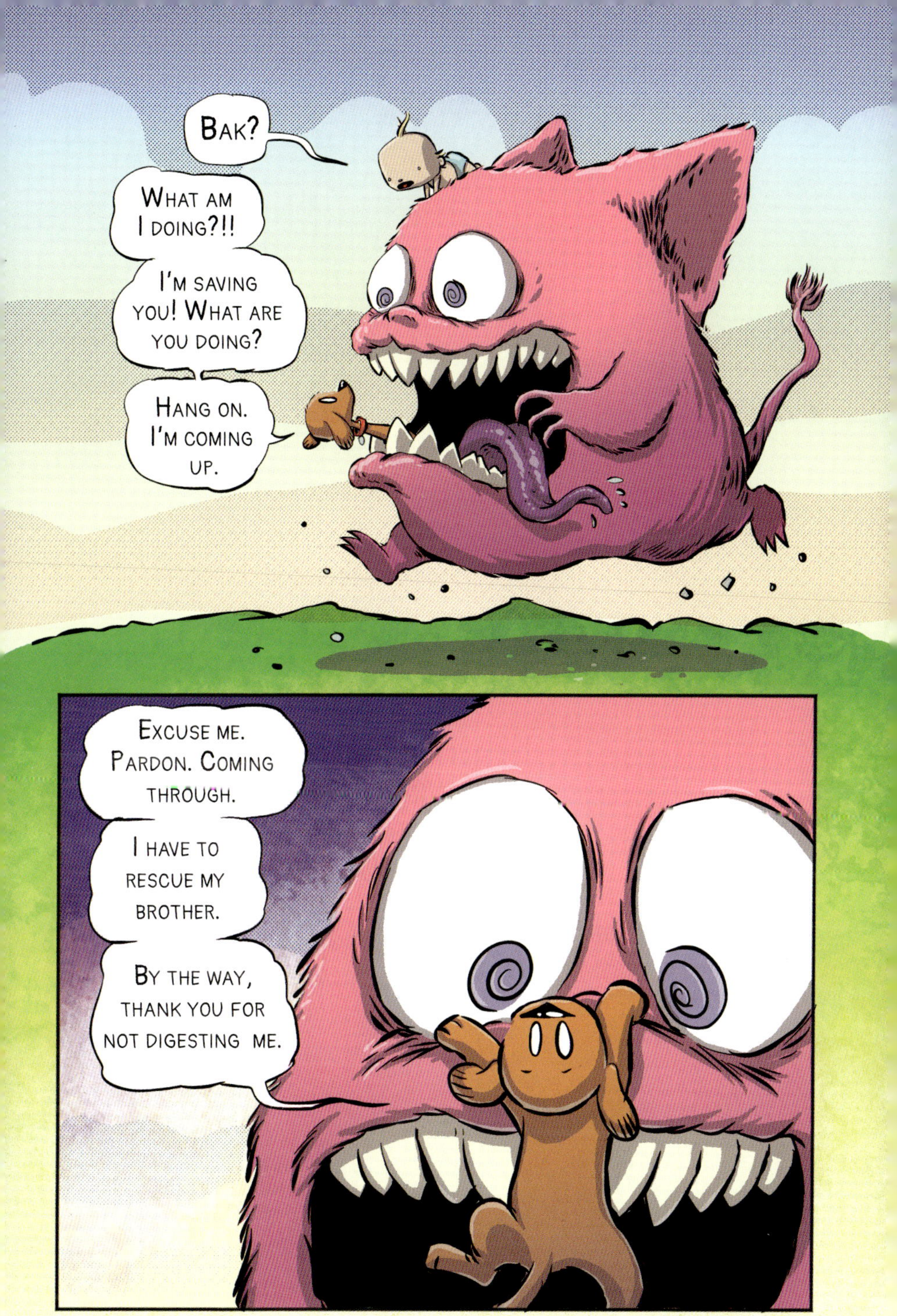
BAK?
WHAT AM I DOING?!!
I'M SAVING YOU! WHAT ARE YOU DOING?
HANG ON. I'M COMING UP.
EXCUSE ME. PARDON. COMING THROUGH.
I HAVE TO RESCUE MY BROTHER.
BY THE WAY, THANK YOU FOR NOT DIGESTING ME.

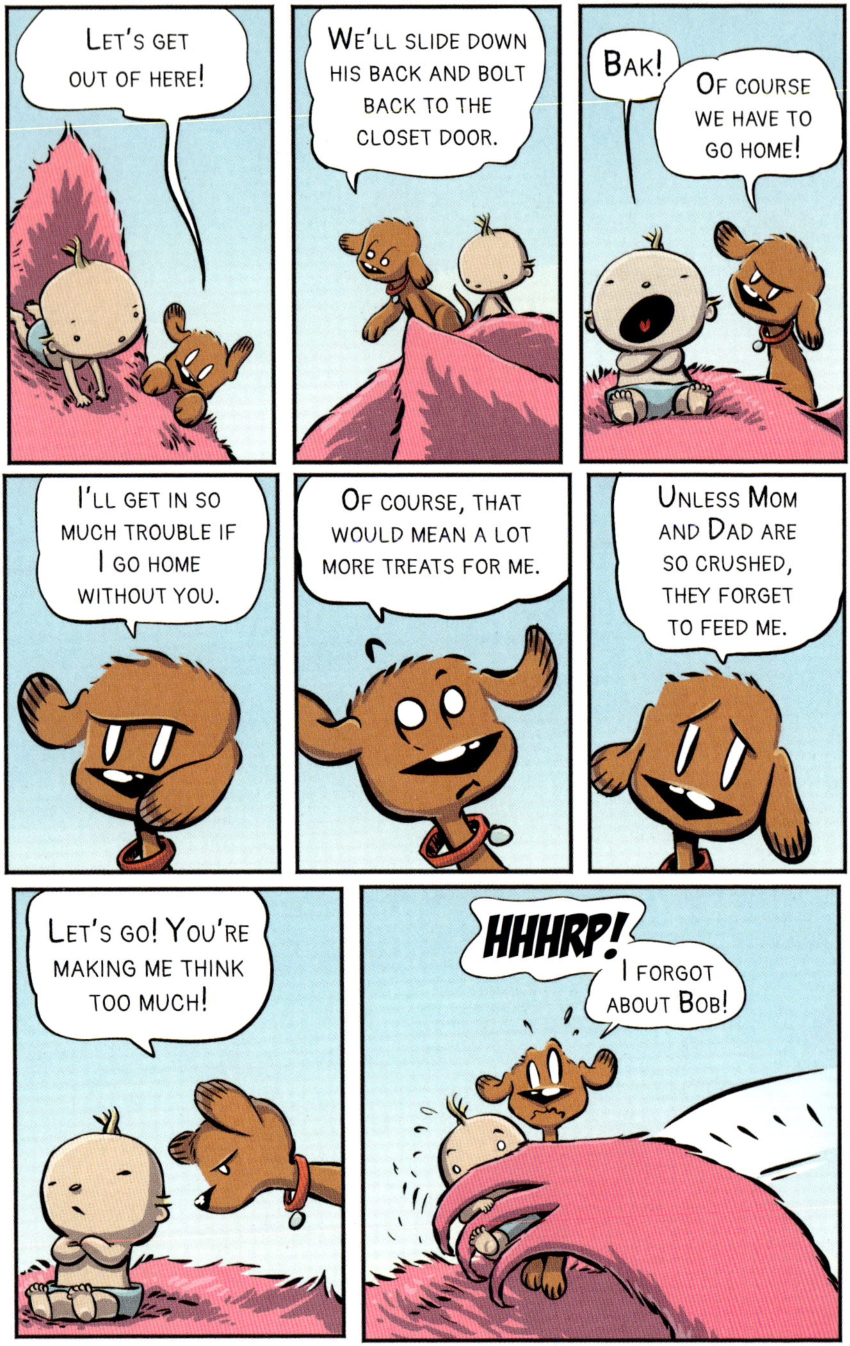
LET'S GET OUT OF HERE!
WE'LL SLIDE DOWN HIS BACK AND BOLT BACK TO THE CLOSET DOOR.
BAK!
OF COURSE WE HAVE TO GO HOME!
I'LL GET IN SO MUCH TROUBLE IF I GO HOME WITHOUT YOU.
OF COURSE, THAT WOULD MEAN A LOT MORE TREATS FOR ME.
UNLESS MOM AND DAD ARE SO CRUSHED, THEY FORGET TO FEED ME.
LET'S GO! YOU'RE MAKING ME THINK TOO MUCH!
HHHRP!
I FORGOT ABOUT BOB!

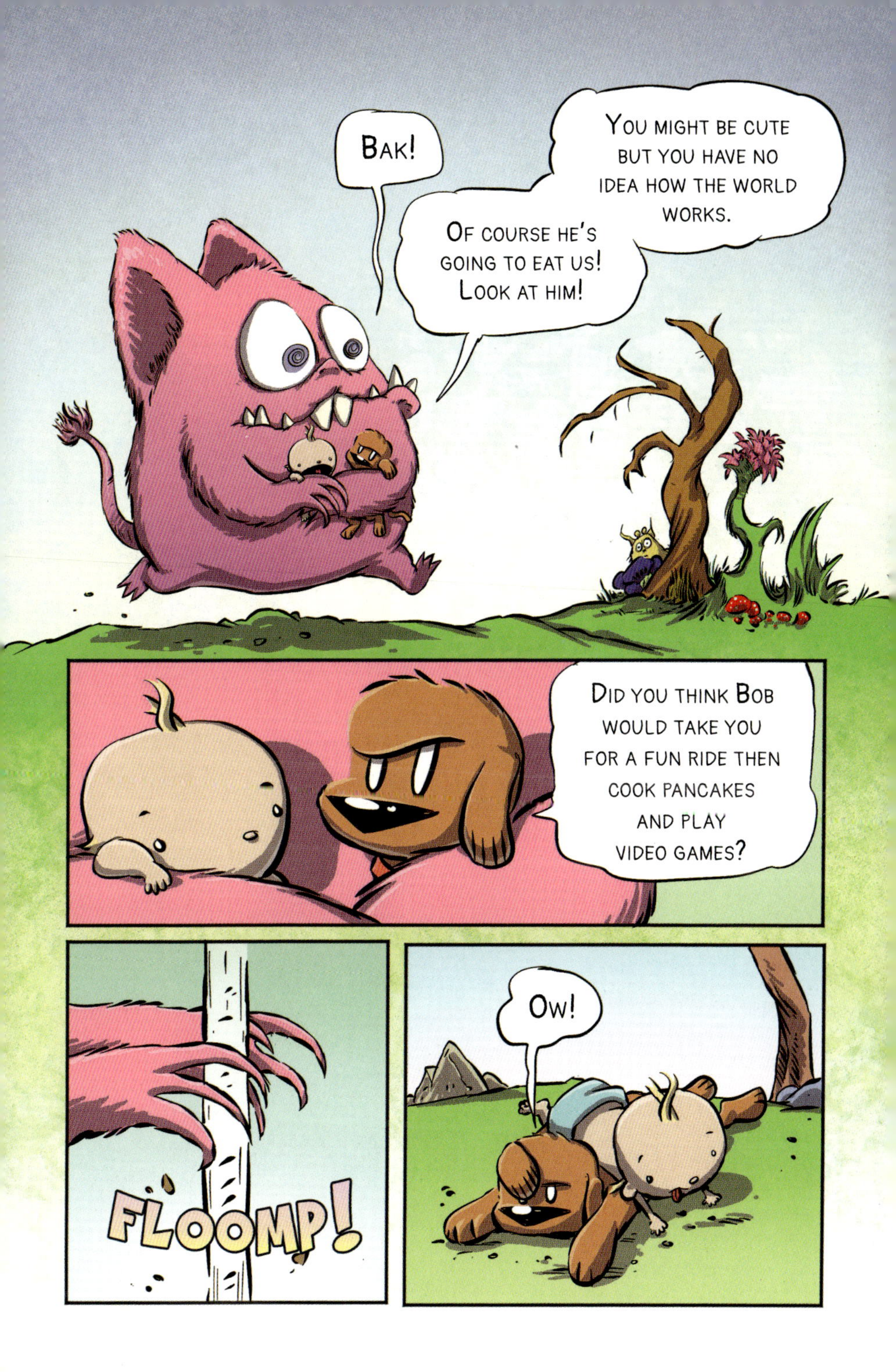
BAK!
YOU MIGHT BE CUTE BUT YOU HAVE NO IDEA HOW THE WORLD WORKS.
OF COURSE HE'S GOING TO EAT US! LOOK AT HIM!
DID YOU THINK BOB WOULD TAKE YOU FOR A FUN RIDE THEN COOK PANCAKES AND PLAY VIDEO GAMES?
FLOOMP!
OW!

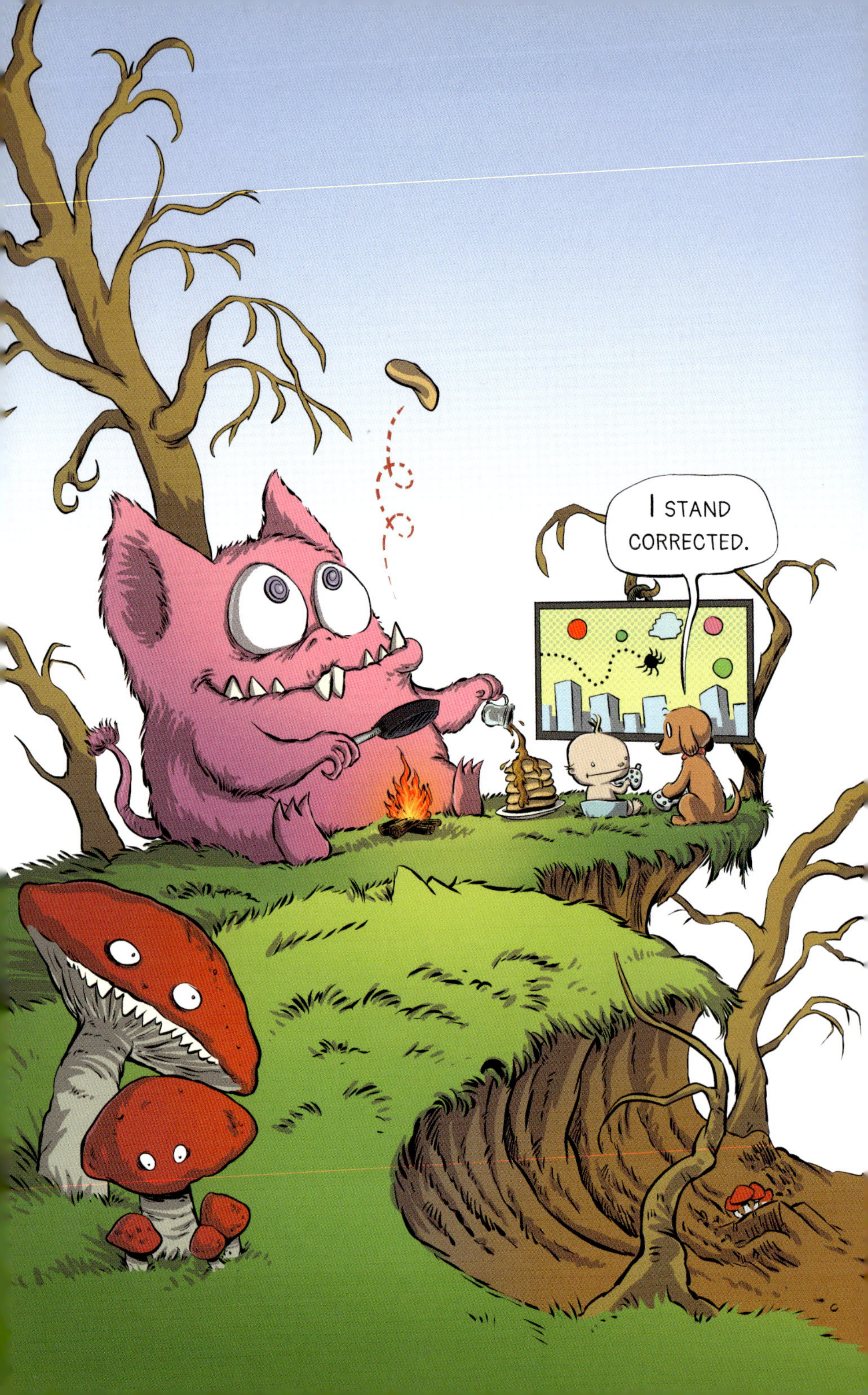
I STAND CORRECTED.

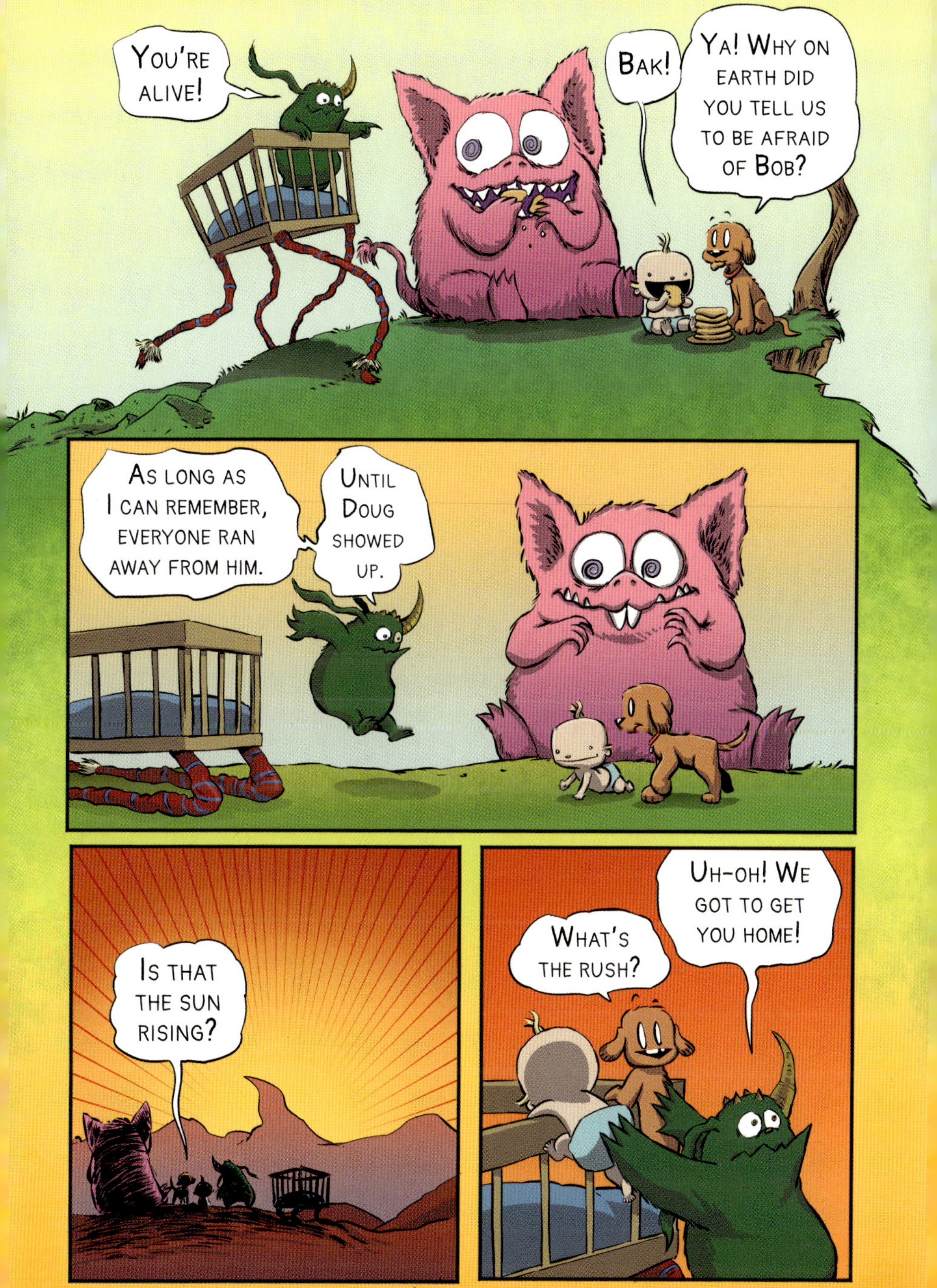
You're alive!
Bak!
Ya! Why on earth did you tell us to be afraid of Bob?
As long as I can remember, everyone ran away from him.
Until Doug showed up.
Is that the sun rising?
What's the rush?
Uh-oh! We got to get you home!

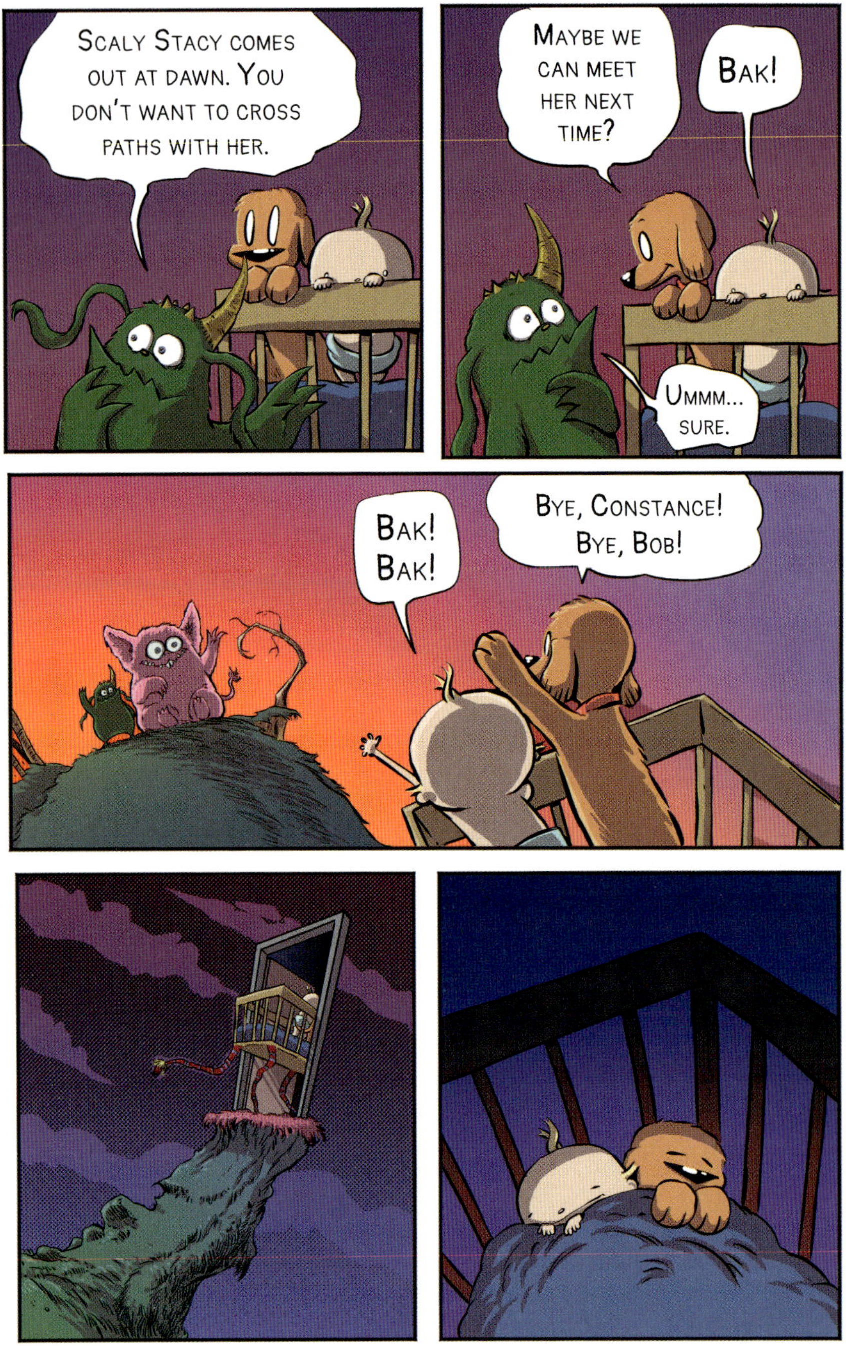
SCALY STACY COMES OUT AT DAWN. YOU DON'T WANT TO CROSS PATHS WITH HER.
MAYBE WE CAN MEET HER NEXT TIME?
BAK!
UMMM... SURE.
BAK! BAK!
BYE, CONSTANCE! BYE, BOB!

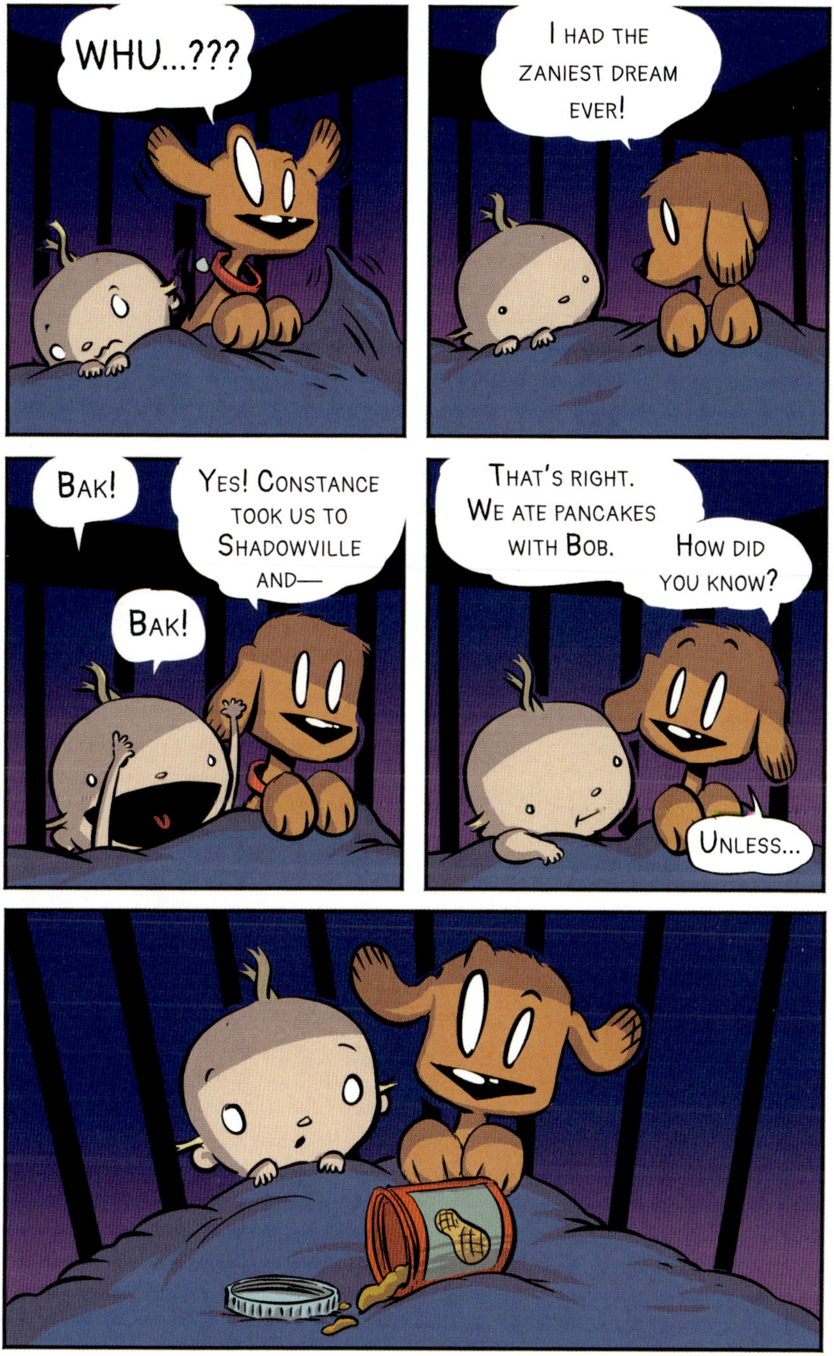
WHU...???
I HAD THE ZANIEST DREAM EVER!
BAK!
YES! CONSTANCE TOOK US TO SHADOWVILLE AND—
BAK!
THAT'S RIGHT. WE ATE PANCAKES WITH BOB.
HOW DID YOU KNOW?
UNLESS...

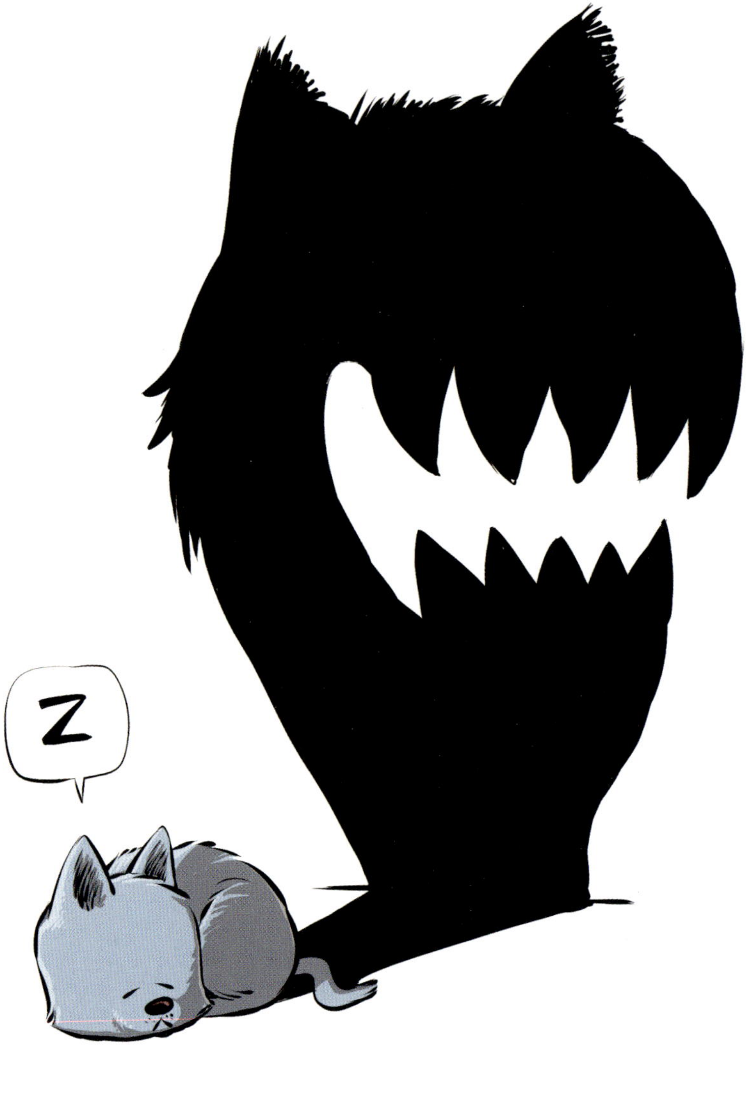
Z

CHAPTER 4

The Time-Traveling Cats

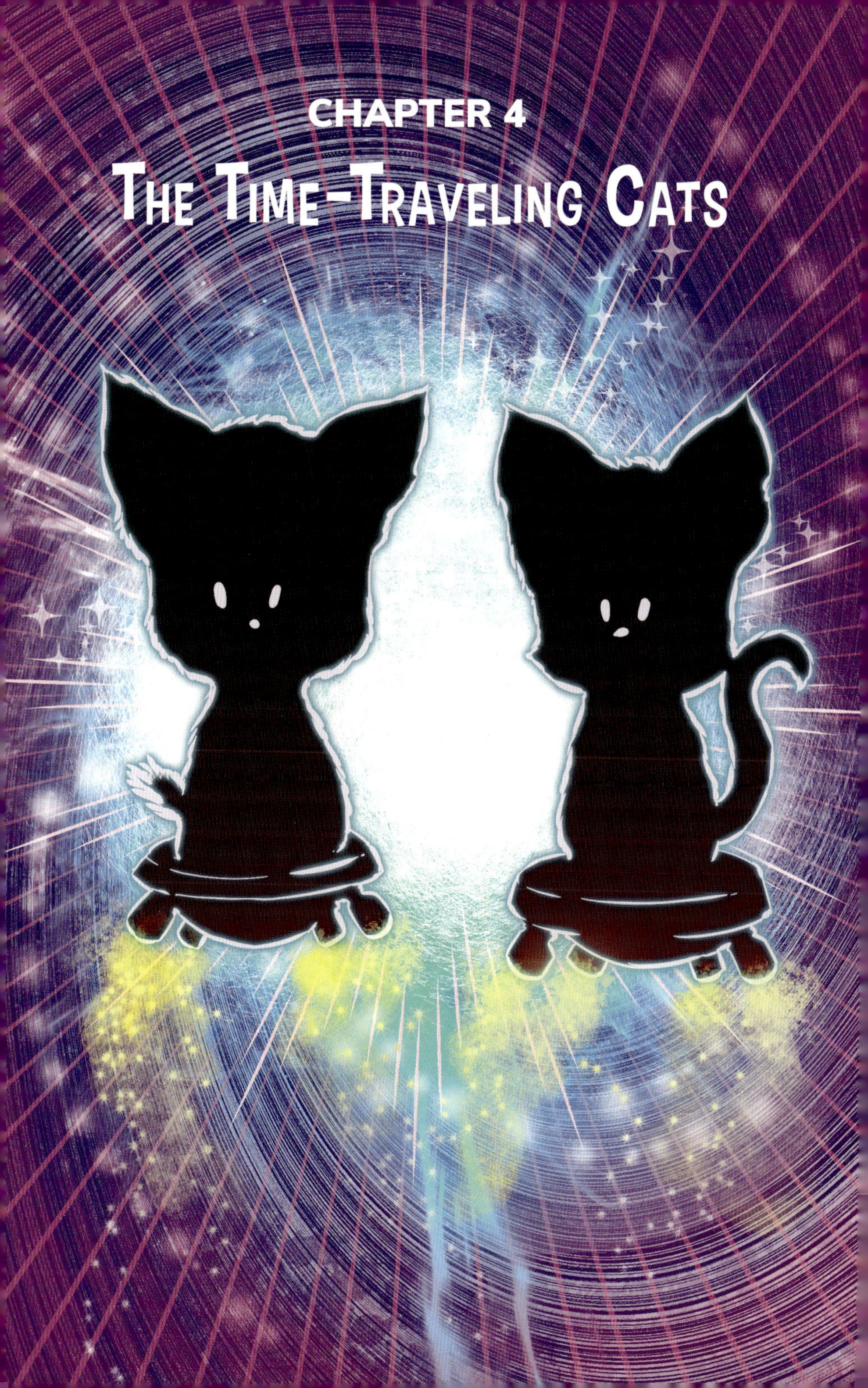

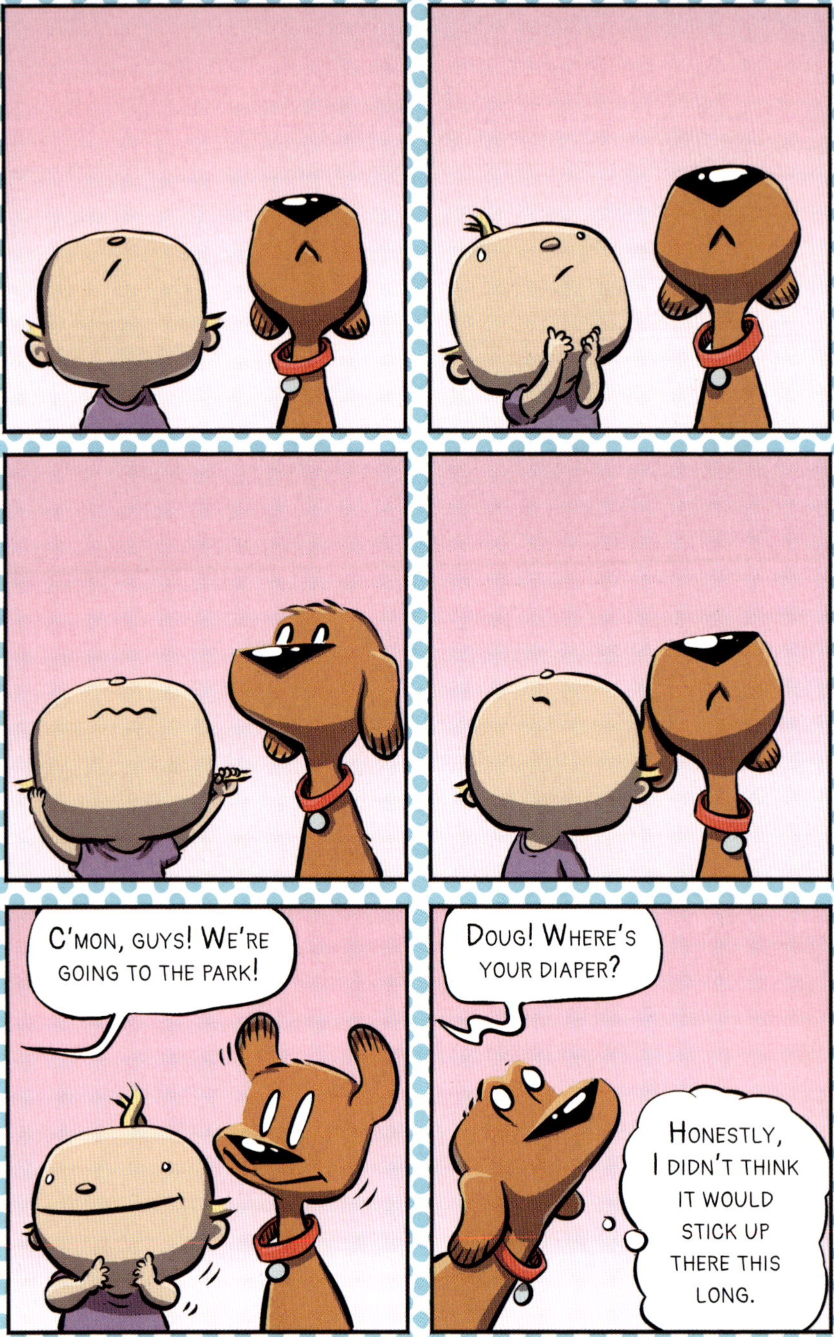
C'MON, GUYS! WE'RE GOING TO THE PARK!
DOUG! WHERE'S YOUR DIAPER?
HONESTLY, I DIDN'T THINK IT WOULD STICK UP THERE THIS LONG.

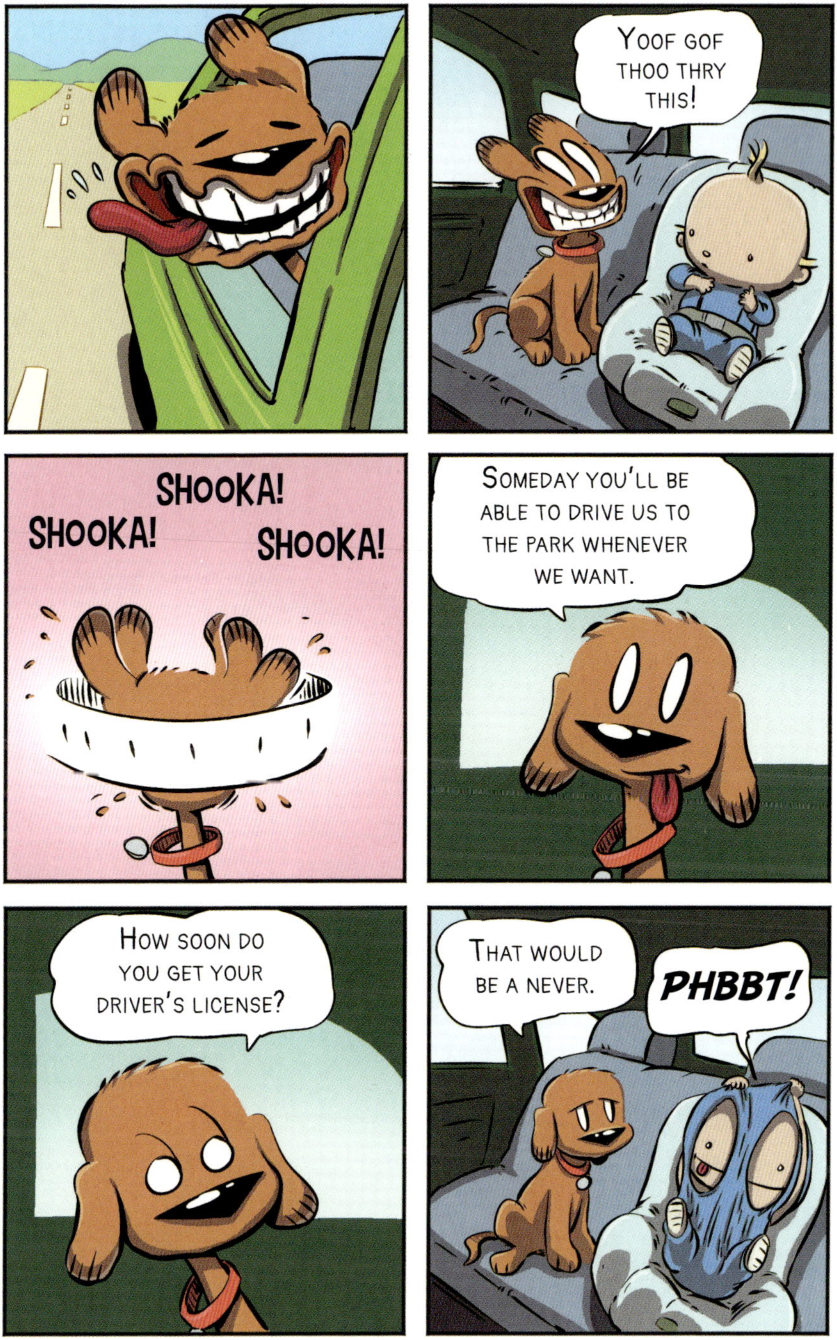
YOOF GOF THOO THRY THIS!
SHOOKA!
SHOOKA!
SHOOKA!
SOMEDAY YOU'LL BE ABLE TO DRIVE US TO THE PARK WHENEVER WE WANT.
HOW SOON DO YOU GET YOUR DRIVER'S LICENSE?
THAT WOULD BE A NEVER.
PHBBT!

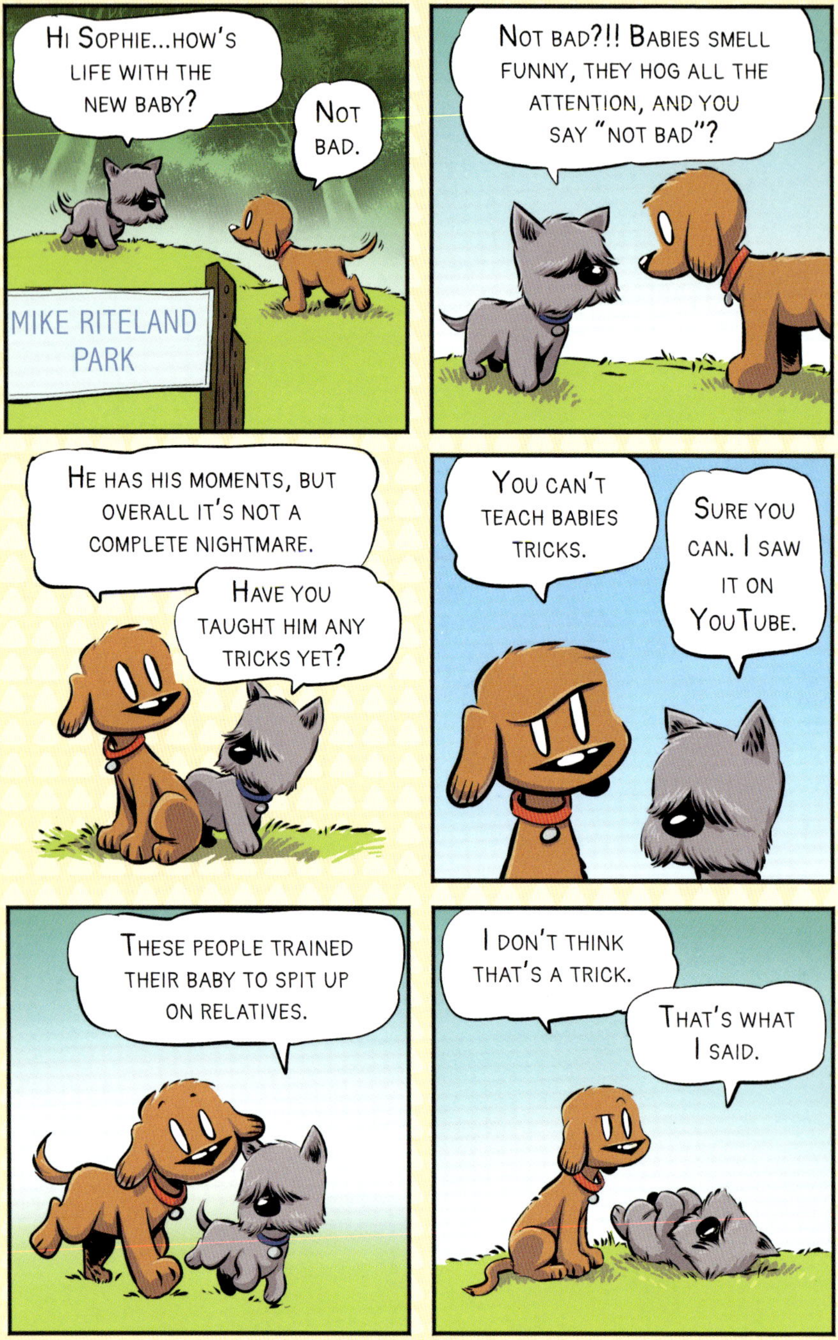
MIKE RITELAND PARK
HI SOPHIE...HOW'S LIFE WITH THE NEW BABY?
NOT BAD.
NOT BAD?!! BABIES SMELL FUNNY, THEY HOG ALL THE ATTENTION, AND YOU SAY "NOT BAD"?
HE HAS HIS MOMENTS, BUT OVERALL IT'S NOT A COMPLETE NIGHTMARE.
HAVE YOU TAUGHT HIM ANY TRICKS YET?
YOU CAN'T TEACH BABIES TRICKS.
SURE YOU CAN. I SAW IT ON YOUTUBE.
THESE PEOPLE TRAINED THEIR BABY TO SPIT UP ON RELATIVES.
I DON'T THINK THAT'S A TRICK.
THAT'S WHAT I SAID.

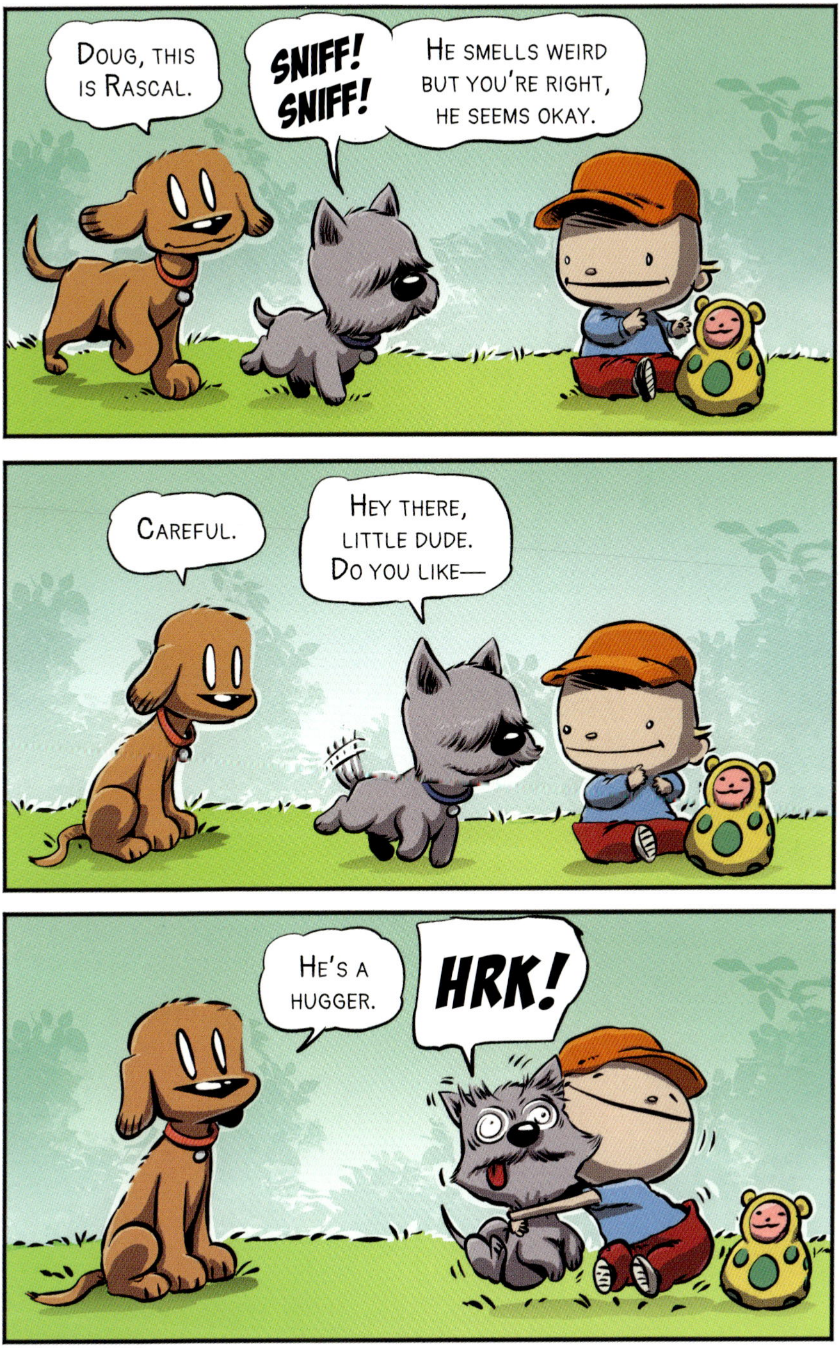
Doug, this is Rascal.
SNIFF! SNIFF!
He smells weird but you're right, he seems okay.
Careful.
Hey there, little dude. Do you like—
He's a hugger.
HRK!

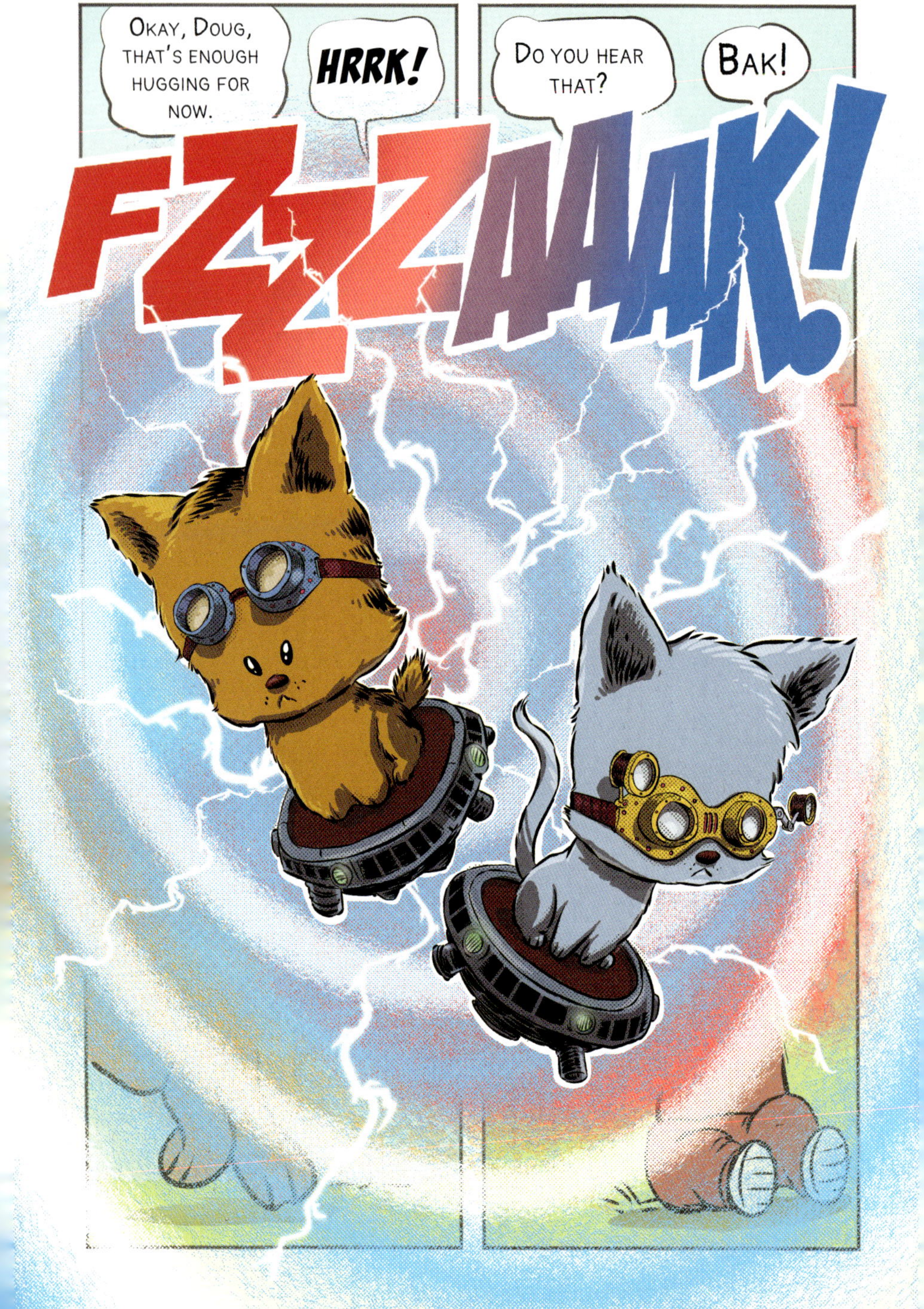
OKAY, DOUG, THAT'S ENOUGH HUGGING FOR NOW.
HRRK!
DO YOU HEAR THAT?
BAK!
FZZZAAAK!

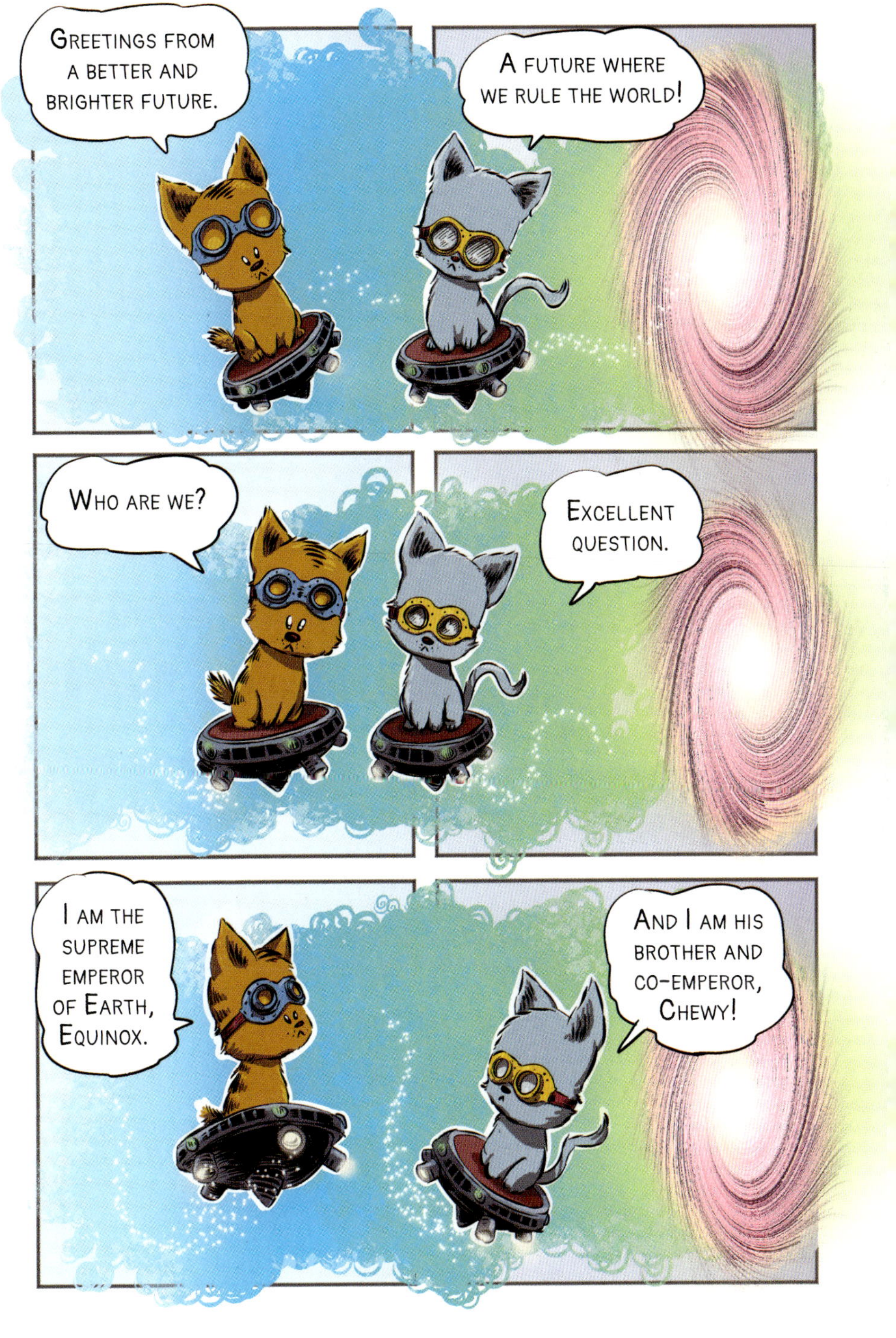
GREETINGS FROM A BETTER AND BRIGHTER FUTURE.
A FUTURE WHERE WE RULE THE WORLD!
WHO ARE WE?
EXCELLENT QUESTION.
I AM THE SUPREME EMPEROR OF EARTH, EQUINOX.
AND I AM HIS BROTHER AND CO-EMPEROR, CHEWY!

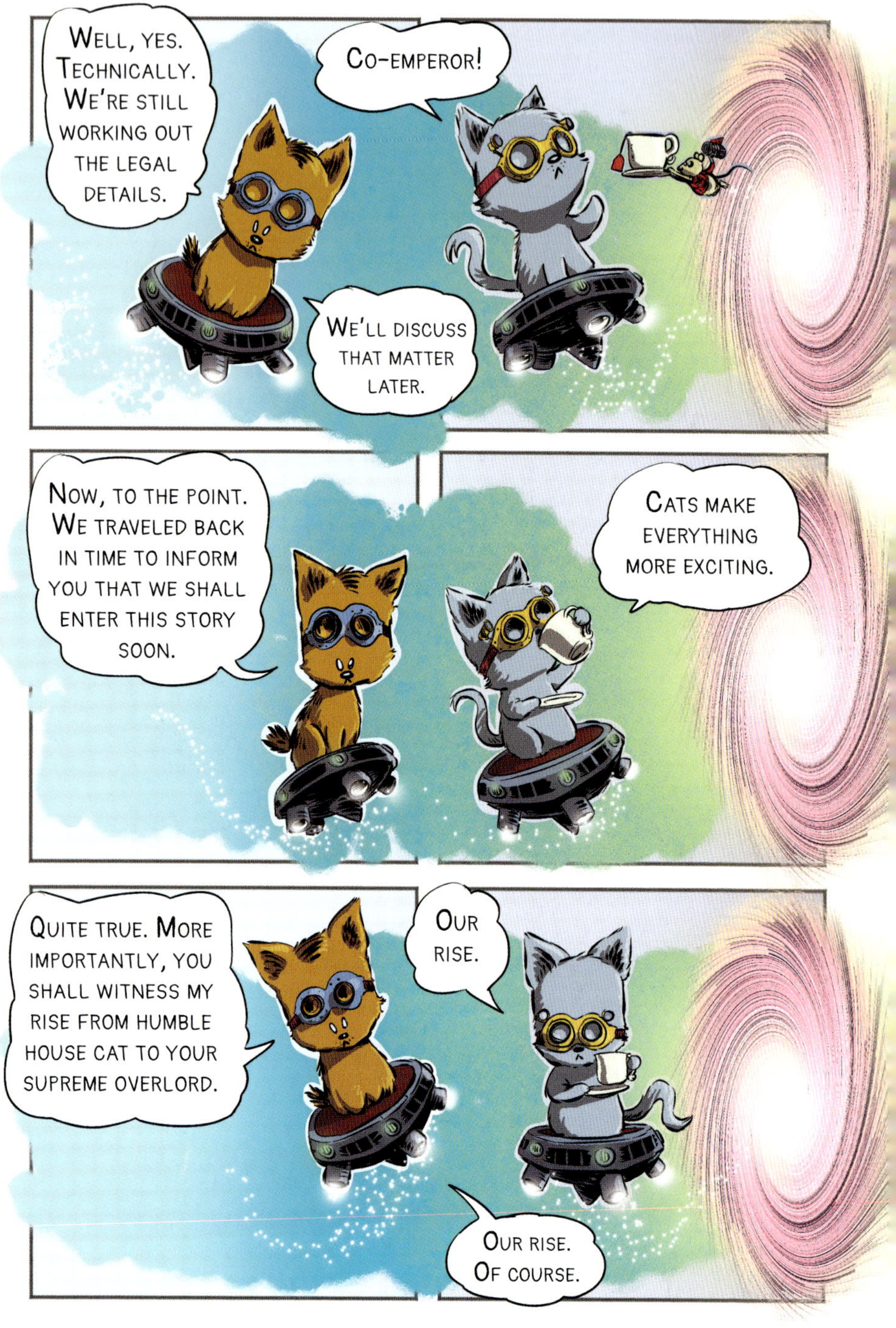
WELL, YES. TECHNICALLY. WE'RE STILL WORKING OUT THE LEGAL DETAILS.
CO-EMPEROR!
WE'LL DISCUSS THAT MATTER LATER.
NOW, TO THE POINT. WE TRAVELED BACK IN TIME TO INFORM YOU THAT WE SHALL ENTER THIS STORY SOON.
CATS MAKE EVERYTHING MORE EXCITING.
QUITE TRUE. MORE IMPORTANTLY, YOU SHALL WITNESS MY RISE FROM HUMBLE HOUSE CAT TO YOUR SUPREME OVERLORD.
OUR RISE.
OUR RISE. OF COURSE.

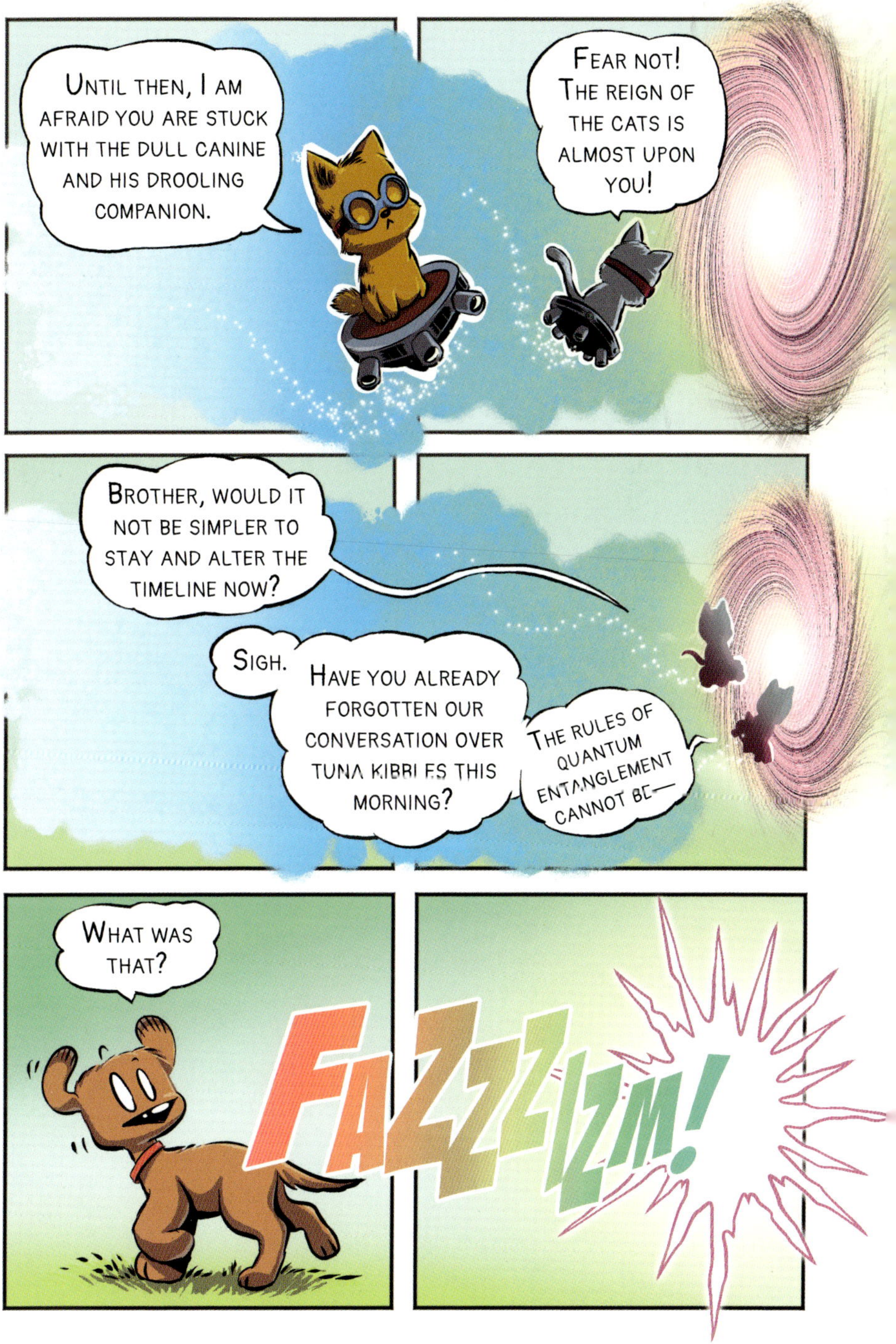
UNTIL THEN, I AM AFRAID YOU ARE STUCK WITH THE DULL CANINE AND HIS DROOLING COMPANION.
FEAR NOT! THE REIGN OF THE CATS IS ALMOST UPON YOU!
BROTHER, WOULD IT NOT BE SIMPLER TO STAY AND ALTER THE TIMELINE NOW?
SIGH.
HAVE YOU ALREADY FORGOTTEN OUR CONVERSATION OVER TUNA KIBBLES THIS MORNING?
THE RULES OF QUANTUM ENTANGLEMENT CANNOT BE—
WHAT WAS THAT?
FAZZZIZM!

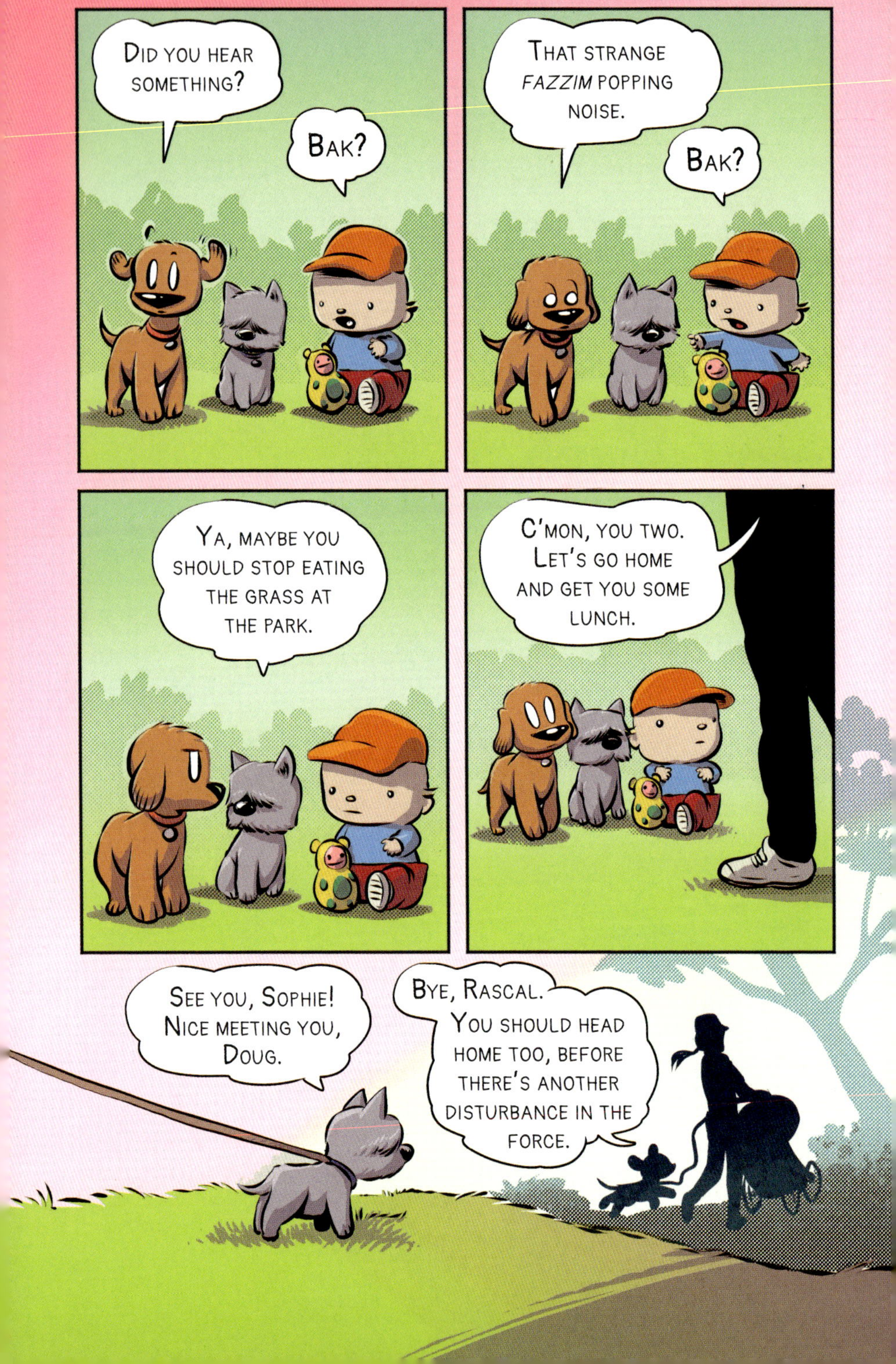
DID YOU HEAR SOMETHING?
BAK?
THAT STRANGE *FAZZIM* POPPING NOISE.
BAK?
YA, MAYBE YOU SHOULD STOP EATING THE GRASS AT THE PARK.
C'MON, YOU TWO. LET'S GO HOME AND GET YOU SOME LUNCH.
SEE YOU, SOPHIE! NICE MEETING YOU, DOUG.
BYE, RASCAL. YOU SHOULD HEAD HOME TOO, BEFORE THERE'S ANOTHER DISTURBANCE IN THE FORCE.

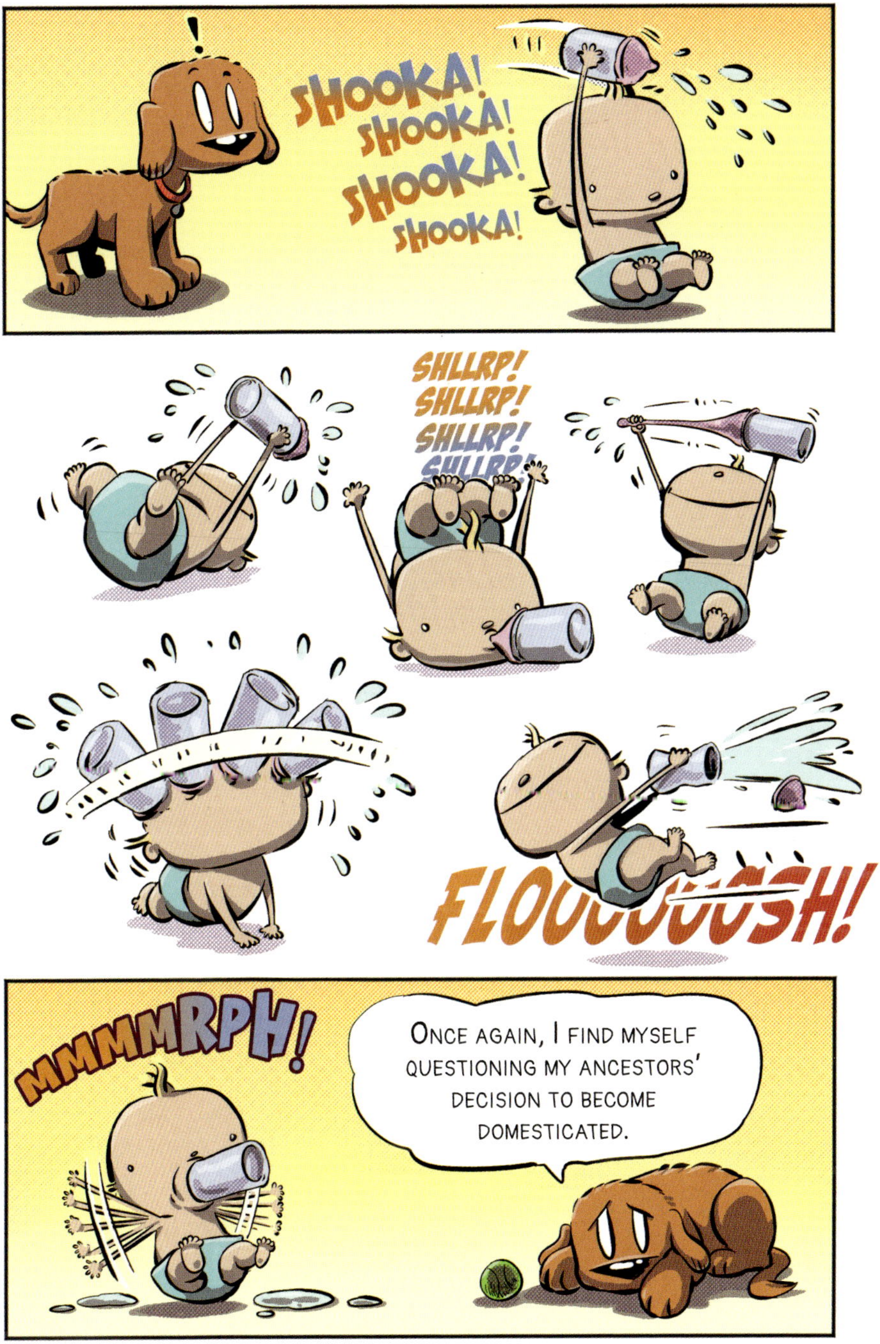
!
SHOOKA! SHOOKA! SHOOKA! SHOOKA!
SHLLRP! SHLLRP! SHLLRP!
FLOOOOOOSH!
MMMMMRPH!
ONCE AGAIN, I FIND MYSELF QUESTIONING MY ANCESTORS' DECISION TO BECOME DOMESTICATED.

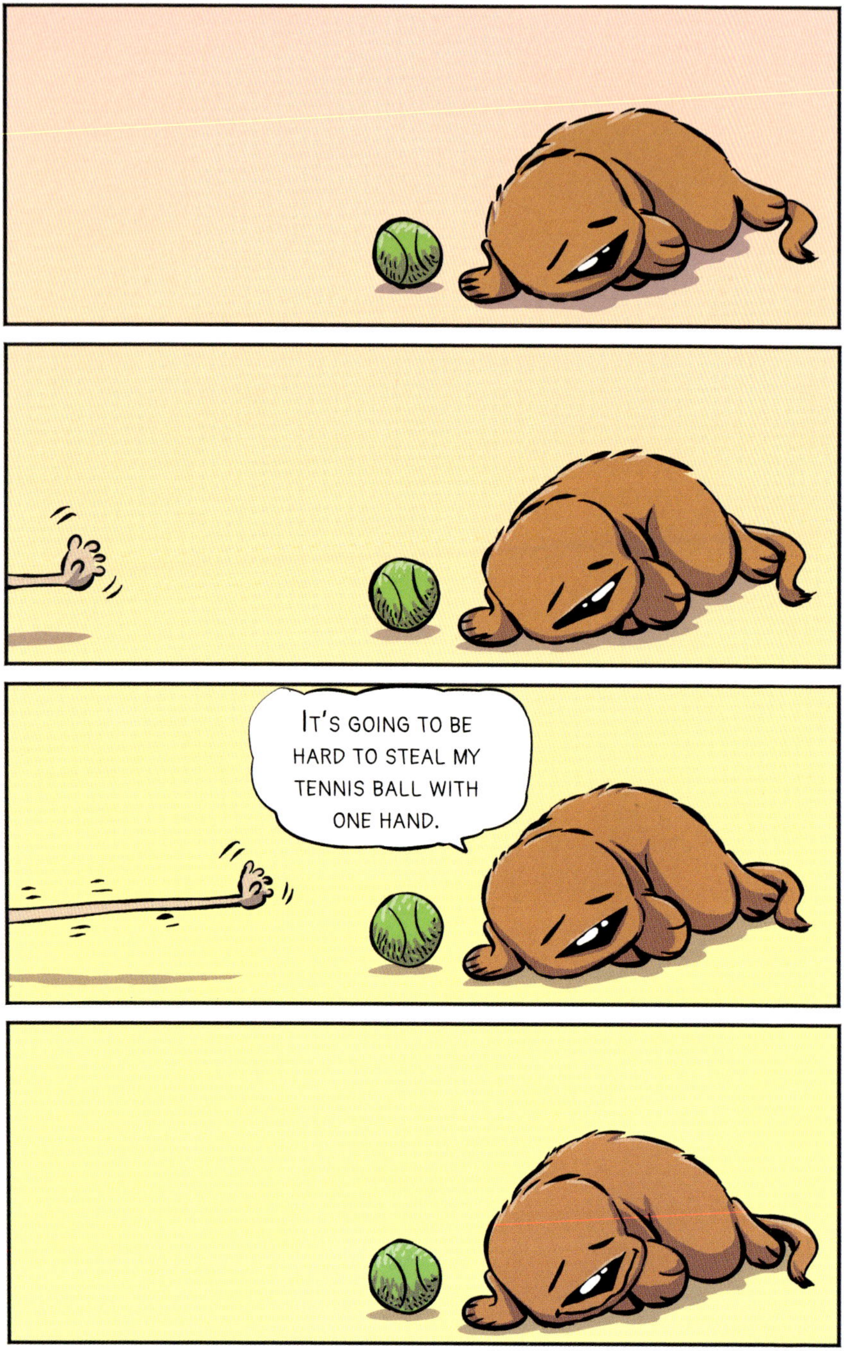
IT'S GOING TO BE HARD TO STEAL MY TENNIS BALL WITH ONE HAND.

CHAPTER 5

Commander Doug vs. the Labradorian

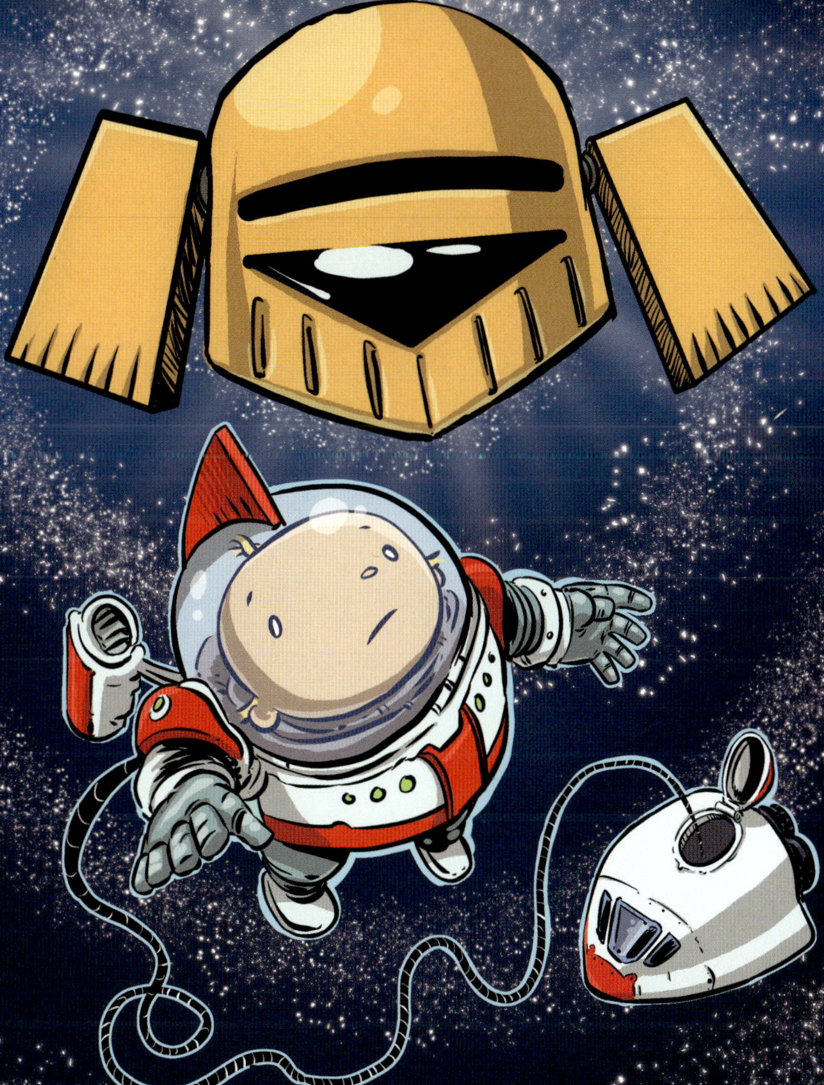

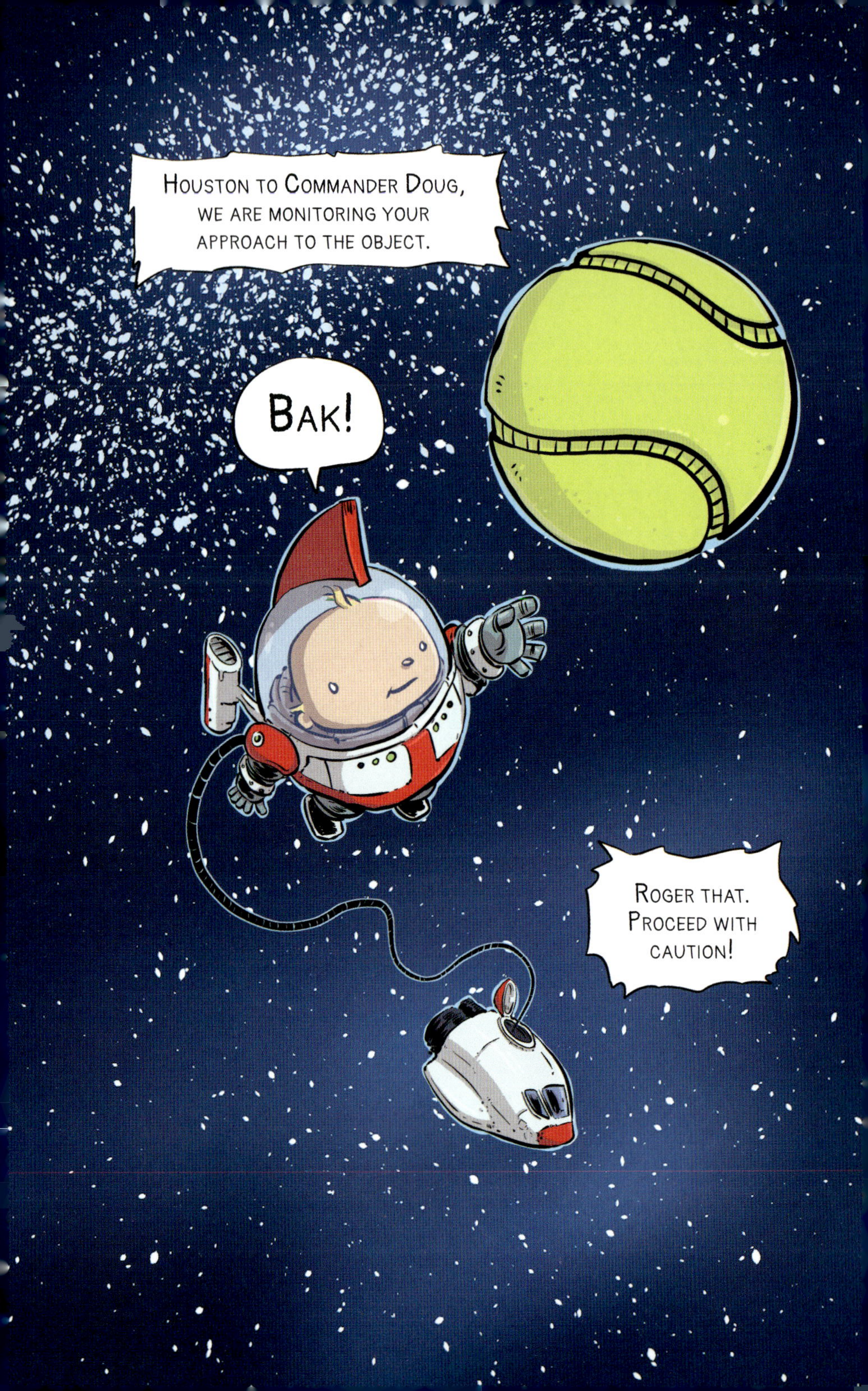
HOUSTON TO COMMANDER DOUG, WE ARE MONITORING YOUR APPROACH TO THE OBJECT.
BAK!
ROGER THAT. PROCEED WITH CAUTION!

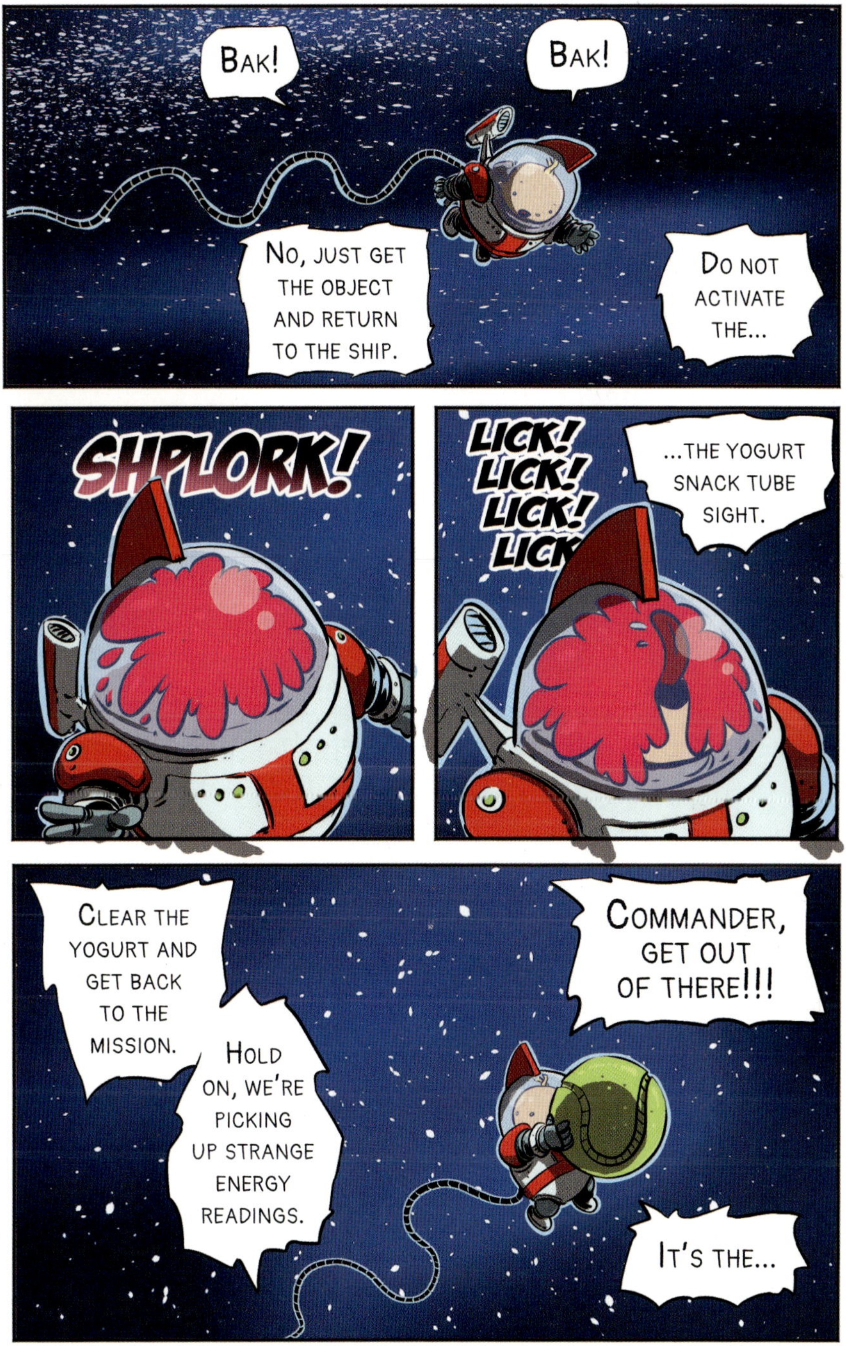
BAK!
BAK!
NO, JUST GET THE OBJECT AND RETURN TO THE SHIP.
DO NOT ACTIVATE THE...
SHPLORK!
LICK! LICK! LICK! LICK
...THE YOGURT SNACK TUBE SIGHT.
CLEAR THE YOGURT AND GET BACK TO THE MISSION.
HOLD ON, WE'RE PICKING UP STRANGE ENERGY READINGS.
COMMANDER, GET OUT OF THERE!!!
IT'S THE...

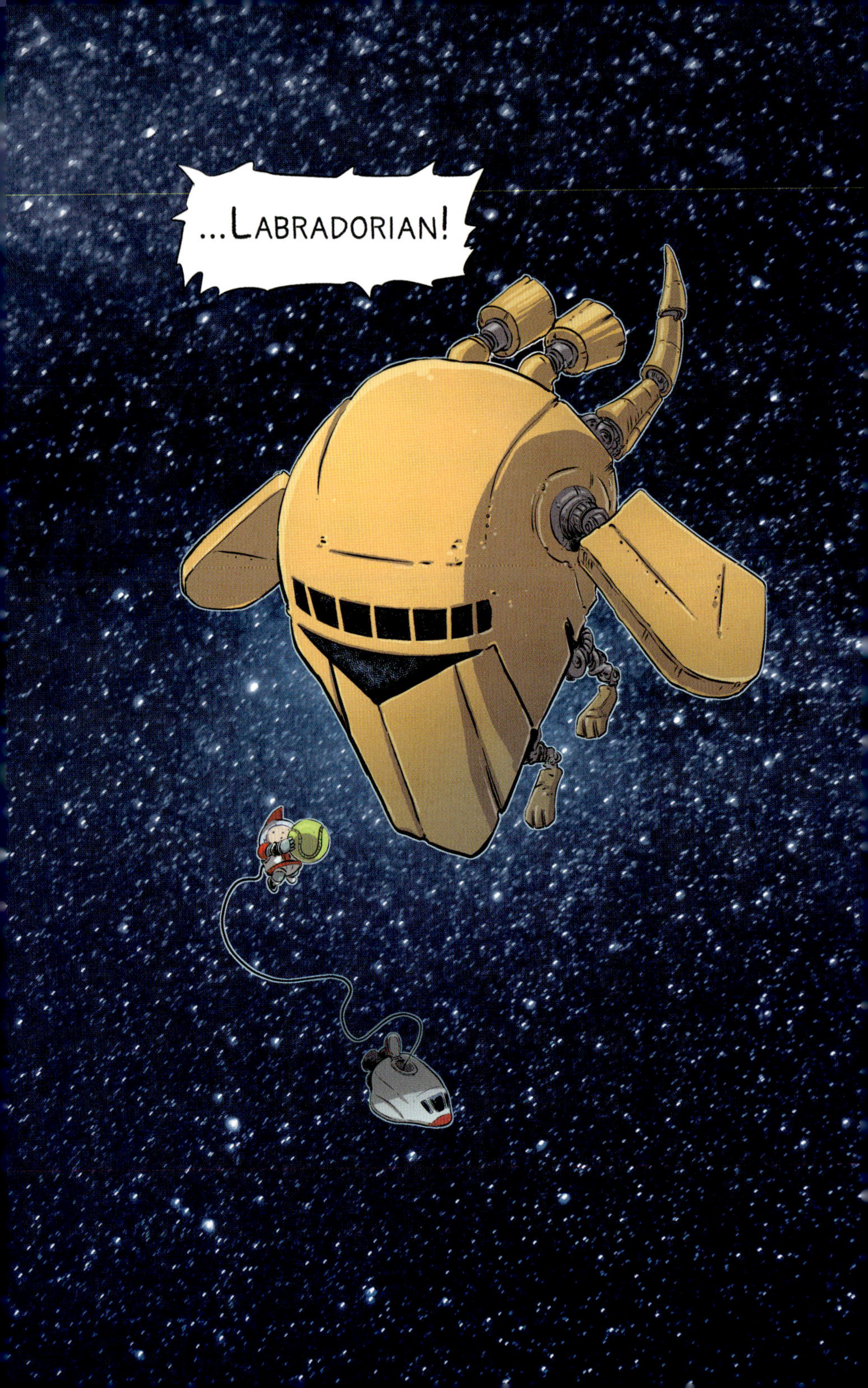
...LABRADORIAN!

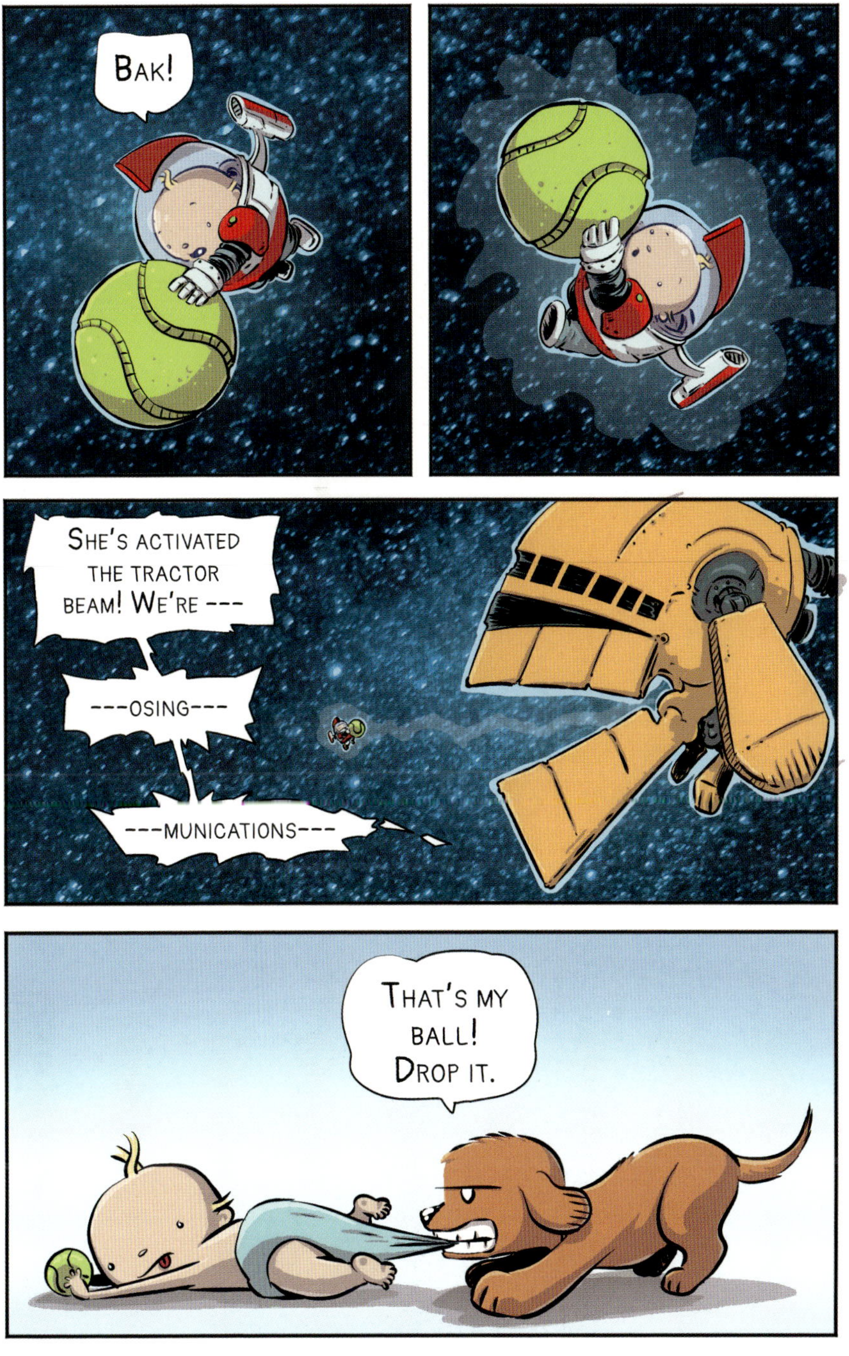
BAK!
SHE'S ACTIVATED THE TRACTOR BEAM! WE'RE ---
---OSING---
---MUNICATIONS---
THAT'S MY BALL! DROP IT.

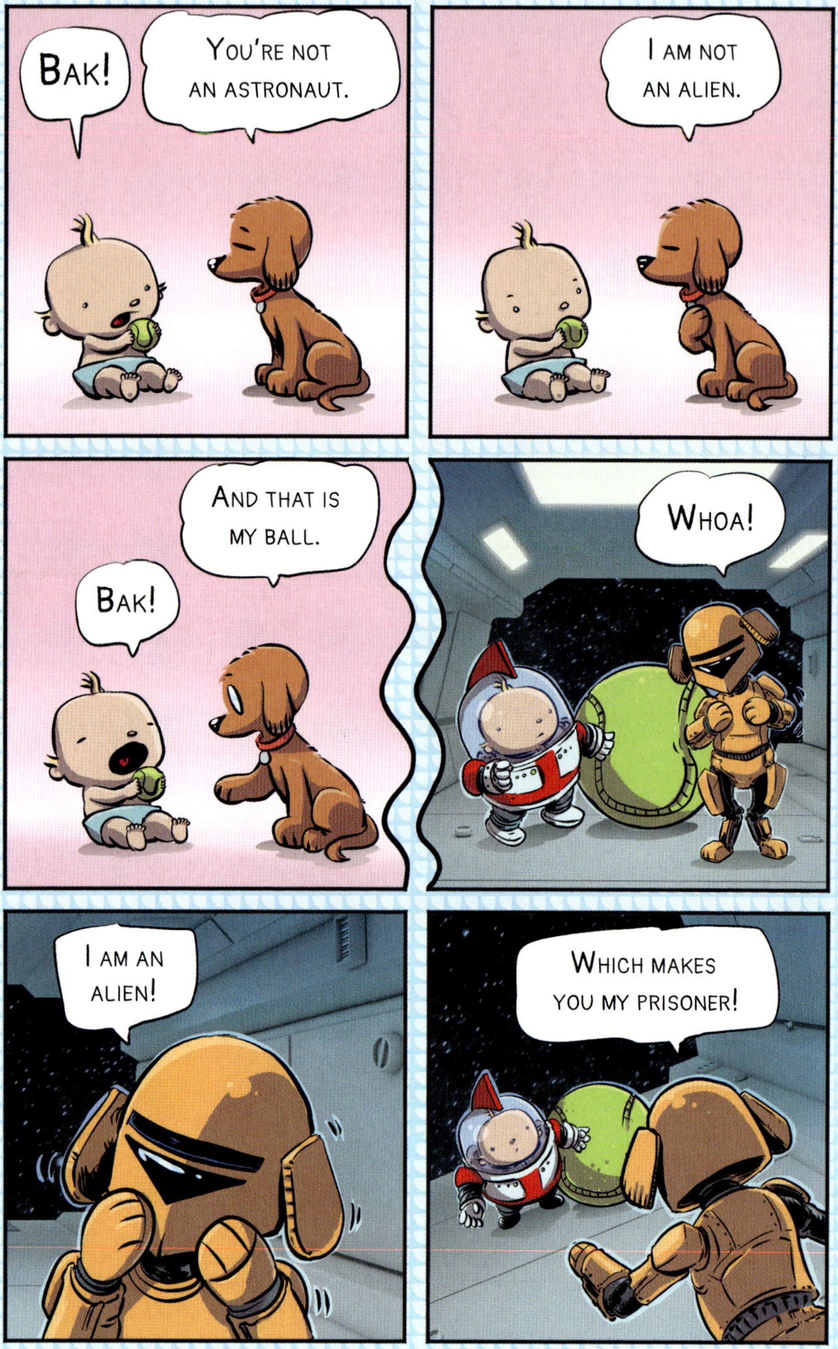
BAK!
YOU'RE NOT AN ASTRONAUT.
I AM NOT AN ALIEN.
AND THAT IS MY BALL.
BAK!
WHOA!
I AM AN ALIEN!
WHICH MAKES YOU MY PRISONER!

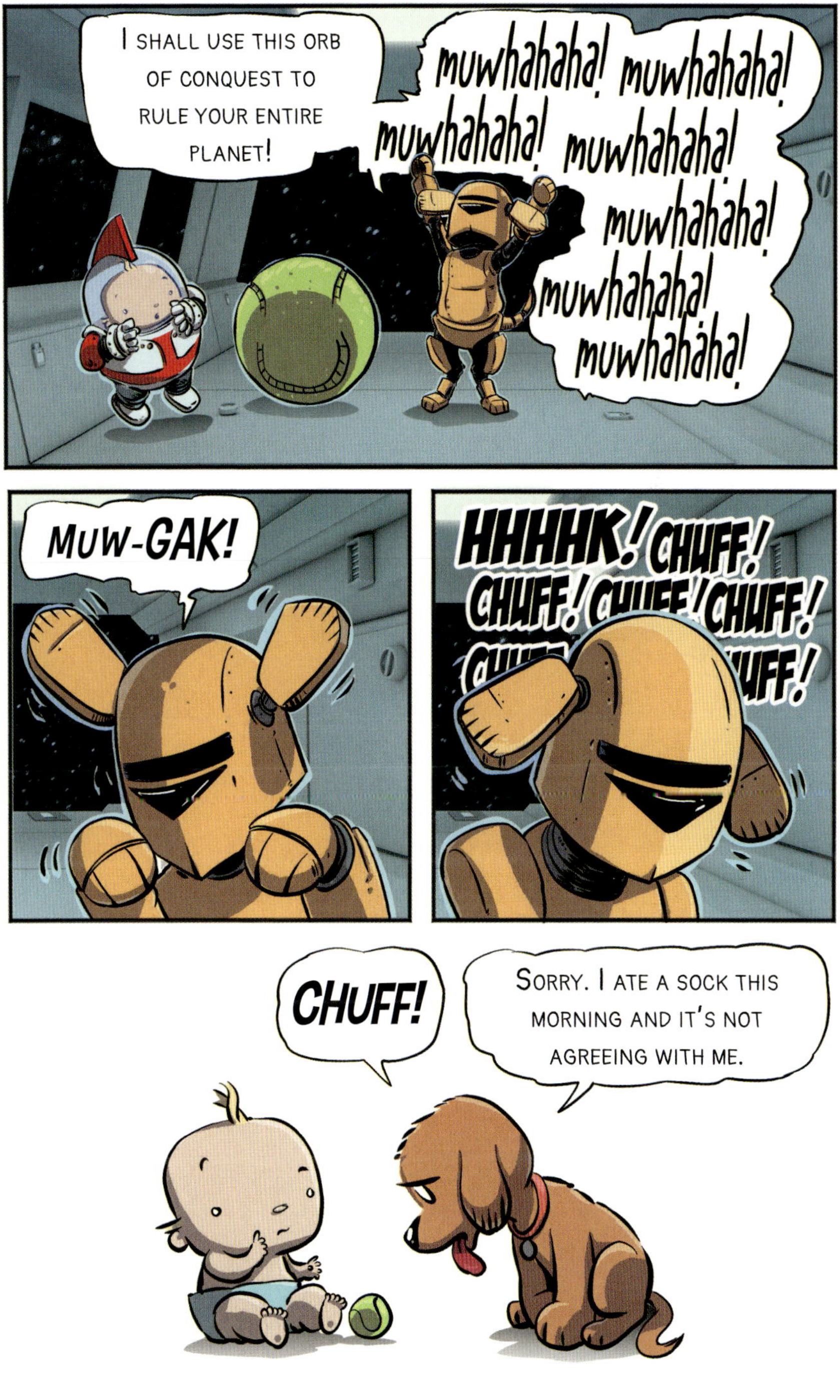
I SHALL USE THIS ORB OF CONQUEST TO RULE YOUR ENTIRE PLANET!
MUWHAHAHA! MUWHAHAHA! MUWHAHAHA! MUWHAHAHA! MUWHAHAHA! MUWHAHAHA! MUWHAHAHA!
MUW-GAK!
HHHHK! CHUFF!
CHUFF! CHUFF!
CHUFF!
SORRY. I ATE A SOCK THIS MORNING AND IT'S NOT AGREEING WITH ME.

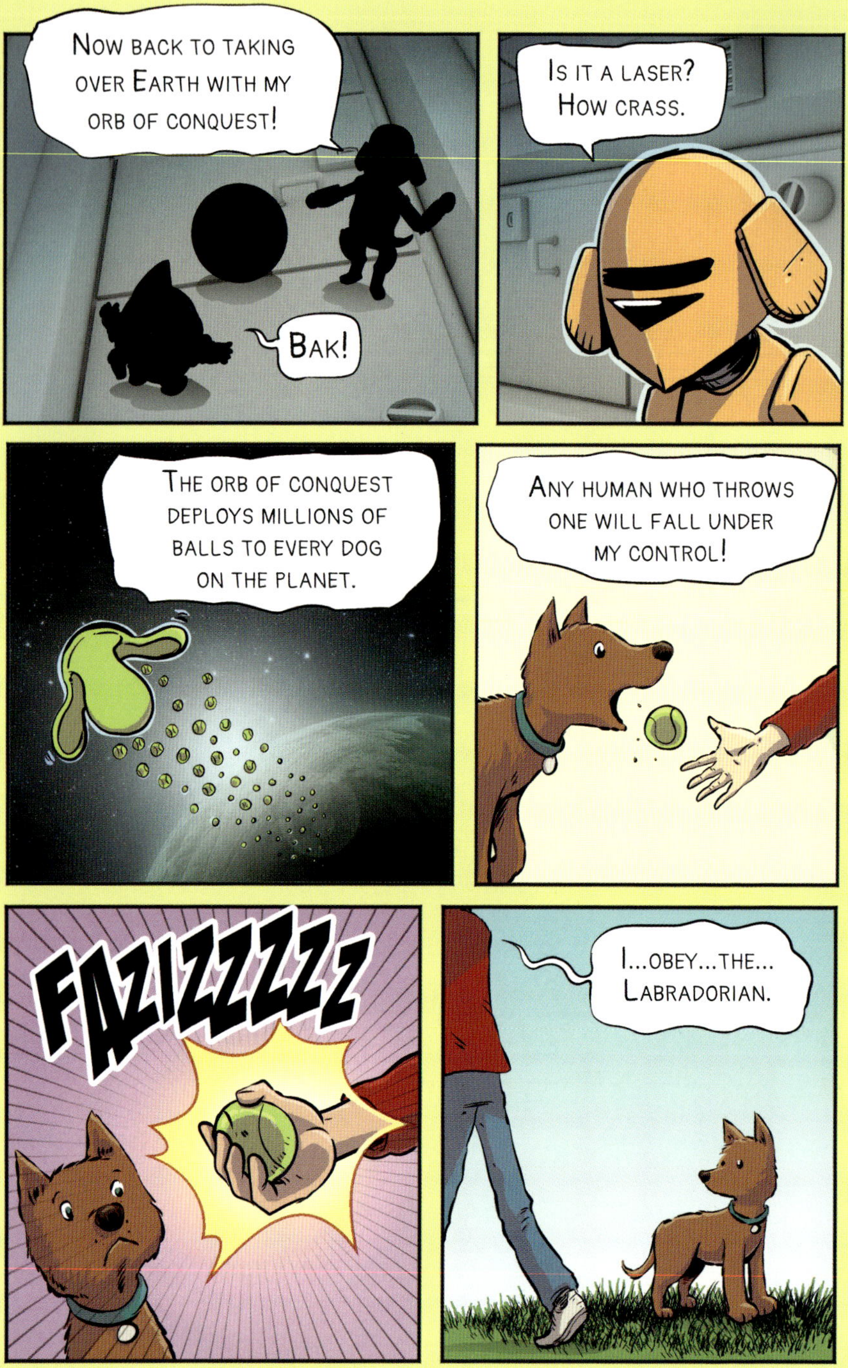
NOW BACK TO TAKING OVER EARTH WITH MY ORB OF CONQUEST!
BAK!
IS IT A LASER? HOW CRASS.
THE ORB OF CONQUEST DEPLOYS MILLIONS OF BALLS TO EVERY DOG ON THE PLANET.
ANY HUMAN WHO THROWS ONE WILL FALL UNDER MY CONTROL!
FAZIZZZZZ
I...OBEY...THE... LABRADORIAN.

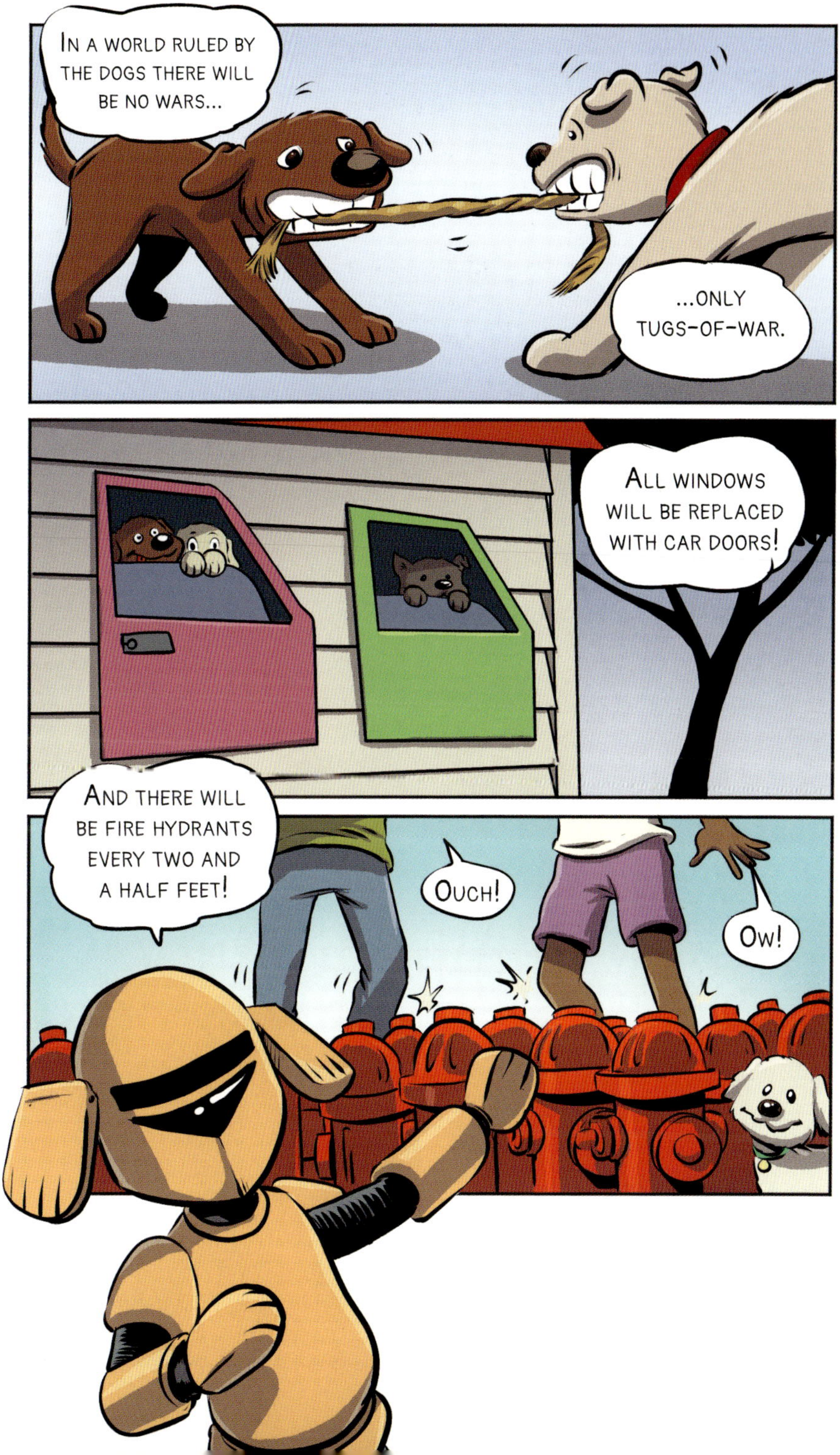
IN A WORLD RULED BY THE DOGS THERE WILL BE NO WARS...
...ONLY TUGS-OF-WAR.
ALL WINDOWS WILL BE REPLACED WITH CAR DOORS!
AND THERE WILL BE FIRE HYDRANTS EVERY TWO AND A HALF FEET!
OUCH!
OW!

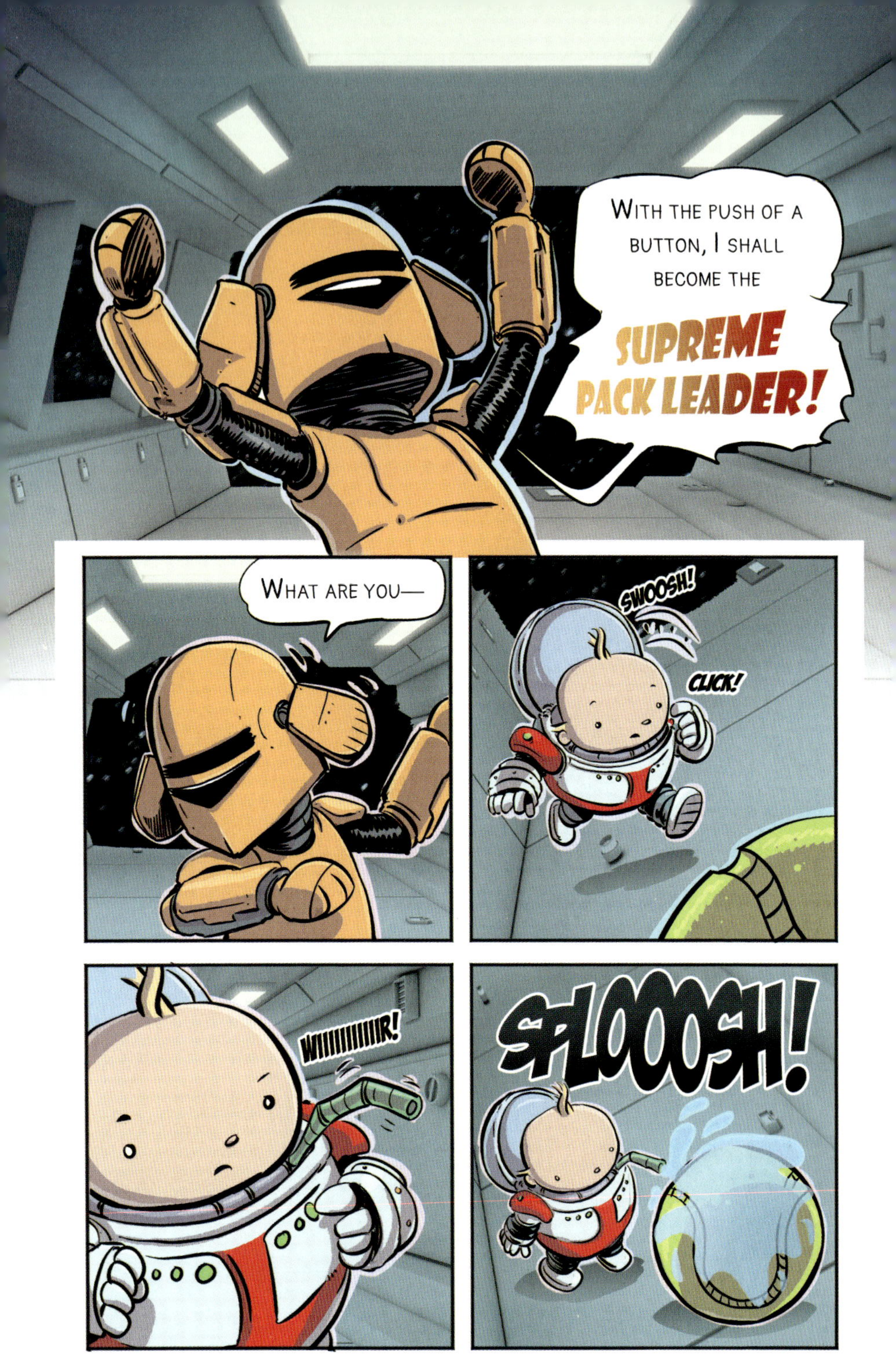
WITH THE PUSH OF A BUTTON, I SHALL BECOME THE
SUPREME PACK LEADER!
WHAT ARE YOU—
SWOOSH!
CLICK!
WIIIIIIIIIIR!
SPLOOOSH!

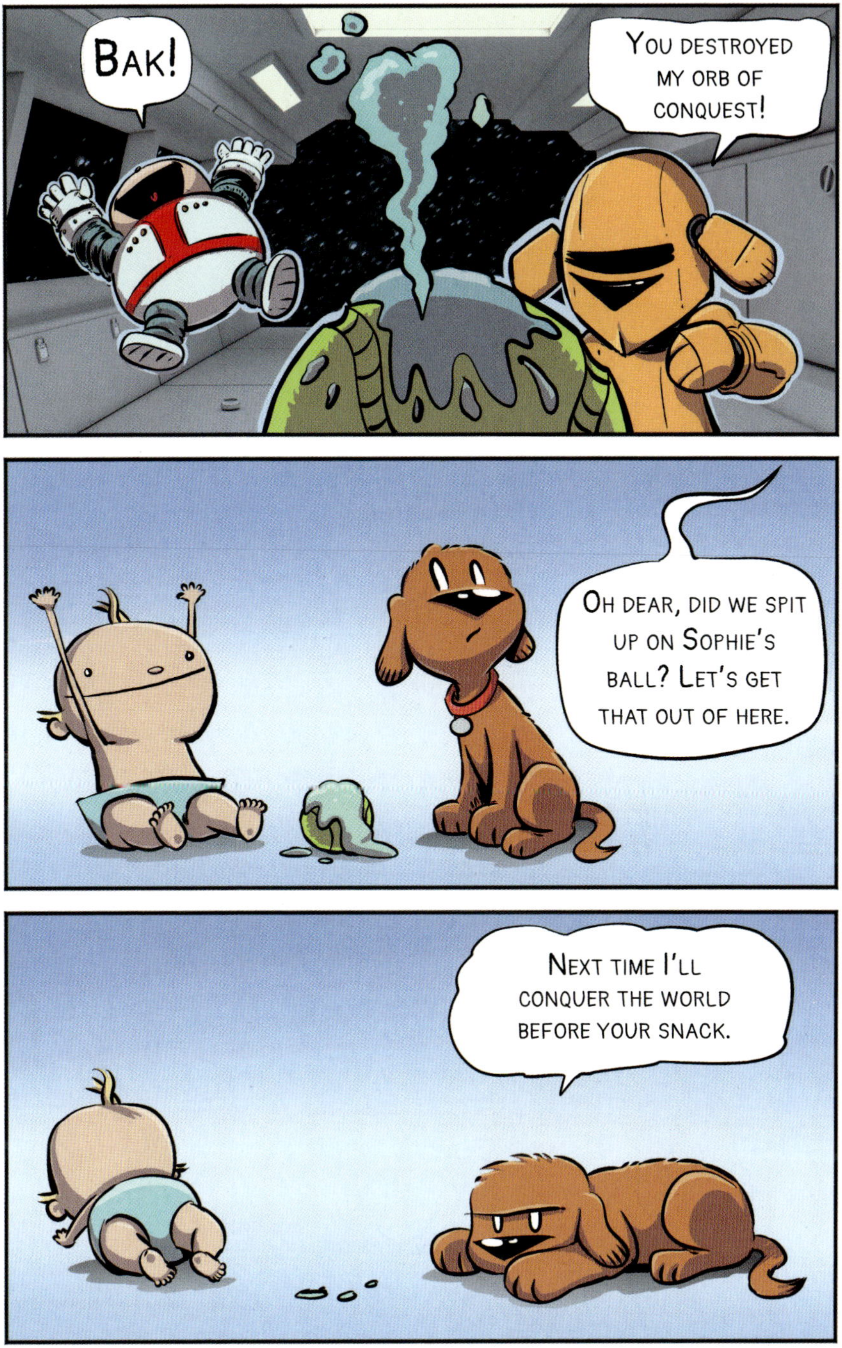
BAK!
YOU DESTROYED MY ORB OF CONQUEST!
OH DEAR, DID WE SPIT UP ON SOPHIE'S BALL? LET'S GET THAT OUT OF HERE.
NEXT TIME I'LL CONQUER THE WORLD BEFORE YOUR SNACK.

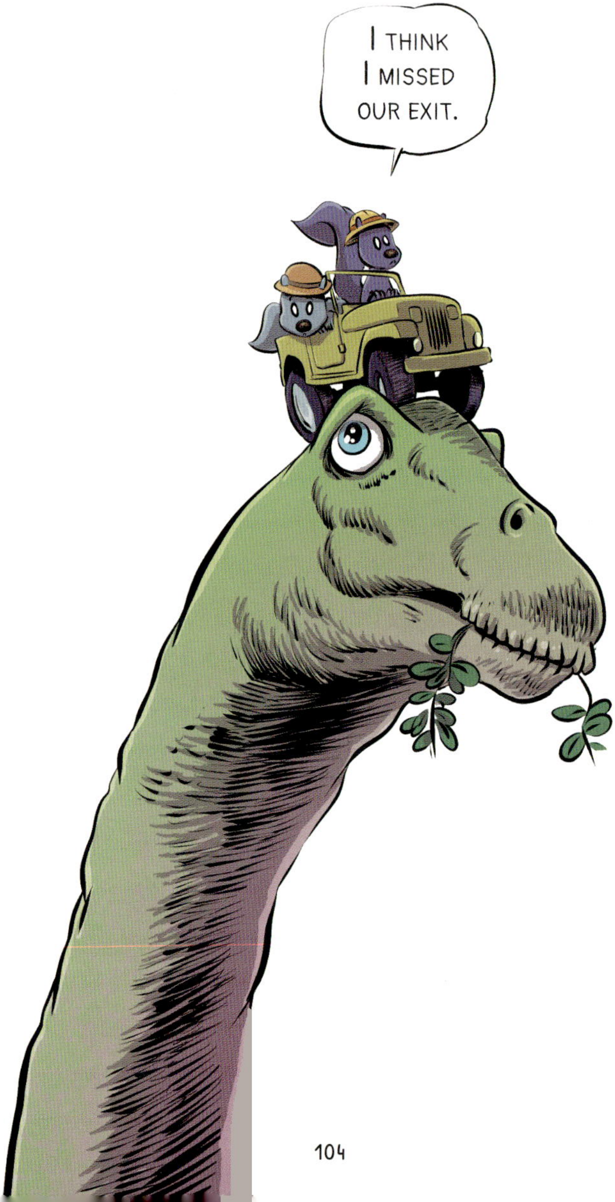
I THINK I MISSED OUR EXIT.

CHAPTER 6

JURASSIC BARK

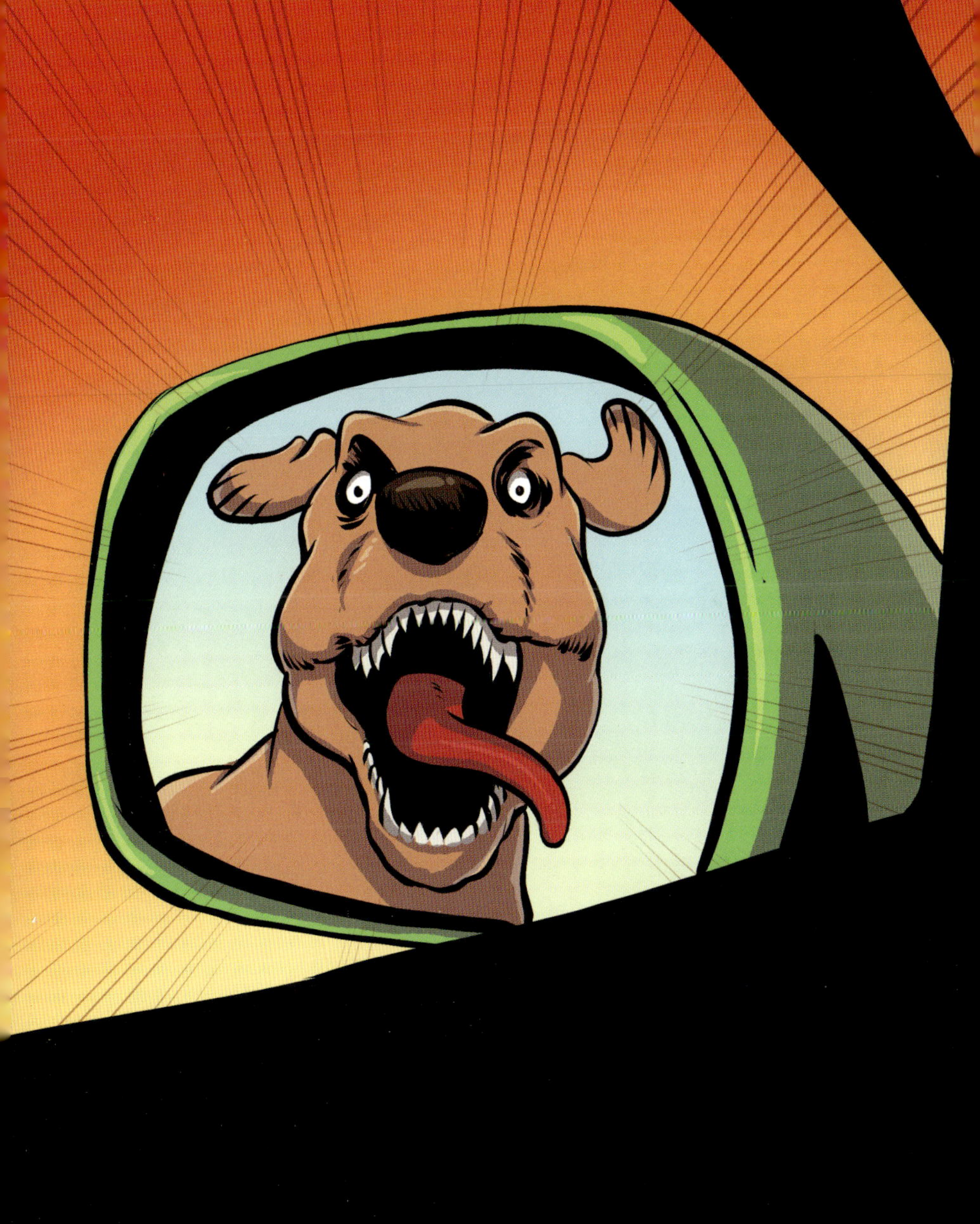

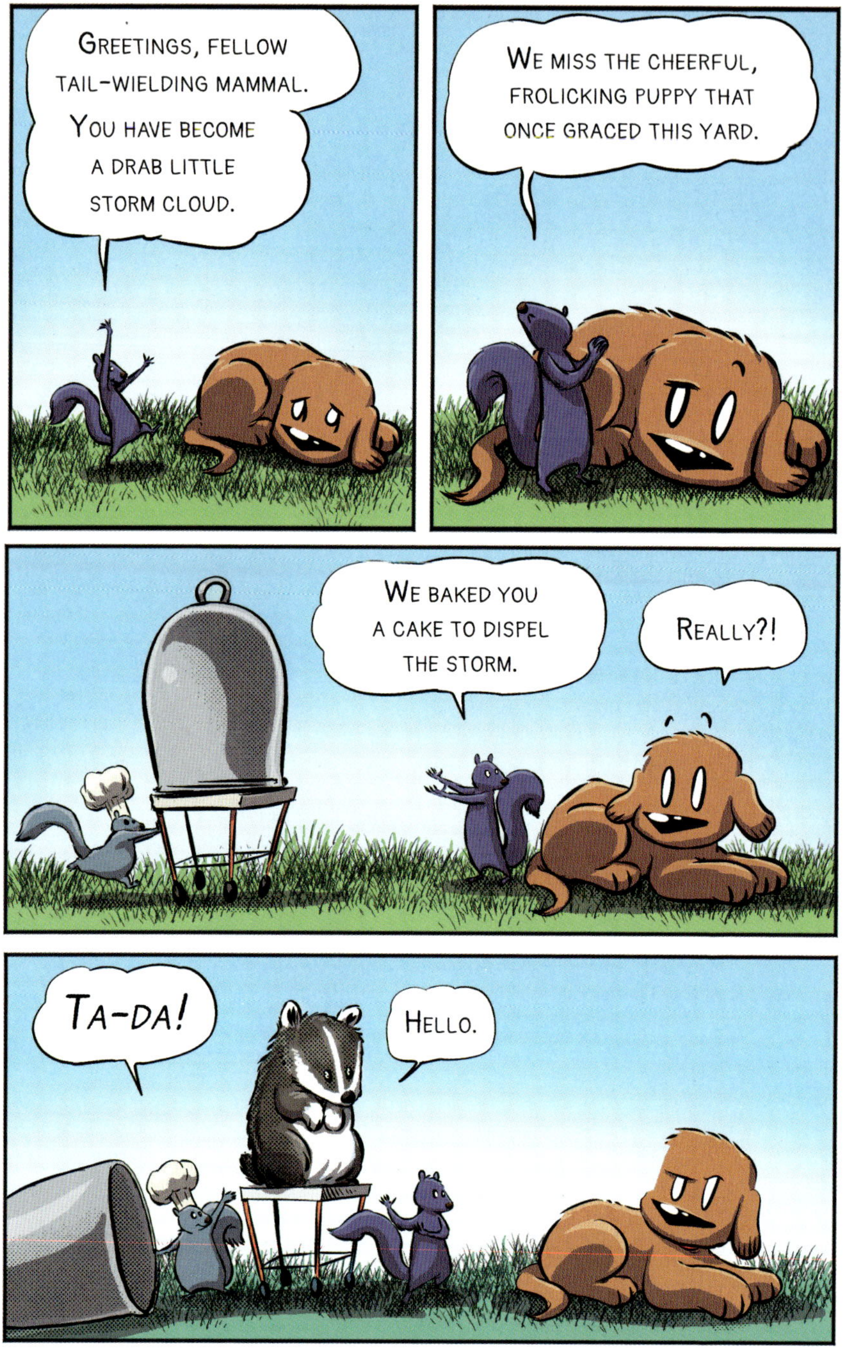
GREETINGS, FELLOW TAIL-WIELDING MAMMAL.
YOU HAVE BECOME A DRAB LITTLE STORM CLOUD.
WE MISS THE CHEERFUL, FROLICKING PUPPY THAT ONCE GRACED THIS YARD.
WE BAKED YOU A CAKE TO DISPEL THE STORM.
REALLY?!
TA-DA!
HELLO.

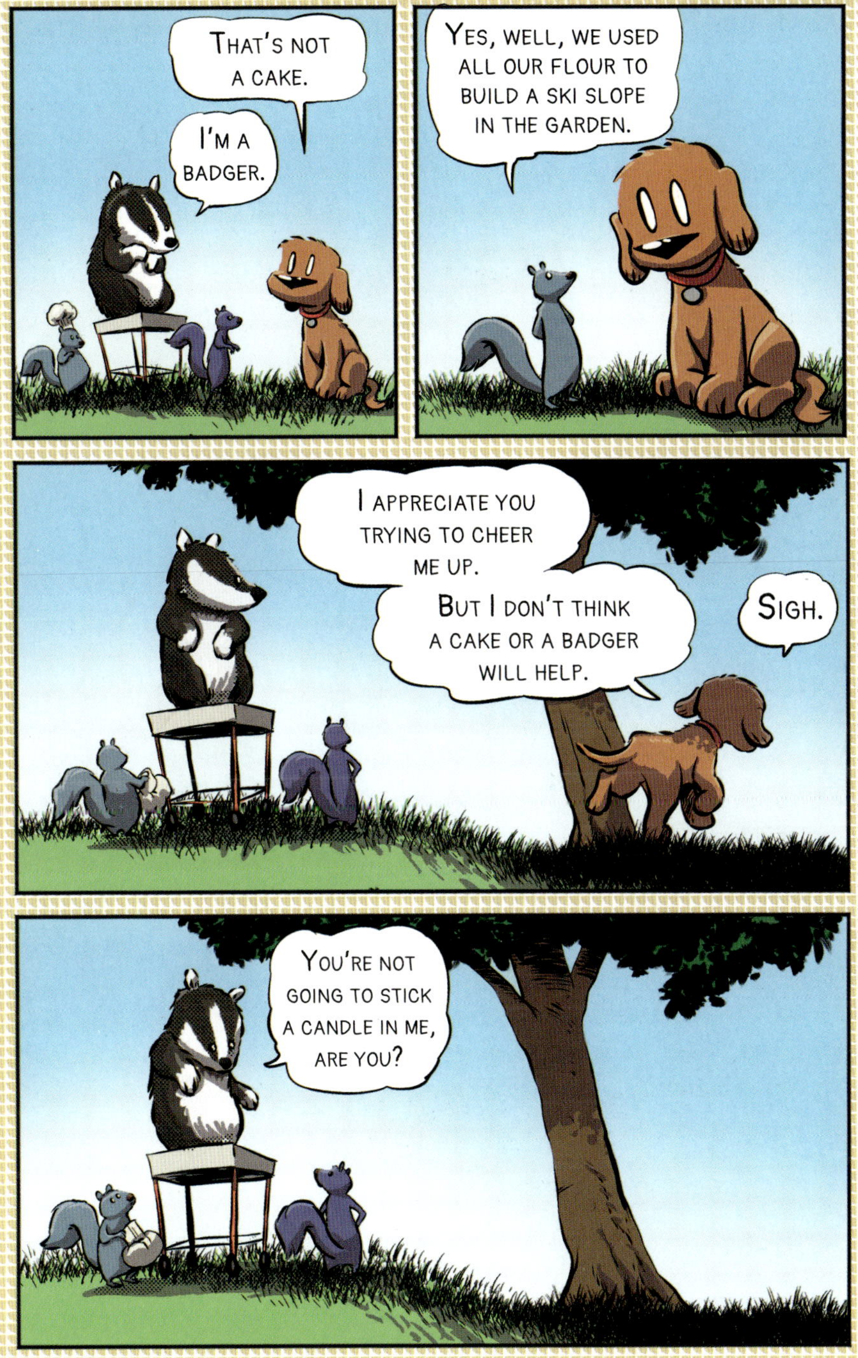
THAT'S NOT A CAKE.
I'M A BADGER.
YES, WELL, WE USED ALL OUR FLOUR TO BUILD A SKI SLOPE IN THE GARDEN.
I APPRECIATE YOU TRYING TO CHEER ME UP.
BUT I DON'T THINK A CAKE OR A BADGER WILL HELP.
SIGH.
YOU'RE NOT GOING TO STICK A CANDLE IN ME, ARE YOU?

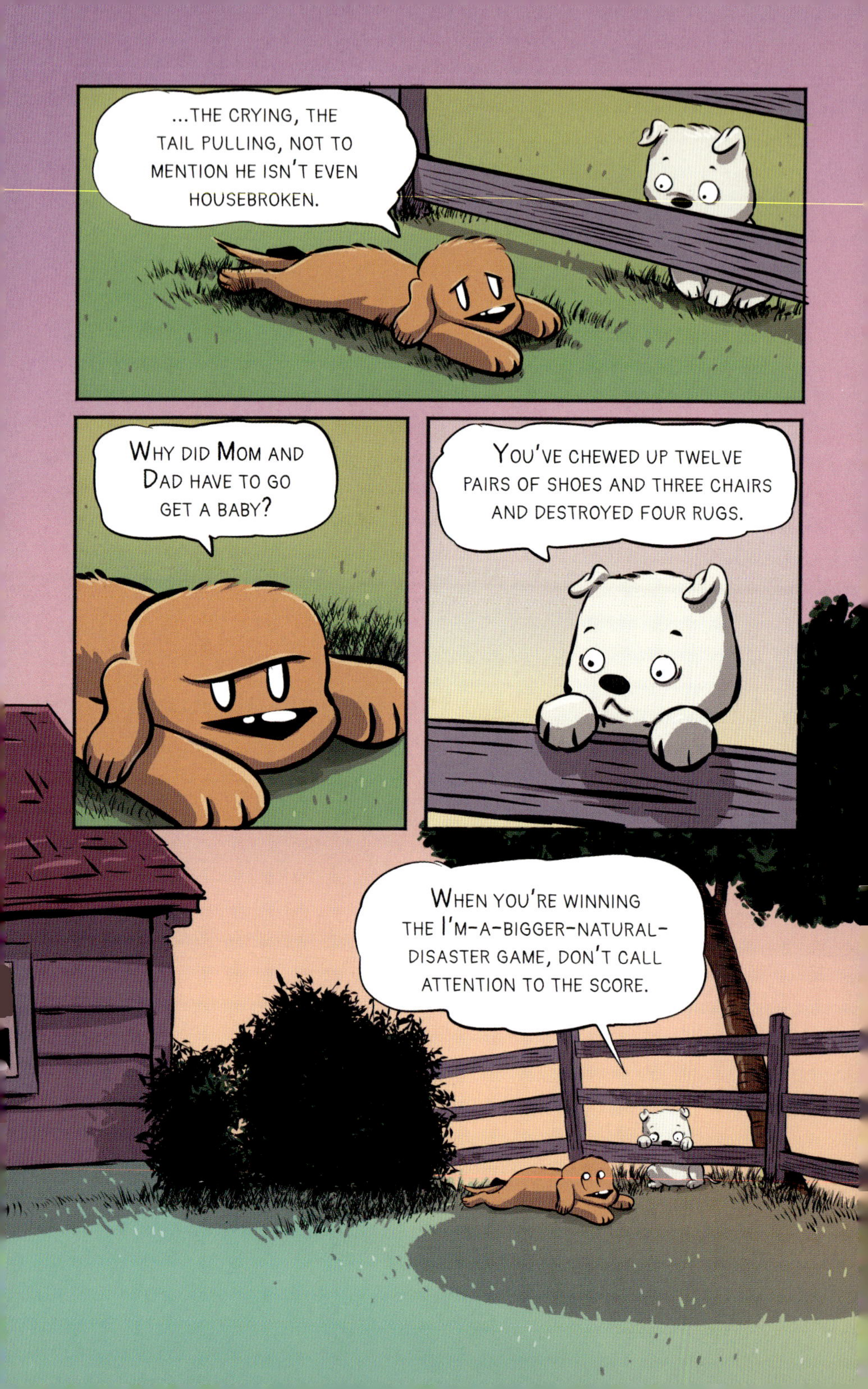
...THE CRYING, THE TAIL PULLING, NOT TO MENTION HE ISN'T EVEN HOUSEBROKEN.
WHY DID MOM AND DAD HAVE TO GO GET A BABY?
YOU'VE CHEWED UP TWELVE PAIRS OF SHOES AND THREE CHAIRS AND DESTROYED FOUR RUGS.
WHEN YOU'RE WINNING THE I'M-A-BIGGER-NATURAL-DISASTER GAME, DON'T CALL ATTENTION TO THE SCORE.

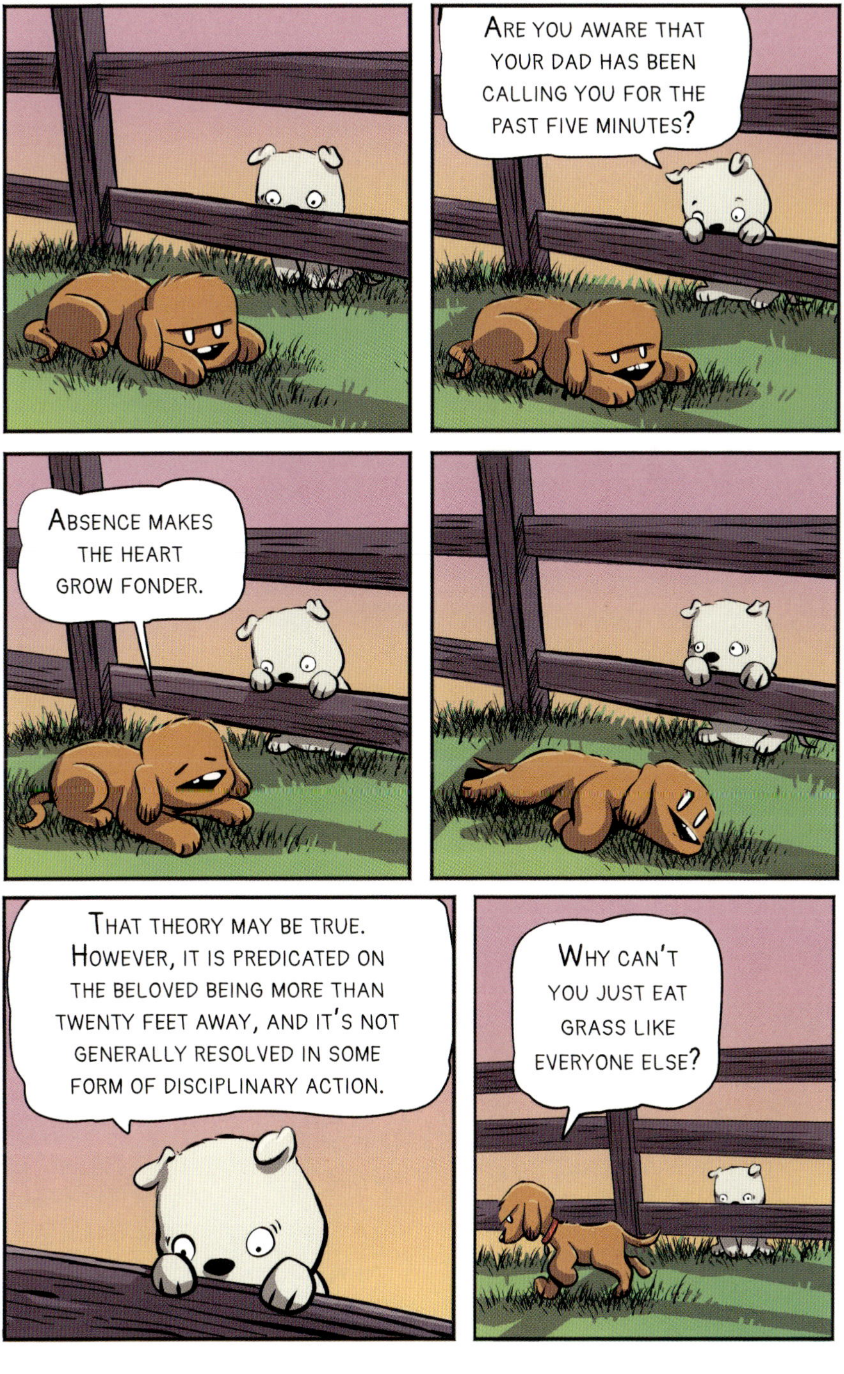
ARE YOU AWARE THAT YOUR DAD HAS BEEN CALLING YOU FOR THE PAST FIVE MINUTES?
ABSENCE MAKES THE HEART GROW FONDER.
THAT THEORY MAY BE TRUE. HOWEVER, IT IS PREDICATED ON THE BELOVED BEING MORE THAN TWENTY FEET AWAY, AND IT'S NOT GENERALLY RESOLVED IN SOME FORM OF DISCIPLINARY ACTION.
WHY CAN'T YOU JUST EAT GRASS LIKE EVERYONE ELSE?

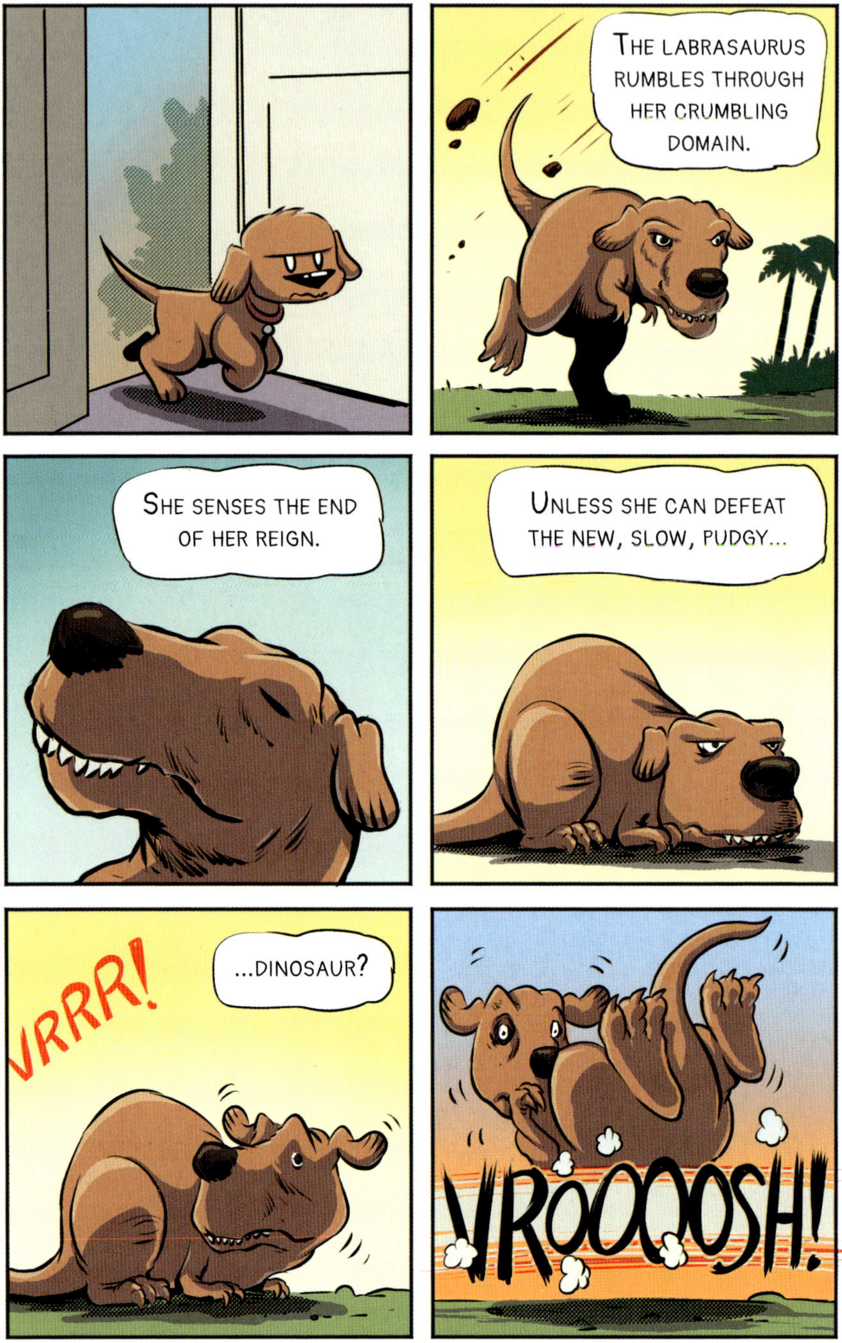
THE LABRASAURUS RUMBLES THROUGH HER CRUMBLING DOMAIN.
SHE SENSES THE END OF HER REIGN.
UNLESS SHE CAN DEFEAT THE NEW, SLOW, PUDGY...
VRRR!
...DINOSAUR?
VROOOOSH!

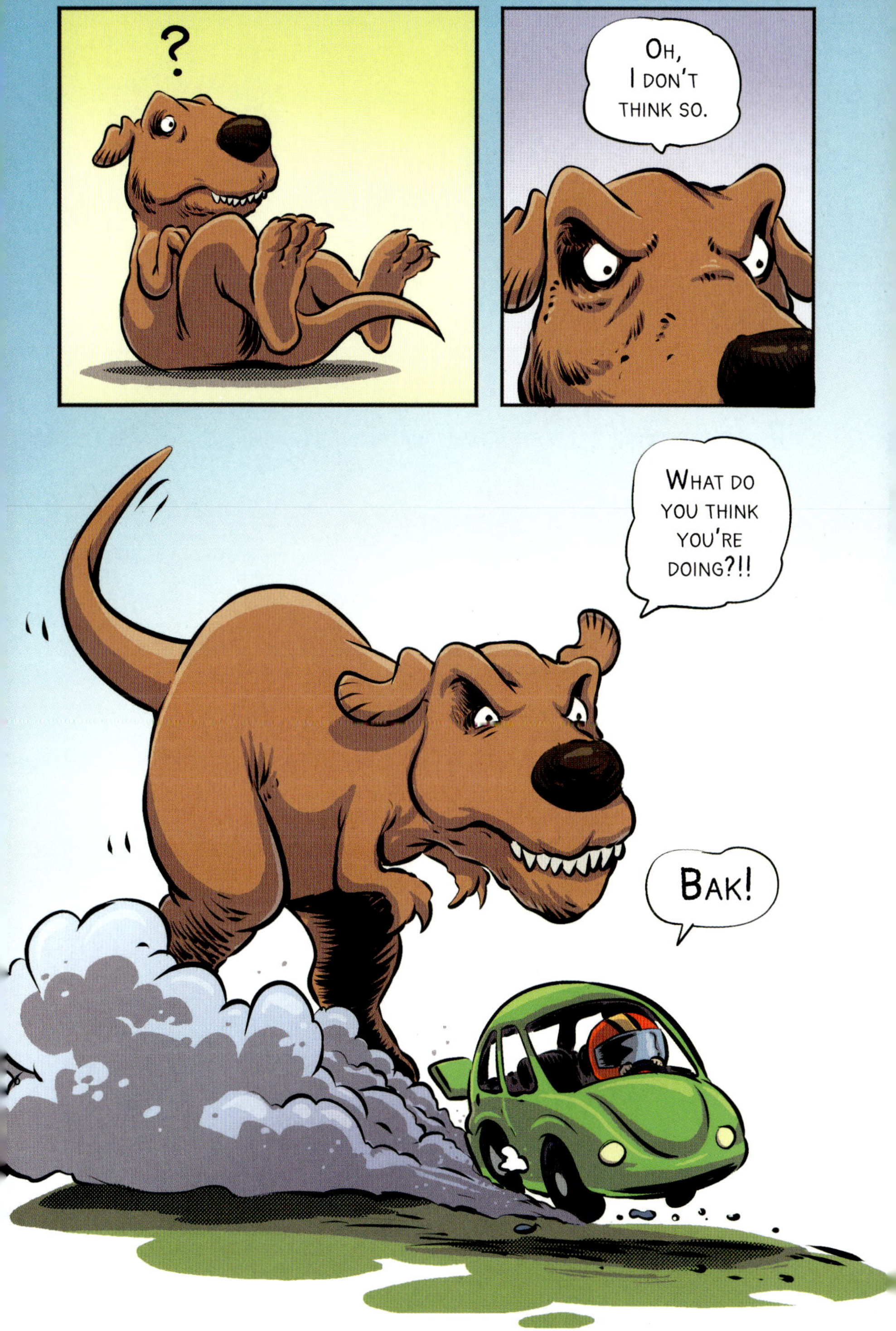
?
OH, I DON'T THINK SO.
WHAT DO YOU THINK YOU'RE DOING?!!
BAK!

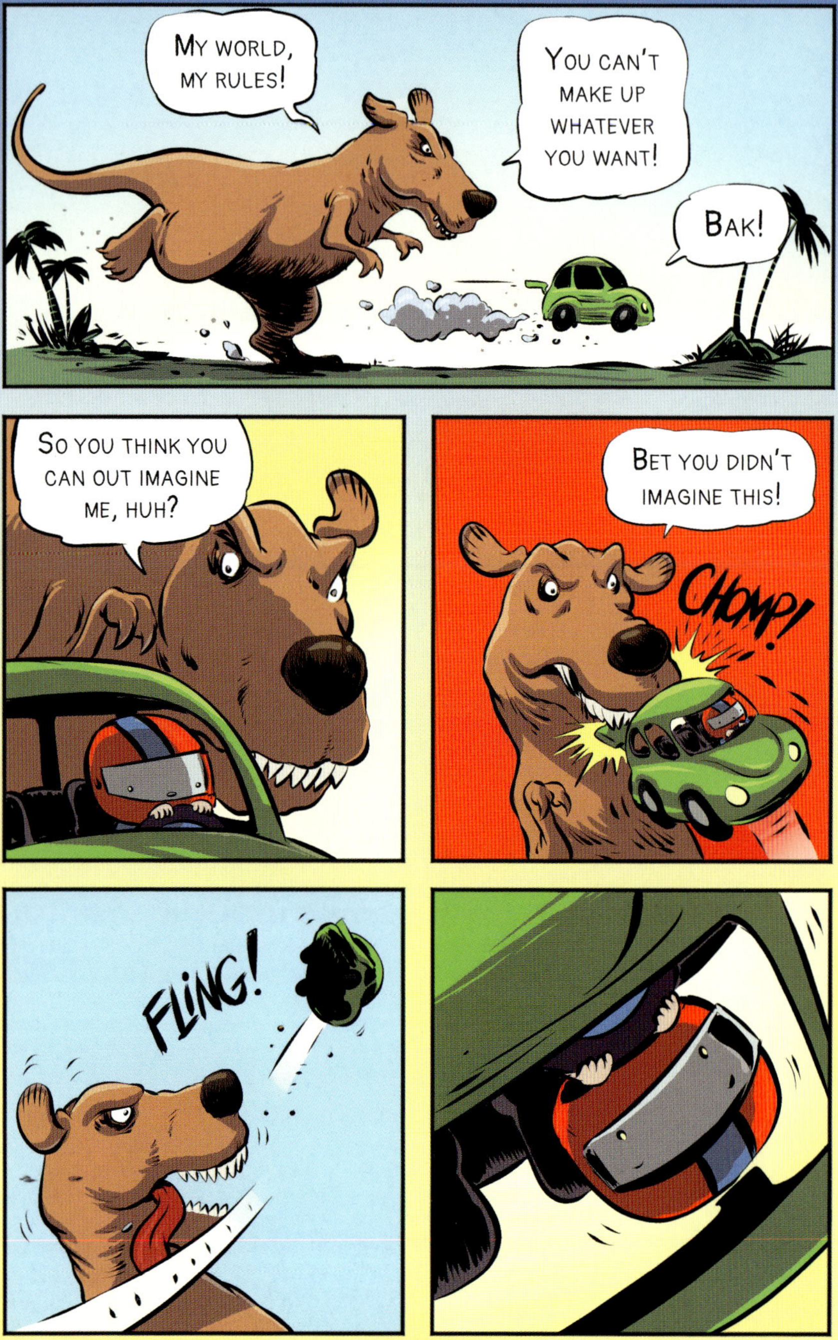
MY WORLD, MY RULES!
YOU CAN'T MAKE UP WHATEVER YOU WANT!
BAK!
SO YOU THINK YOU CAN OUT IMAGINE ME, HUH?
BET YOU DIDN'T IMAGINE THIS!
CHOMP!
FLING!

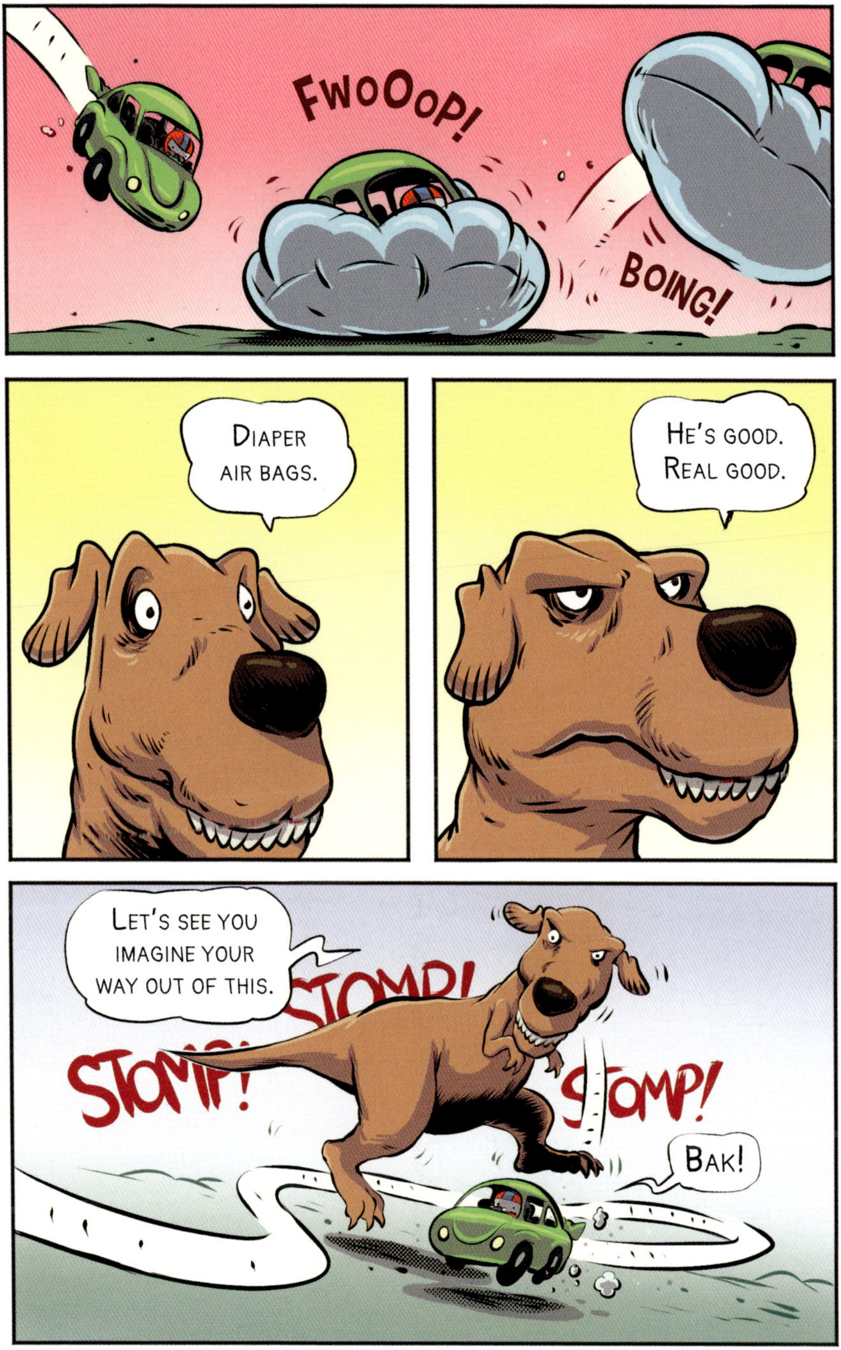
FWOOOP!
BOING!
DIAPER AIR BAGS.
HE'S GOOD. REAL GOOD.
LET'S SEE YOU IMAGINE YOUR WAY OUT OF THIS.
STOMP!
STOMP!
STOMP!
BAK!

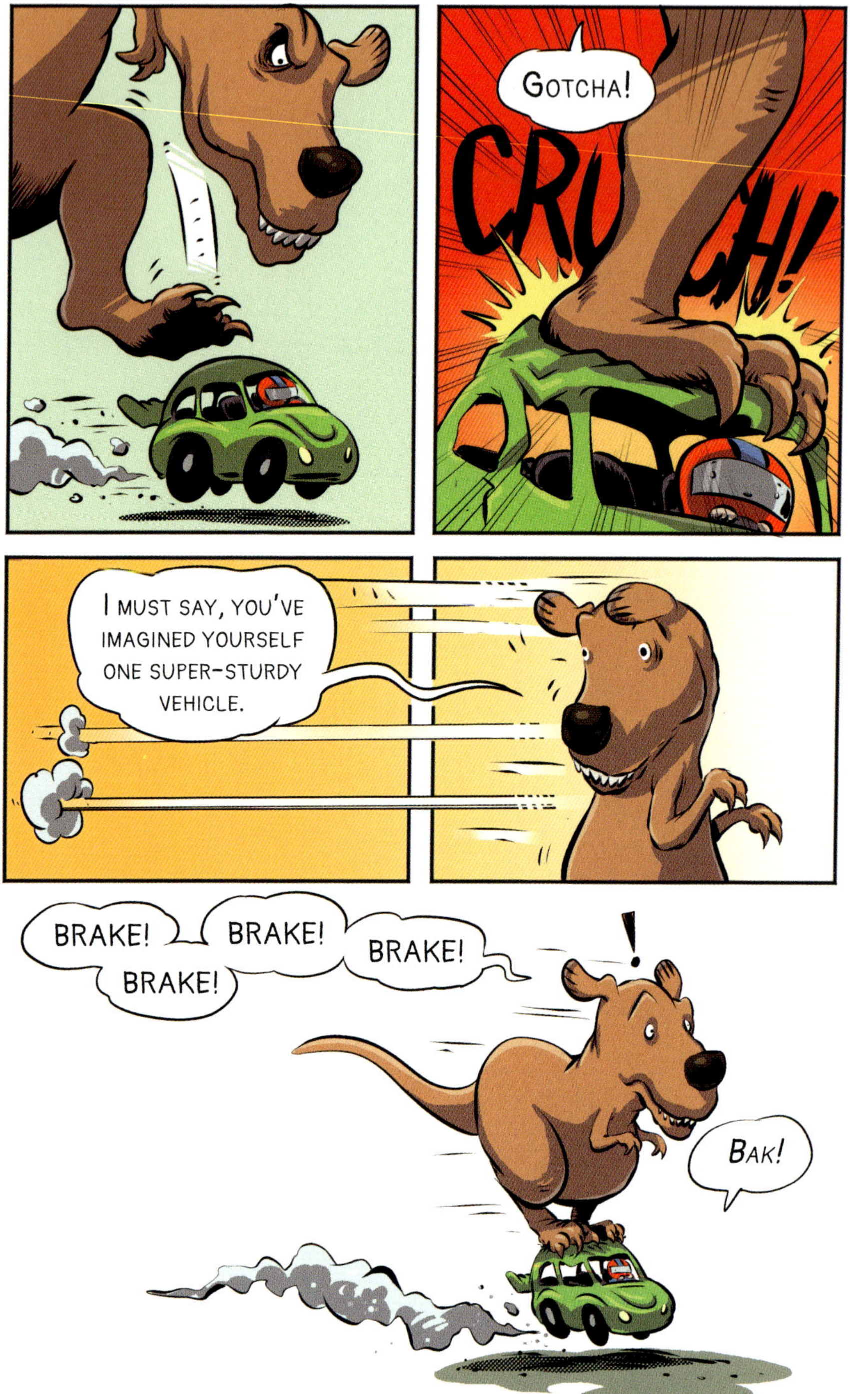

GOTCHA!
CRUNCH!
I MUST SAY, YOU'VE IMAGINED YOURSELF ONE SUPER-STURDY VEHICLE.
BRAKE!
BRAKE!
BRAKE!
BRAKE!
!
BAK!

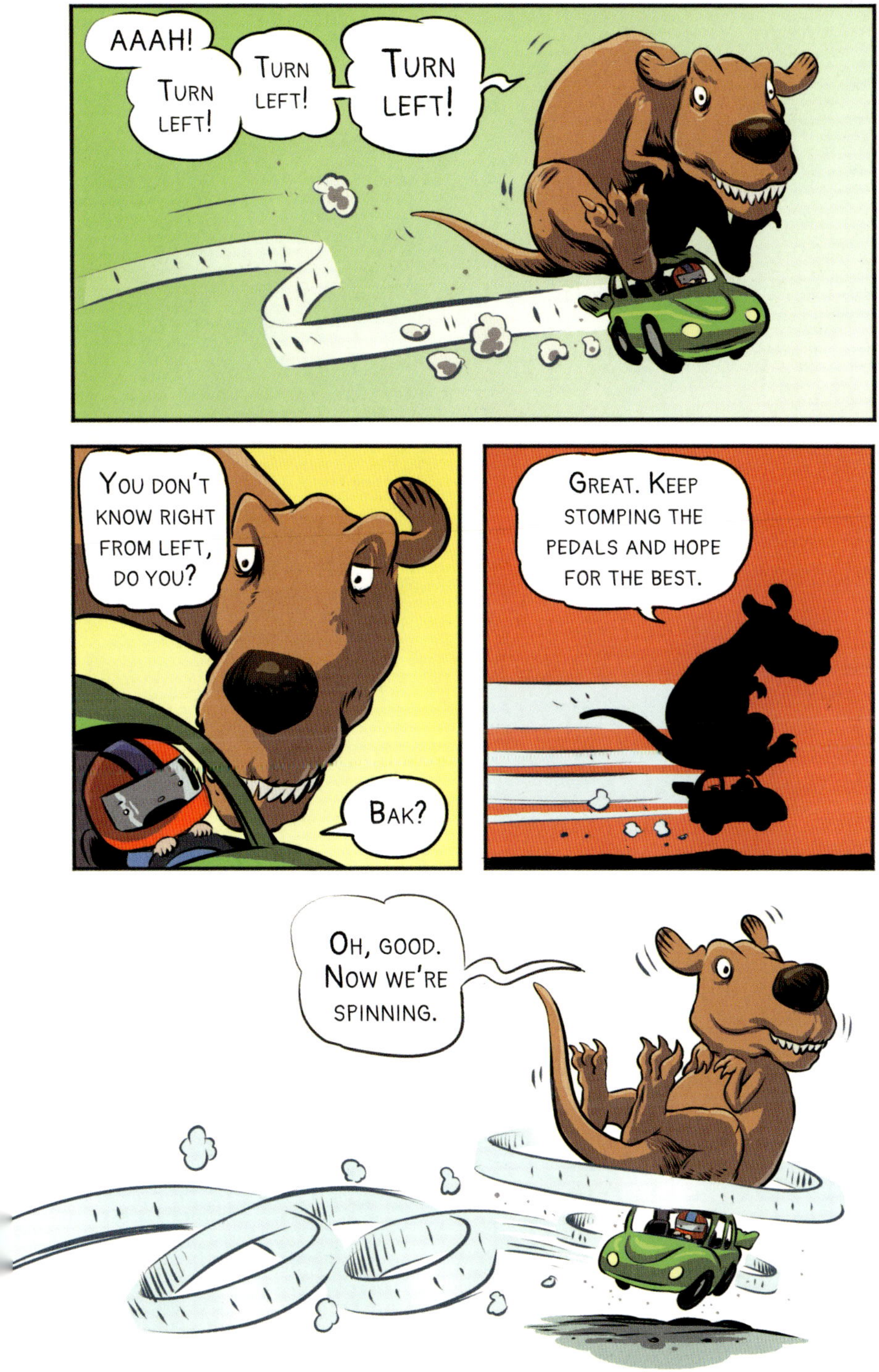
AAAH!
TURN LEFT!
TURN LEFT!
TURN LEFT!
YOU DON'T KNOW RIGHT FROM LEFT, DO YOU?
BAK?
GREAT. KEEP STOMPING THE PEDALS AND HOPE FOR THE BEST.
OH, GOOD. NOW WE'RE SPINNING.

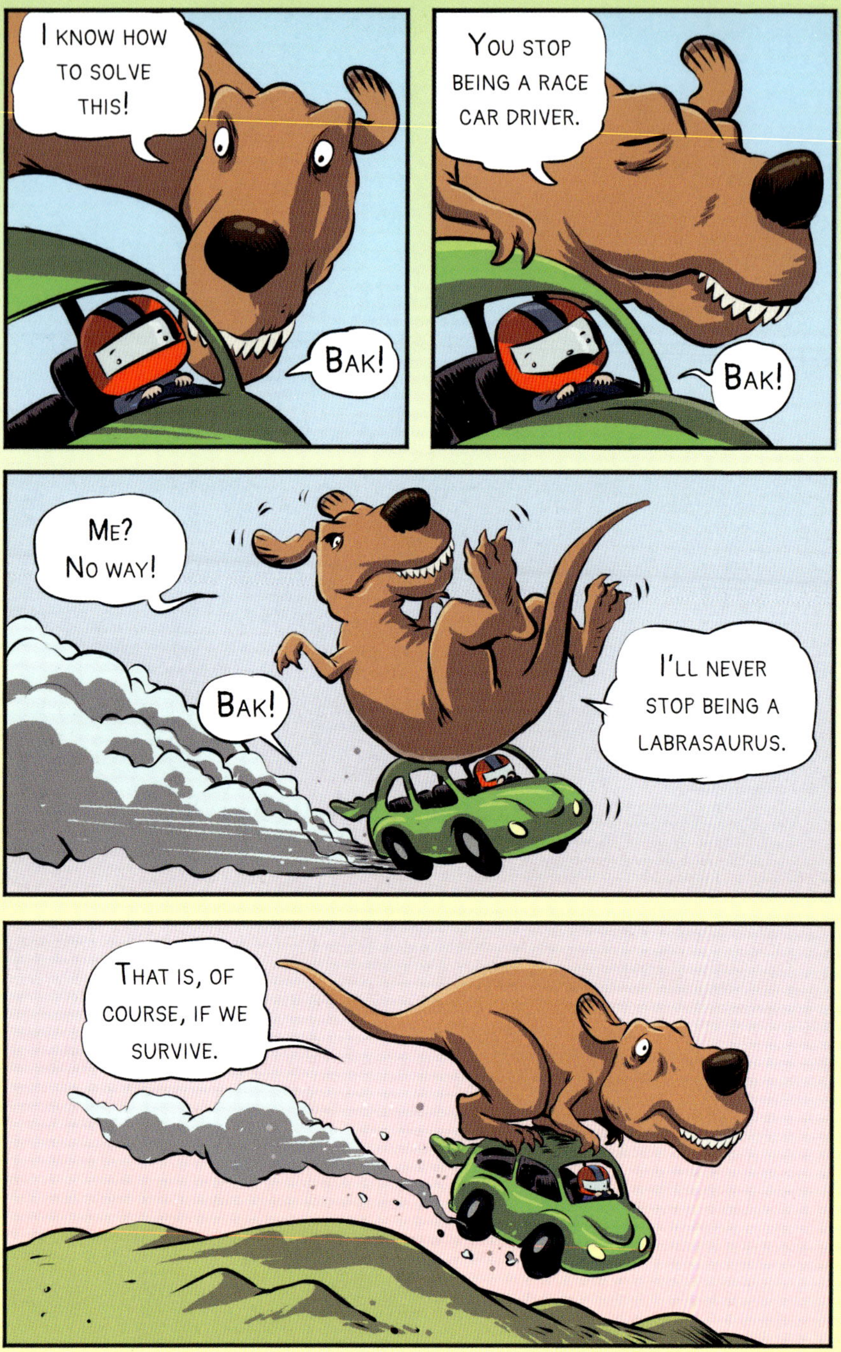
I KNOW HOW TO SOLVE THIS!
BAK!
YOU STOP BEING A RACE CAR DRIVER.
BAK!
ME? NO WAY!
BAK!
I'LL NEVER STOP BEING A LABRASAURUS.
THAT IS, OF COURSE, IF WE SURVIVE.

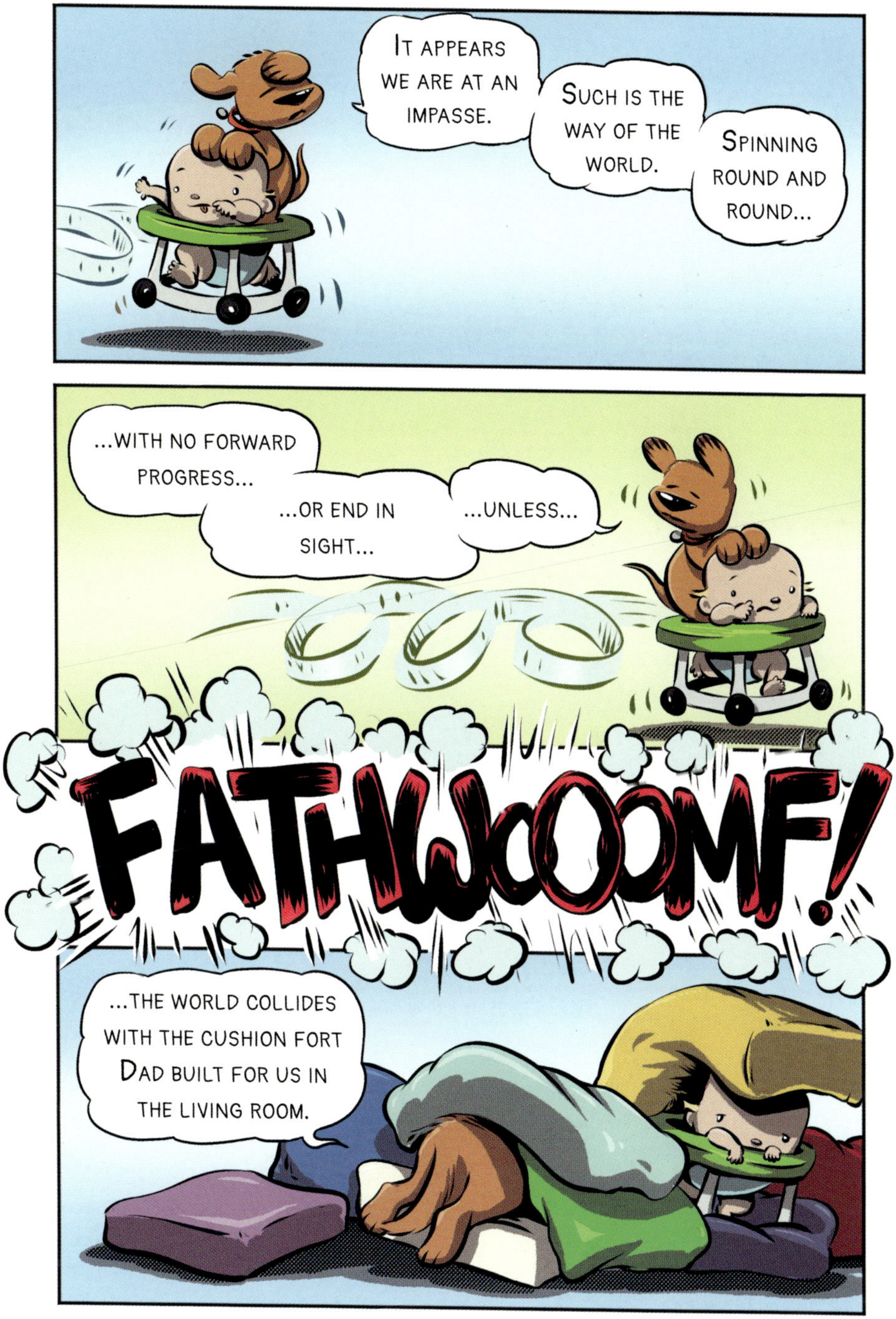
It appears we are at an impasse.
Such is the way of the world.
Spinning round and round...
...with no forward progress...
...or end in sight...
...unless...
FATHWOOOMF!
...the world collides with the cushion fort Dad built for us in the living room.

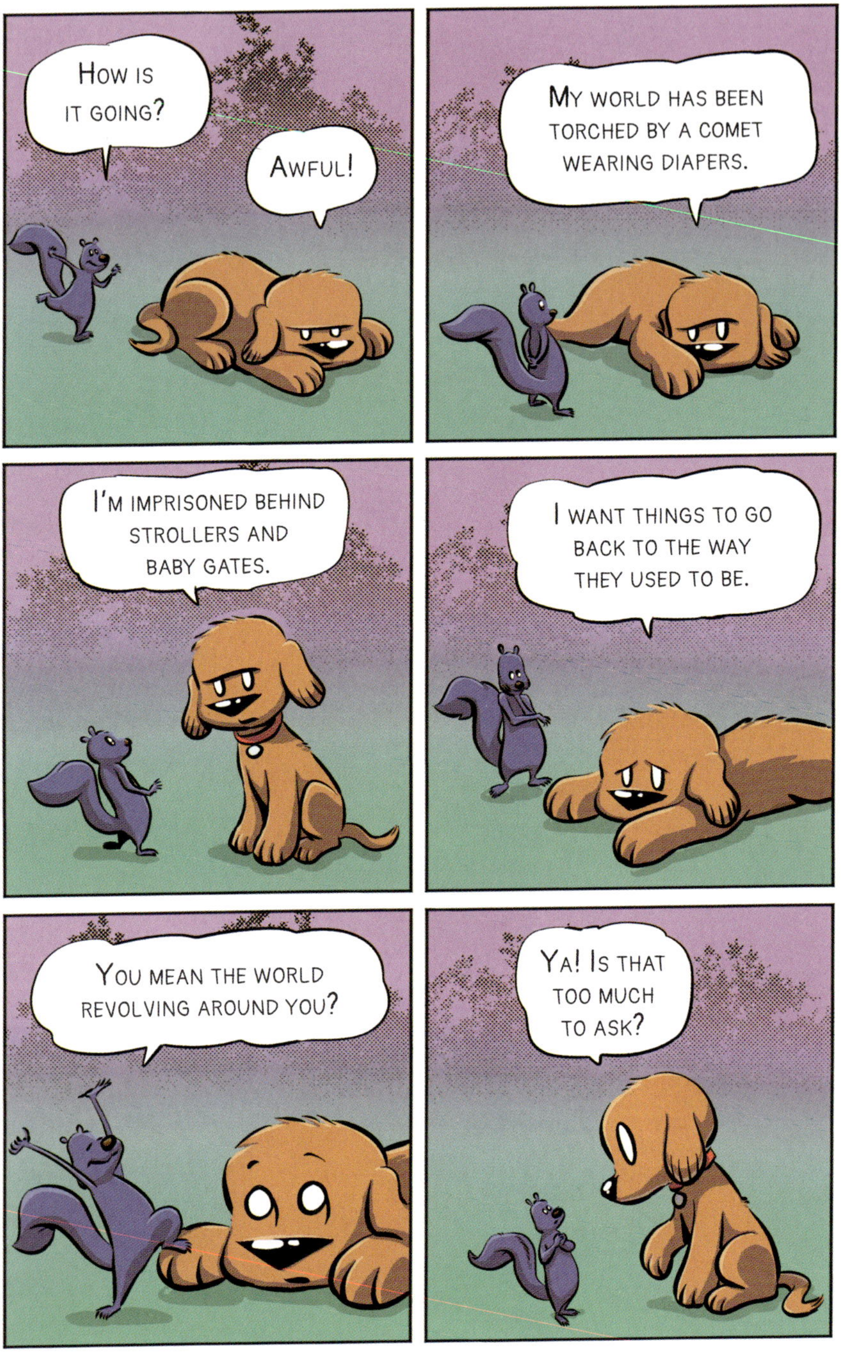
HOW IS IT GOING?
AWFUL!
MY WORLD HAS BEEN TORCHED BY A COMET WEARING DIAPERS.
I'M IMPRISONED BEHIND STROLLERS AND BABY GATES.
I WANT THINGS TO GO BACK TO THE WAY THEY USED TO BE.
YOU MEAN THE WORLD REVOLVING AROUND YOU?
YA! IS THAT TOO MUCH TO ASK?

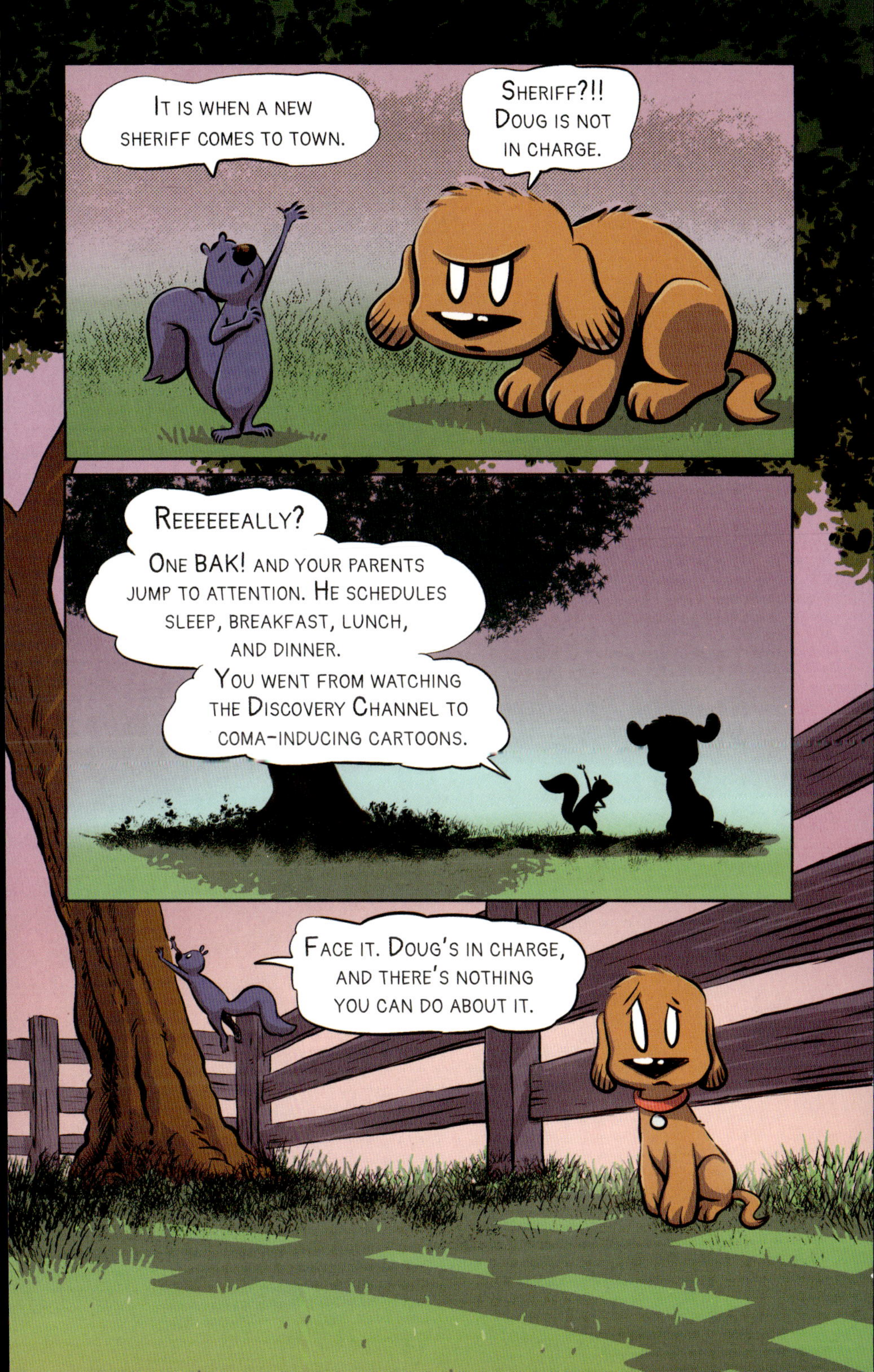
It is when a new sheriff comes to town.
Sheriff?!! Doug is not in charge.
Reeeeeeally?
One BAK! and your parents jump to attention. He schedules sleep, breakfast, lunch, and dinner.
You went from watching the Discovery Channel to coma-inducing cartoons.
Face it. Doug's in charge, and there's nothing you can do about it.

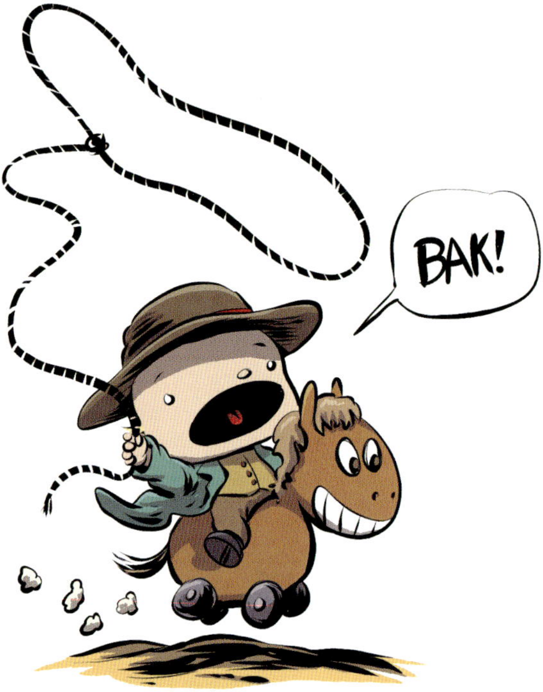
BAK!

CHAPTER 7

The Binky Bandit

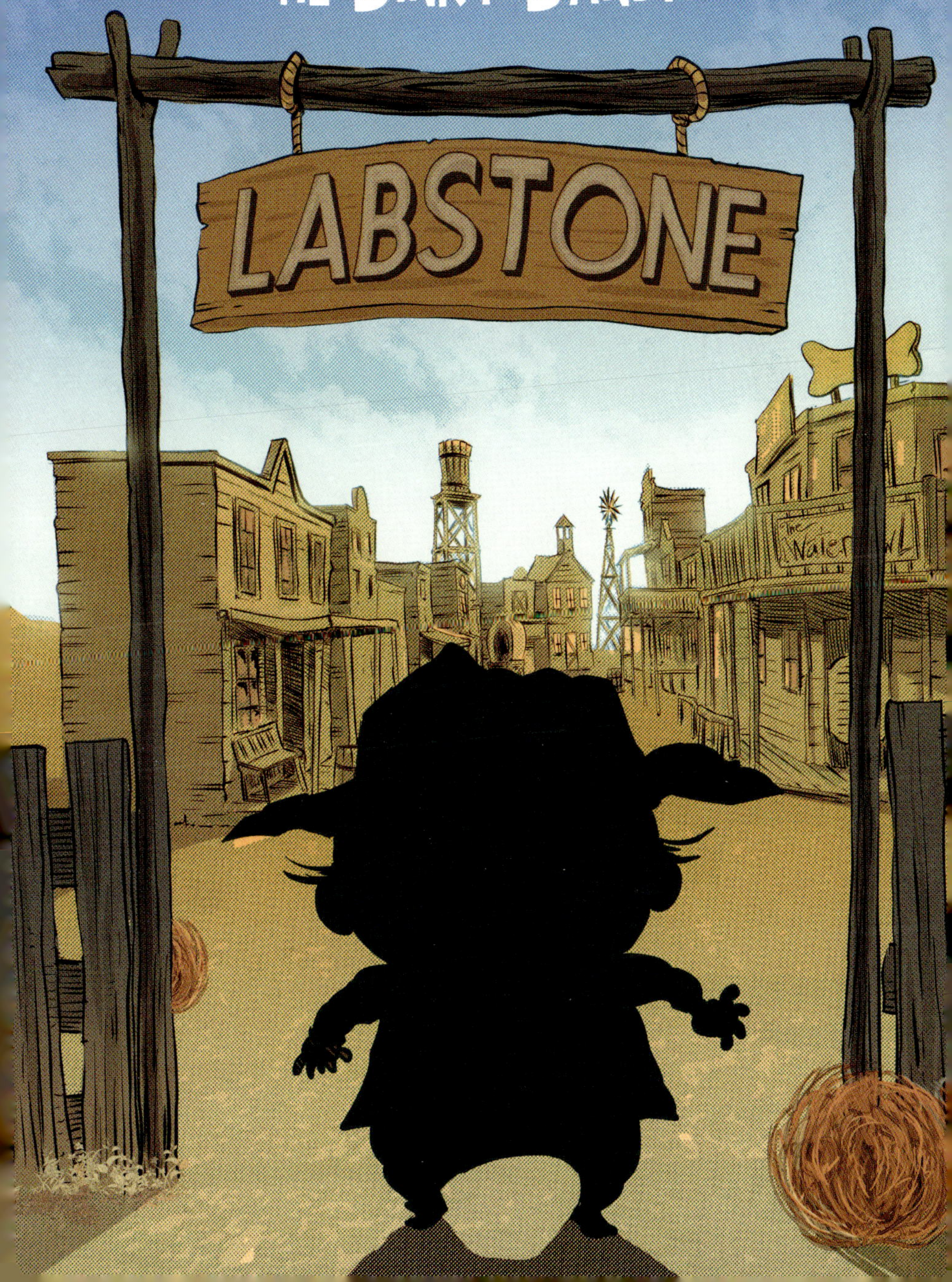
LABSTONE

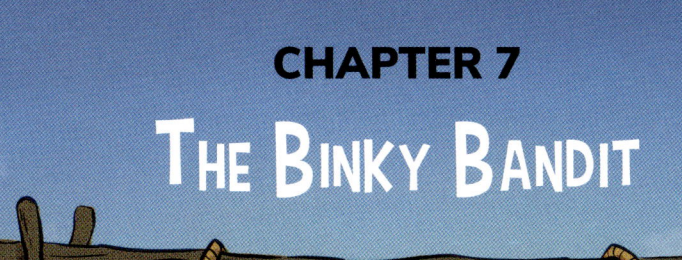

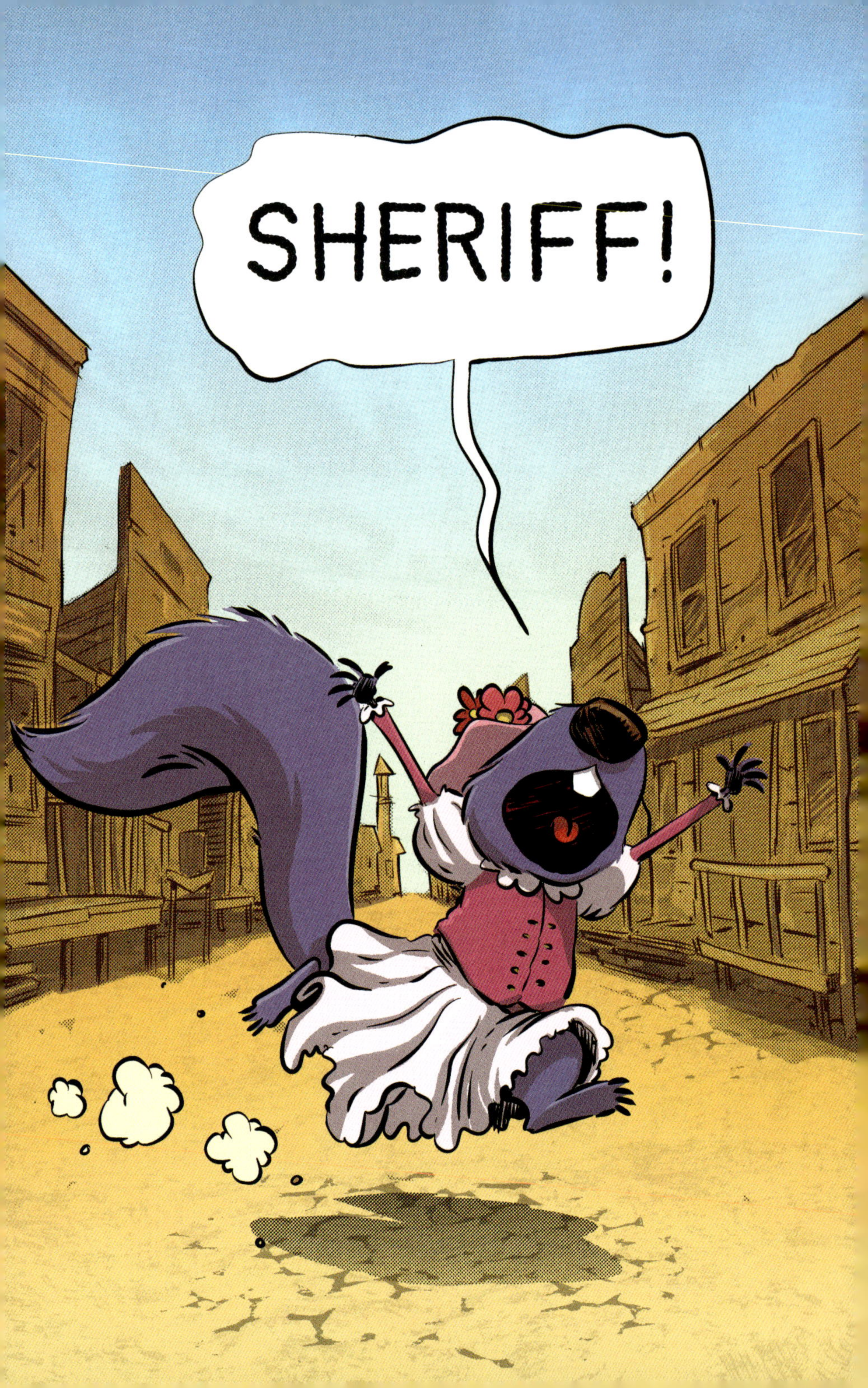
SHERIFF!

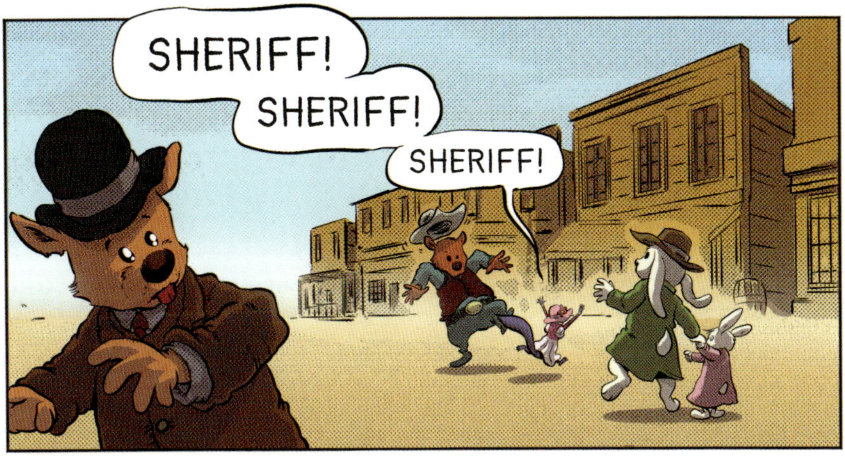
SHERIFF!
SHERIFF!
SHERIFF!

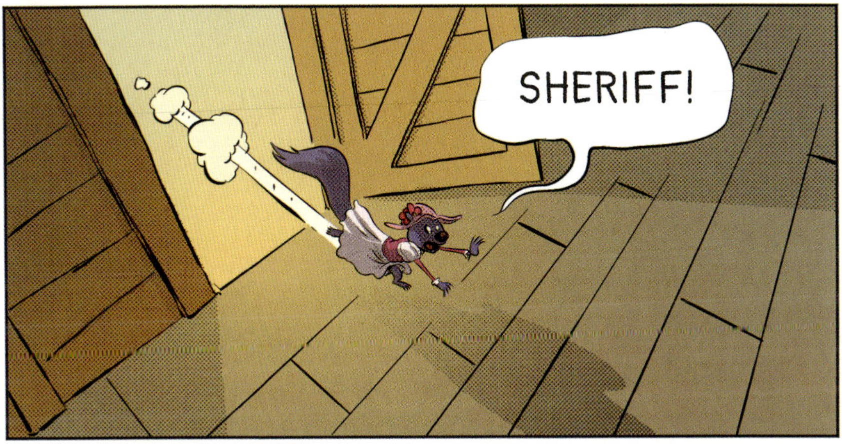
SHERIFF!

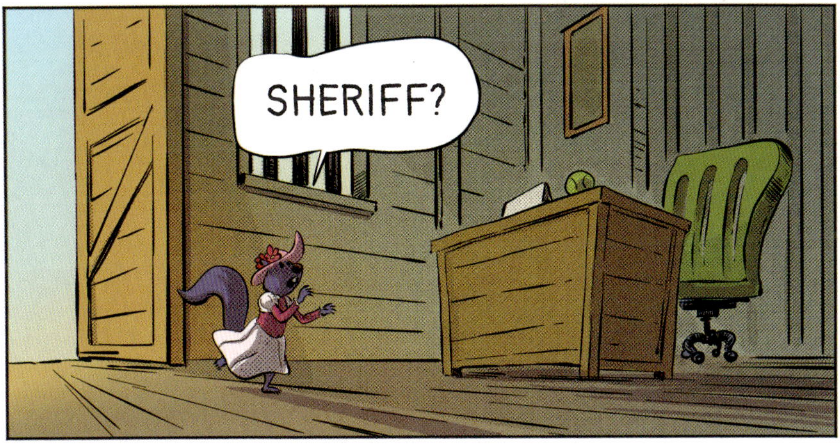
SHERIFF?

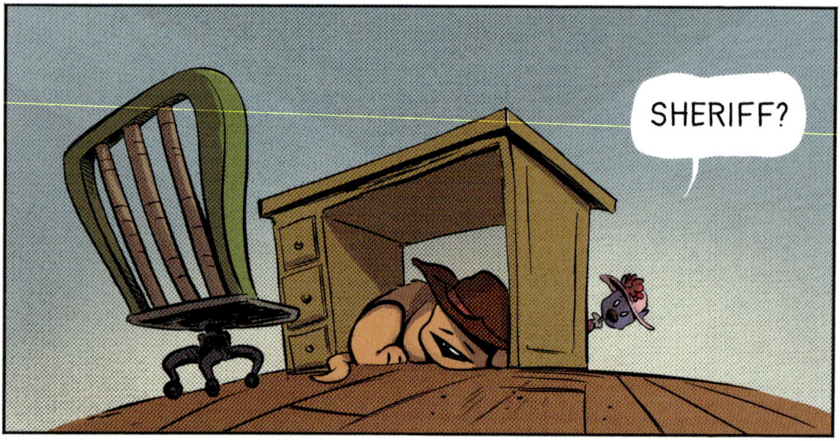
SHERIFF?

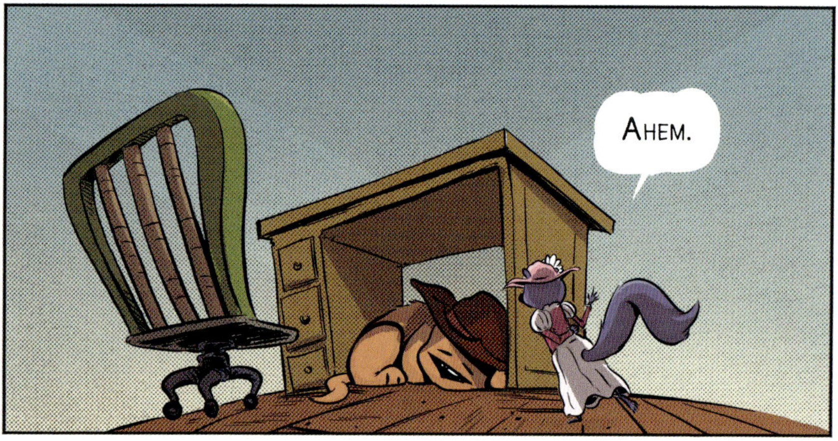
AHEM.

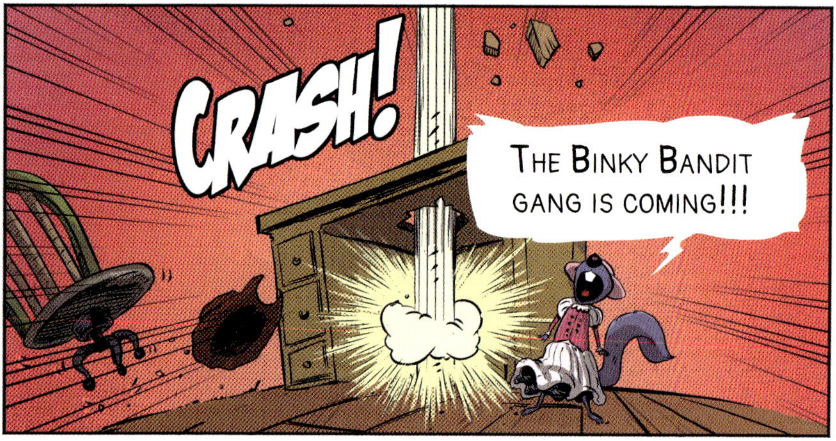
CRASH!
THE BINKY BANDIT GANG IS COMING!!!

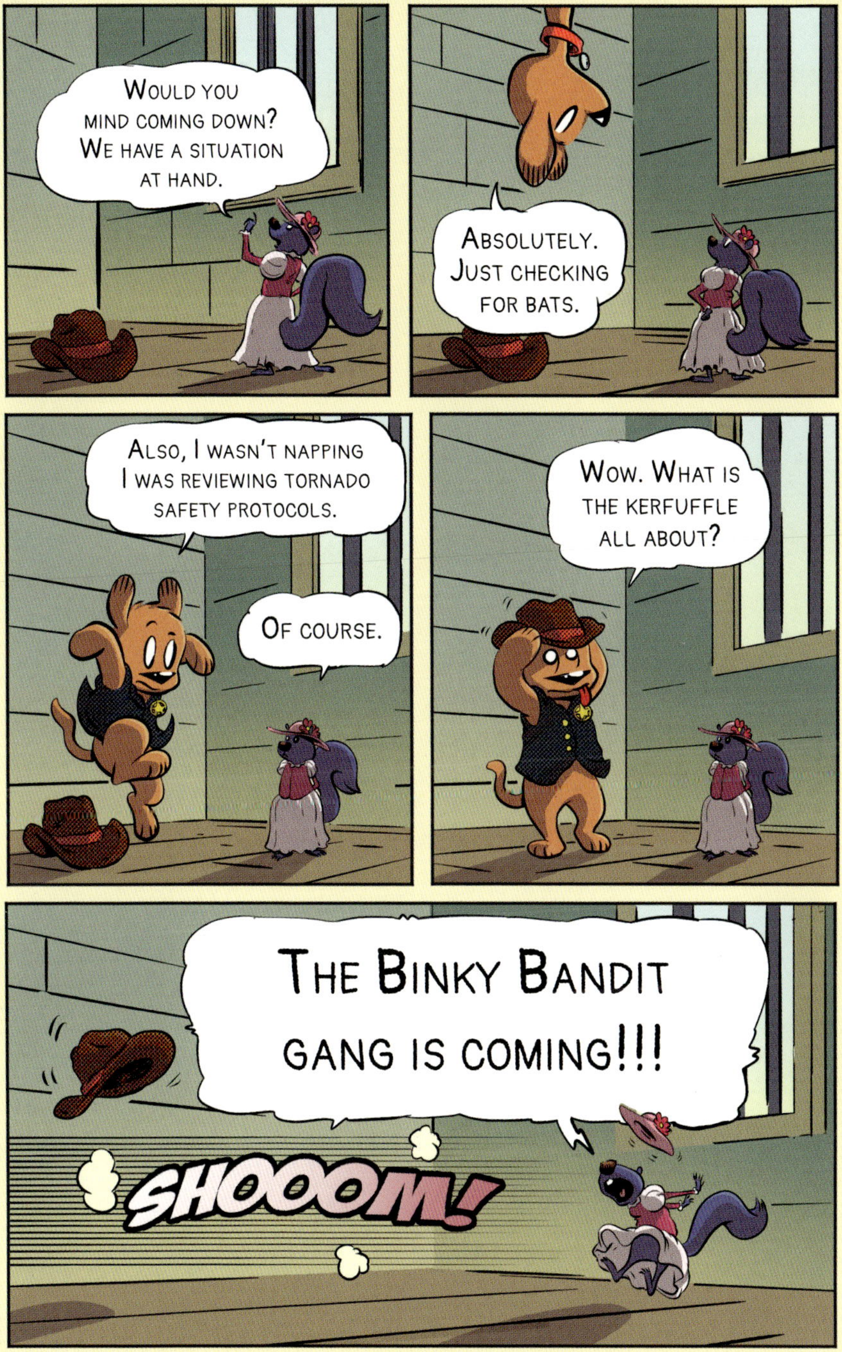
WOULD YOU MIND COMING DOWN? WE HAVE A SITUATION AT HAND.
ABSOLUTELY. JUST CHECKING FOR BATS.
ALSO, I WASN'T NAPPING I WAS REVIEWING TORNADO SAFETY PROTOCOLS.
OF COURSE.
WOW. WHAT IS THE KERFUFFLE ALL ABOUT?
THE BINKY BANDIT GANG IS COMING!!!
SHOOOM!

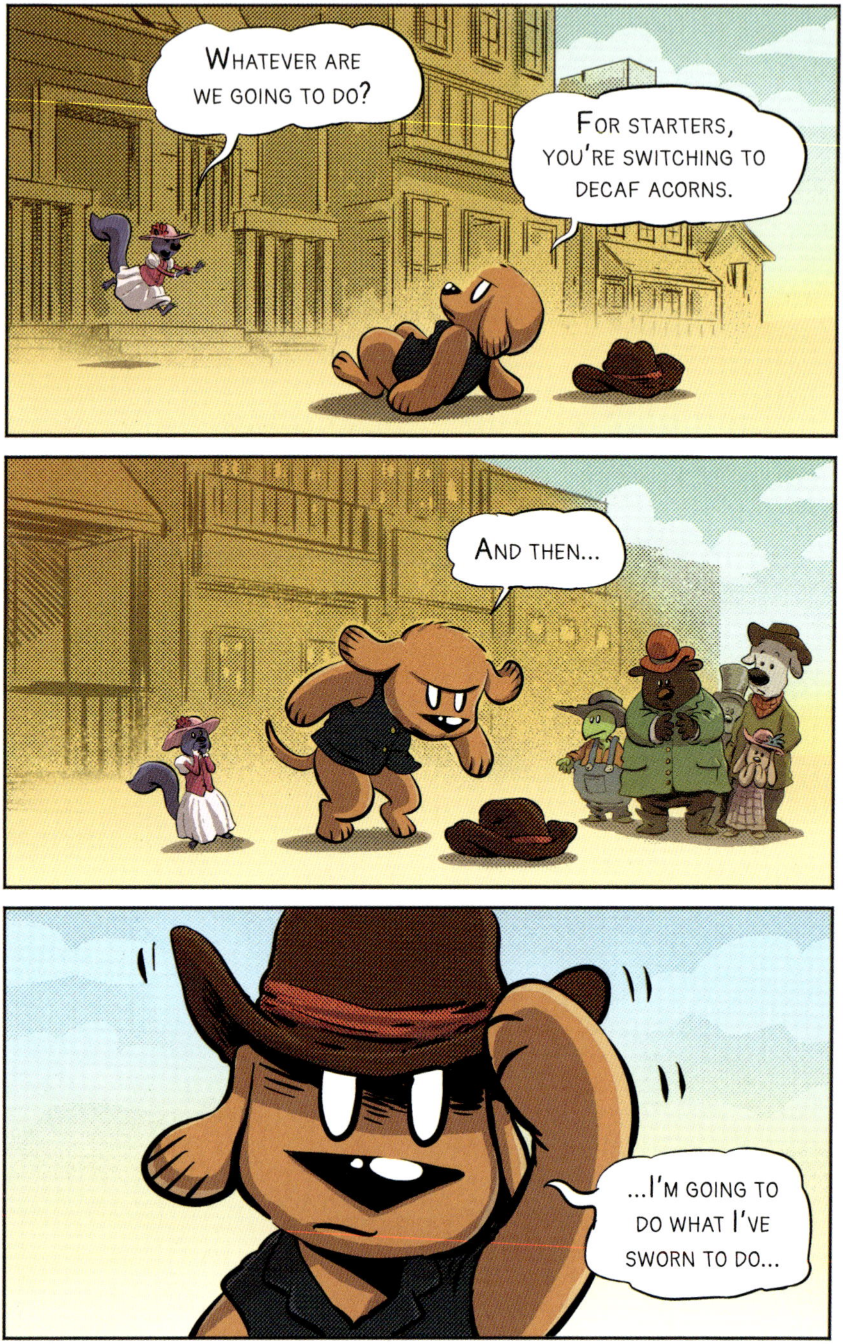
WHATEVER ARE WE GOING TO DO?
FOR STARTERS, YOU'RE SWITCHING TO DECAF ACORNS.
AND THEN...
...I'M GOING TO DO WHAT I'VE SWORN TO DO...

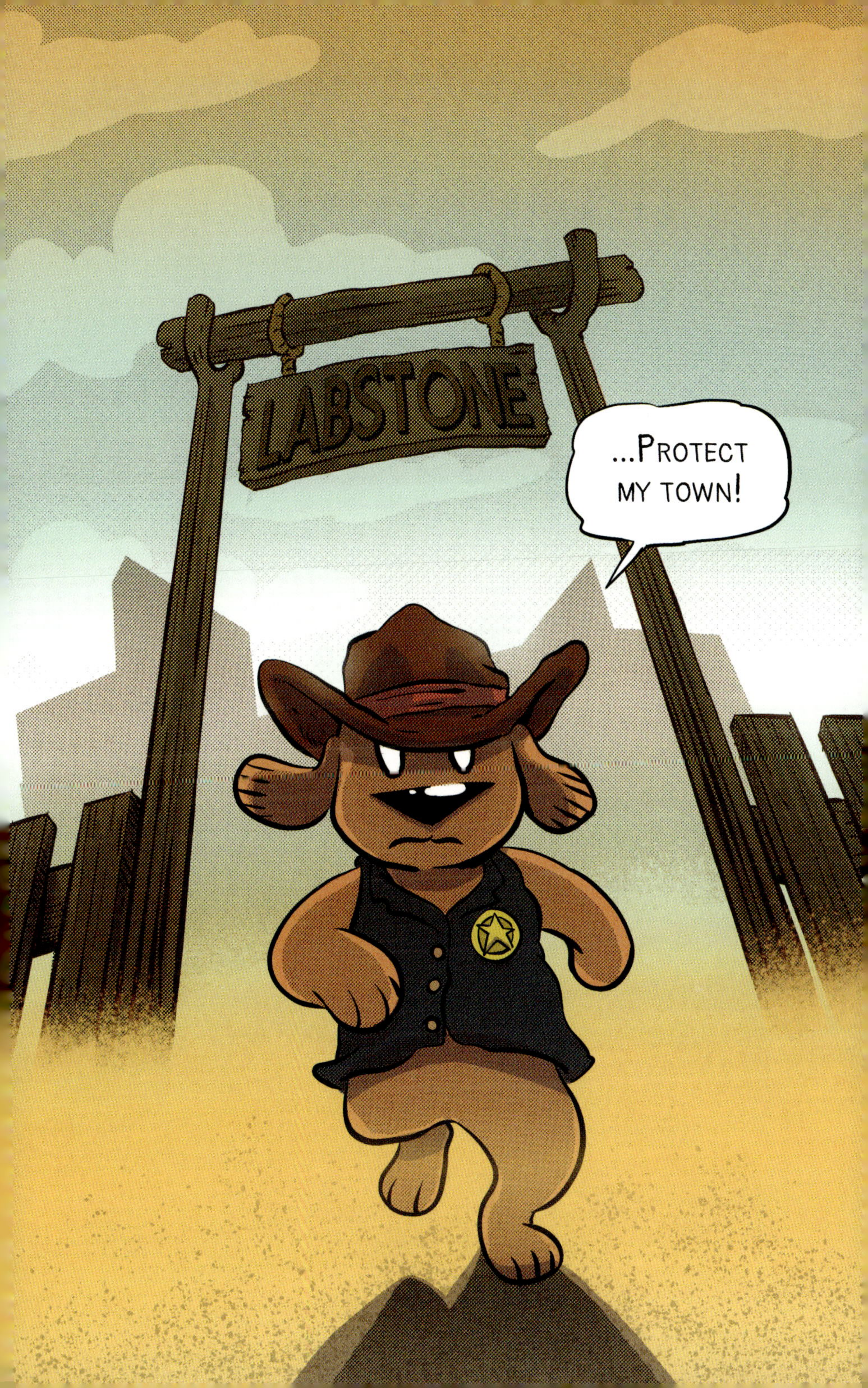
LABSTONE
...PROTECT MY TOWN!

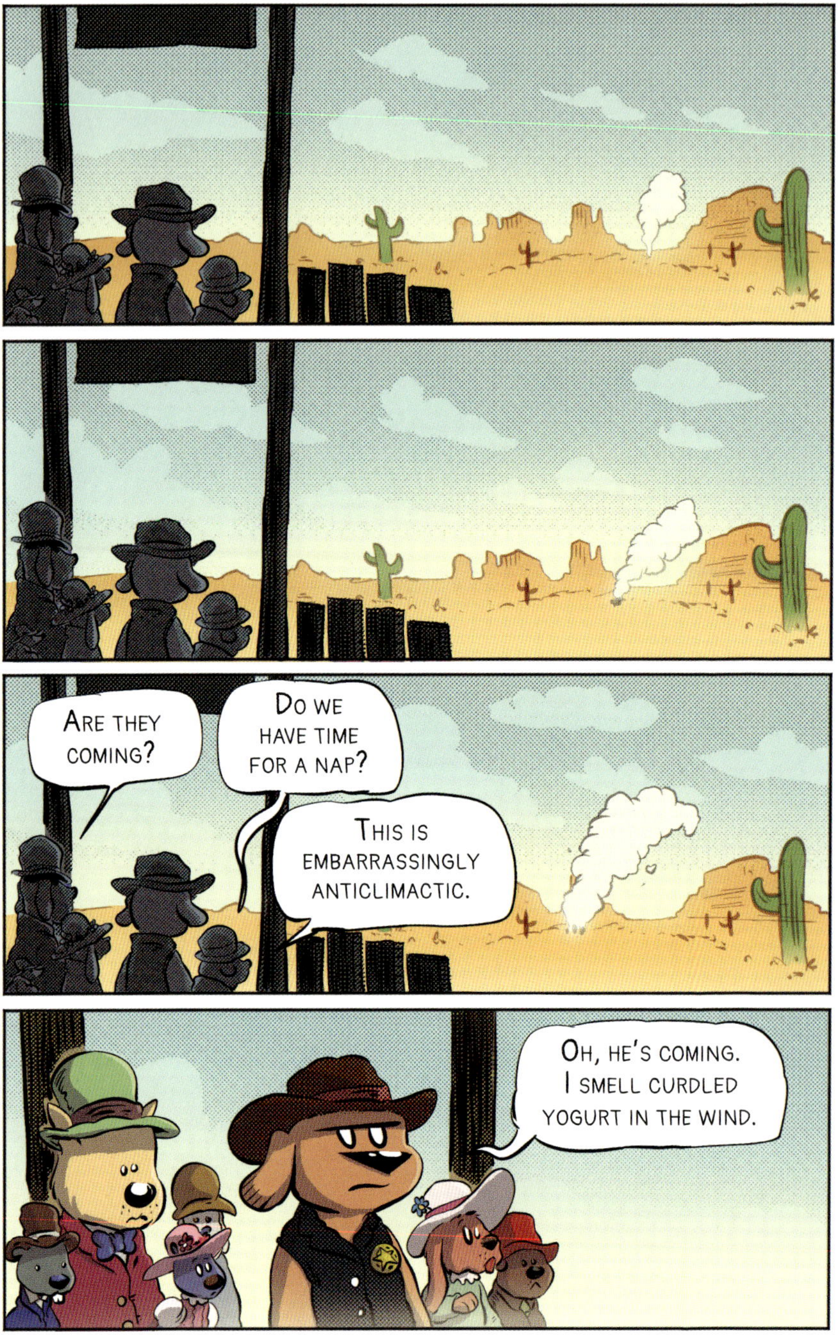
ARE THEY COMING?
DO WE HAVE TIME FOR A NAP?
THIS IS EMBARRASSINGLY ANTICLIMACTIC.
OH, HE'S COMING. I SMELL CURDLED YOGURT IN THE WIND.

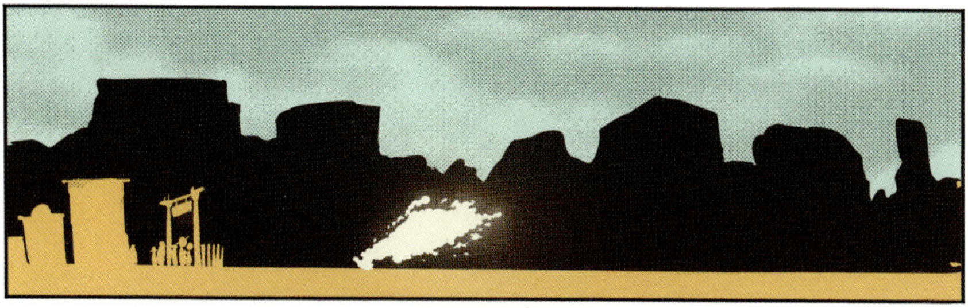

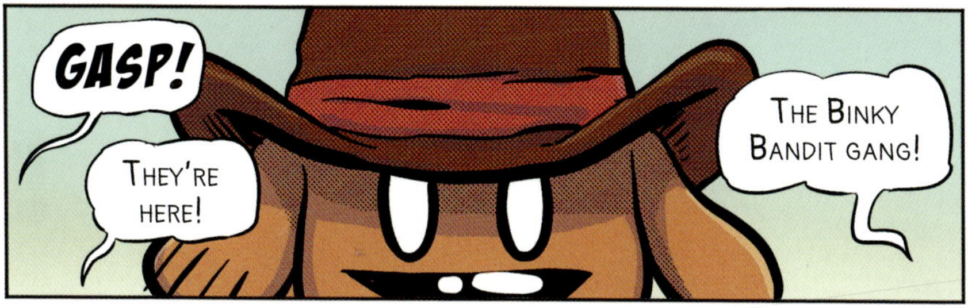
GASP!
THEY'RE HERE!
THE BINKY BANDIT GANG!

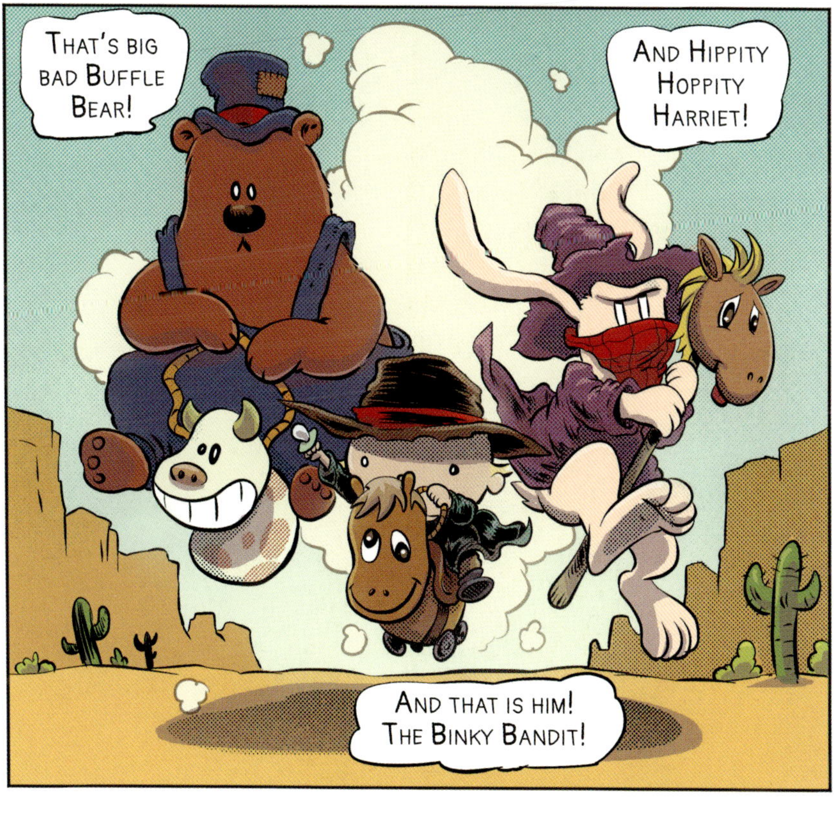
THAT'S BIG BAD BUFFLE BEAR!
AND HIPPITY HOPPITY HARRIET!
AND THAT IS HIM! THE BINKY BANDIT!

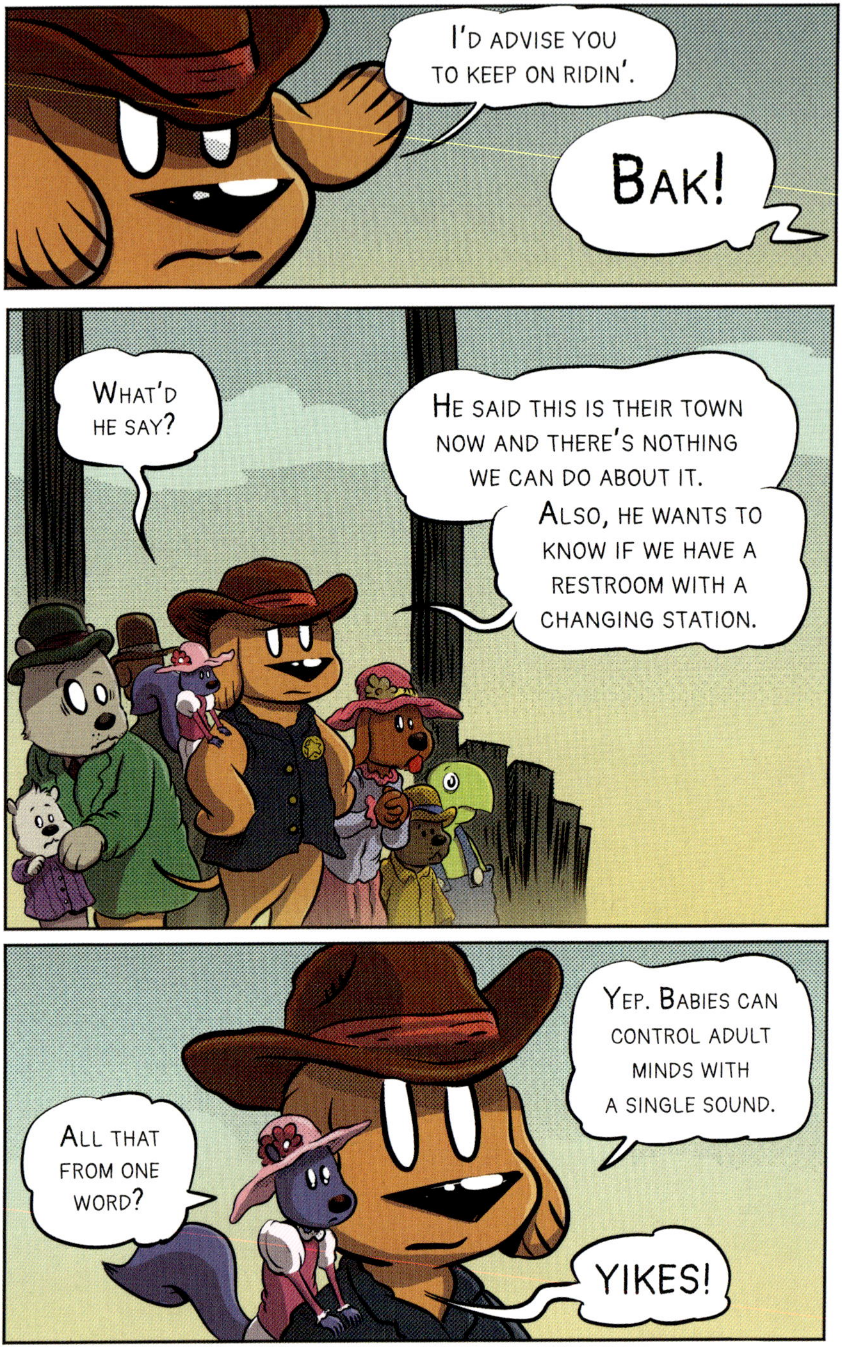
I'D ADVISE YOU TO KEEP ON RIDIN'.
BAK!
WHAT'D HE SAY?
HE SAID THIS IS THEIR TOWN NOW AND THERE'S NOTHING WE CAN DO ABOUT IT.
ALSO, HE WANTS TO KNOW IF WE HAVE A RESTROOM WITH A CHANGING STATION.
YEP. BABIES CAN CONTROL ADULT MINDS WITH A SINGLE SOUND.
ALL THAT FROM ONE WORD?
YIKES!

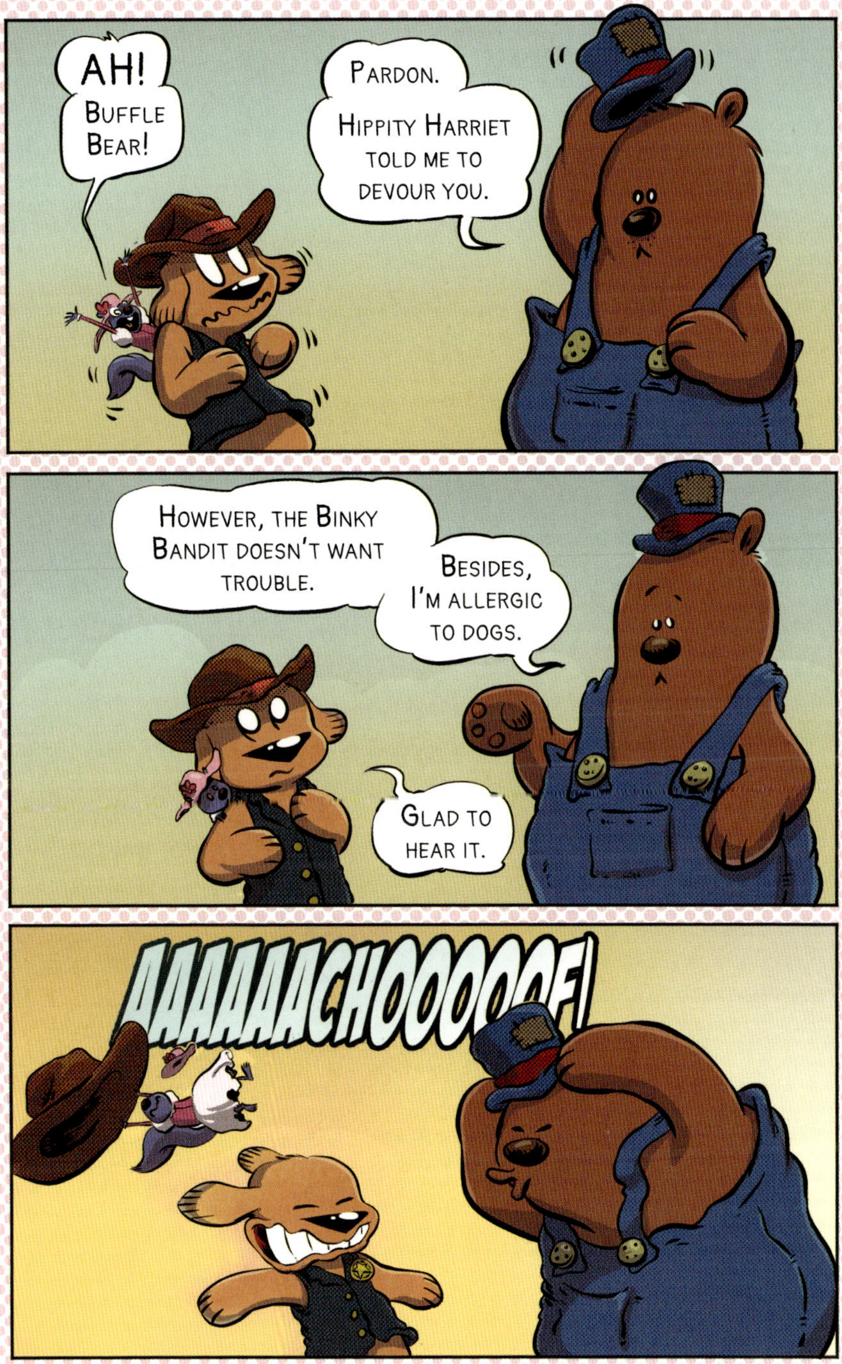
AH! BUFFLE BEAR!
PARDON.
HIPPITY HARRIET TOLD ME TO DEVOUR YOU.
HOWEVER, THE BINKY BANDIT DOESN'T WANT TROUBLE.
BESIDES, I'M ALLERGIC TO DOGS.
GLAD TO HEAR IT.
AAAAACHOOOOOF!

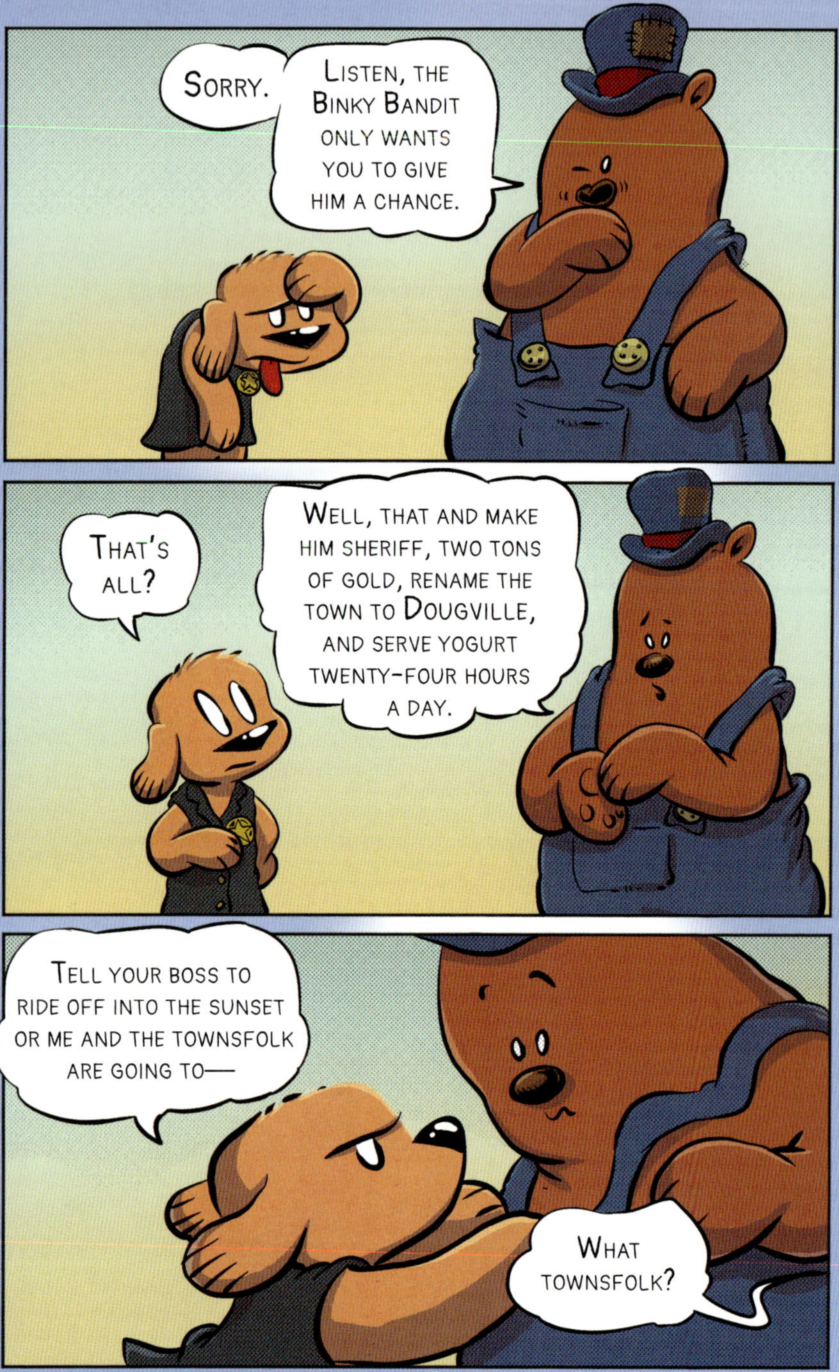
SORRY.
LISTEN, THE BINKY BANDIT ONLY WANTS YOU TO GIVE HIM A CHANCE.
THAT'S ALL?
WELL, THAT AND MAKE HIM SHERIFF, TWO TONS OF GOLD, RENAME THE TOWN TO DOUGVILLE, AND SERVE YOGURT TWENTY-FOUR HOURS A DAY.
TELL YOUR BOSS TO RIDE OFF INTO THE SUNSET OR ME AND THE TOWNSFOLK ARE GOING TO—
WHAT TOWNSFOLK?

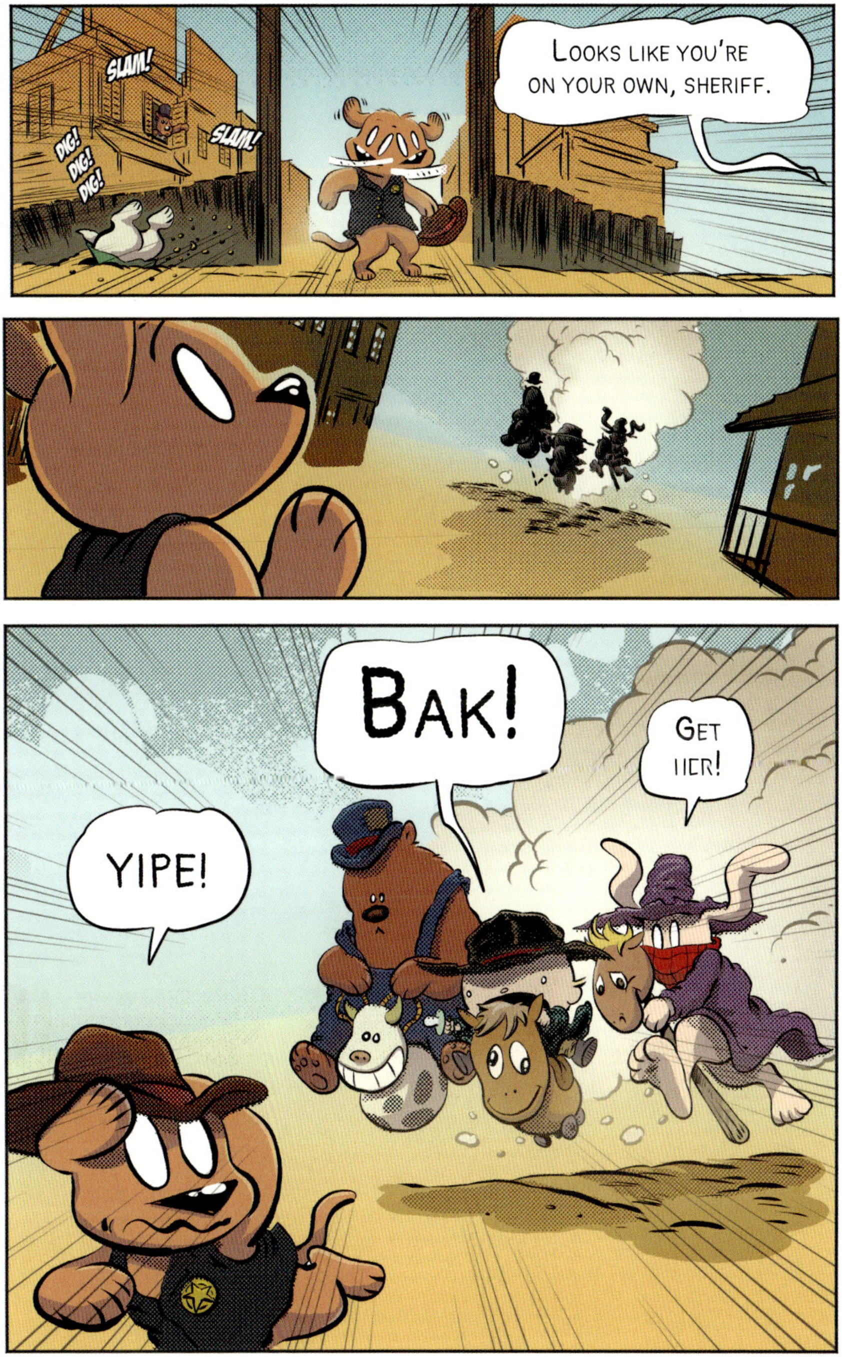
SLAM!
DIG! DIG! DIG!
SLAM!
LOOKS LIKE YOU'RE ON YOUR OWN, SHERIFF.
BAK!
GET HER!
YIPE!

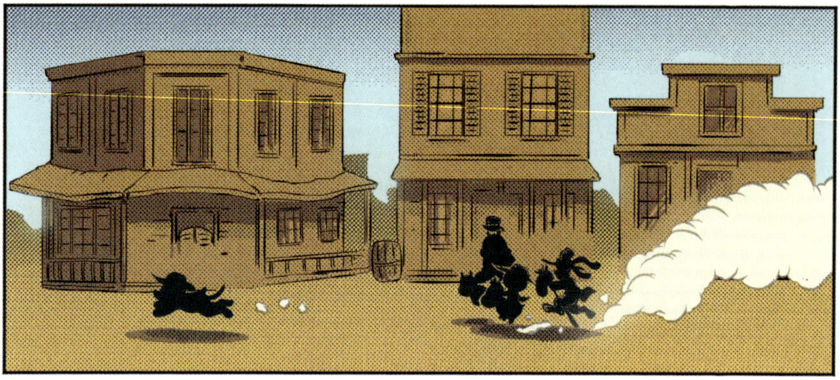

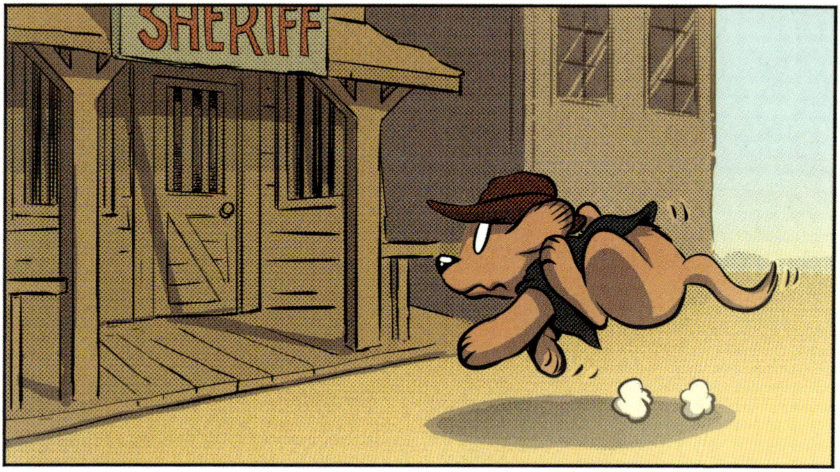
SHERIFF

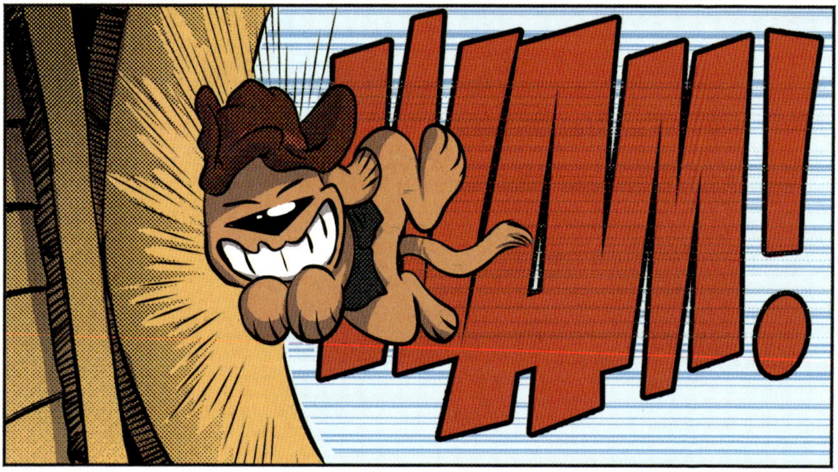
WHAM!

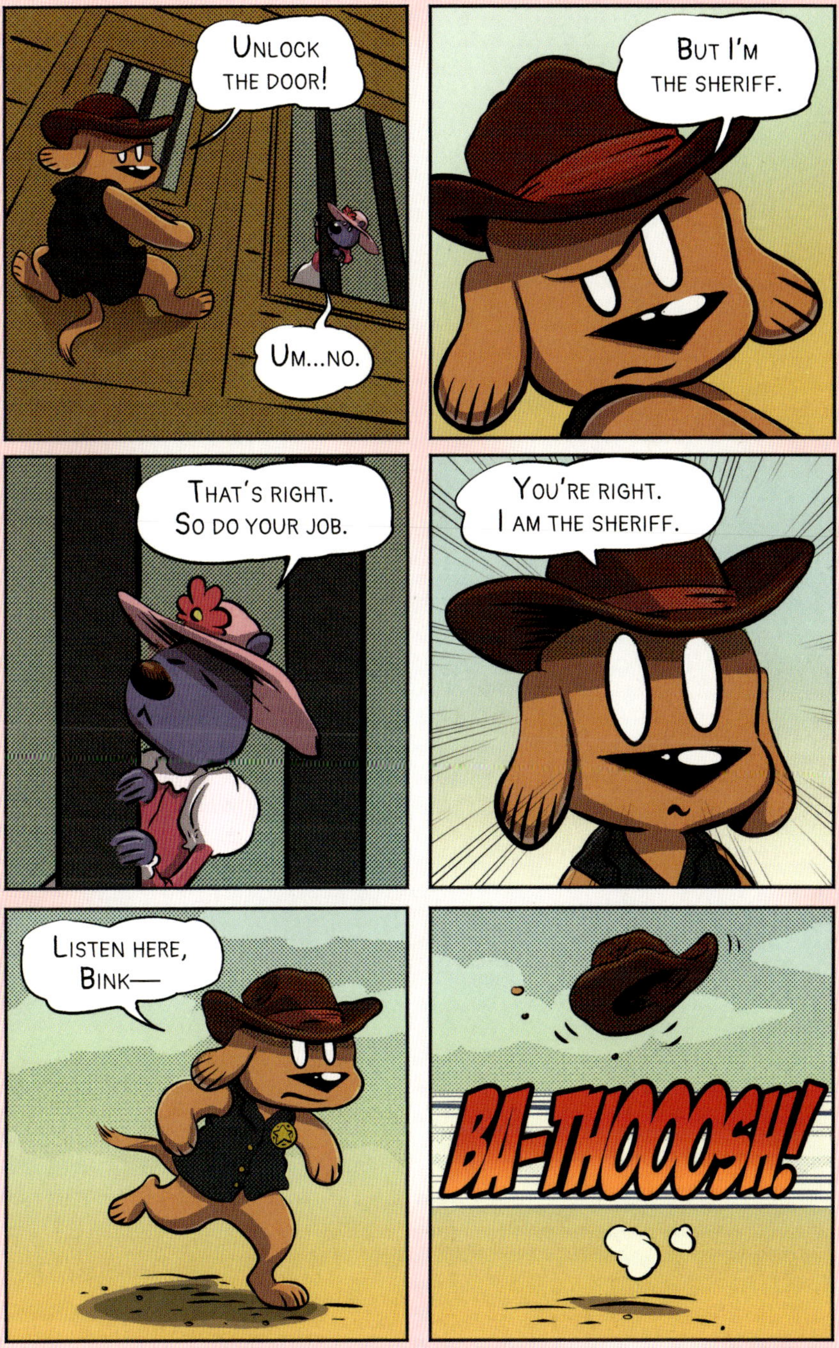
UNLOCK THE DOOR!
UM...NO.
BUT I'M THE SHERIFF.
THAT'S RIGHT. SO DO YOUR JOB.
YOU'RE RIGHT. I AM THE SHERIFF.
LISTEN HERE, BINK—
BA-THOOOSH!

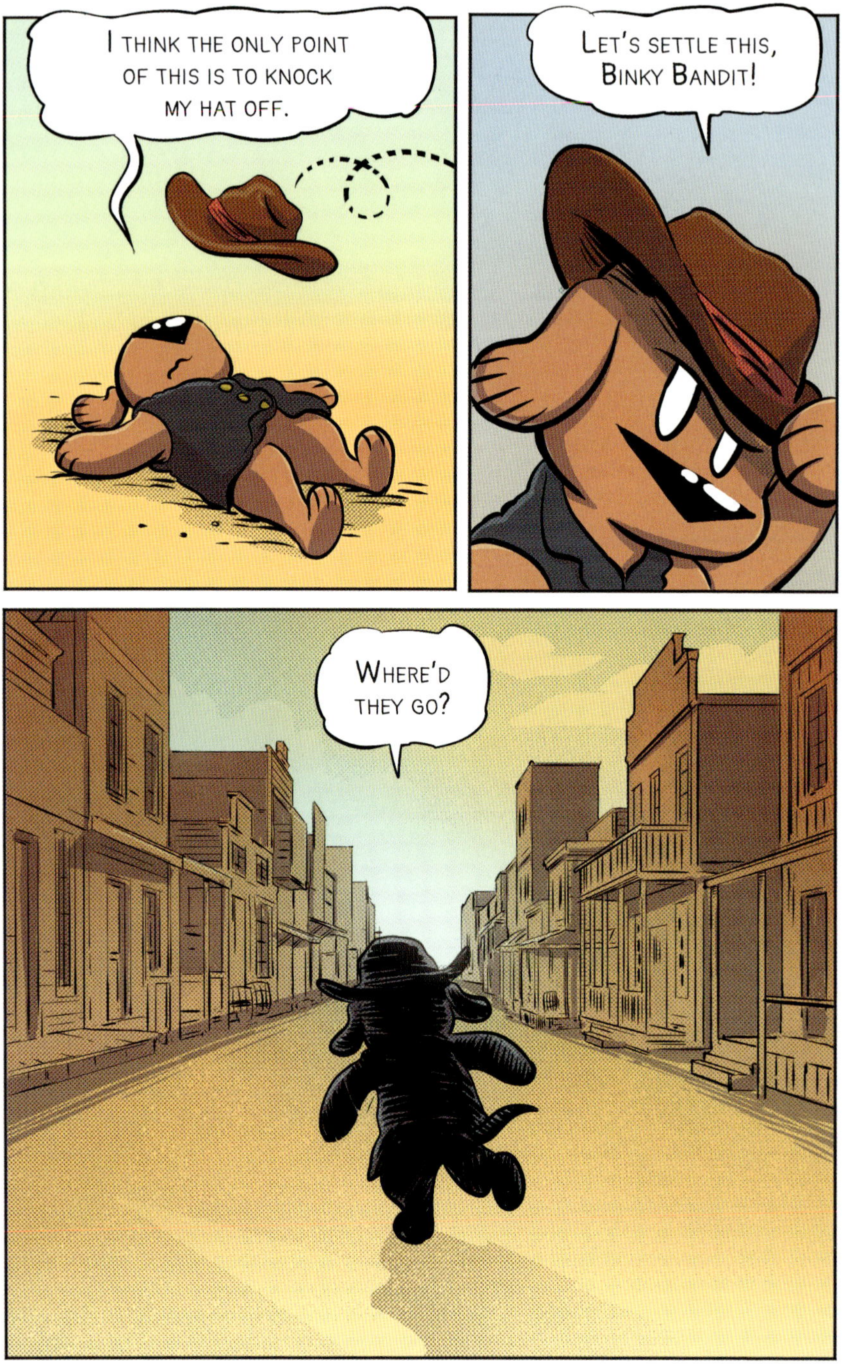
I THINK THE ONLY POINT OF THIS IS TO KNOCK MY HAT OFF.
LET'S SETTLE THIS, BINKY BANDIT!
WHERE'D THEY GO?

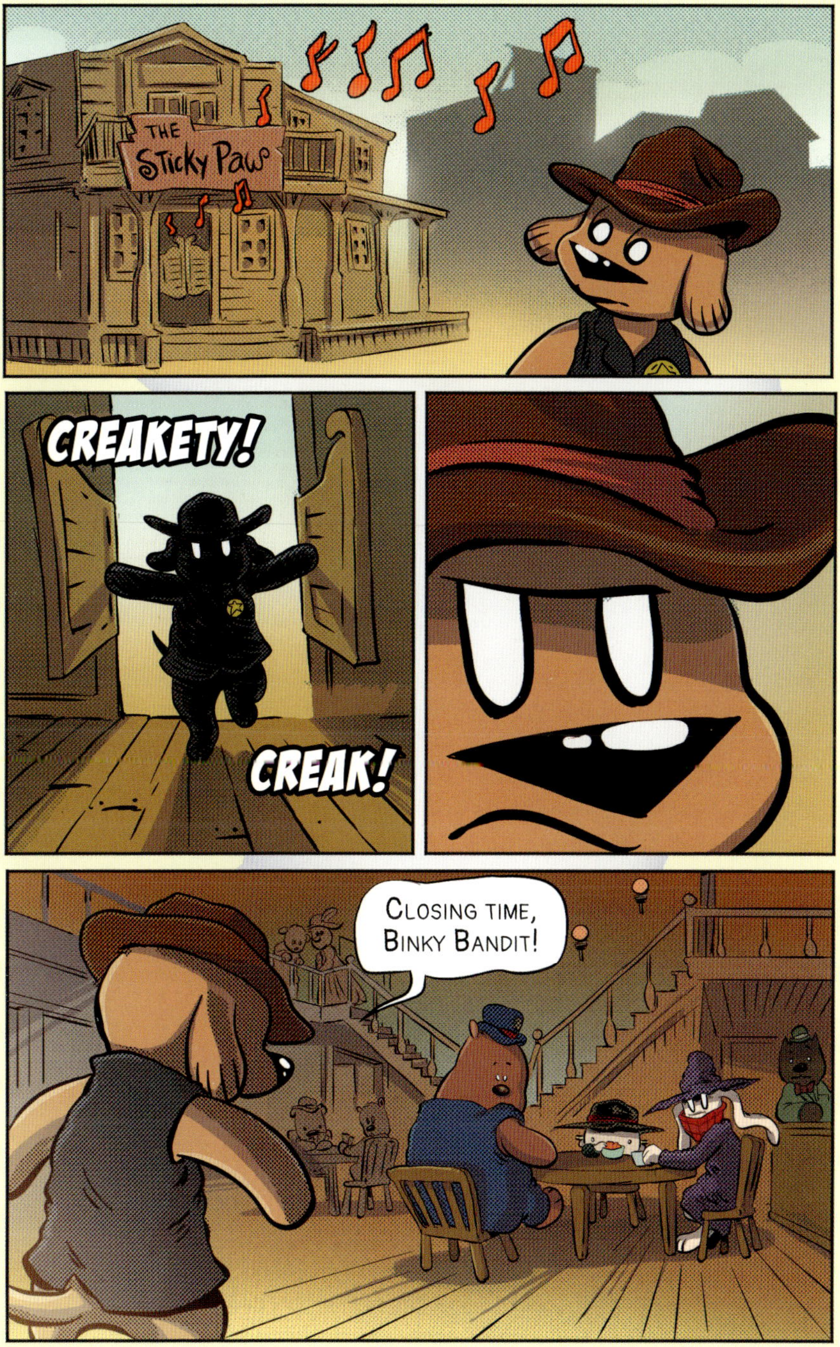
THE Sticky Paws
CREAKETY!
CREAK!
CLOSING TIME, BINKY BANDIT!

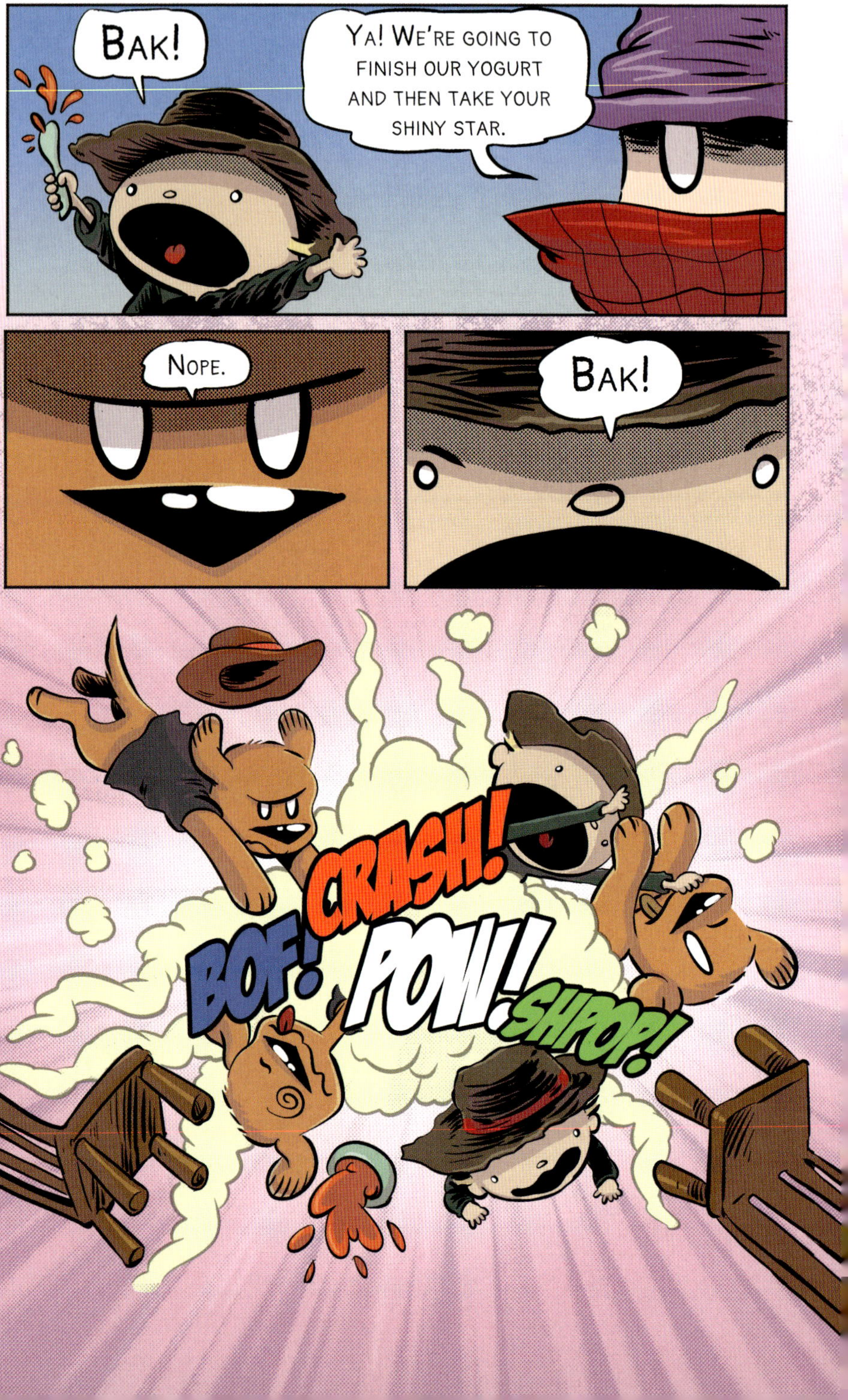
BAK!
YA! WE'RE GOING TO FINISH OUR YOGURT AND THEN TAKE YOUR SHINY STAR.
NOPE.
BAK!
CRASH!
BOF!
POW!
SHPOP!

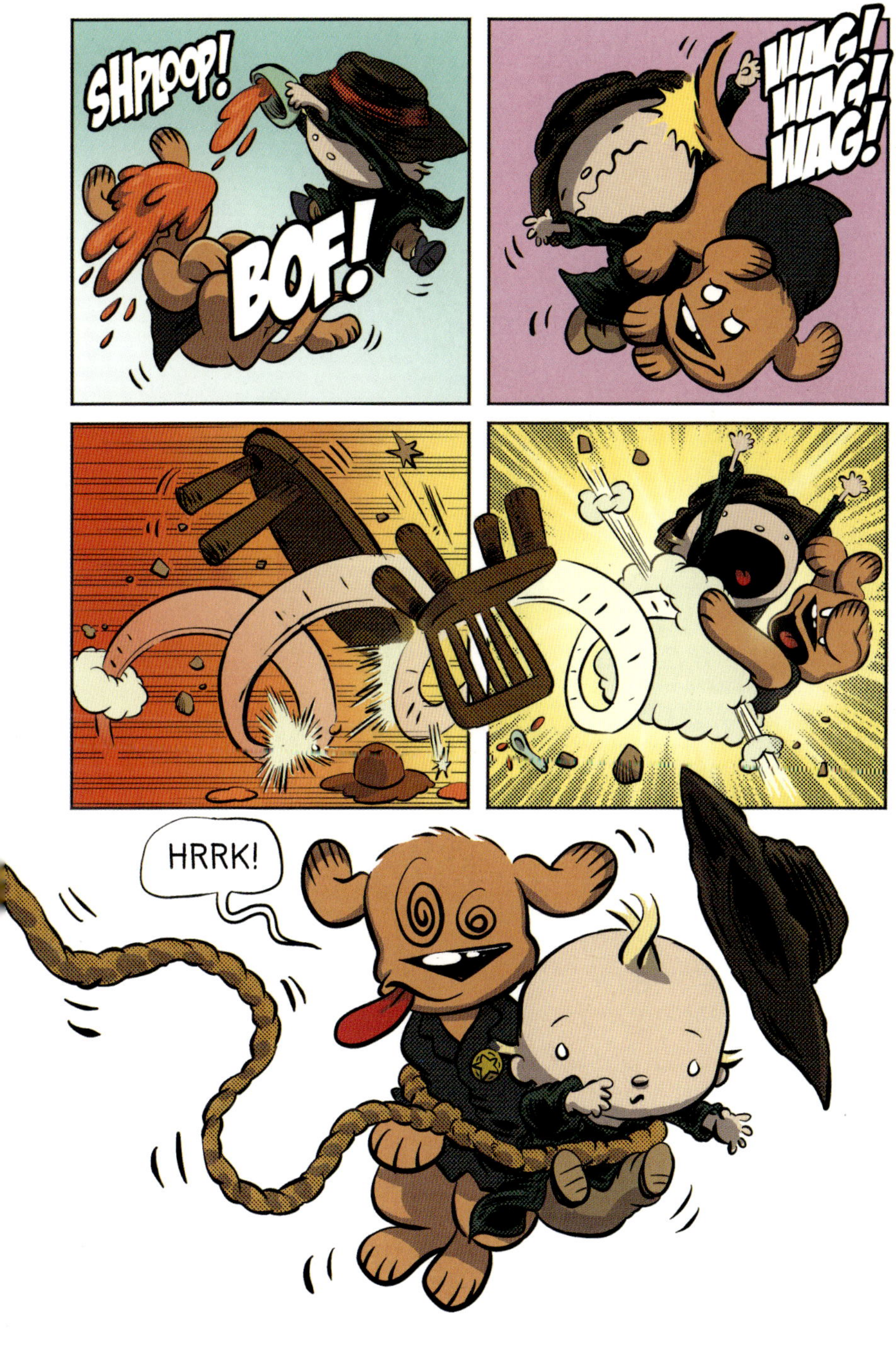
SHPLOOP!
BOF!
WAG! WAG! WAG!
HRRK!

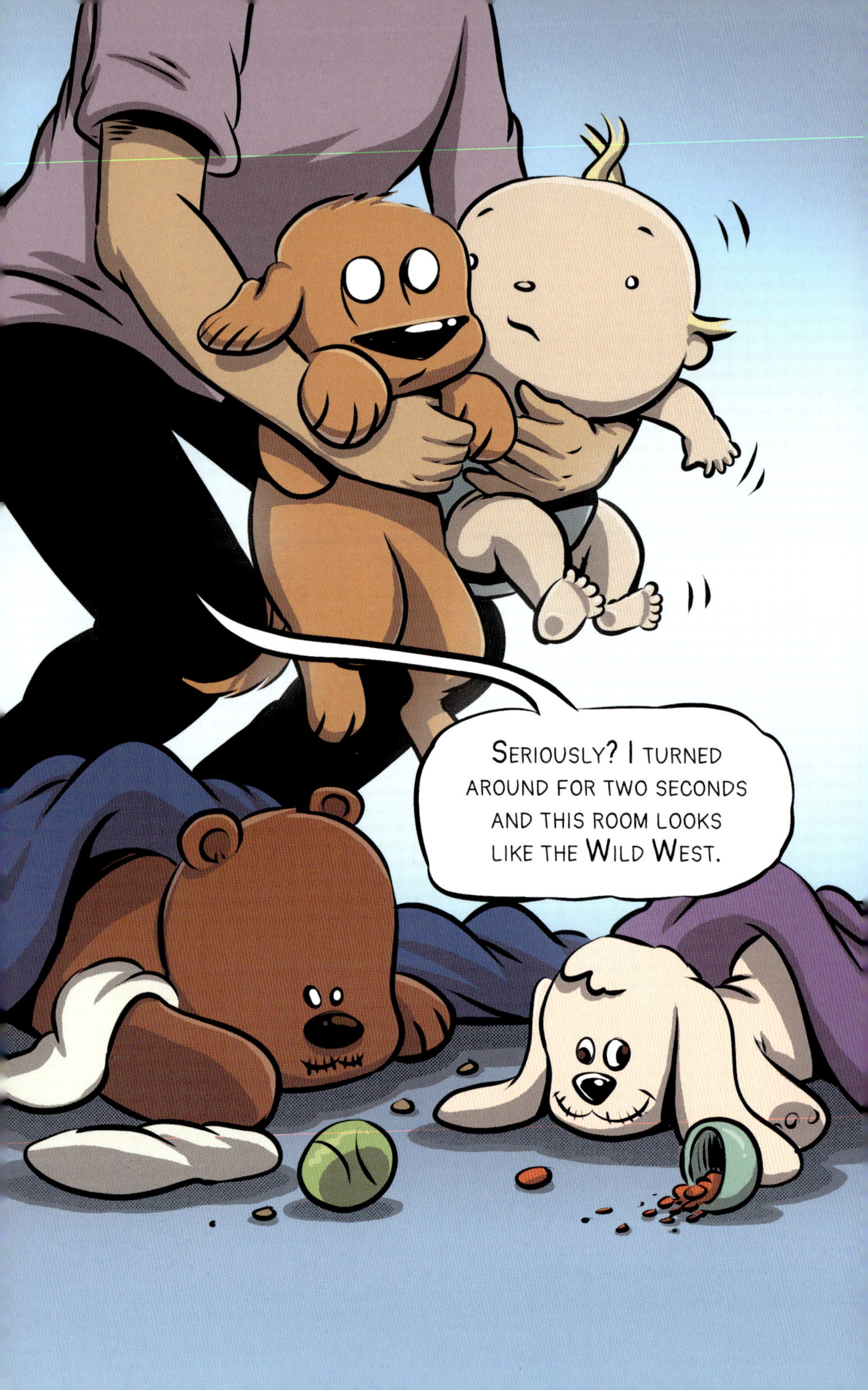
SERIOUSLY? I TURNED AROUND FOR TWO SECONDS AND THIS ROOM LOOKS LIKE THE WILD WEST.

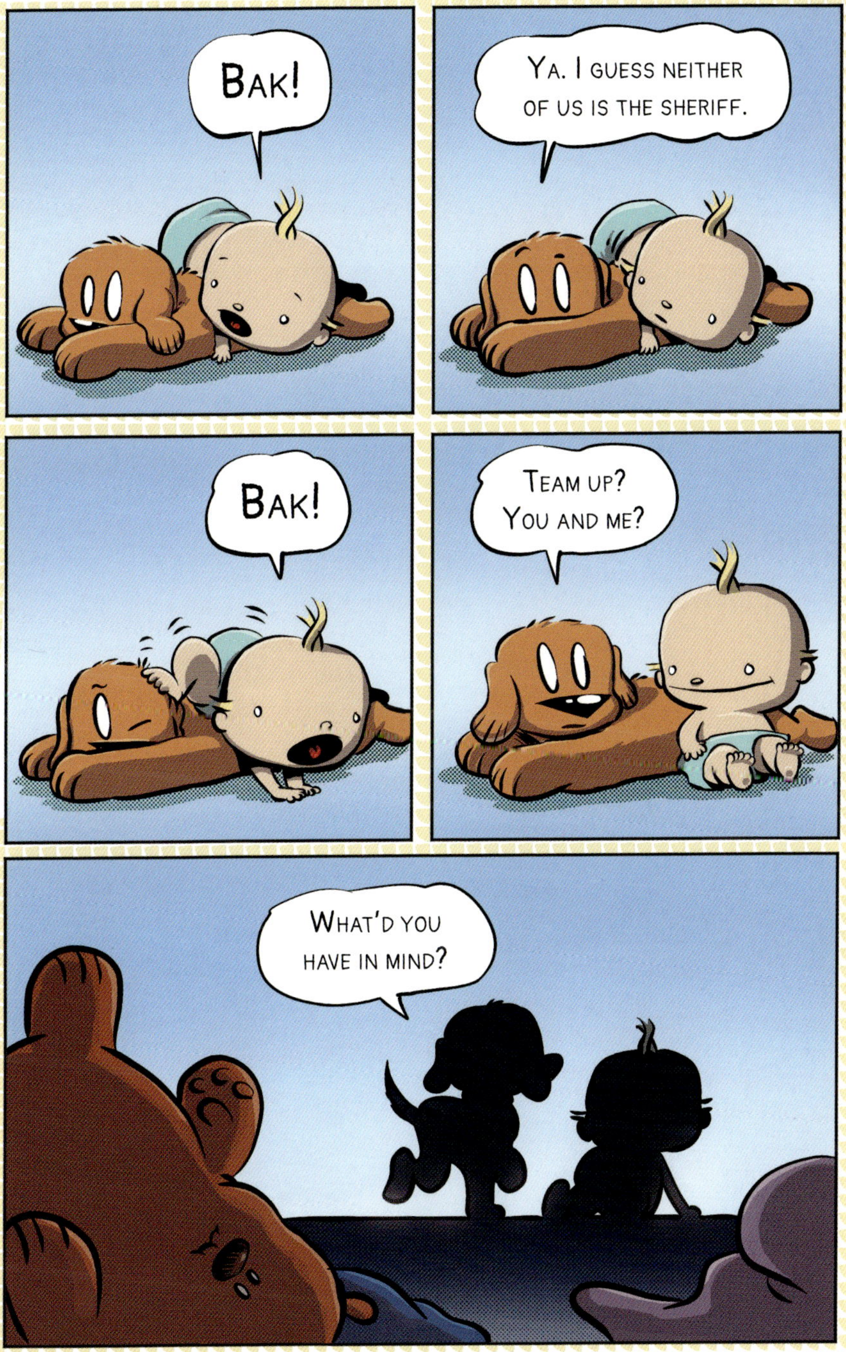
BAK!
YA. I GUESS NEITHER OF US IS THE SHERIFF.
BAK!
TEAM UP? YOU AND ME?
WHAT'D YOU HAVE IN MIND?

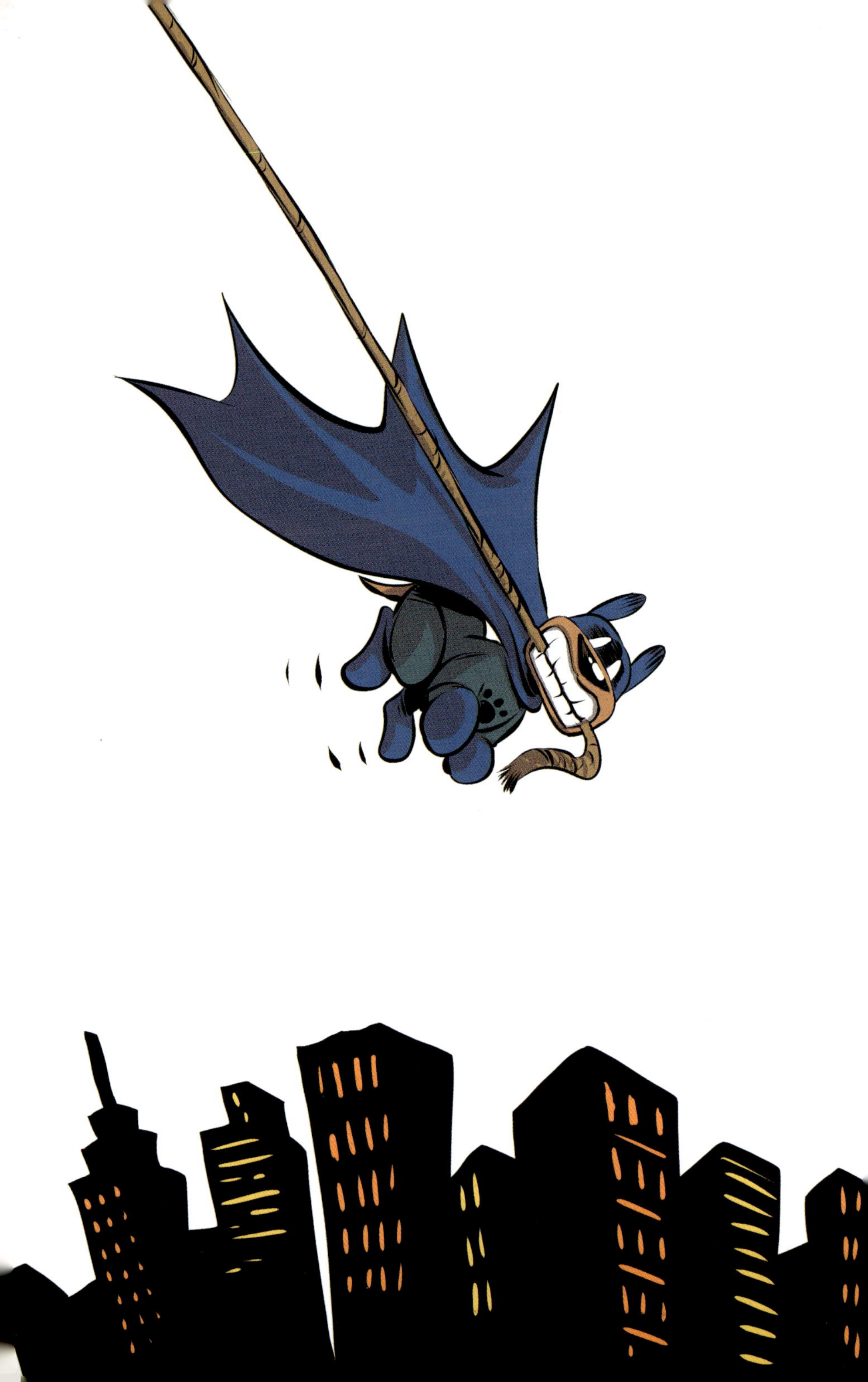

CHAPTER 8

The Canine Crusader

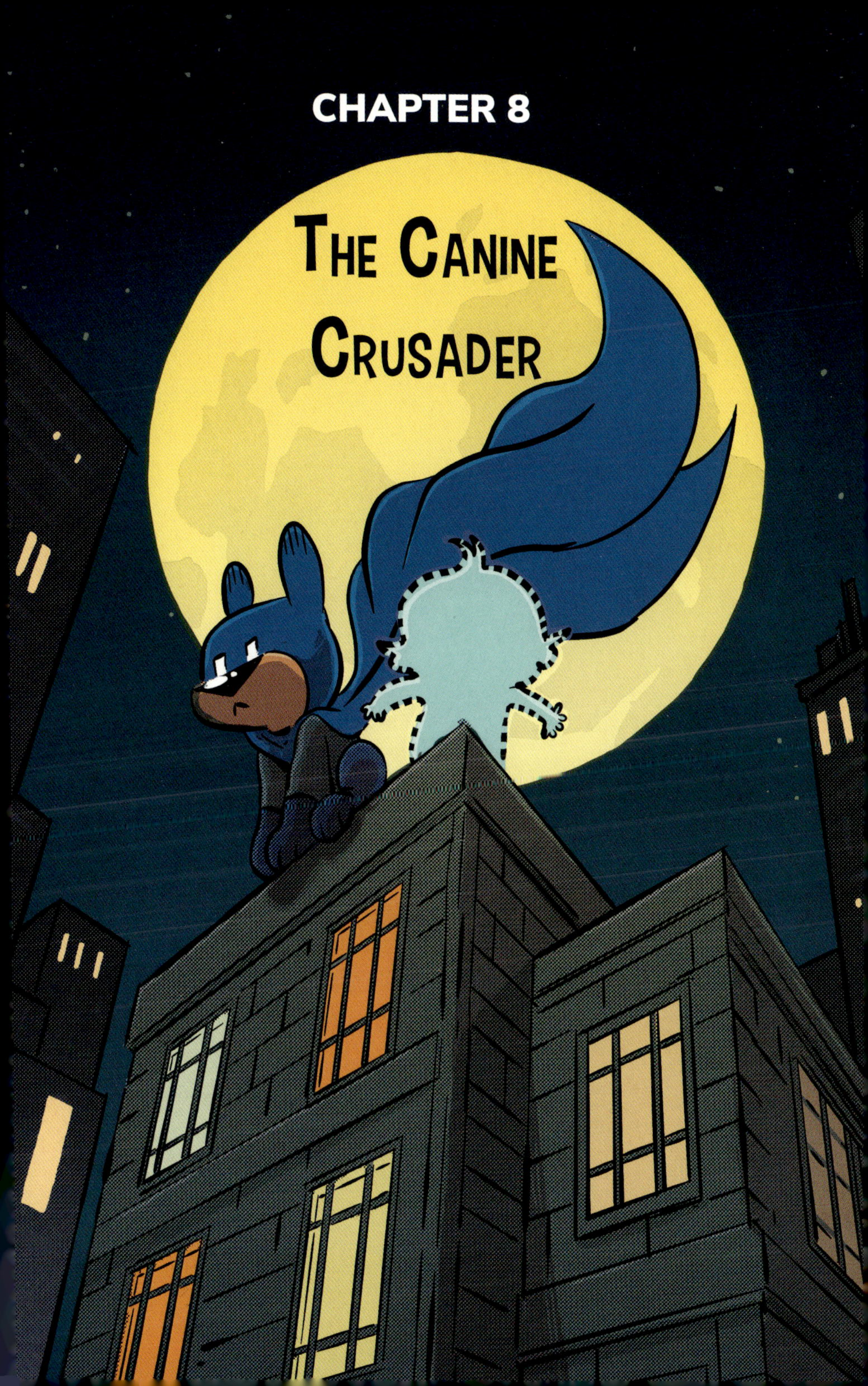

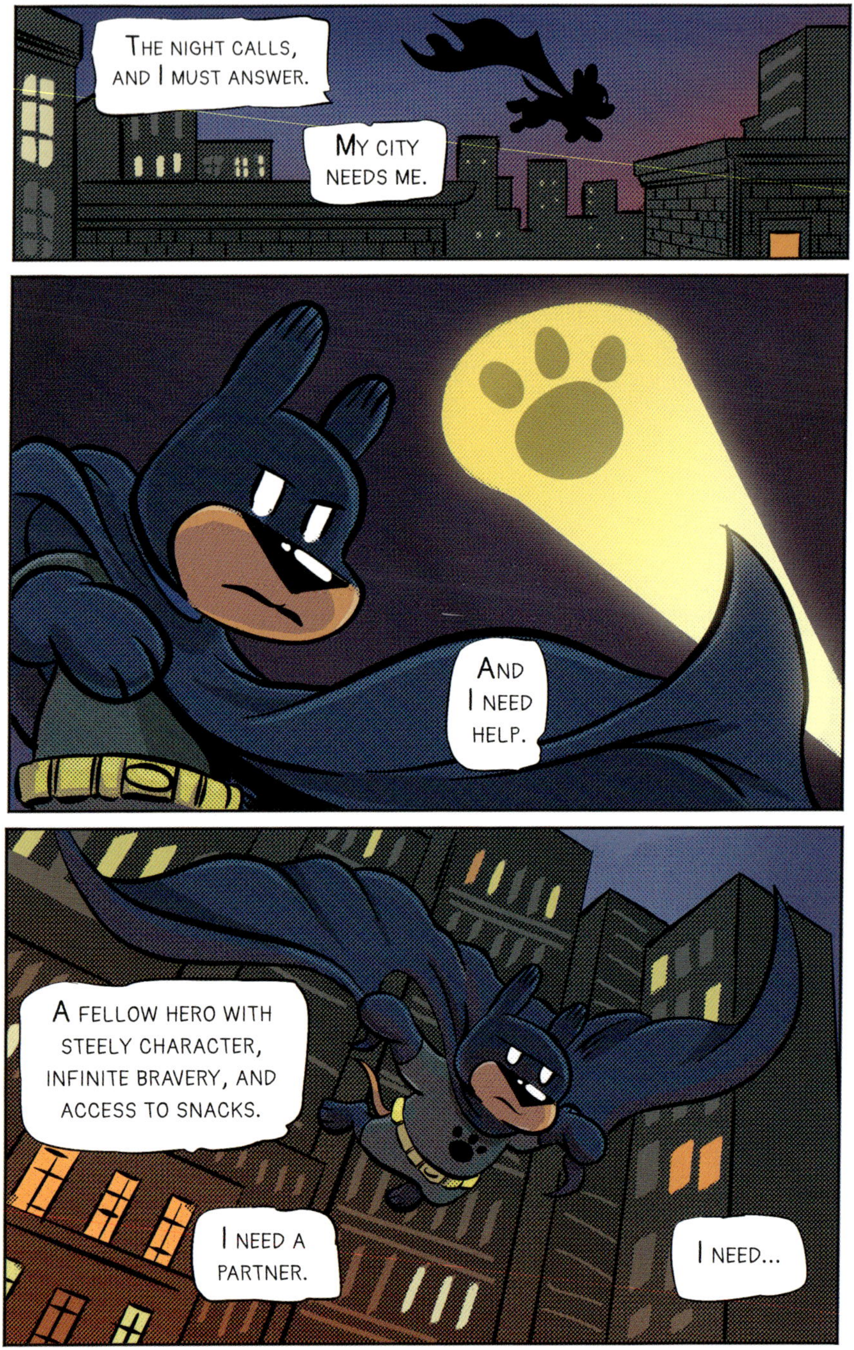
THE NIGHT CALLS, AND I MUST ANSWER.
MY CITY NEEDS ME.
AND I NEED HELP.
A FELLOW HERO WITH STEELY CHARACTER, INFINITE BRAVERY, AND ACCESS TO SNACKS.
I NEED A PARTNER.
I NEED...

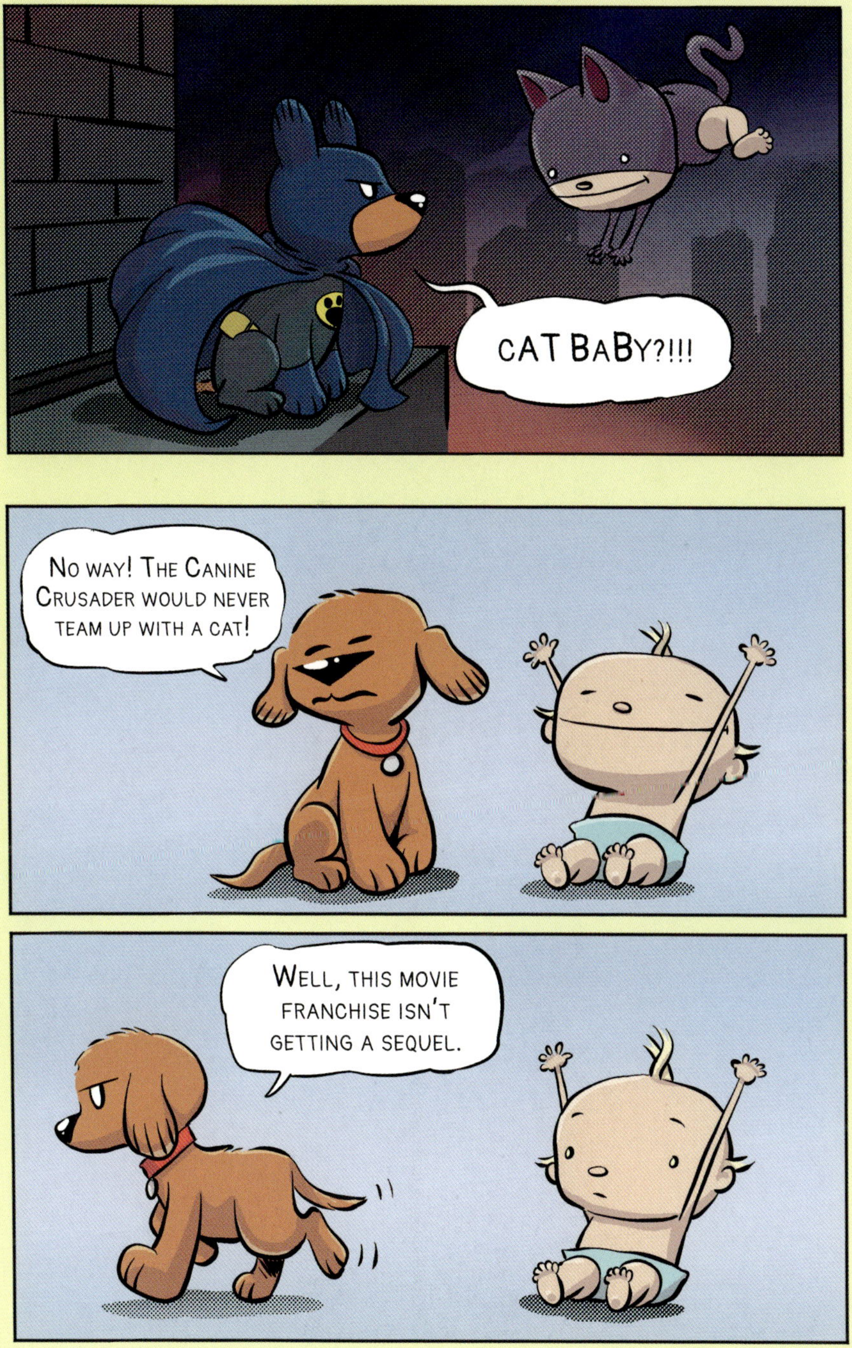
CAT BABY?!!!
NO WAY! THE CANINE CRUSADER WOULD NEVER TEAM UP WITH A CAT!
WELL, THIS MOVIE FRANCHISE ISN'T GETTING A SEQUEL.

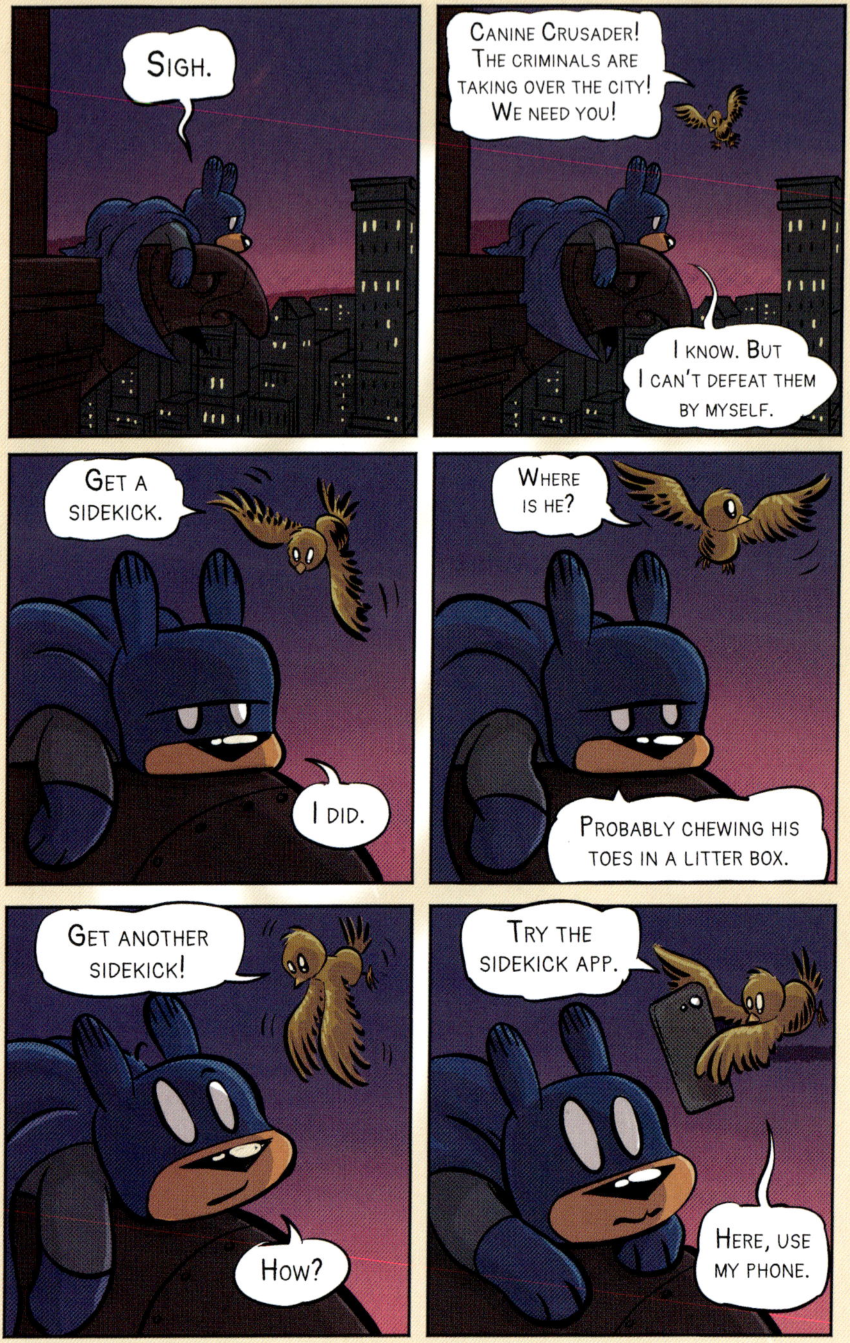
SIGH.
CANINE CRUSADER! THE CRIMINALS ARE TAKING OVER THE CITY! WE NEED YOU!
I KNOW. BUT I CAN'T DEFEAT THEM BY MYSELF.
GET A SIDEKICK.
I DID.
WHERE IS HE?
PROBABLY CHEWING HIS TOES IN A LITTER BOX.
GET ANOTHER SIDEKICK!
HOW?
TRY THE SIDEKICK APP.
HERE, USE MY PHONE.

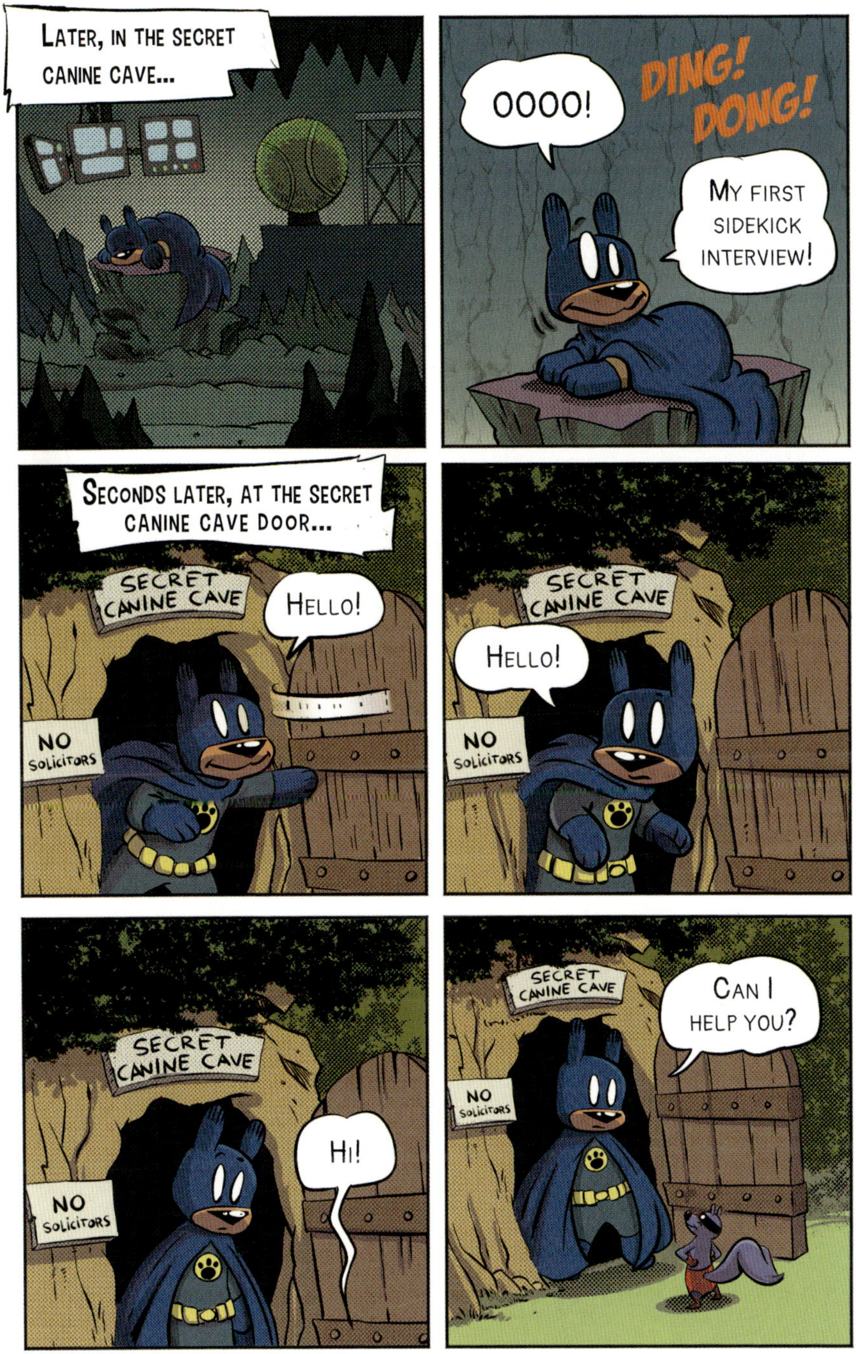
LATER, IN THE SECRET CANINE CAVE...
OOOO!
DING! DONG!
MY FIRST SIDEKICK INTERVIEW!
SECONDS LATER, AT THE SECRET CANINE CAVE DOOR...
SECRET CANINE CAVE
NO SOLICITORS
HELLO!
SECRET CANINE CAVE
NO SOLICITORS
HELLO!
SECRET CANINE CAVE
NO SOLICITORS
HI!
SECRET CANINE CAVE
NO SOLICITORS
CAN I HELP YOU?

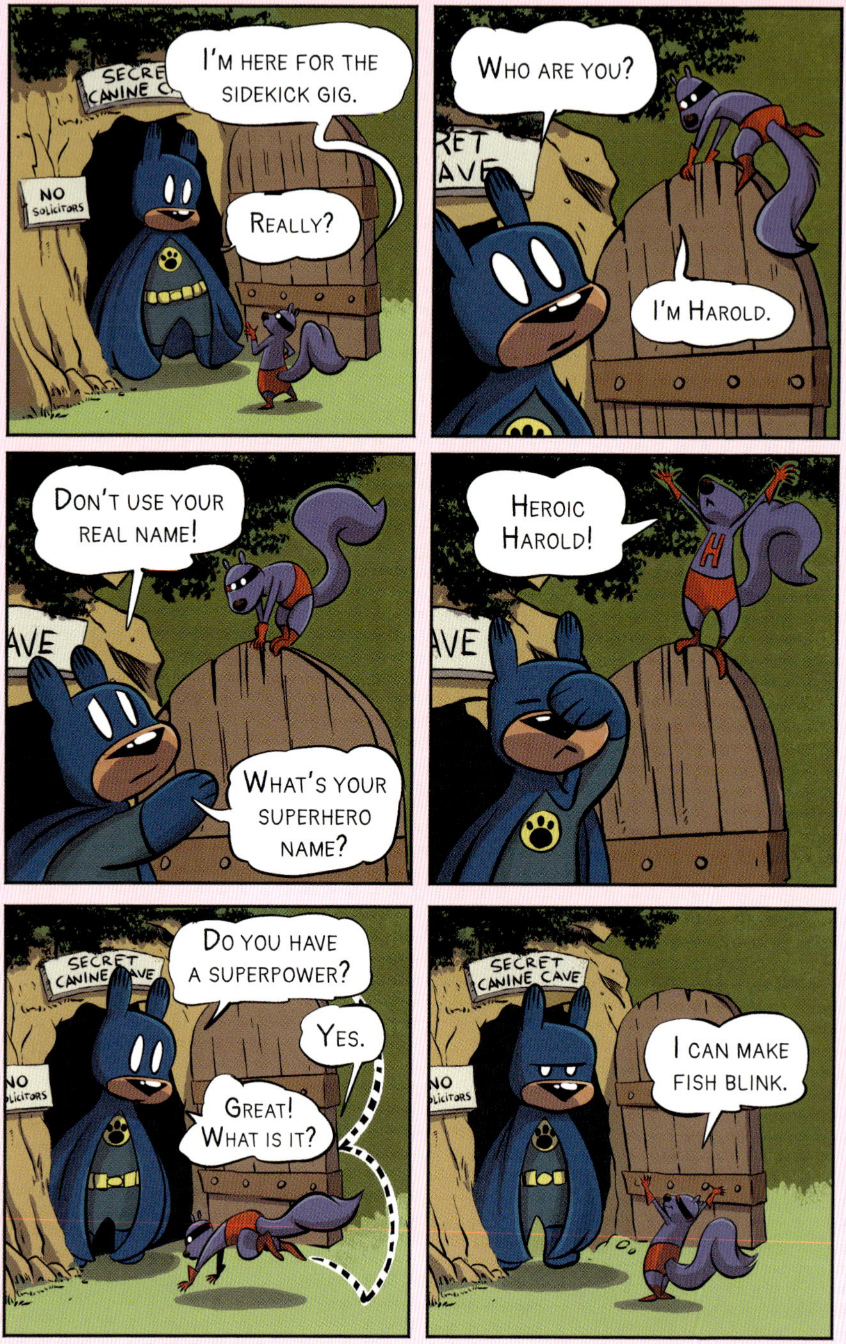
SECRET CANINE C
NO SOLICITORS
I'M HERE FOR THE SIDEKICK GIG.
REALLY?
WHO ARE YOU?
I'M HAROLD.
DON'T USE YOUR REAL NAME!
WHAT'S YOUR SUPERHERO NAME?
HEROIC HAROLD!
SECRET CANINE CAVE
DO YOU HAVE A SUPERPOWER?
YES.
GREAT! WHAT IS IT?
SECRET CANINE CAVE
I CAN MAKE FISH BLINK.

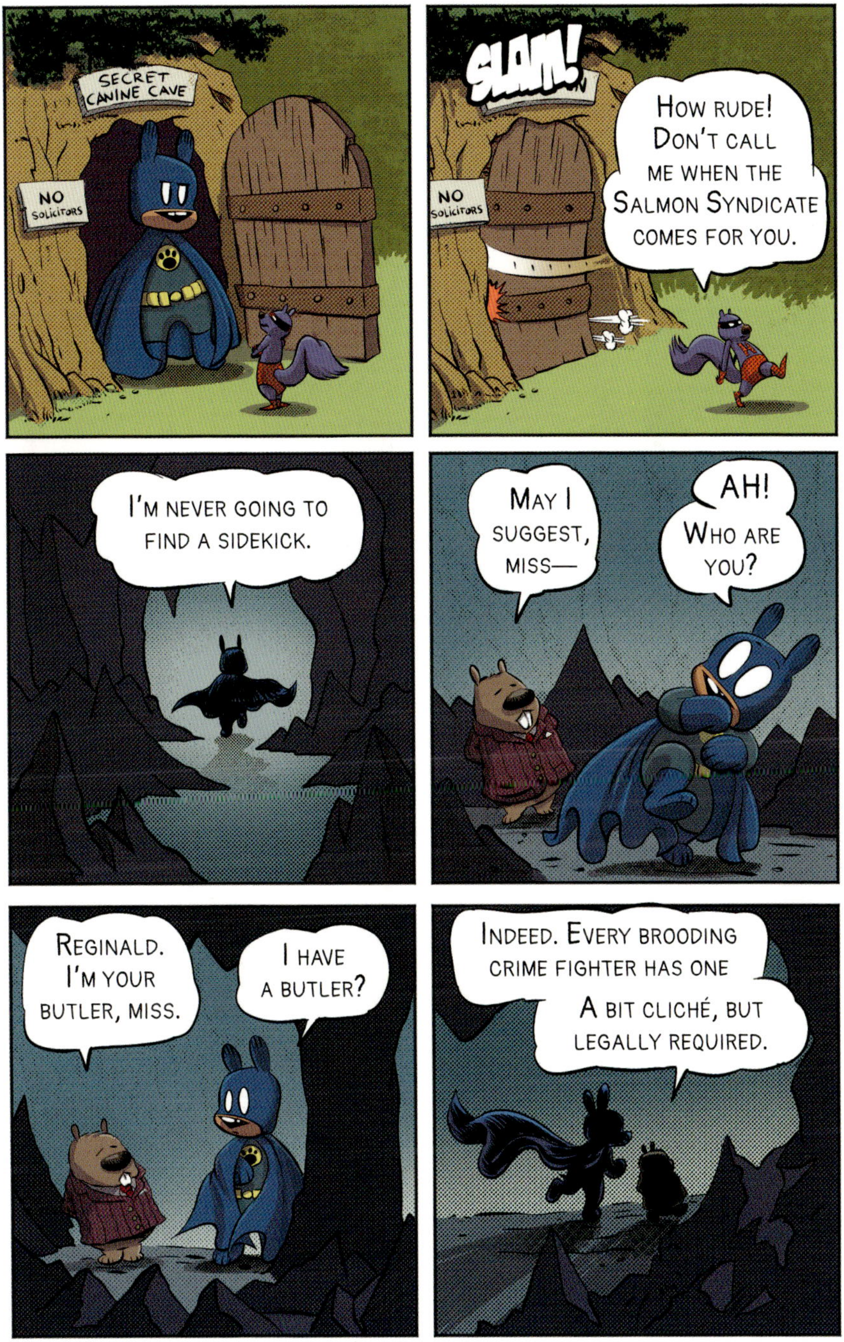
SECRET CANINE CAVE
NO SOLICITORS
SLAM!
NO SOLICITORS
HOW RUDE! DON'T CALL ME WHEN THE SALMON SYNDICATE COMES FOR YOU.
I'M NEVER GOING TO FIND A SIDEKICK.
MAY I SUGGEST, MISS—
AH! WHO ARE YOU?
REGINALD. I'M YOUR BUTLER, MISS.
I HAVE A BUTLER?
INDEED. EVERY BROODING CRIME FIGHTER HAS ONE
A BIT CLICHÉ, BUT LEGALLY REQUIRED.

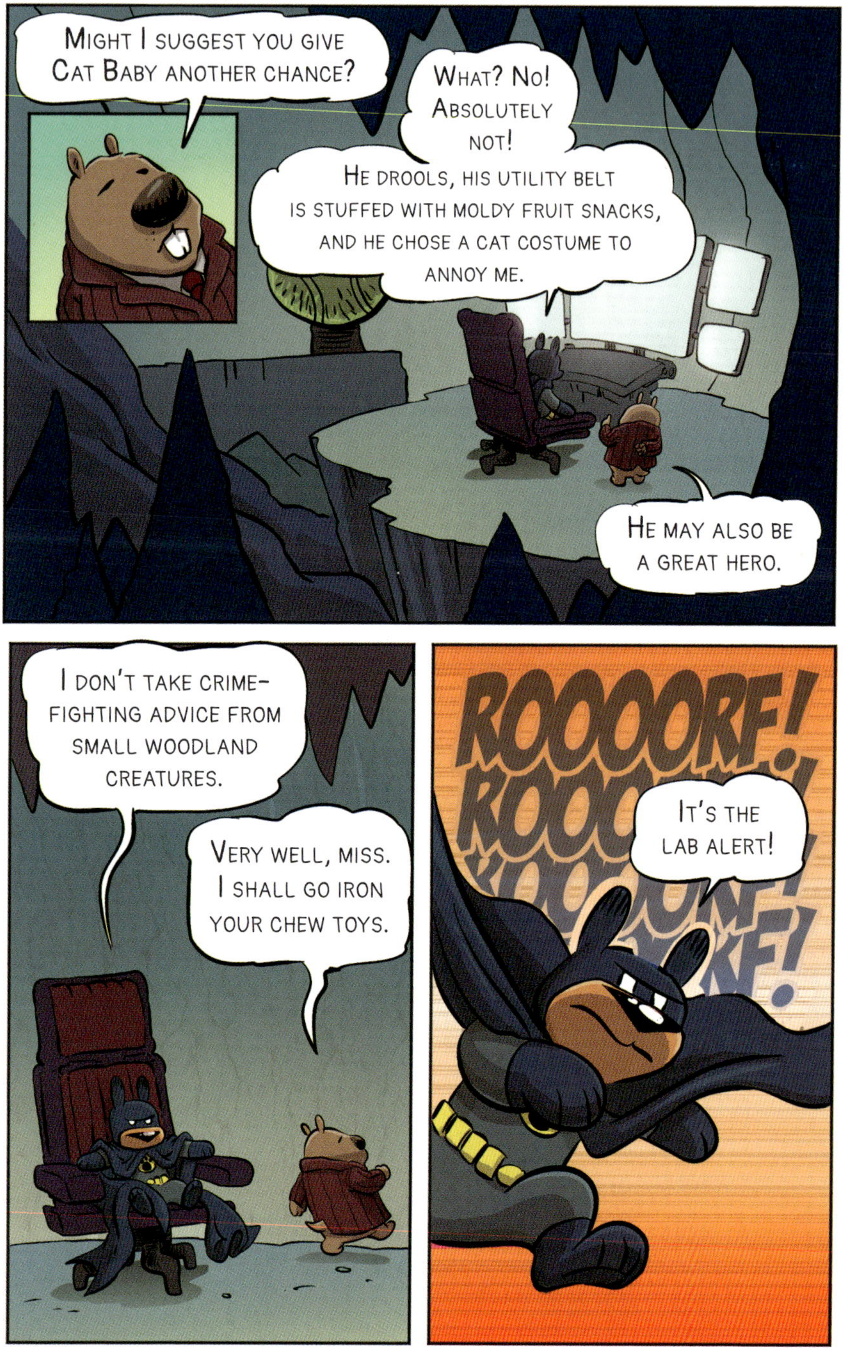
MIGHT I SUGGEST YOU GIVE CAT BABY ANOTHER CHANCE?
WHAT? NO! ABSOLUTELY NOT!
HE DROOLS, HIS UTILITY BELT IS STUFFED WITH MOLDY FRUIT SNACKS, AND HE CHOSE A CAT COSTUME TO ANNOY ME.
HE MAY ALSO BE A GREAT HERO.
I DON'T TAKE CRIME-FIGHTING ADVICE FROM SMALL WOODLAND CREATURES.
VERY WELL, MISS. I SHALL GO IRON YOUR CHEW TOYS.
ROOOORF!
IT'S THE LAB ALERT!

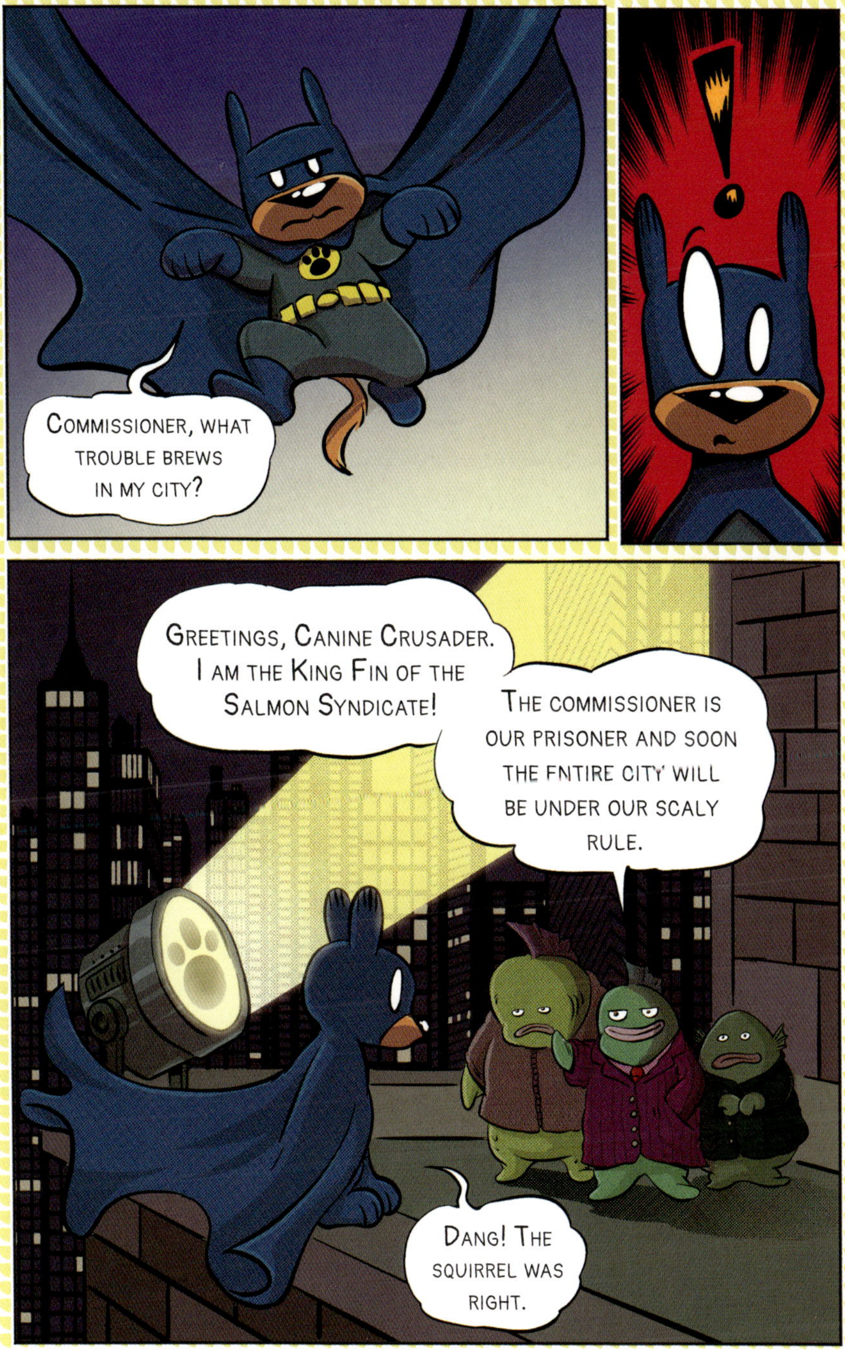
COMMISSIONER, WHAT TROUBLE BREWS IN MY CITY?
!
GREETINGS, CANINE CRUSADER. I AM THE KING FIN OF THE SALMON SYNDICATE!
THE COMMISSIONER IS OUR PRISONER AND SOON THE ENTIRE CITY WILL BE UNDER OUR SCALY RULE.
DANG! THE SQUIRREL WAS RIGHT.

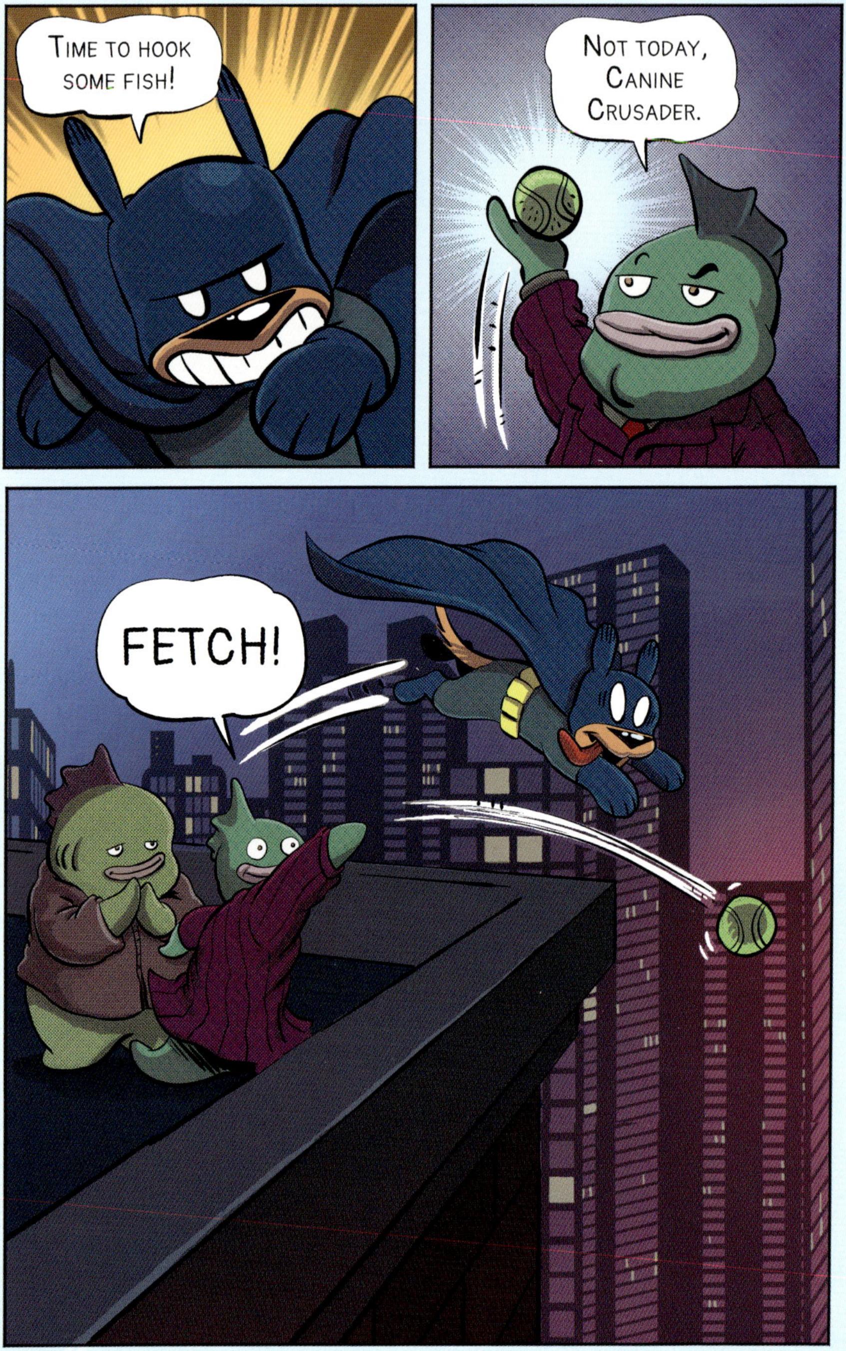
TIME TO HOOK SOME FISH!
NOT TODAY, CANINE CRUSADER.
FETCH!

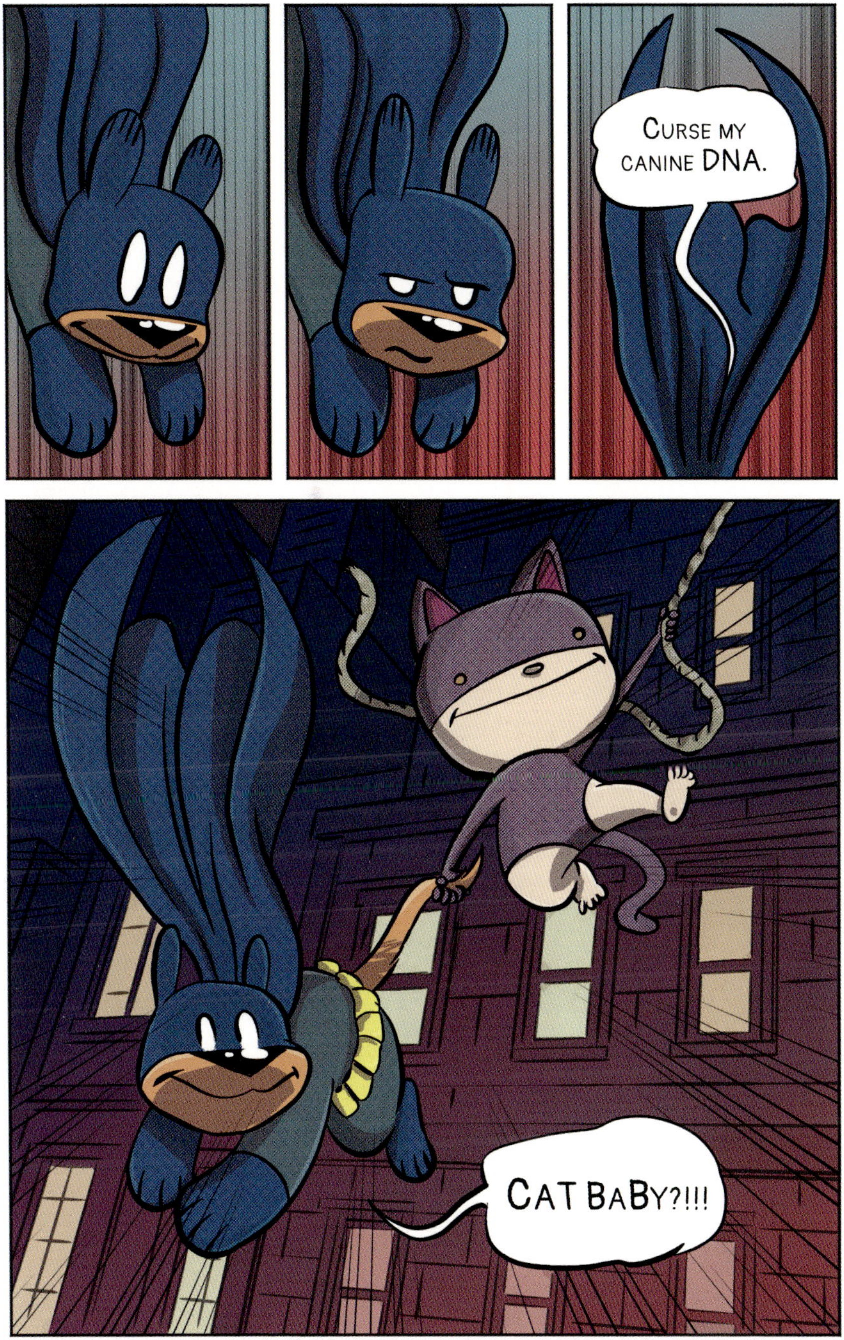
CURSE MY CANINE DNA.
CAT BABY?!!!

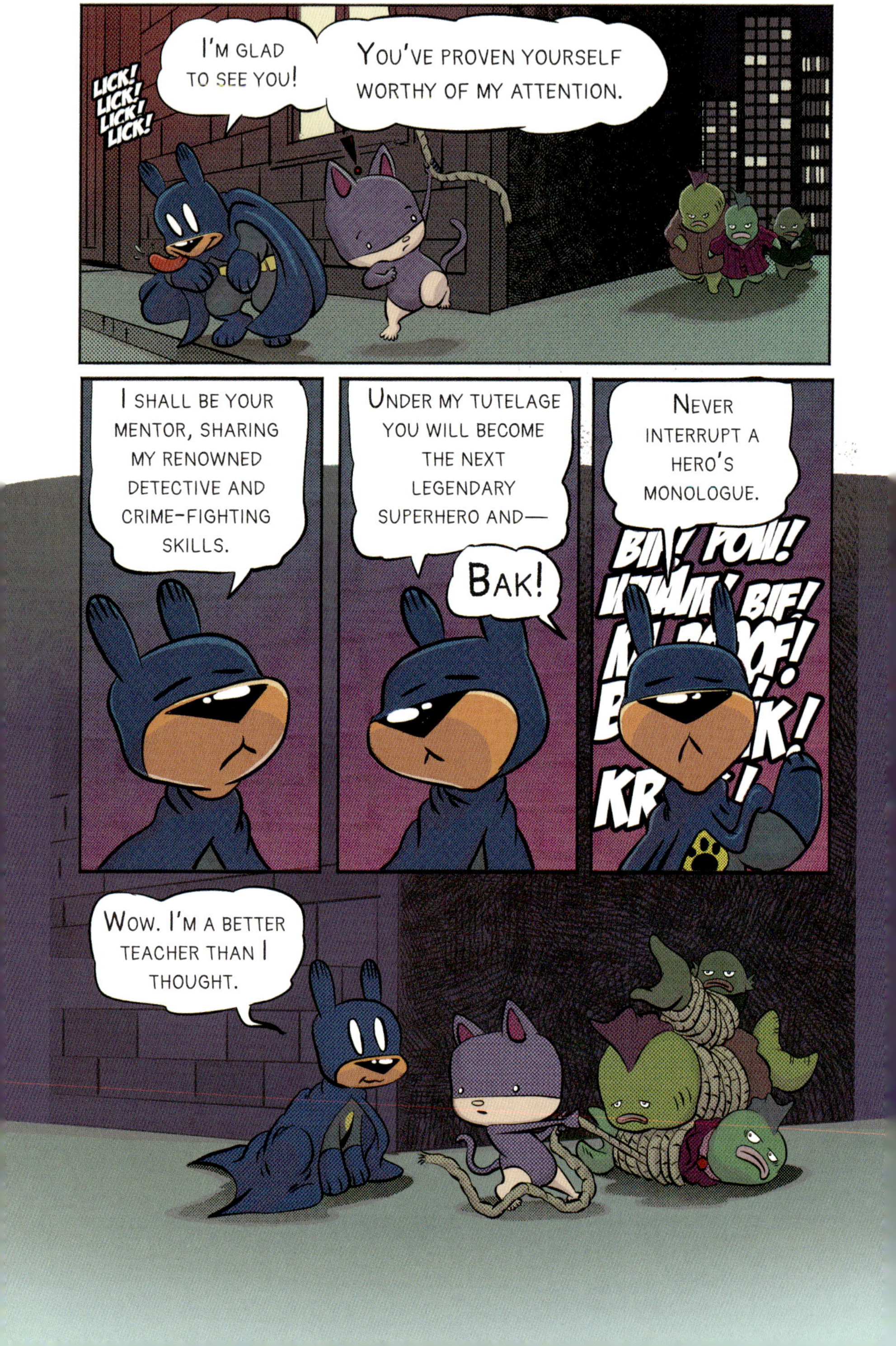
LICK! LICK! LICK! LICK!
I'M GLAD TO SEE YOU!
YOU'VE PROVEN YOURSELF WORTHY OF MY ATTENTION.
I SHALL BE YOUR MENTOR, SHARING MY RENOWNED DETECTIVE AND CRIME-FIGHTING SKILLS.
UNDER MY TUTELAGE YOU WILL BECOME THE NEXT LEGENDARY SUPERHERO AND—
BAK!
NEVER INTERRUPT A HERO'S MONOLOGUE.
POW!
BIF!
WOW. I'M A BETTER TEACHER THAN I THOUGHT.

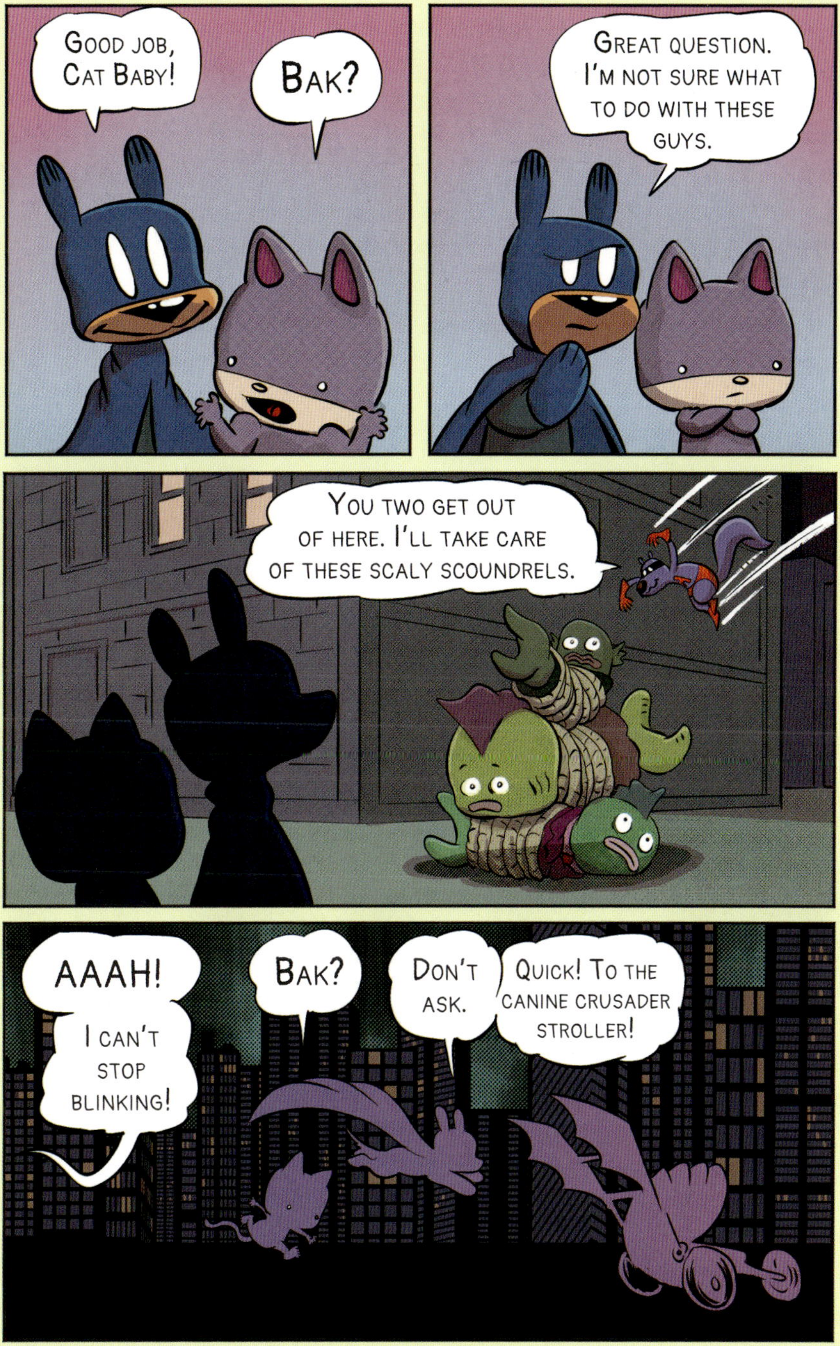
GOOD JOB, CAT BABY!
BAK?
GREAT QUESTION. I'M NOT SURE WHAT TO DO WITH THESE GUYS.
YOU TWO GET OUT OF HERE. I'LL TAKE CARE OF THESE SCALY SCOUNDRELS.
AAAH!
I CAN'T STOP BLINKING!
BAK?
DON'T ASK.
QUICK! TO THE CANINE CRUSADER STROLLER!

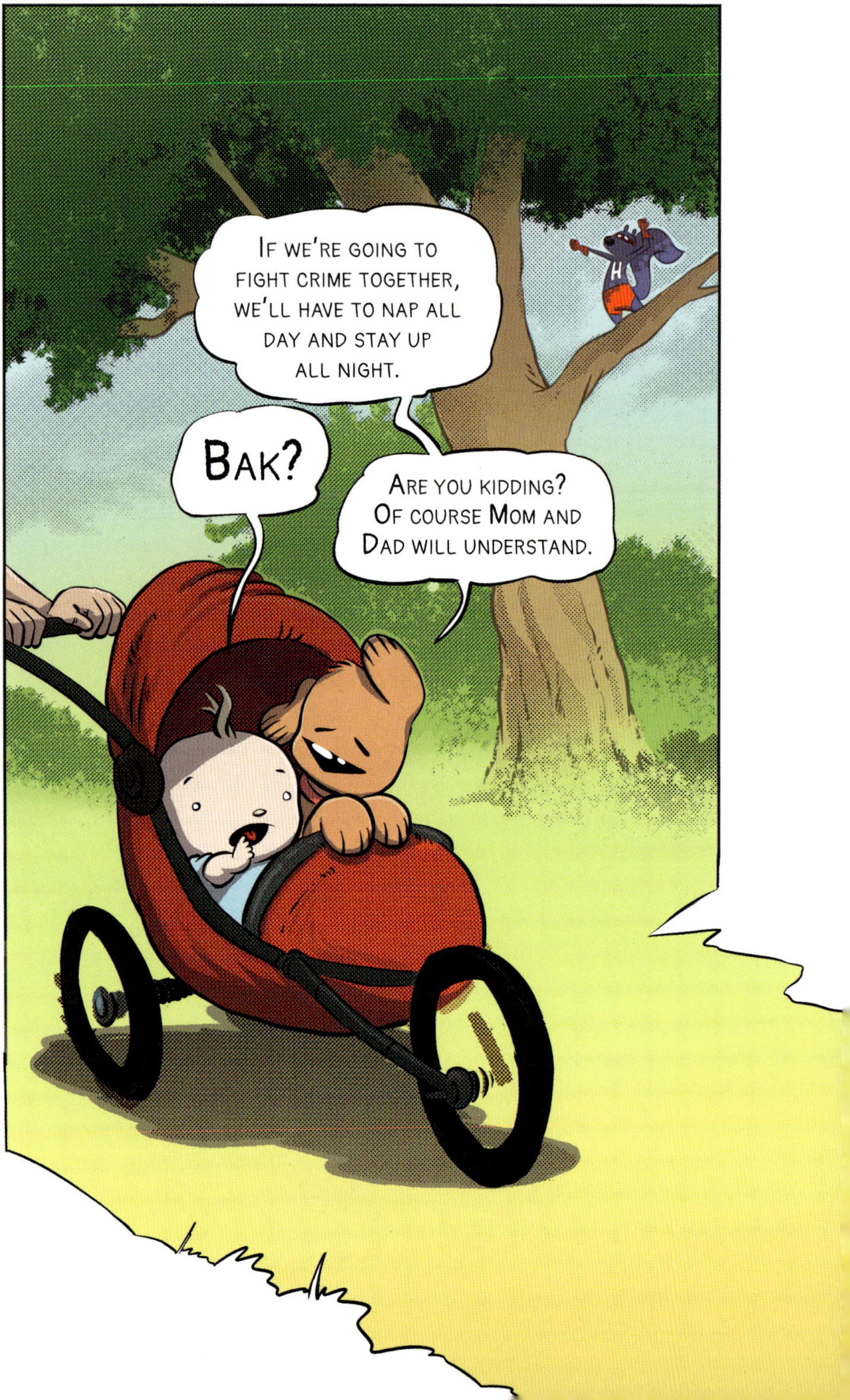
IF WE'RE GOING TO FIGHT CRIME TOGETHER, WE'LL HAVE TO NAP ALL DAY AND STAY UP ALL NIGHT.
BAK?
ARE YOU KIDDING? OF COURSE MOM AND DAD WILL UNDERSTAND.

CHAPTER 9

The Adorable Doom

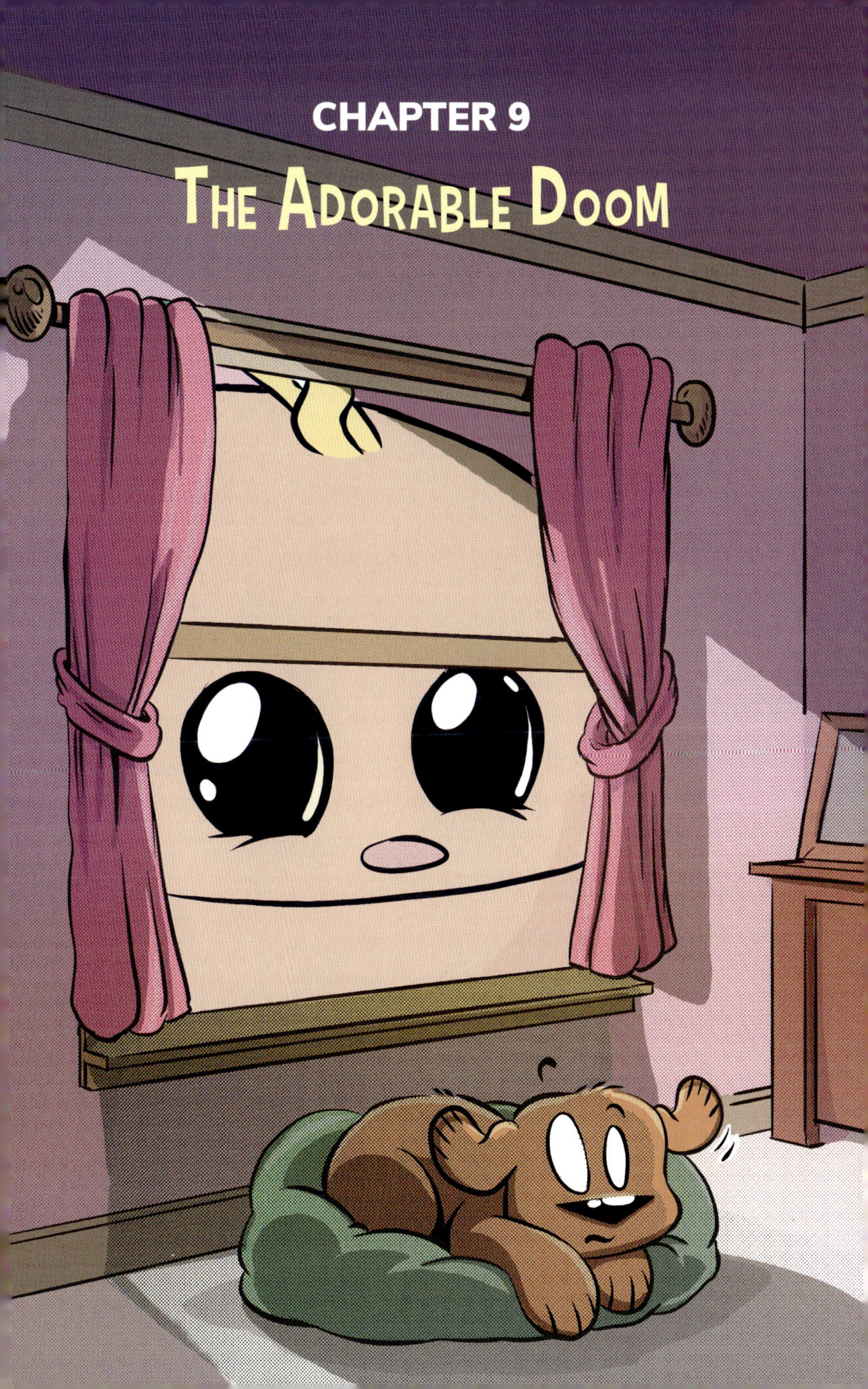

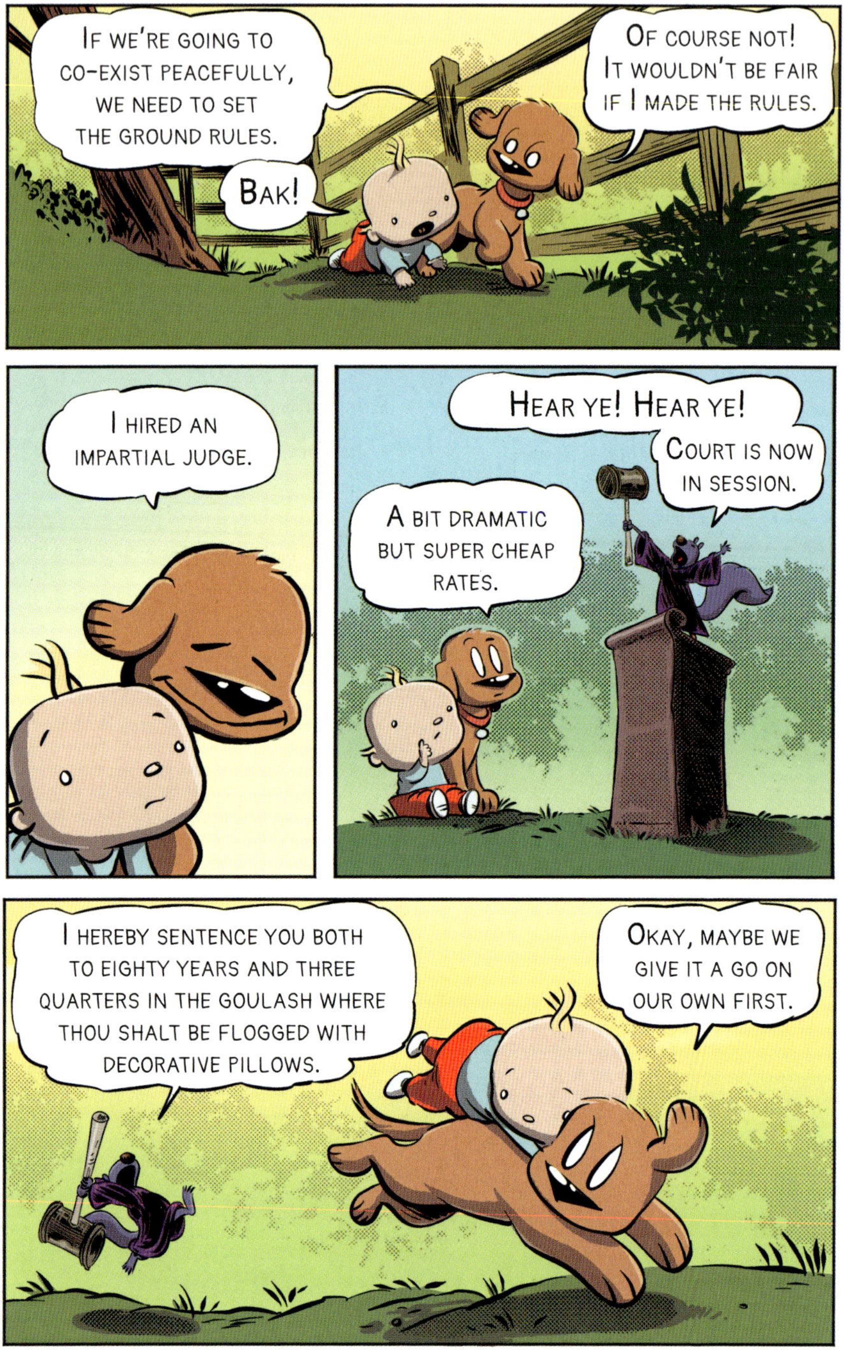

IF WE'RE GOING TO CO-EXIST PEACEFULLY, WE NEED TO SET THE GROUND RULES.
OF COURSE NOT! IT WOULDN'T BE FAIR IF I MADE THE RULES.
BAK!
I HIRED AN IMPARTIAL JUDGE.
HEAR YE! HEAR YE!
COURT IS NOW IN SESSION.
A BIT DRAMATIC BUT SUPER CHEAP RATES.
I HEREBY SENTENCE YOU BOTH TO EIGHTY YEARS AND THREE QUARTERS IN THE GOULASH WHERE THOU SHALT BE FLOGGED WITH DECORATIVE PILLOWS.
OKAY, MAYBE WE GIVE IT A GO ON OUR OWN FIRST.

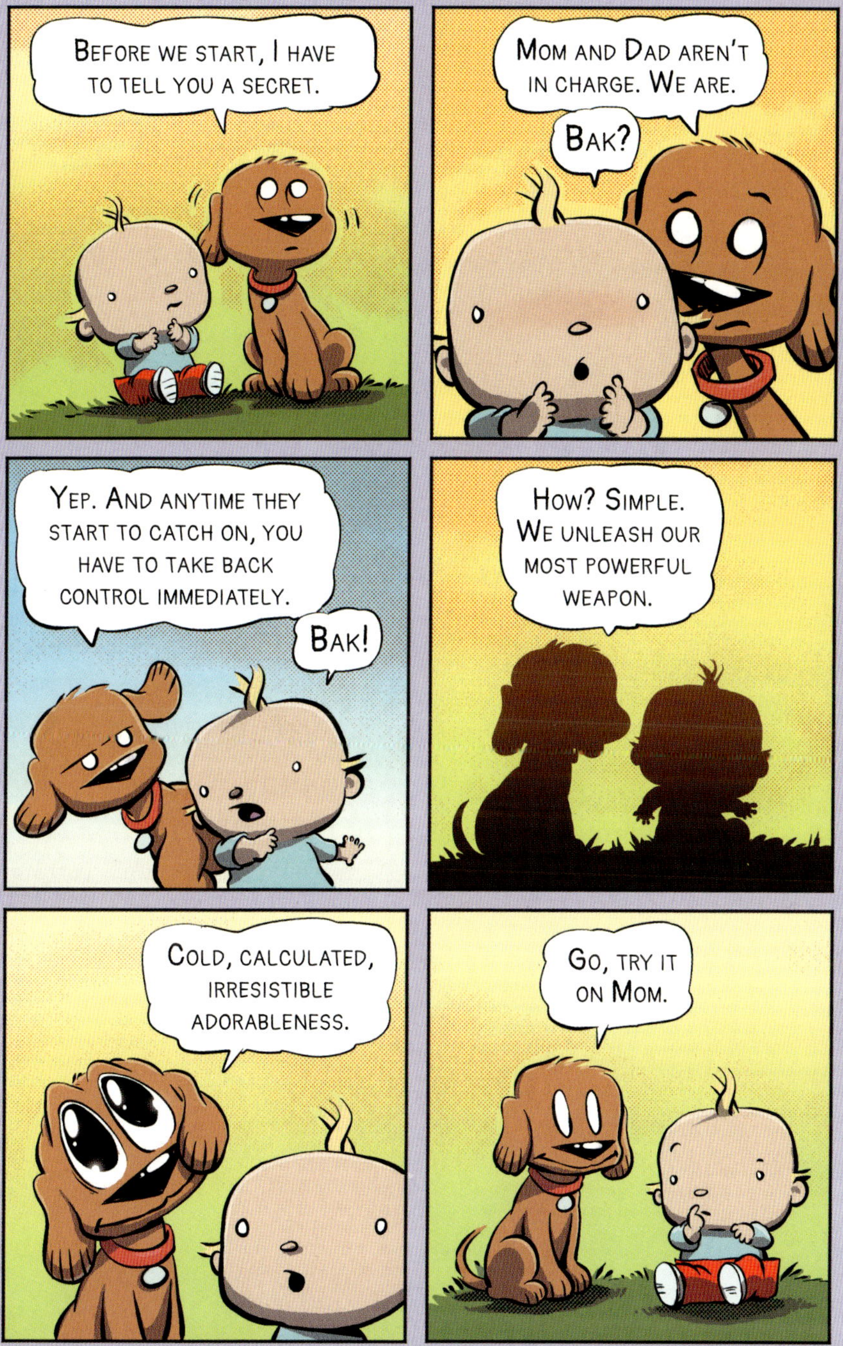
BEFORE WE START, I HAVE TO TELL YOU A SECRET.
MOM AND DAD AREN'T IN CHARGE. WE ARE.
BAK?
YEP. AND ANYTIME THEY START TO CATCH ON, YOU HAVE TO TAKE BACK CONTROL IMMEDIATELY.
BAK!
HOW? SIMPLE. WE UNLEASH OUR MOST POWERFUL WEAPON.
COLD, CALCULATED, IRRESISTIBLE ADORABLENESS.
GO, TRY IT ON MOM.

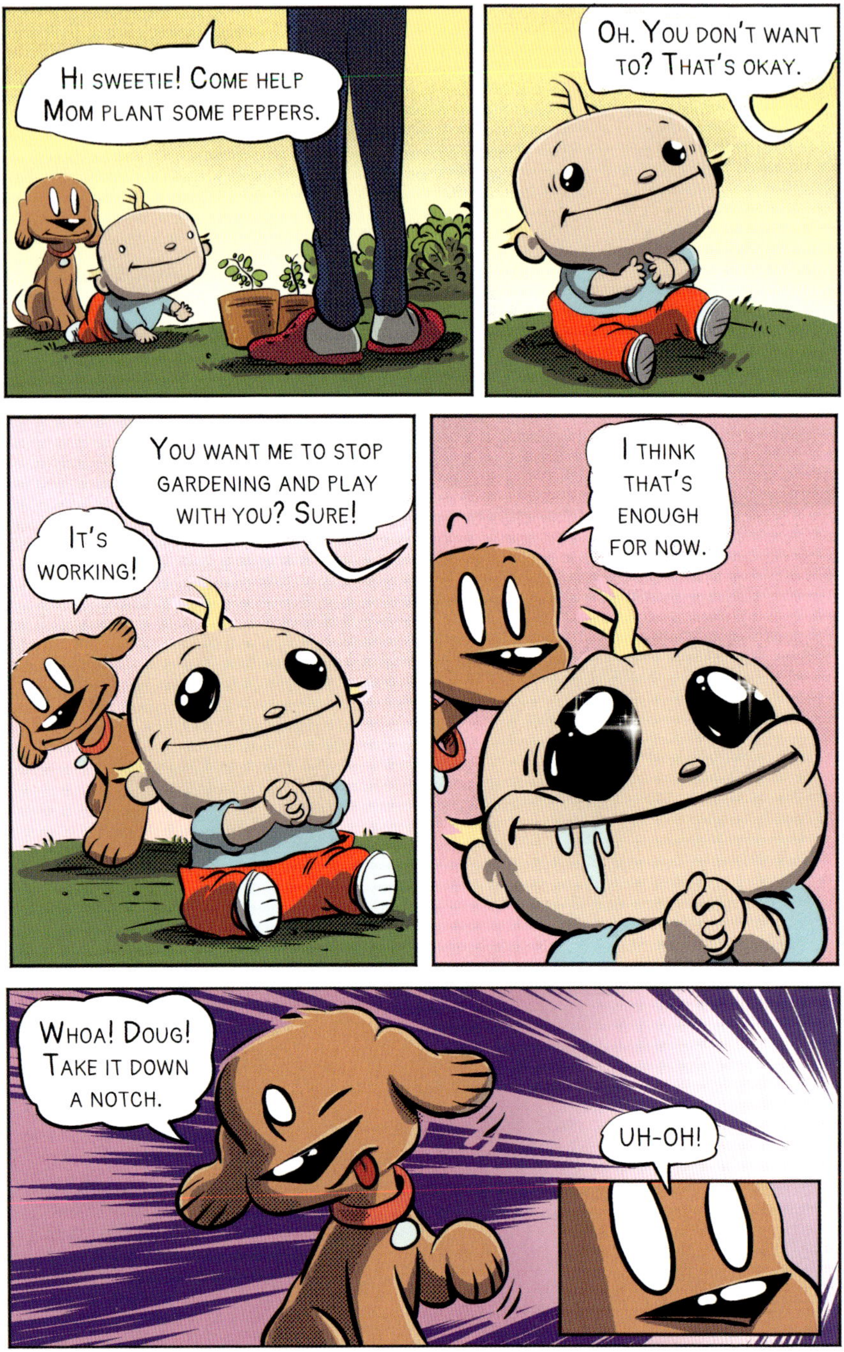
HI SWEETIE! COME HELP MOM PLANT SOME PEPPERS.
OH. YOU DON'T WANT TO? THAT'S OKAY.
YOU WANT ME TO STOP GARDENING AND PLAY WITH YOU? SURE!
IT'S WORKING!
I THINK THAT'S ENOUGH FOR NOW.
WHOA! DOUG! TAKE IT DOWN A NOTCH.
UH-OH!

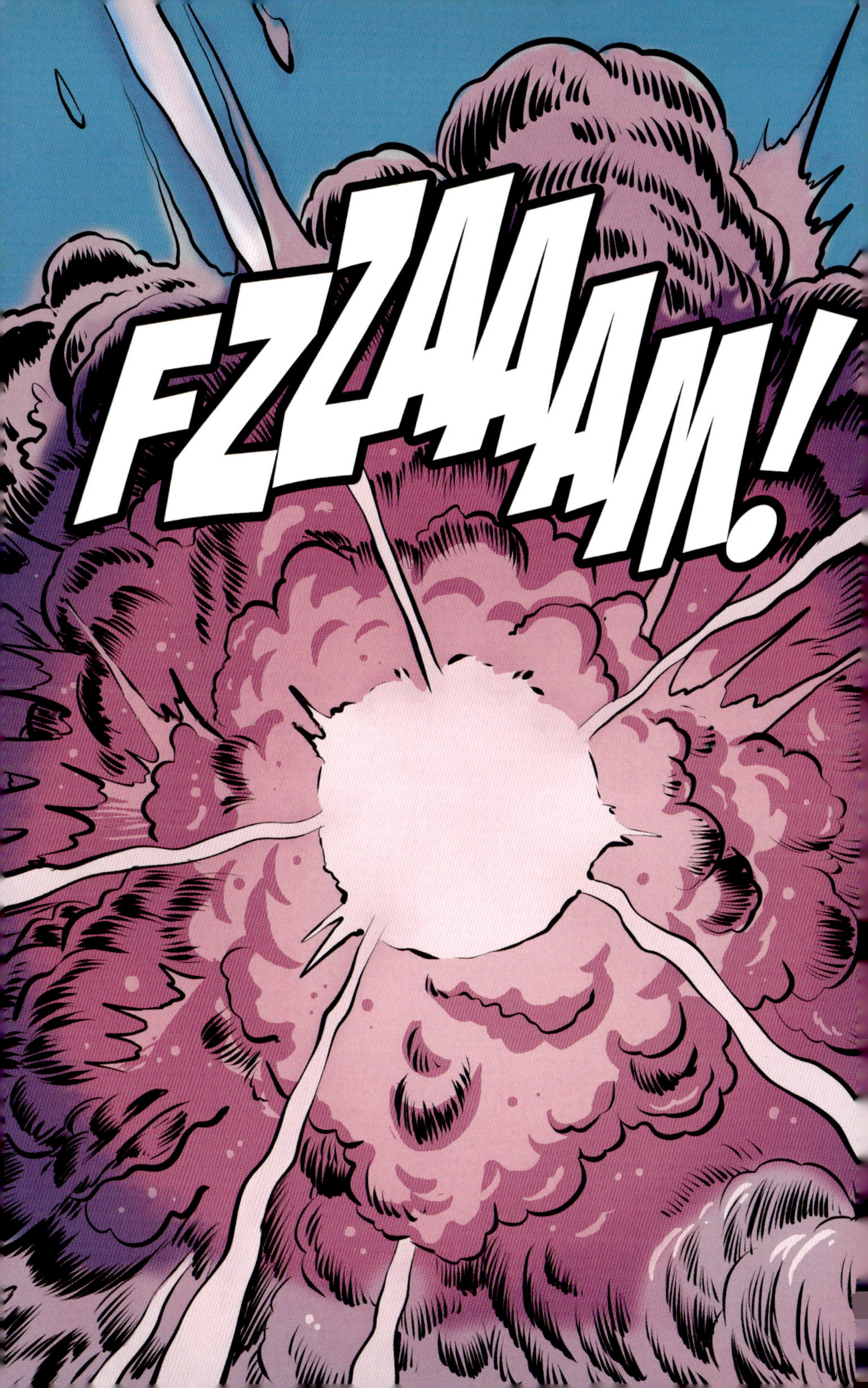
FZZAAAM!

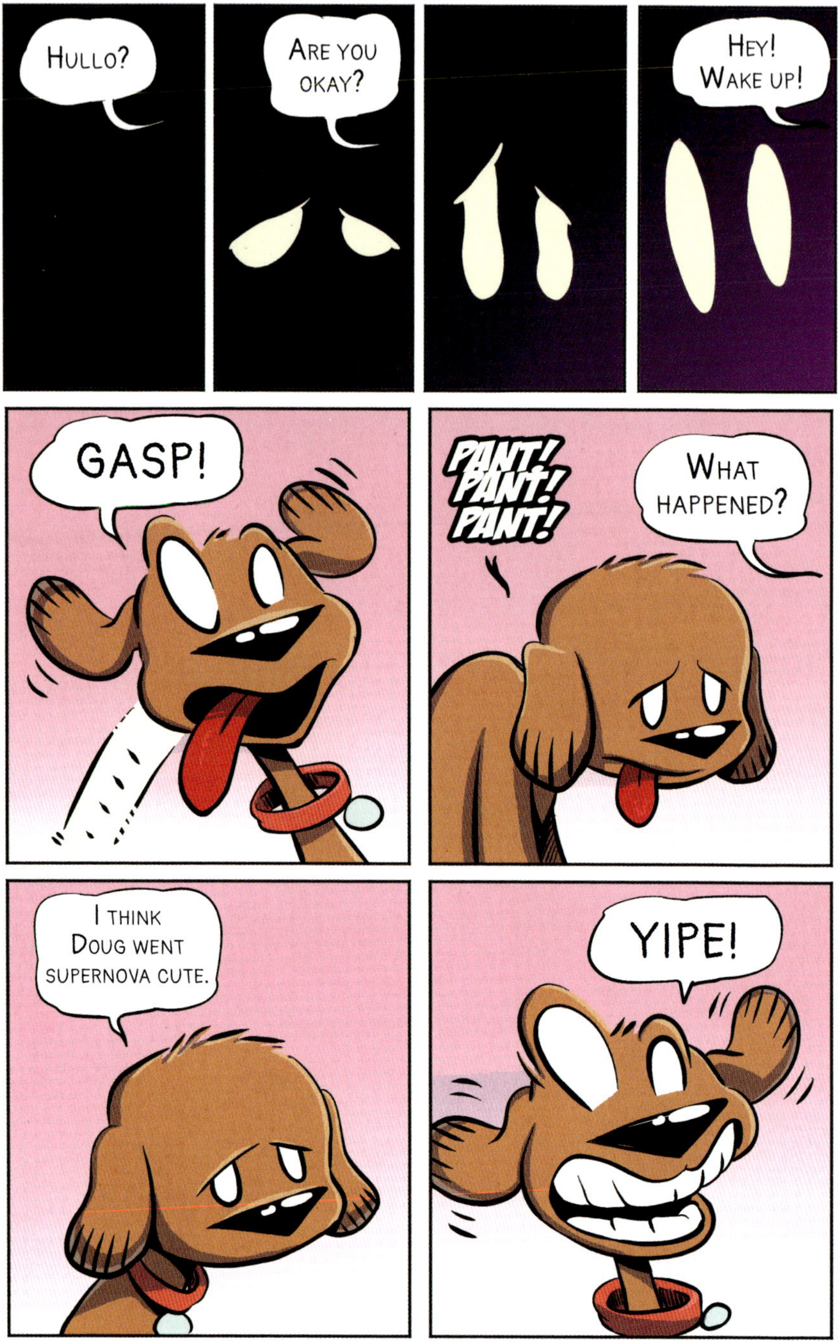
HULLO?
ARE YOU OKAY?
HEY! WAKE UP!
GASP!
PANT! PANT! PANT!
WHAT HAPPENED?
I THINK DOUG WENT SUPERNOVA CUTE.
YIPE!

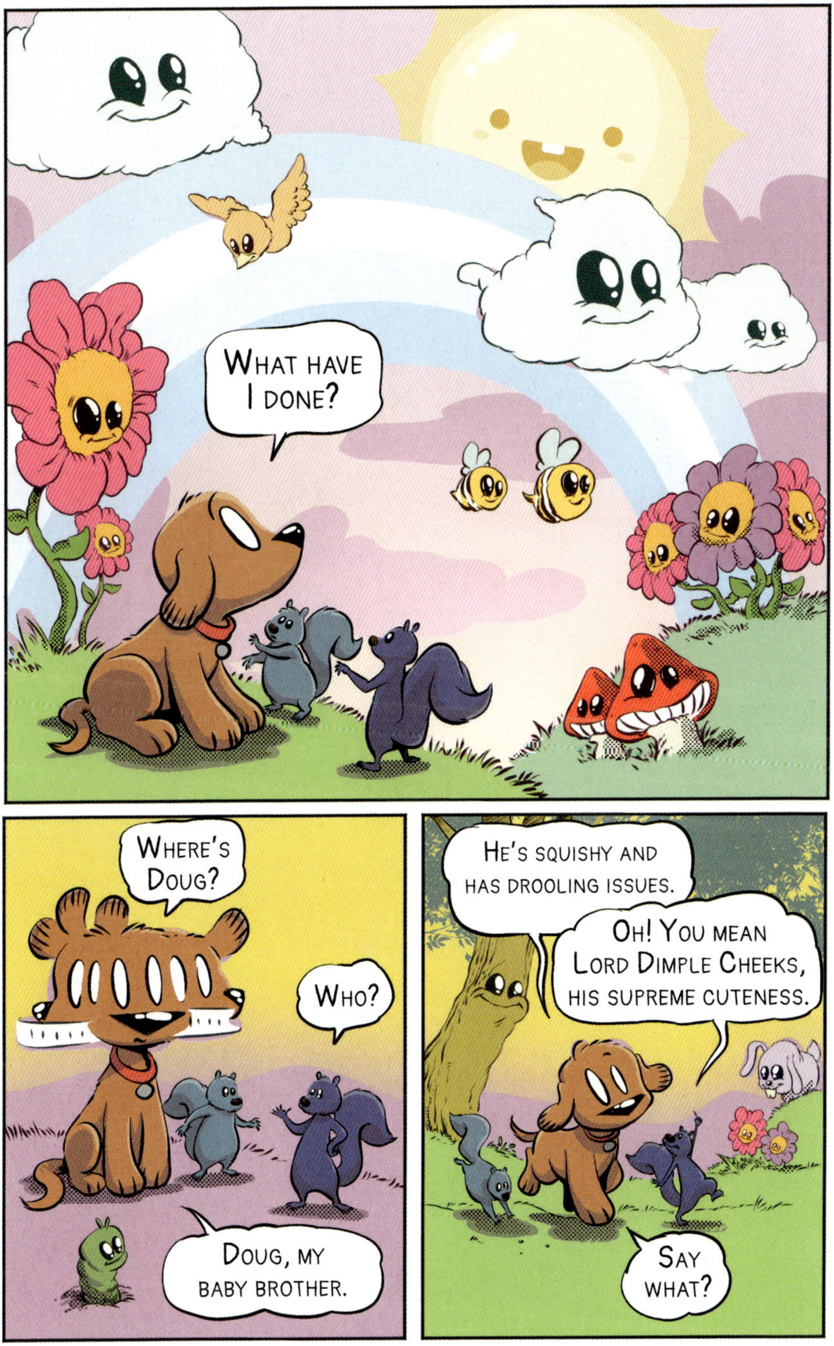
WHAT HAVE I DONE?
WHERE'S DOUG?
WHO?
DOUG, MY BABY BROTHER.
HE'S SQUISHY AND HAS DROOLING ISSUES.
OH! YOU MEAN LORD DIMPLE CHEEKS, HIS SUPREME CUTENESS.
SAY WHAT?

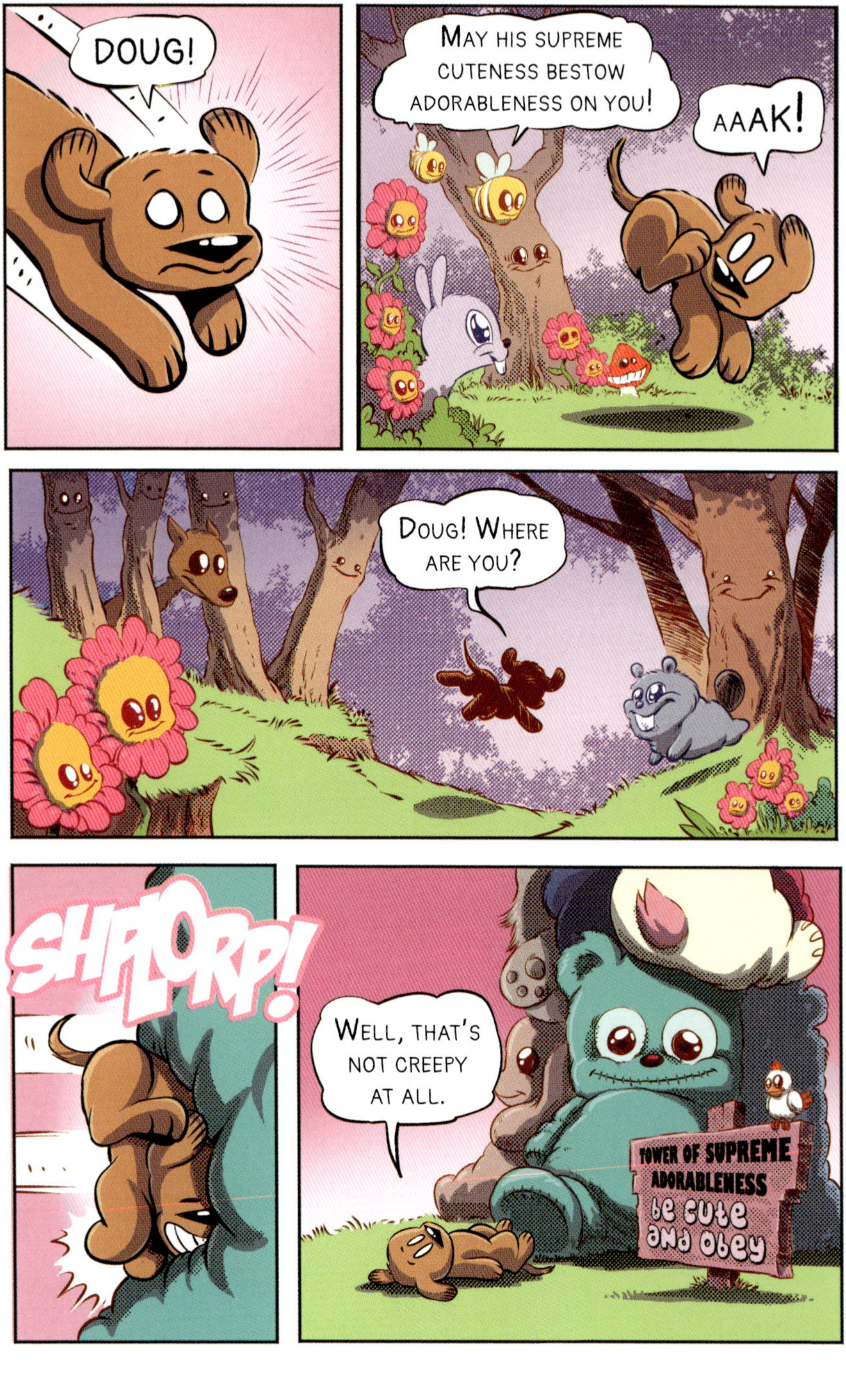
DOUG!
MAY HIS SUPREME CUTENESS BESTOW ADORABLENESS ON YOU!
AAAK!
DOUG! WHERE ARE YOU?
SHPLORP!
WELL, THAT'S NOT CREEPY AT ALL.
TOWER OF SUPREME ADORABLENESS
be cute and obey

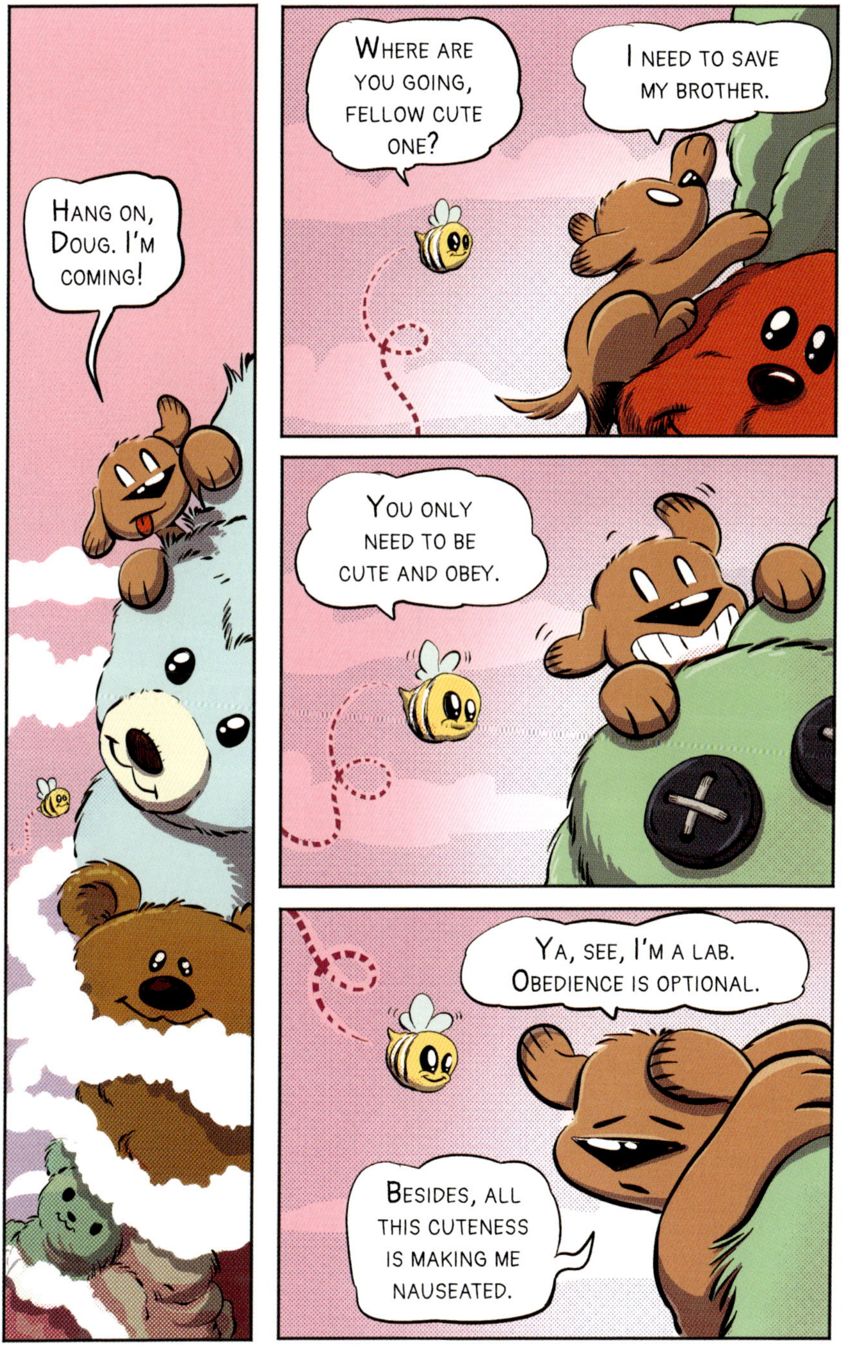
Hang on, Doug. I'm coming!
Where are you going, fellow cute one?
I need to save my brother.
You only need to be cute and obey.
Ya, see, I'm a lab. Obedience is optional.
Besides, all this cuteness is making me nauseated.

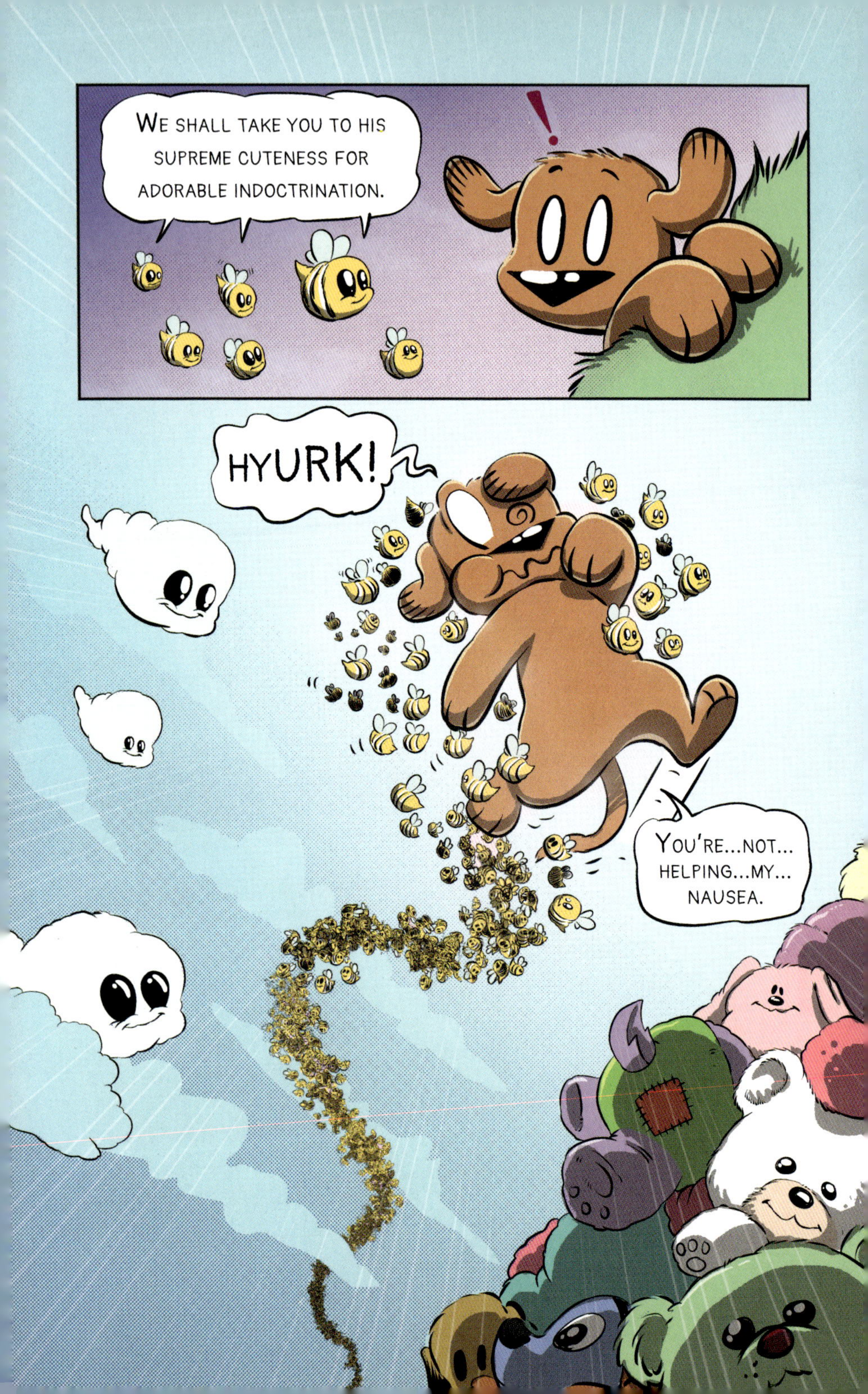
WE SHALL TAKE YOU TO HIS SUPREME CUTENESS FOR ADORABLE INDOCTRINATION.
!
HYURK!
YOU'RE...NOT... HELPING...MY... NAUSEA.

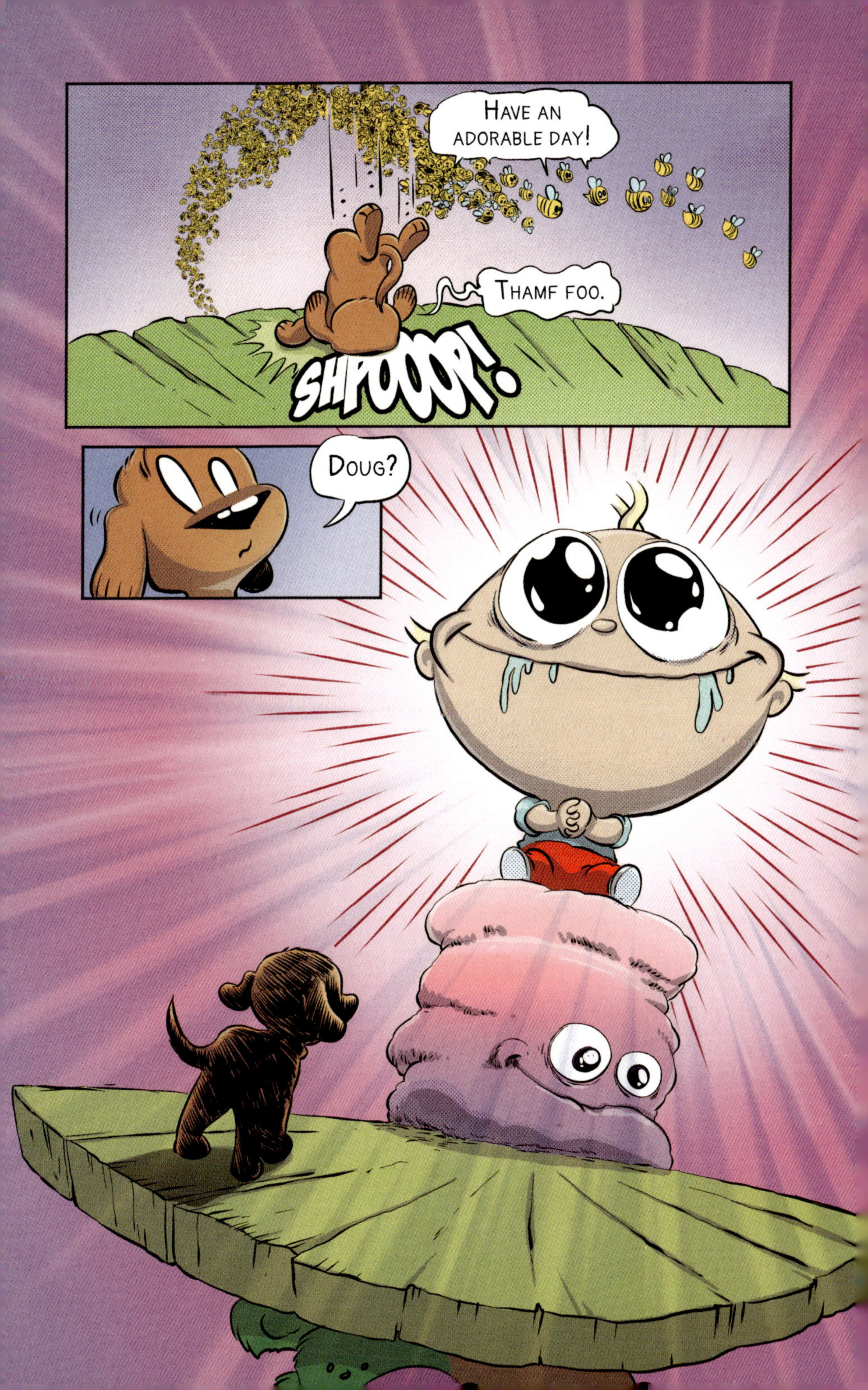
HAVE AN ADORABLE DAY!
THAMF FOO.
SHPOOOP!
DOUG?

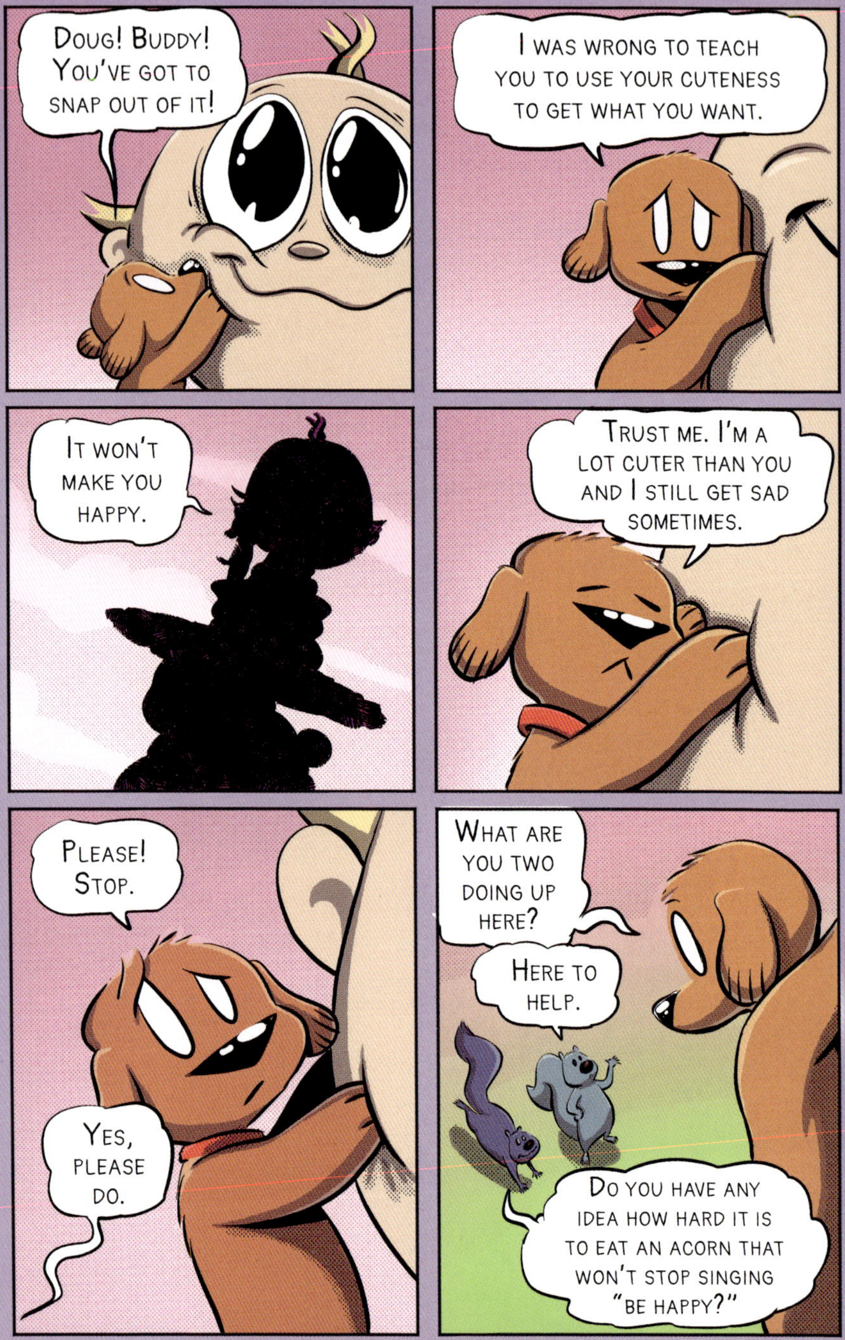
DOUG! BUDDY! YOU'VE GOT TO SNAP OUT OF IT!
I WAS WRONG TO TEACH YOU TO USE YOUR CUTENESS TO GET WHAT YOU WANT.
IT WON'T MAKE YOU HAPPY.
TRUST ME. I'M A LOT CUTER THAN YOU AND I STILL GET SAD SOMETIMES.
PLEASE! STOP.
YES, PLEASE DO.
WHAT ARE YOU TWO DOING UP HERE?
HERE TO HELP.
DO YOU HAVE ANY IDEA HOW HARD IT IS TO EAT AN ACORN THAT WON'T STOP SINGING "BE HAPPY?"

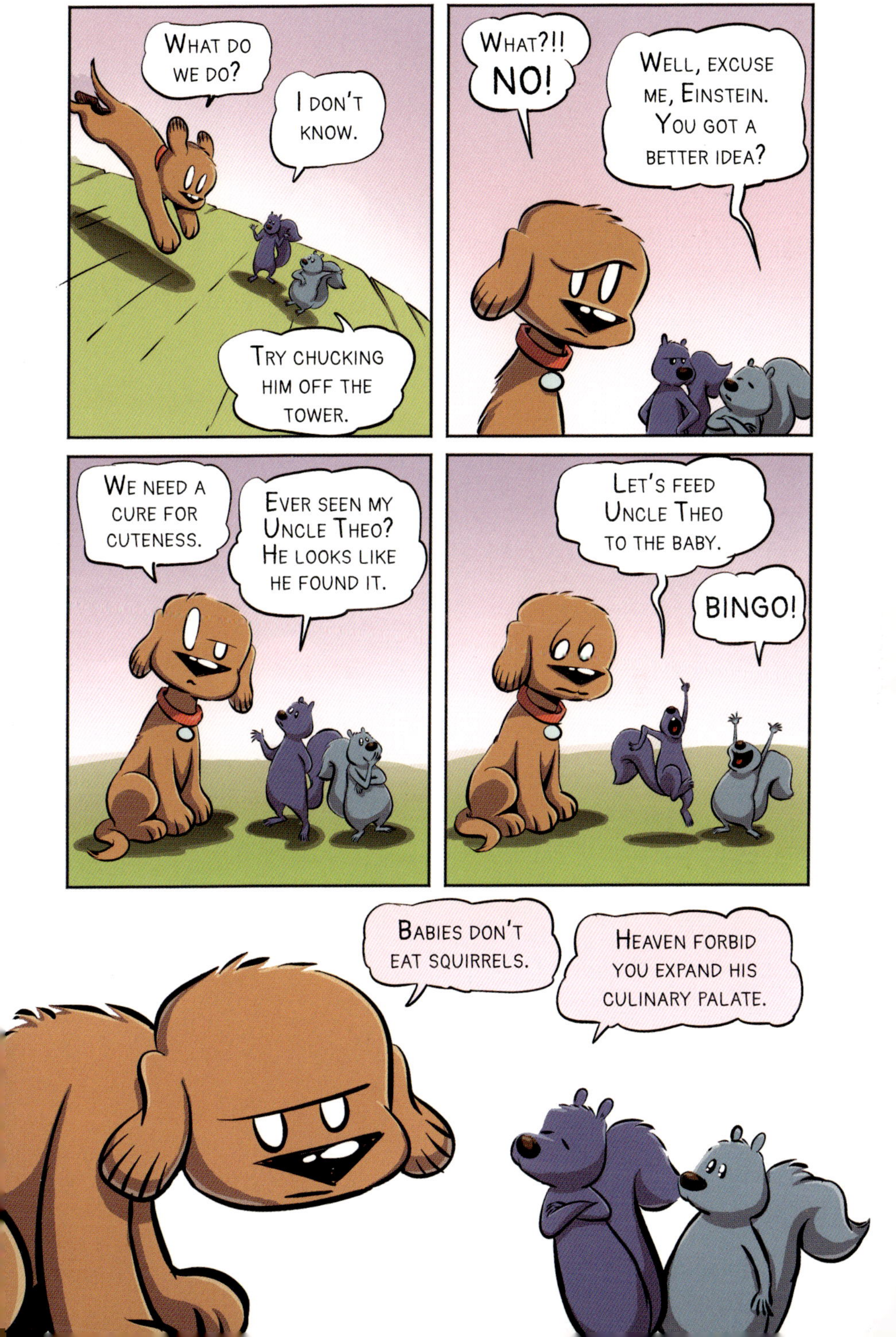

WHAT DO WE DO?
I DON'T KNOW.
TRY CHUCKING HIM OFF THE TOWER.
WHAT?!! NO!
WELL, EXCUSE ME, EINSTEIN. YOU GOT A BETTER IDEA?
WE NEED A CURE FOR CUTENESS.
EVER SEEN MY UNCLE THEO? HE LOOKS LIKE HE FOUND IT.
LET'S FEED UNCLE THEO TO THE BABY.
BINGO!
BABIES DON'T EAT SQUIRRELS.
HEAVEN FORBID YOU EXPAND HIS CULINARY PALATE.

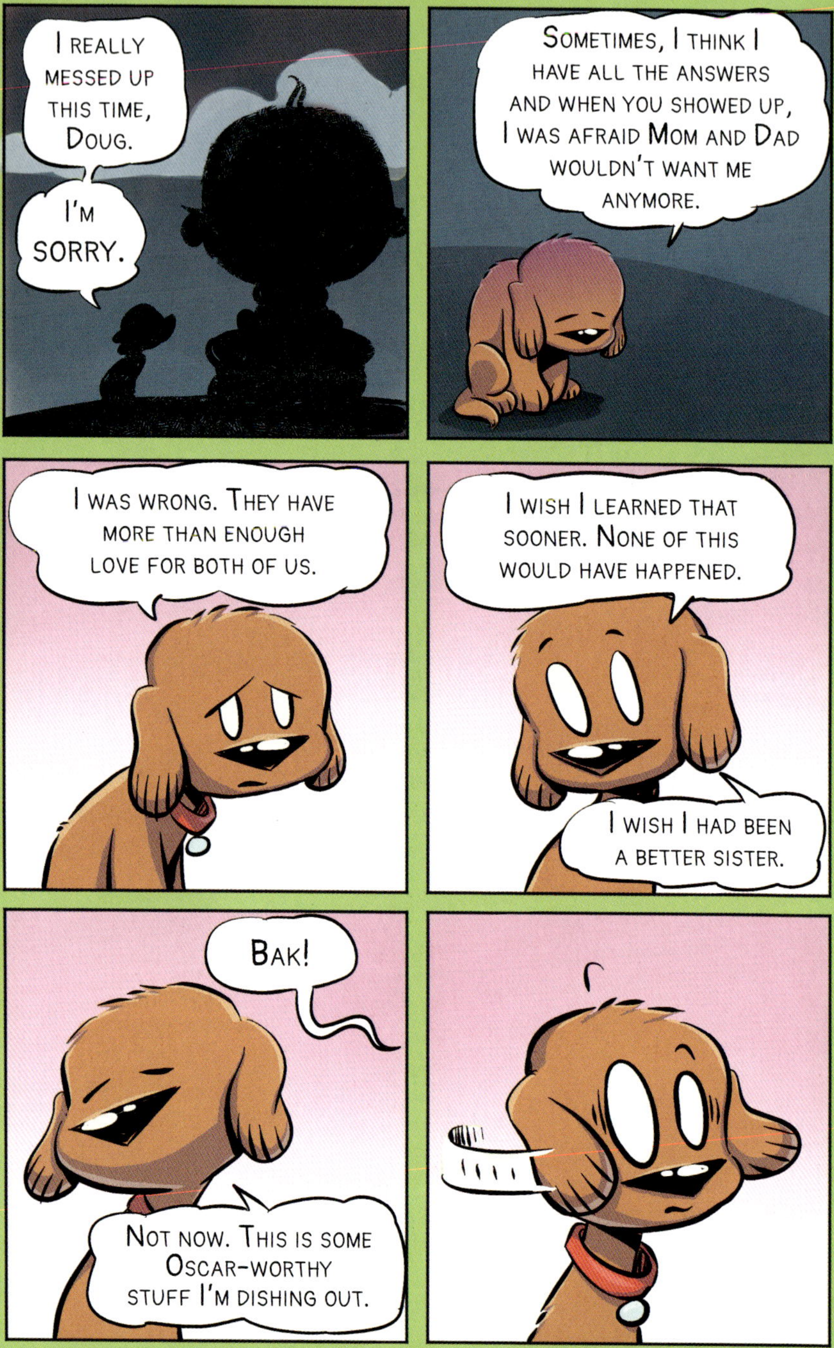
I REALLY MESSED UP THIS TIME, DOUG.
I'M SORRY.
SOMETIMES, I THINK I HAVE ALL THE ANSWERS AND WHEN YOU SHOWED UP, I WAS AFRAID MOM AND DAD WOULDN'T WANT ME ANYMORE.
I WAS WRONG. THEY HAVE MORE THAN ENOUGH LOVE FOR BOTH OF US.
I WISH I LEARNED THAT SOONER. NONE OF THIS WOULD HAVE HAPPENED.
I WISH I HAD BEEN A BETTER SISTER.
BAK!
NOT NOW. THIS IS SOME OSCAR-WORTHY STUFF I'M DISHING OUT.

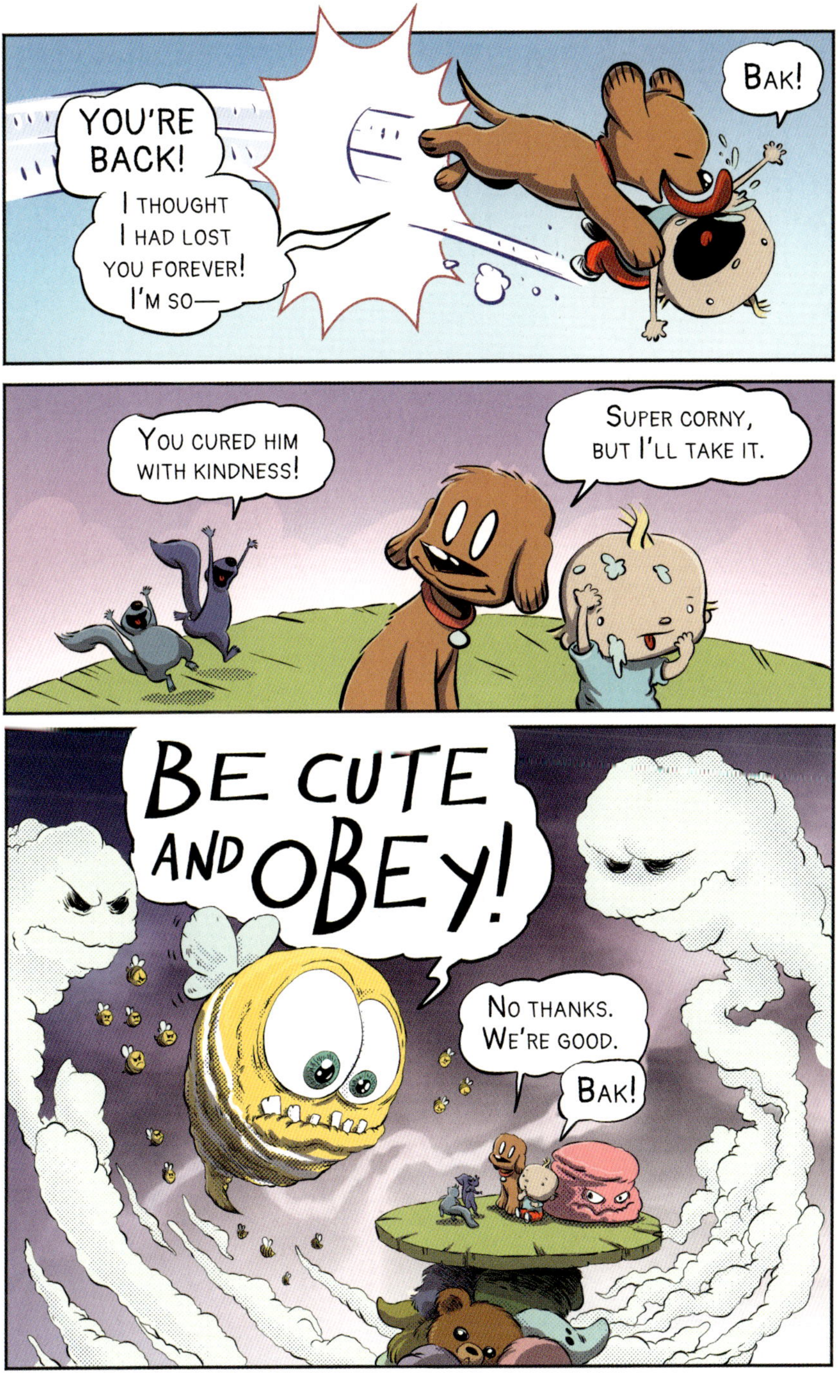
YOU'RE BACK!
I THOUGHT I HAD LOST YOU FOREVER! I'M SO—
BAK!
YOU CURED HIM WITH KINDNESS!
SUPER CORNY, BUT I'LL TAKE IT.
BE CUTE AND OBEY!
NO THANKS. WE'RE GOOD.
BAK!

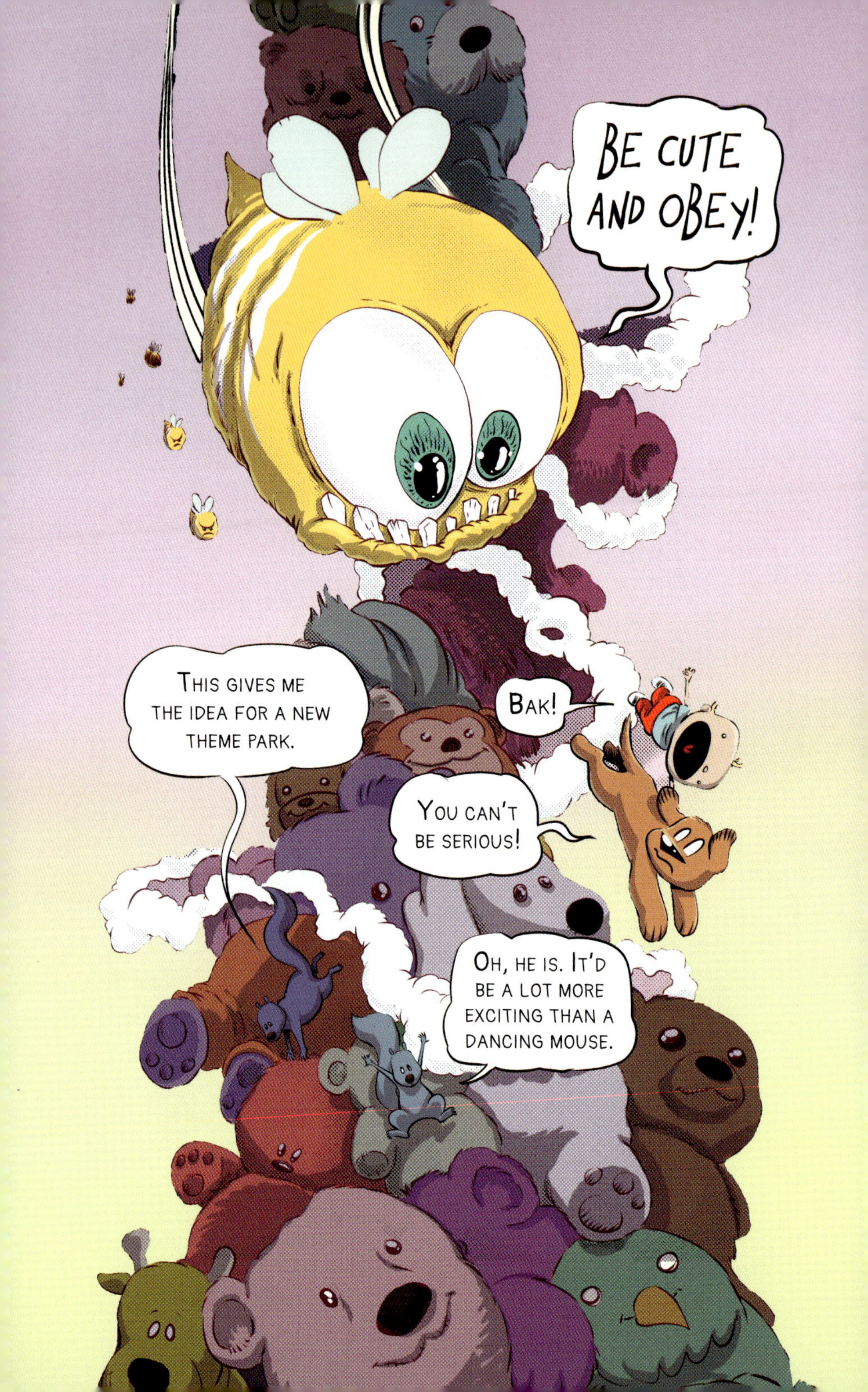
BE CUTE AND OBEY!
THIS GIVES ME THE IDEA FOR A NEW THEME PARK.
BAK!
YOU CAN'T BE SERIOUS!
OH, HE IS. IT'D BE A LOT MORE EXCITING THAN A DANCING MOUSE.

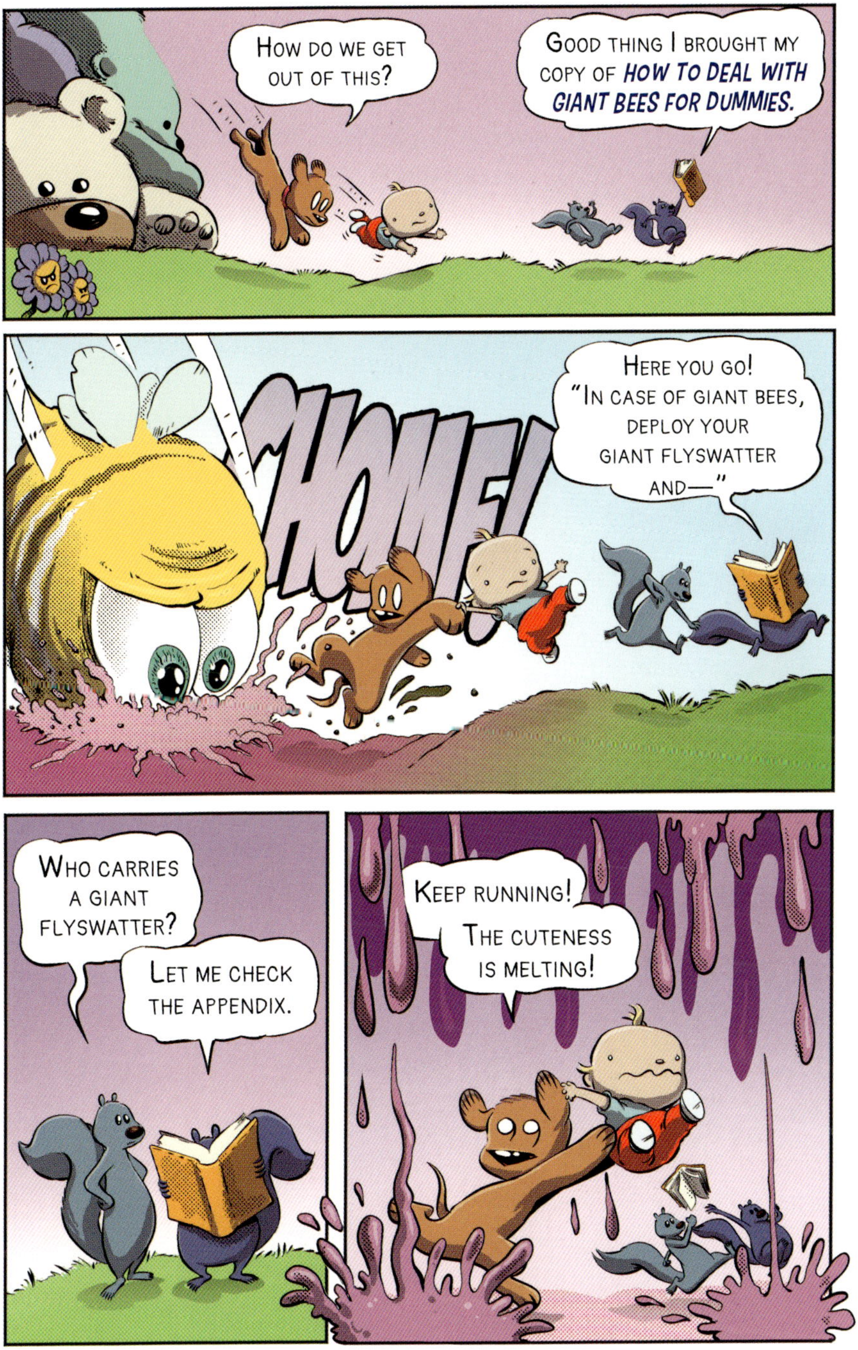

How do we get out of this?
Good thing I brought my copy of *How to Deal with Giant Bees for Dummies.*
CHOMF!
Here you go! "In case of giant bees, deploy your giant flyswatter and—"
Who carries a giant flyswatter?
Let me check the appendix.
Keep running!
The cuteness is melting!

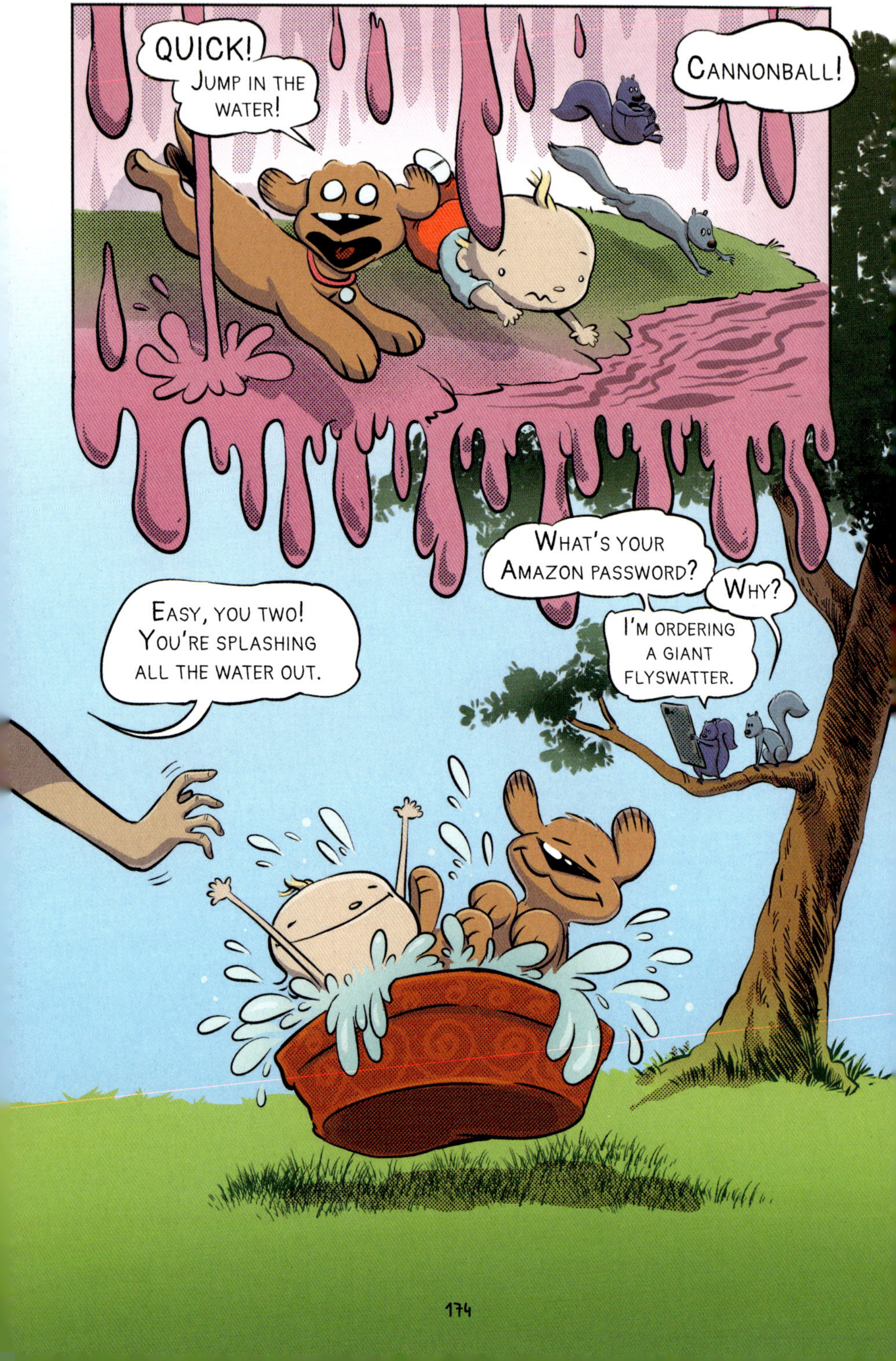
QUICK! JUMP IN THE WATER!
CANNONBALL!
WHAT'S YOUR AMAZON PASSWORD?
WHY?
I'M ORDERING A GIANT FLYSWATTER.
EASY, YOU TWO! YOU'RE SPLASHING ALL THE WATER OUT.

CHAPTER 10

Claws Encounters

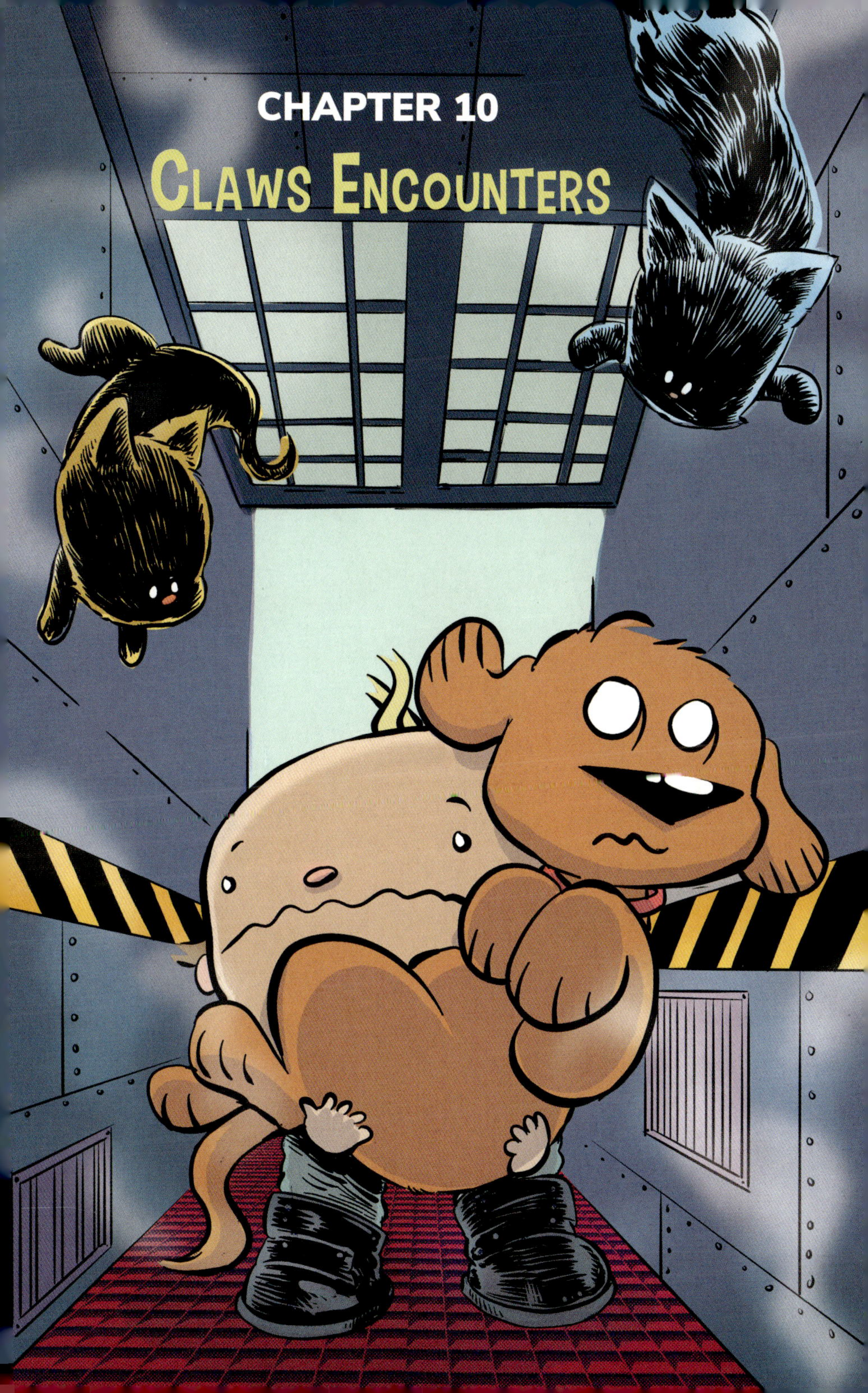

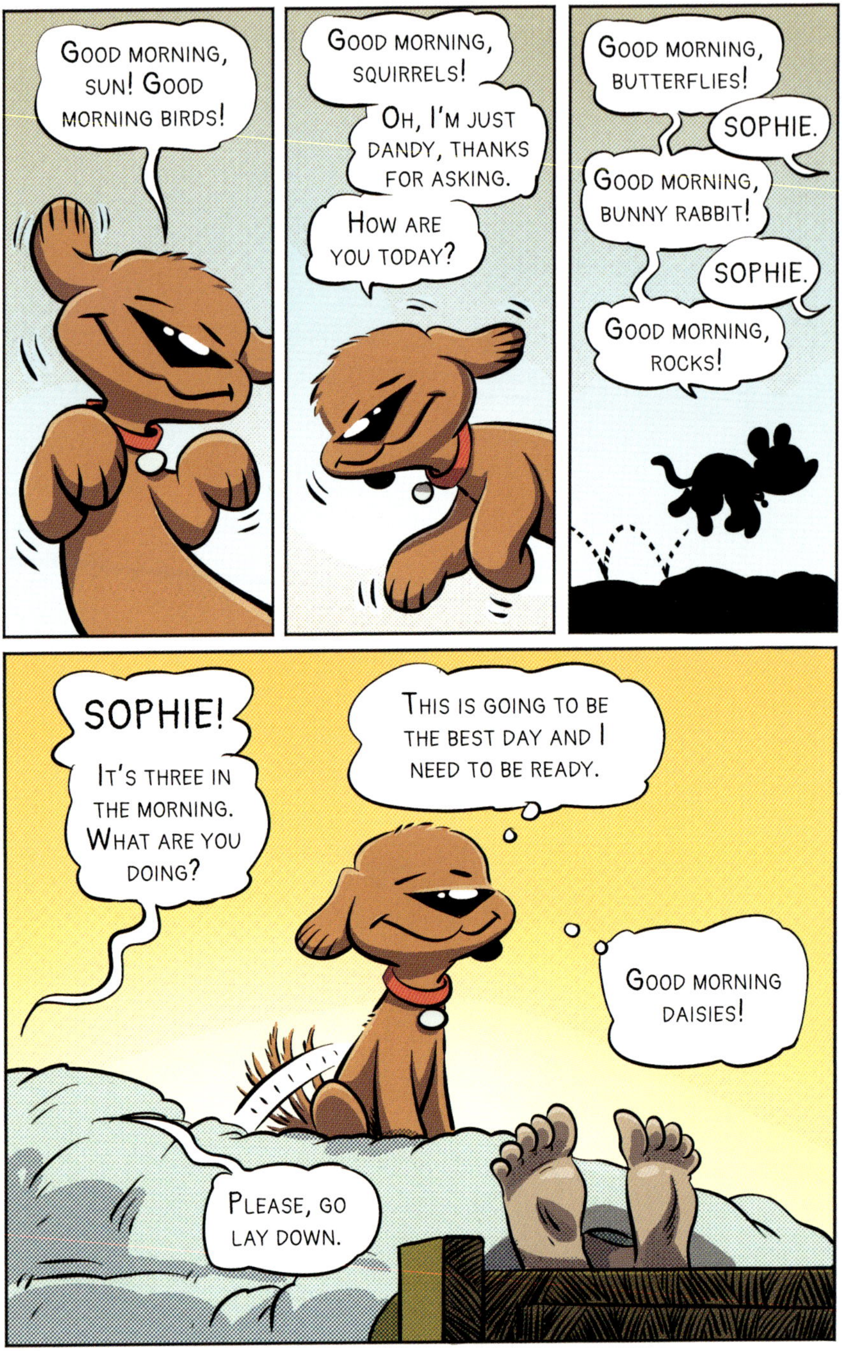
Good morning, sun! Good morning birds!
Good morning, squirrels!
How are you today?
Oh, I'm just dandy, thanks for asking.
Good morning, butterflies!
Sophie.
Good morning, bunny rabbit!
Sophie.
Good morning, rocks!
SOPHIE!
It's three in the morning. What are you doing?
This is going to be the best day and I need to be ready.
Good morning daisies!
Please, go lay down.

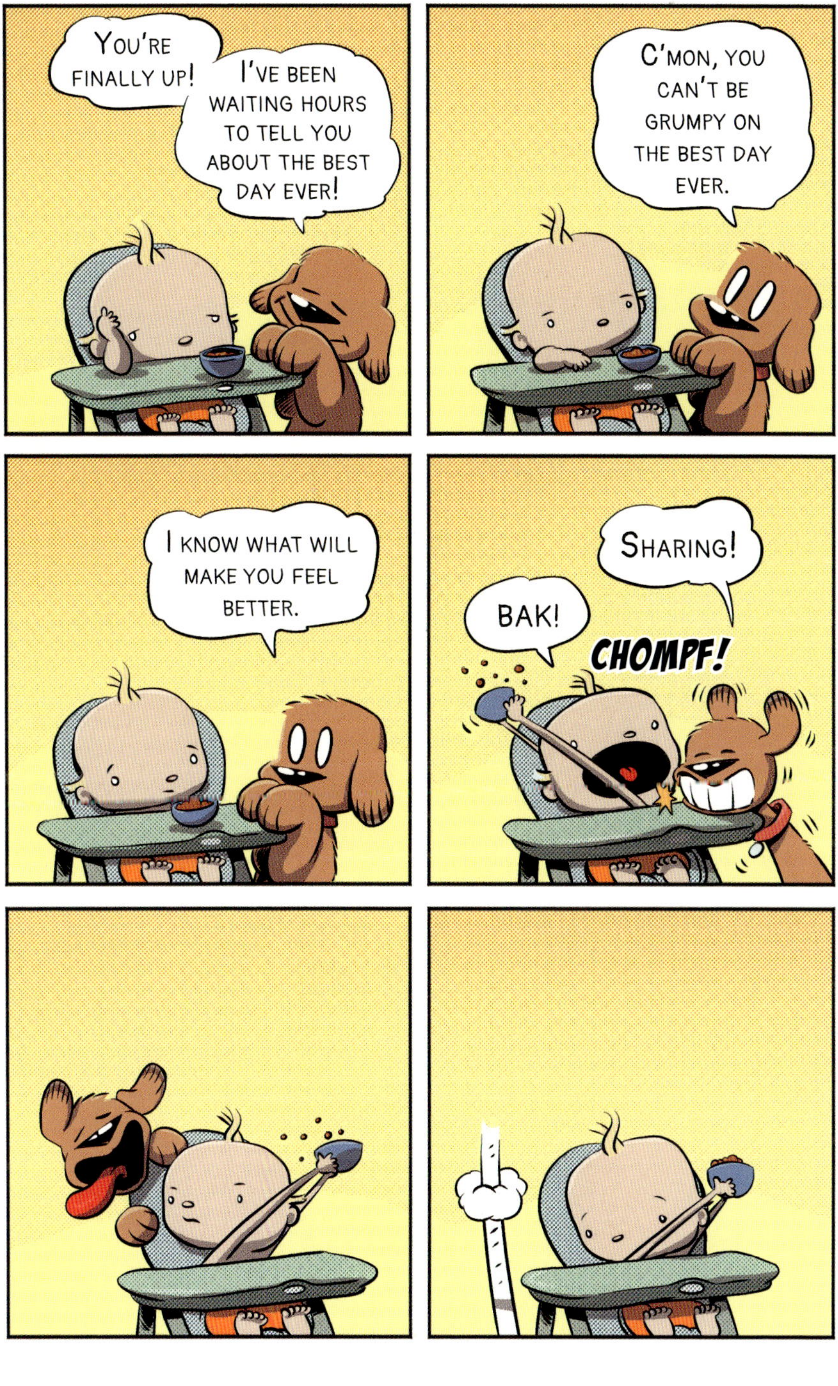
YOU'RE FINALLY UP!
I'VE BEEN WAITING HOURS TO TELL YOU ABOUT THE BEST DAY EVER!
C'MON, YOU CAN'T BE GRUMPY ON THE BEST DAY EVER.
I KNOW WHAT WILL MAKE YOU FEEL BETTER.
SHARING!
BAK!
CHOMPF!

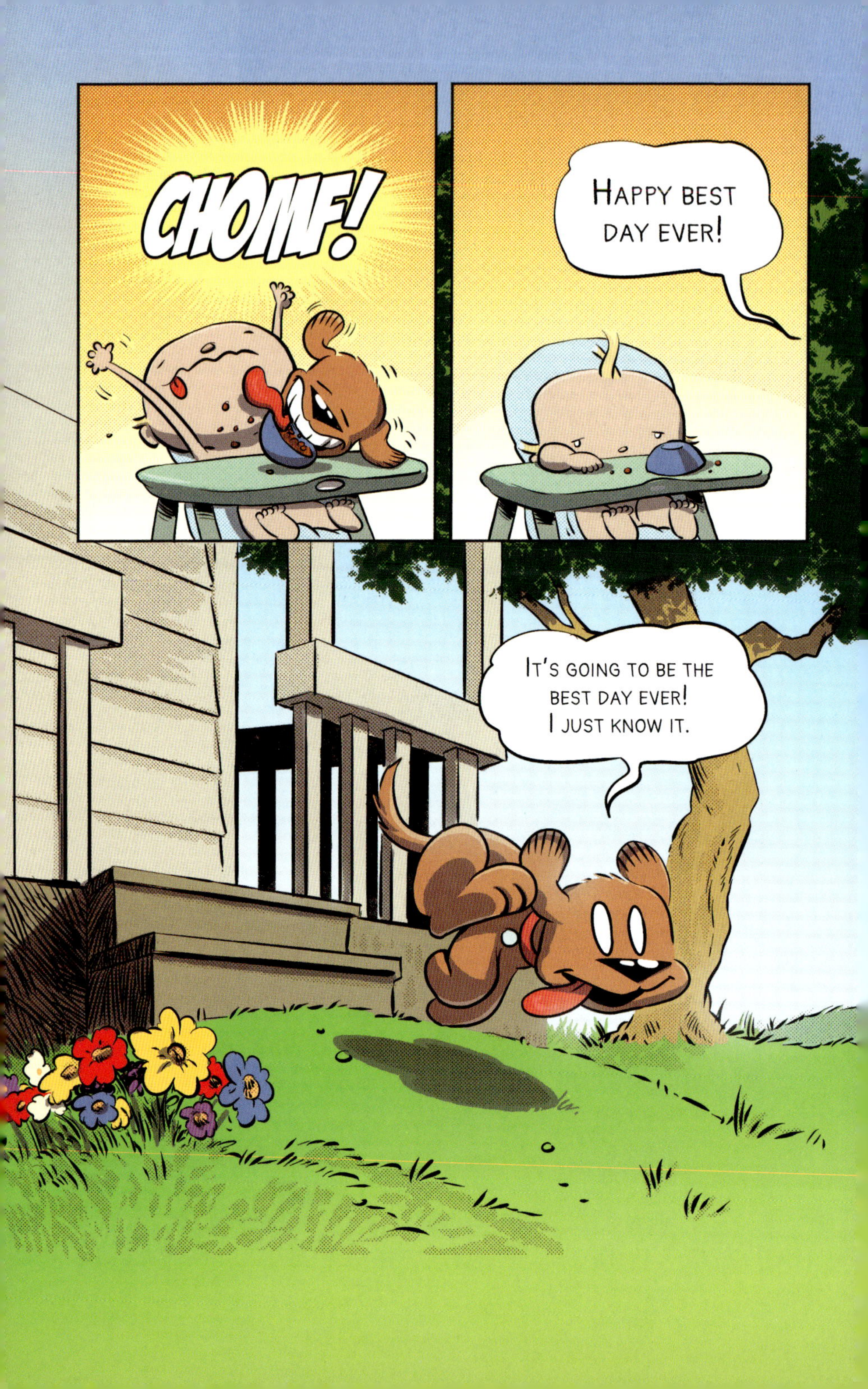
CHOMF!
HAPPY BEST DAY EVER!
IT'S GOING TO BE THE BEST DAY EVER! I JUST KNOW IT.

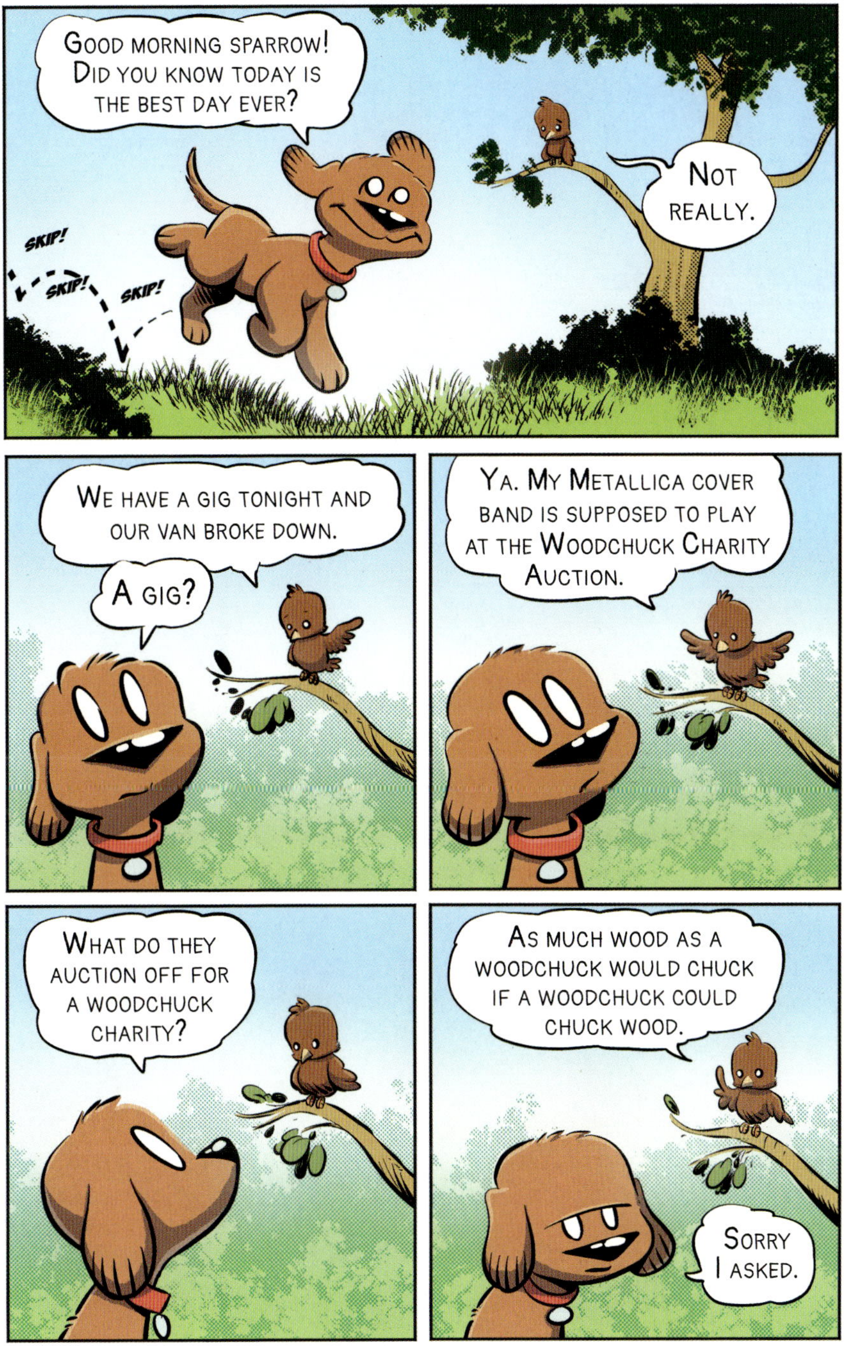
GOOD MORNING SPARROW! DID YOU KNOW TODAY IS THE BEST DAY EVER?
NOT REALLY.
SKIP! SKIP! SKIP!
WE HAVE A GIG TONIGHT AND OUR VAN BROKE DOWN.
A GIG?
YA. MY METALLICA COVER BAND IS SUPPOSED TO PLAY AT THE WOODCHUCK CHARITY AUCTION.
WHAT DO THEY AUCTION OFF FOR A WOODCHUCK CHARITY?
AS MUCH WOOD AS A WOODCHUCK WOULD CHUCK IF A WOODCHUCK COULD CHUCK WOOD.
SORRY I ASKED.

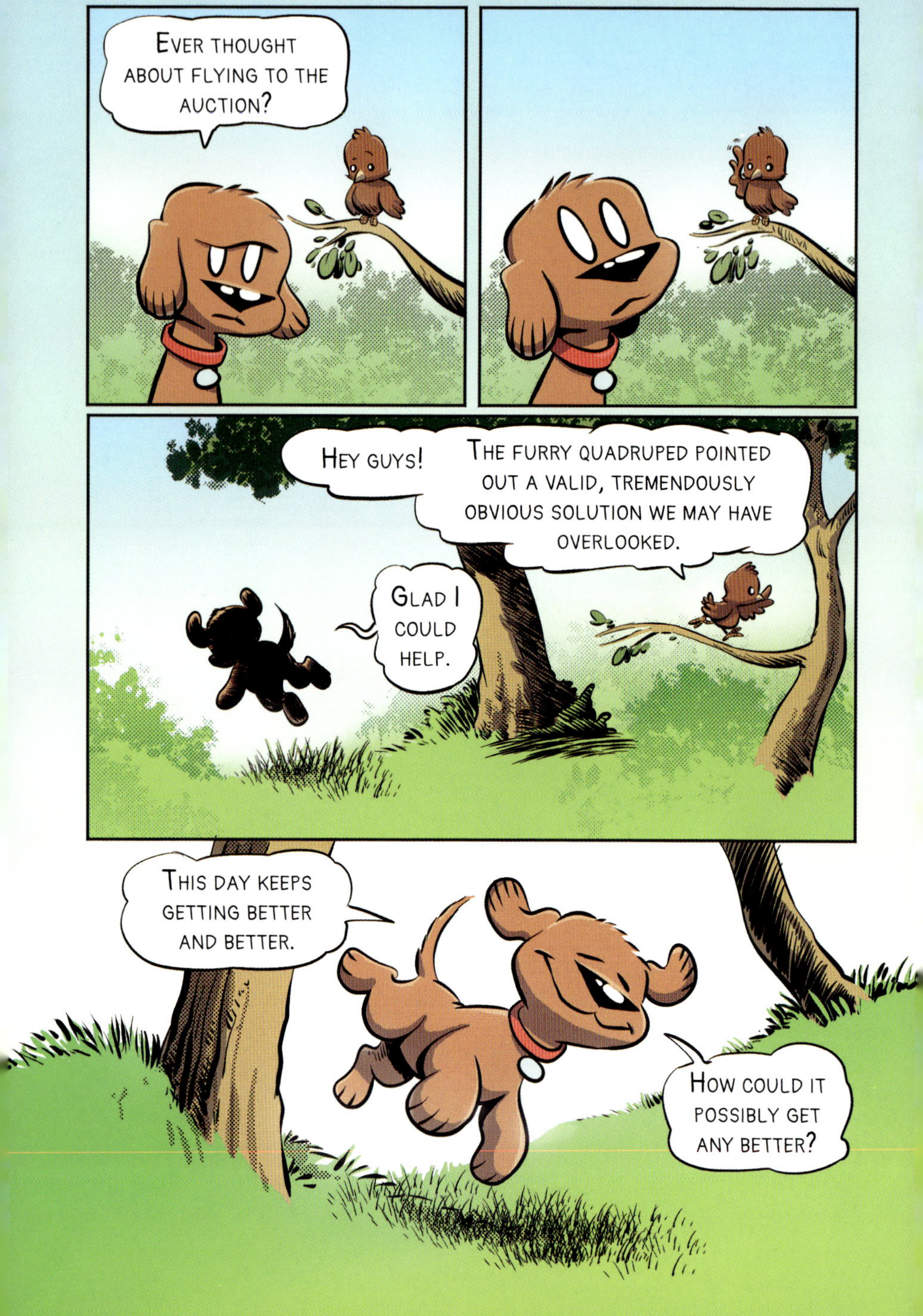
EVER THOUGHT ABOUT FLYING TO THE AUCTION?
HEY GUYS!
THE FURRY QUADRUPED POINTED OUT A VALID, TREMENDOUSLY OBVIOUS SOLUTION WE MAY HAVE OVERLOOKED.
GLAD I COULD HELP.
THIS DAY KEEPS GETTING BETTER AND BETTER.
HOW COULD IT POSSIBLY GET ANY BETTER?

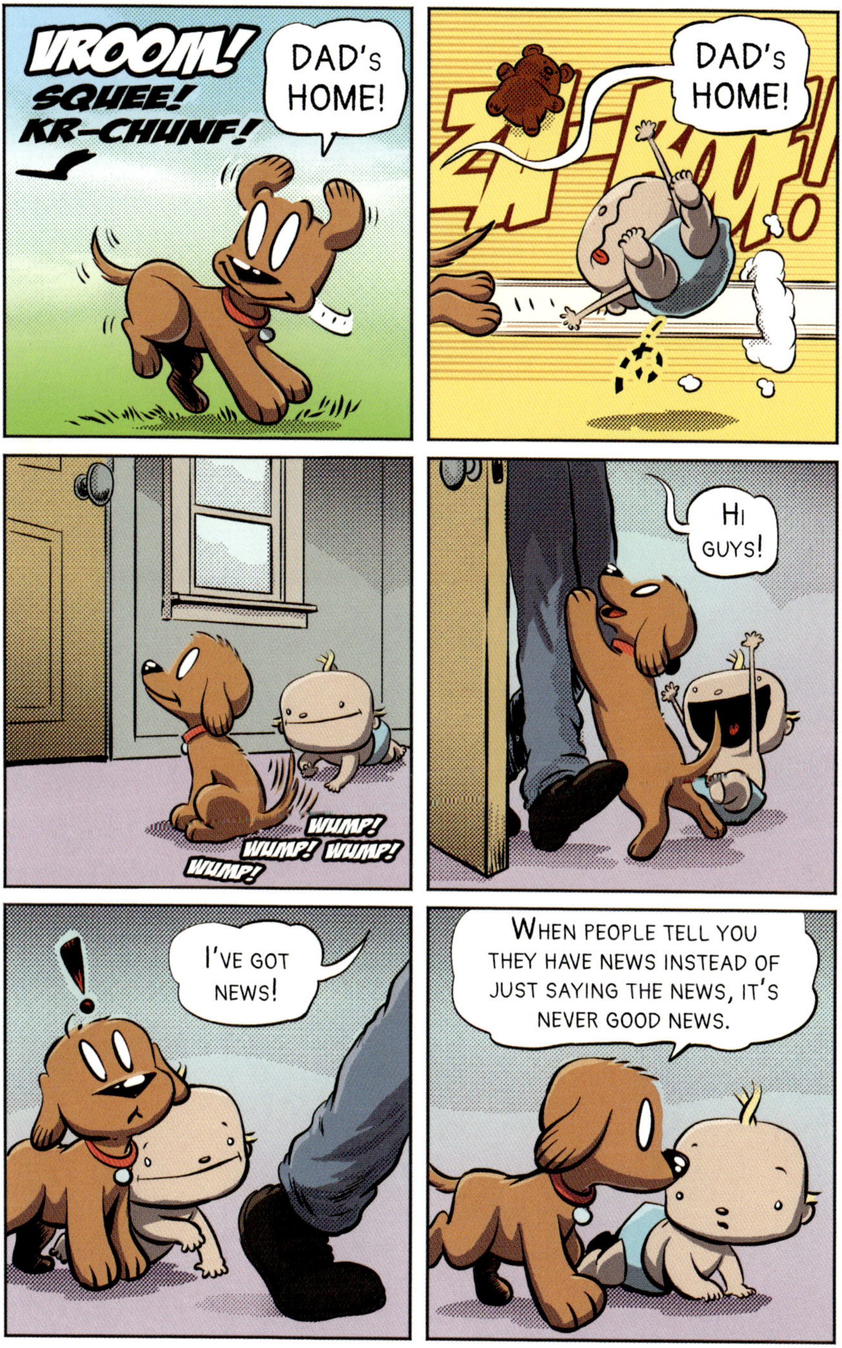
VROOM!
SQUEE!
KR-CHUNF!
DAD's HOME!
DAD's HOME!
WUMP!
WUMP! WUMP!
WUMP!
HI GUYS!
!
I'VE GOT NEWS!
WHEN PEOPLE TELL YOU THEY HAVE NEWS INSTEAD OF JUST SAYING THE NEWS, IT'S NEVER GOOD NEWS.

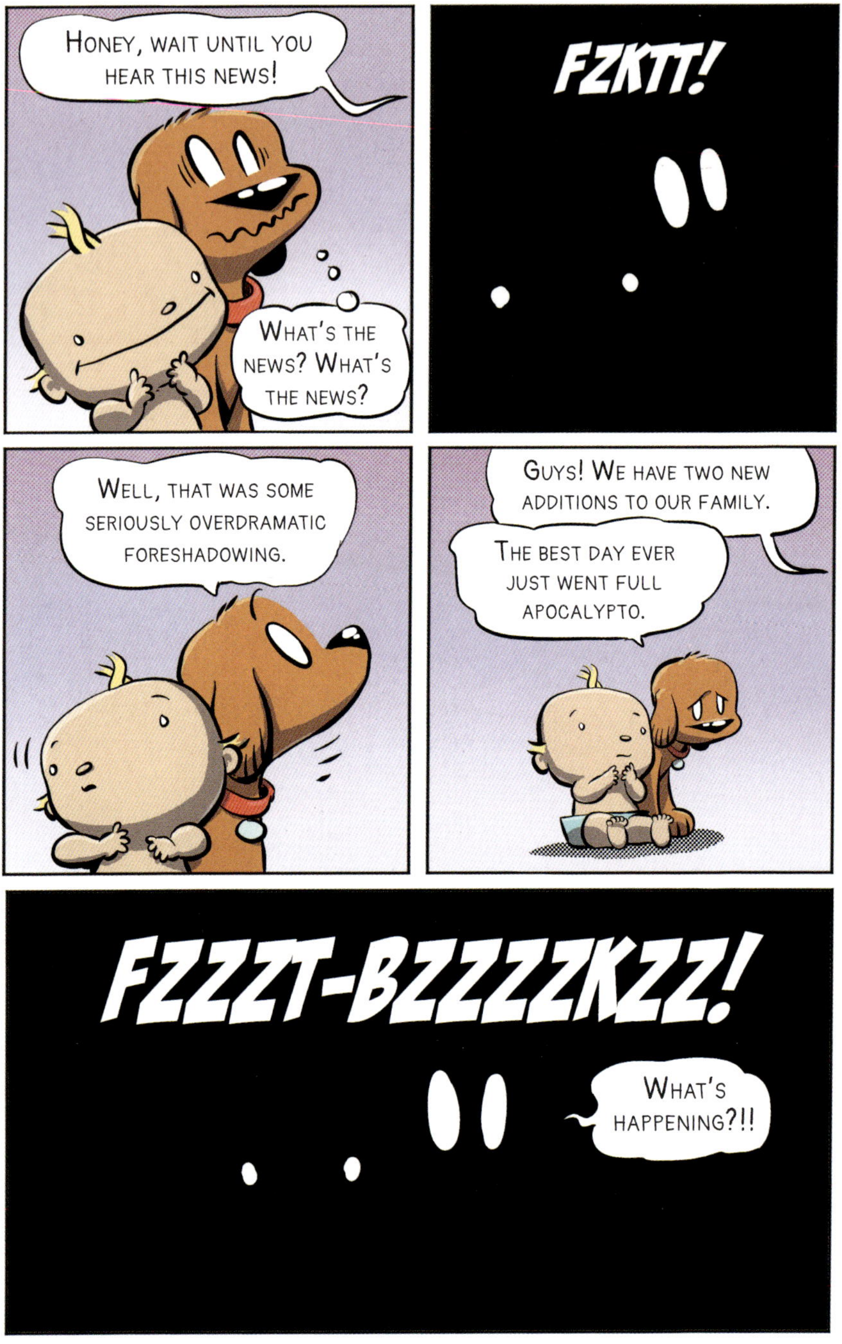
HONEY, WAIT UNTIL YOU HEAR THIS NEWS!
WHAT'S THE NEWS? WHAT'S THE NEWS?
FZKTT!
WELL, THAT WAS SOME SERIOUSLY OVERDRAMATIC FORESHADOWING.
GUYS! WE HAVE TWO NEW ADDITIONS TO OUR FAMILY.
THE BEST DAY EVER JUST WENT FULL APOCALYPTO.
FZZZT-BZZZZKZZ!
WHAT'S HAPPENING?!!

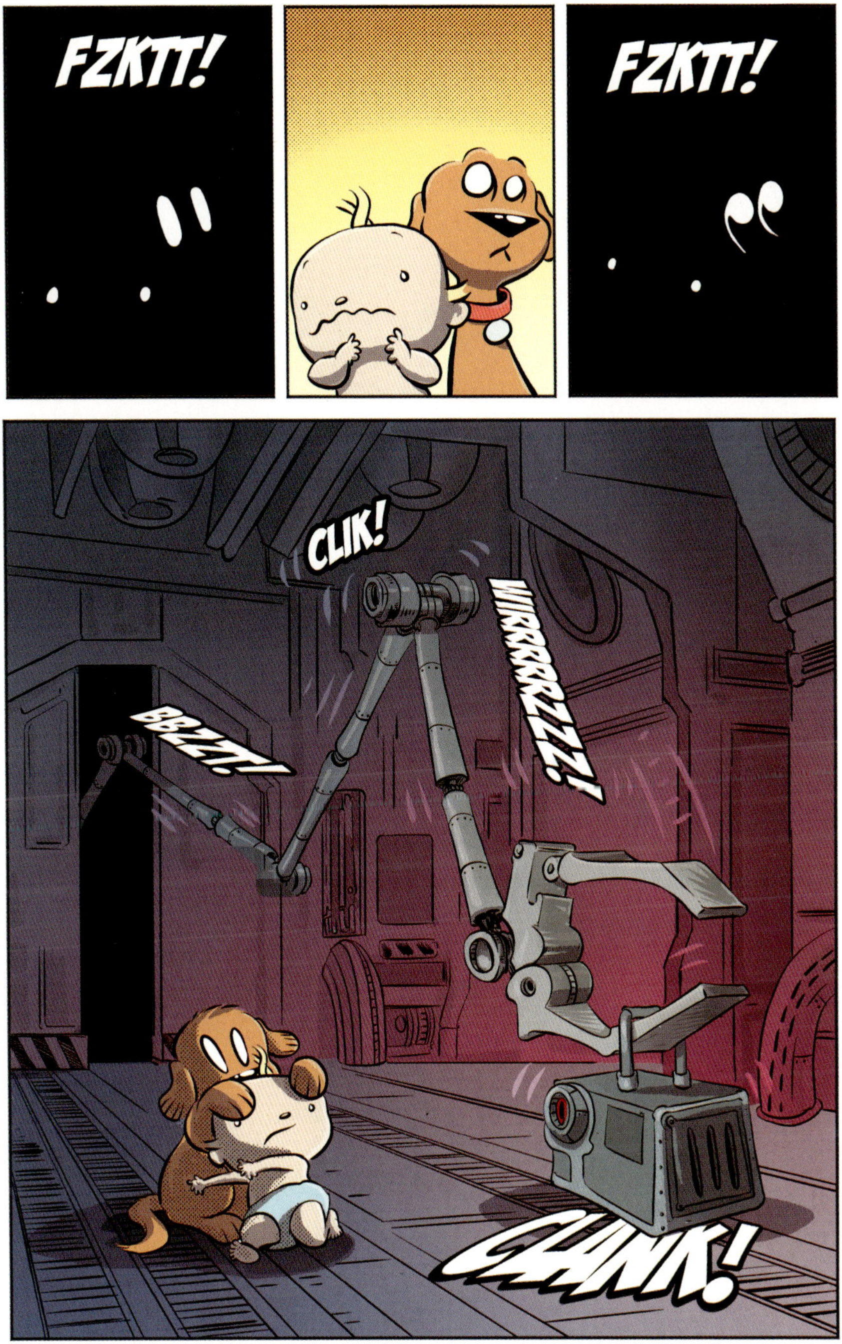
FZKTT!
FZKTT!
CLIK!
WIRRRRRZZZ!
BBZZT!
CLANK!

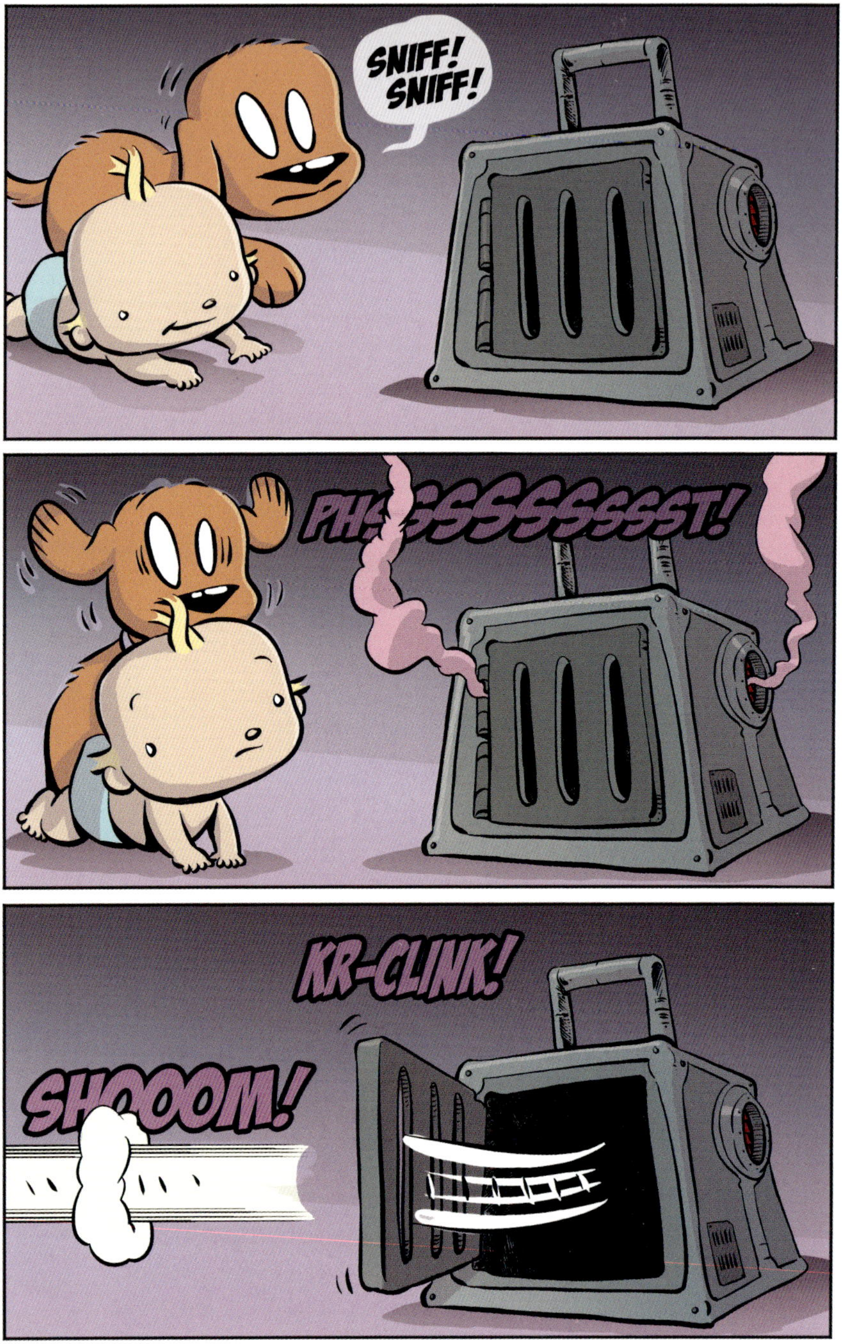
SNIFF! SNIFF!
PHSSSSSSSSST!
KR-CLINK!
SHOOOM!

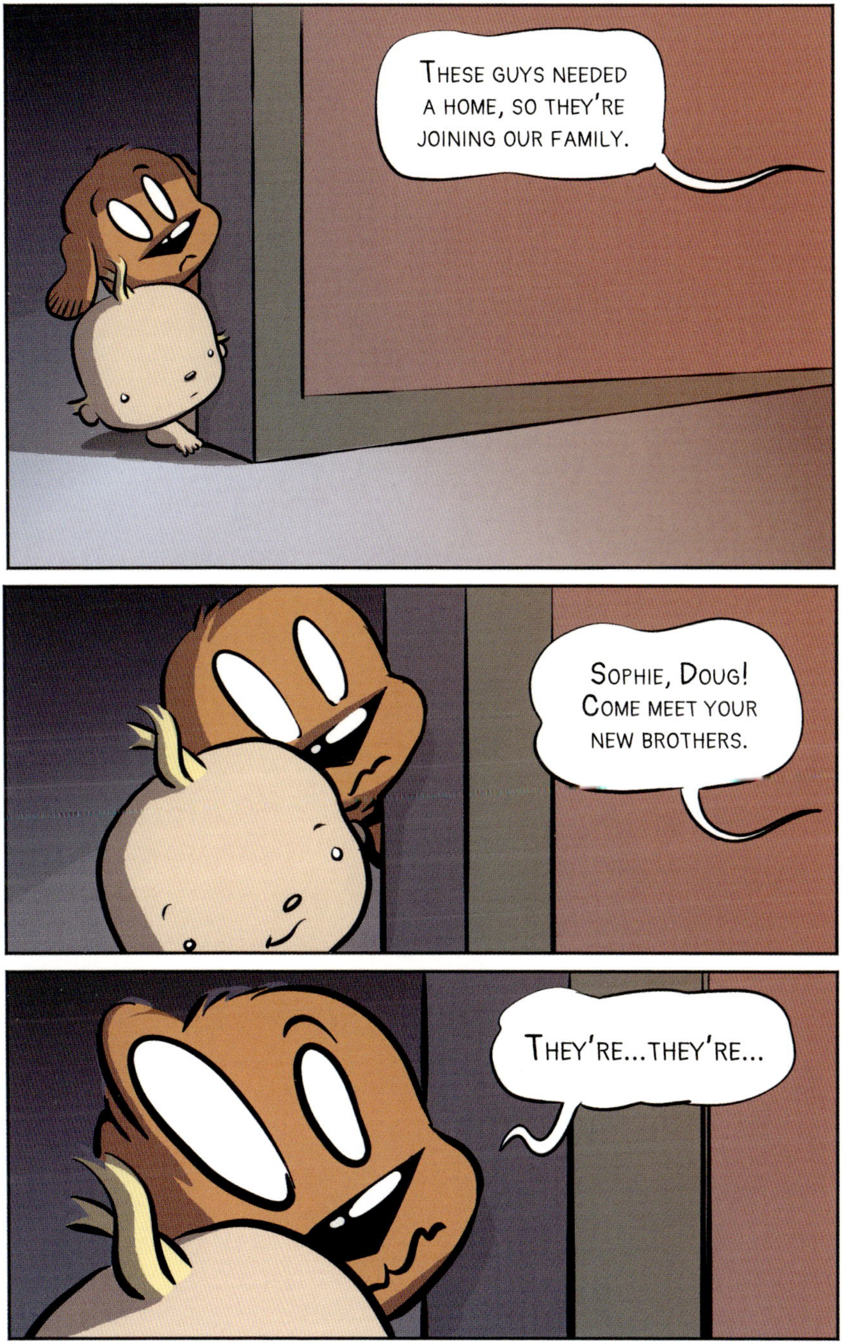
THESE GUYS NEEDED A HOME, SO THEY'RE JOINING OUR FAMILY.
SOPHIE, DOUG! COME MEET YOUR NEW BROTHERS.
THEY'RE...THEY'RE...

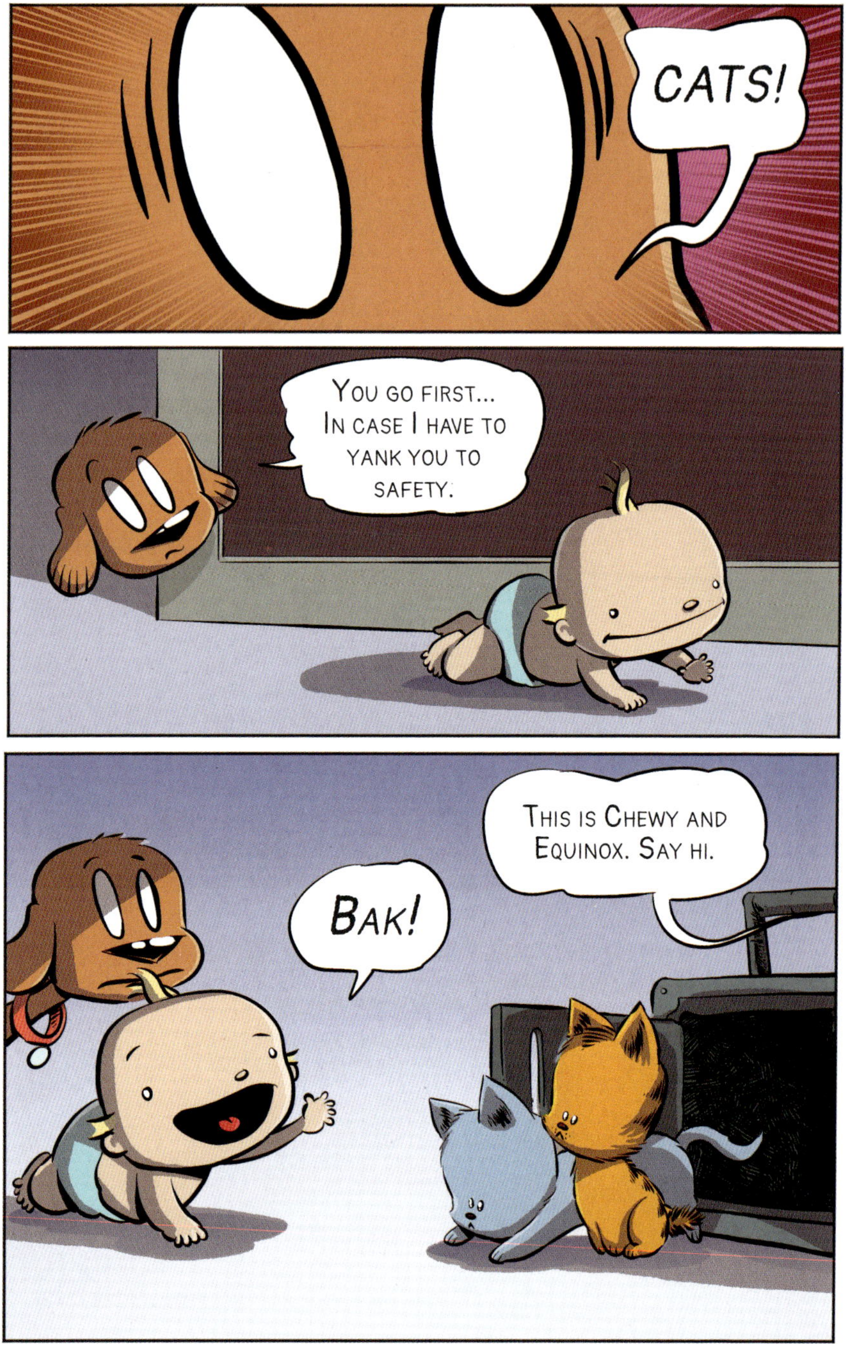
CATS!
YOU GO FIRST... IN CASE I HAVE TO YANK YOU TO SAFETY.
THIS IS CHEWY AND EQUINOX. SAY HI.
BAK!

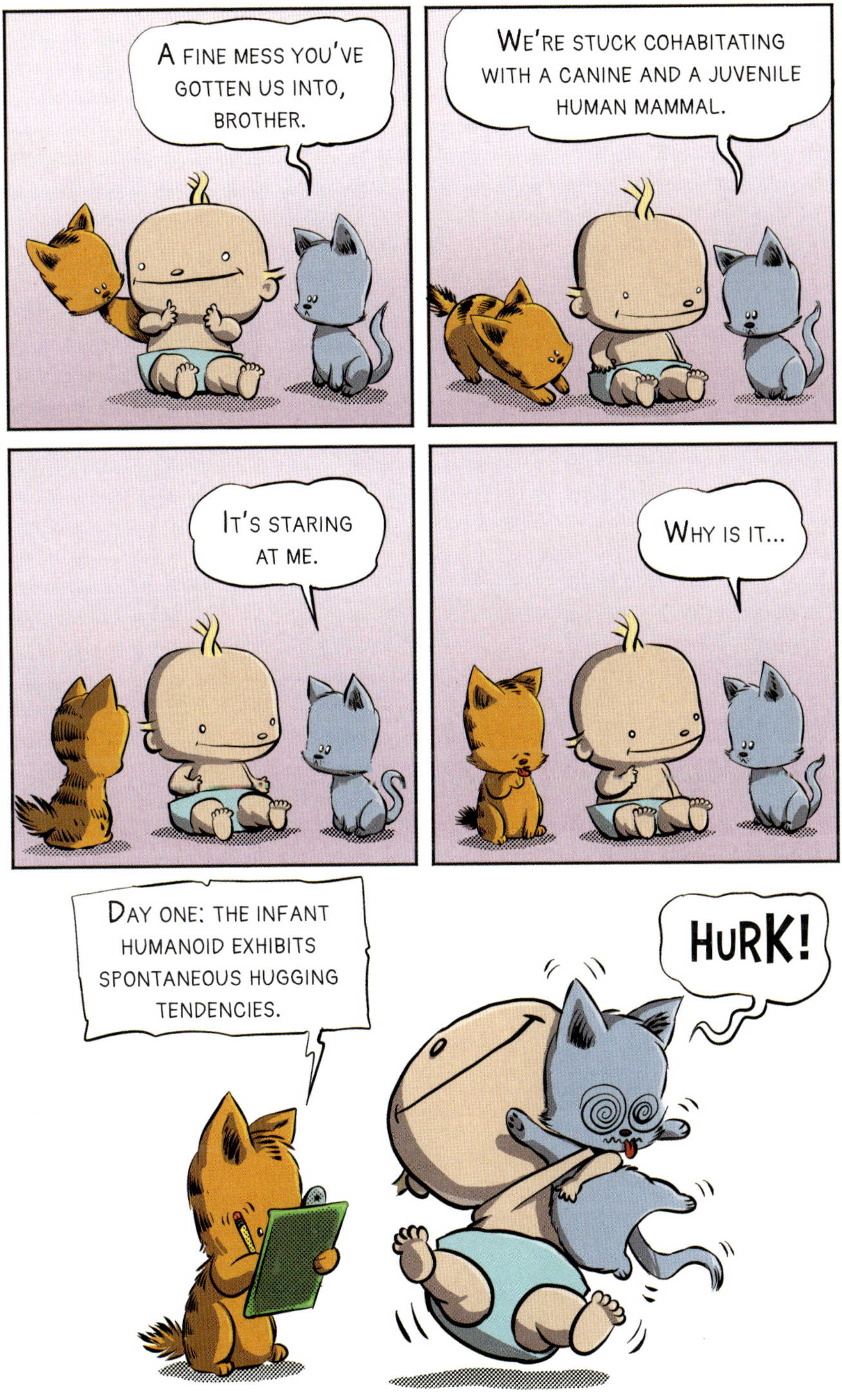
A FINE MESS YOU'VE GOTTEN US INTO, BROTHER.
WE'RE STUCK COHABITATING WITH A CANINE AND A JUVENILE HUMAN MAMMAL.
IT'S STARING AT ME.
WHY IS IT...
DAY ONE: THE INFANT HUMANOID EXHIBITS SPONTANEOUS HUGGING TENDENCIES.
HURK!

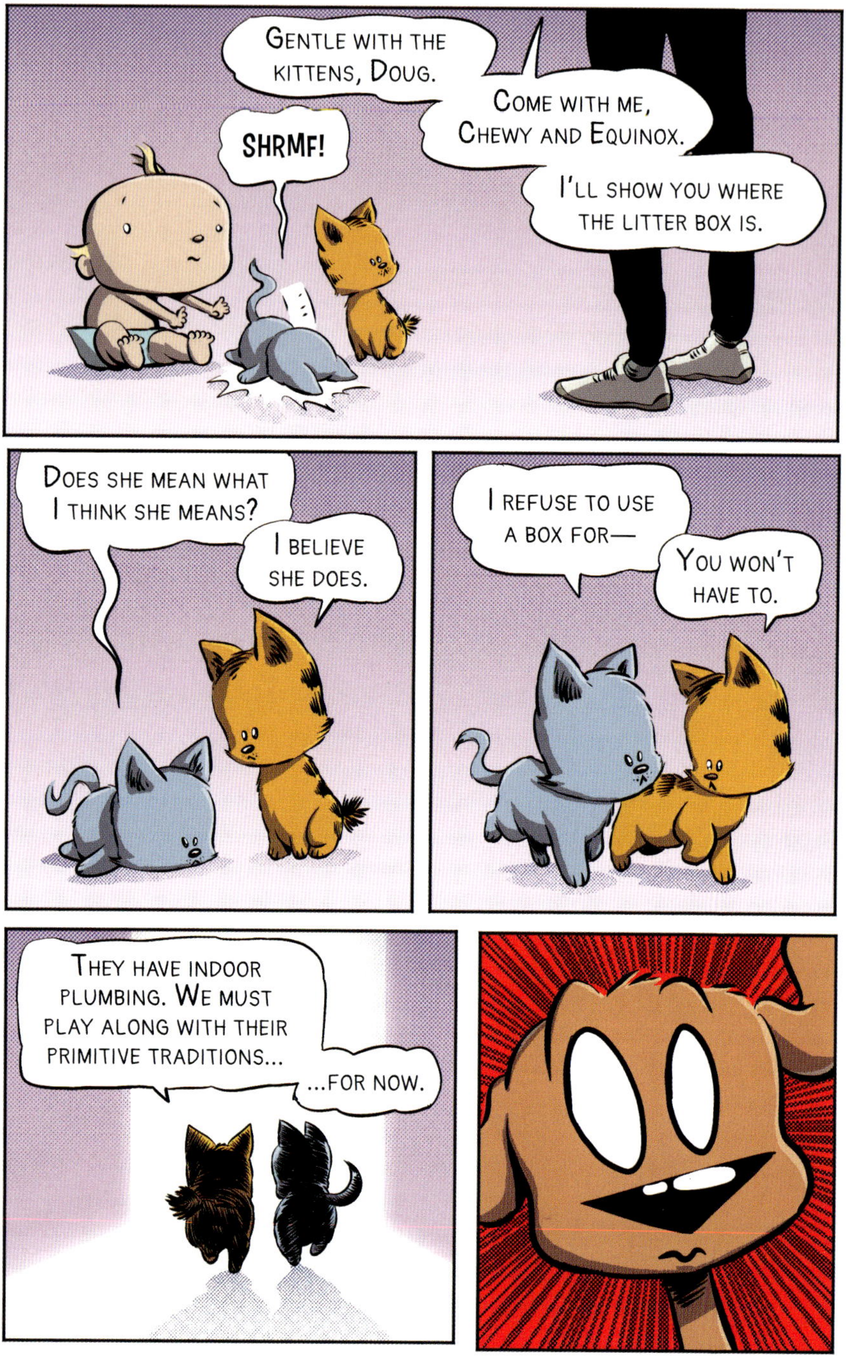
GENTLE WITH THE KITTENS, DOUG.
COME WITH ME, CHEWY AND EQUINOX.
SHRMF!
I'LL SHOW YOU WHERE THE LITTER BOX IS.
DOES SHE MEAN WHAT I THINK SHE MEANS?
I BELIEVE SHE DOES.
I REFUSE TO USE A BOX FOR—
YOU WON'T HAVE TO.
THEY HAVE INDOOR PLUMBING. WE MUST PLAY ALONG WITH THEIR PRIMITIVE TRADITIONS...
...FOR NOW.

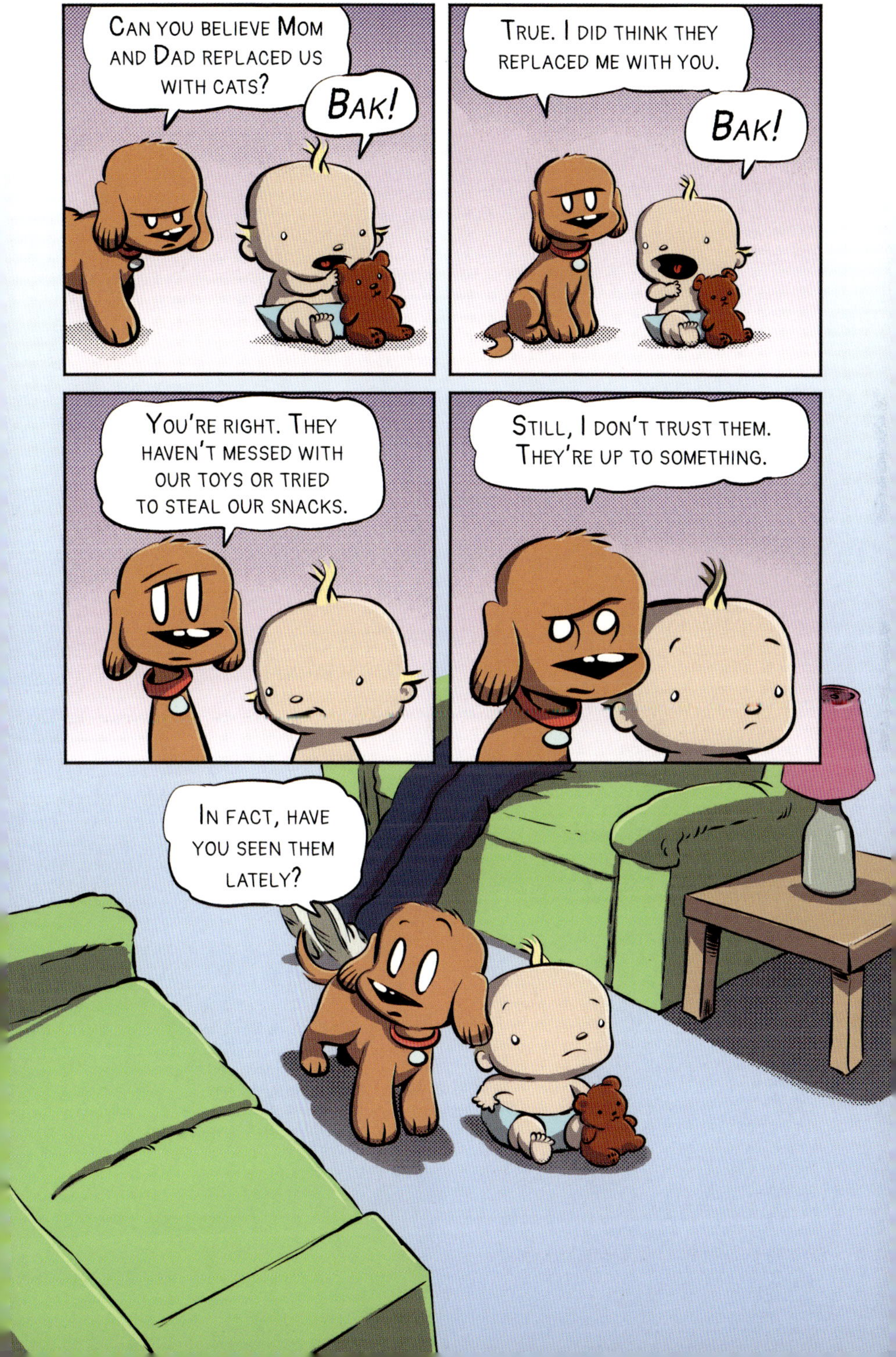
CAN YOU BELIEVE MOM AND DAD REPLACED US WITH CATS?
BAK!
TRUE. I DID THINK THEY REPLACED ME WITH YOU.
BAK!
YOU'RE RIGHT. THEY HAVEN'T MESSED WITH OUR TOYS OR TRIED TO STEAL OUR SNACKS.
STILL, I DON'T TRUST THEM. THEY'RE UP TO SOMETHING.
IN FACT, HAVE YOU SEEN THEM LATELY?

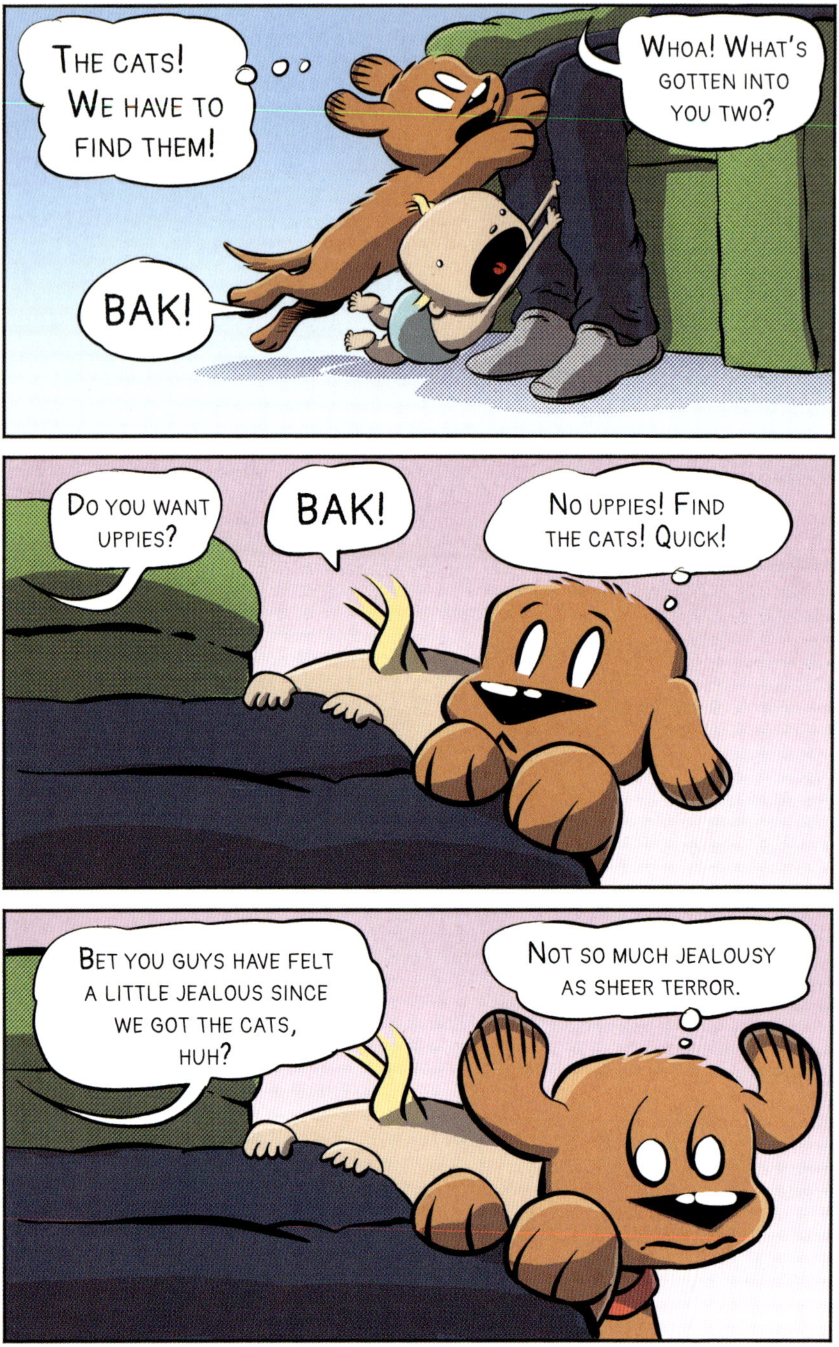
THE CATS! WE HAVE TO FIND THEM!
WHOA! WHAT'S GOTTEN INTO YOU TWO?
BAK!
DO YOU WANT UPPIES?
BAK!
NO UPPIES! FIND THE CATS! QUICK!
BET YOU GUYS HAVE FELT A LITTLE JEALOUS SINCE WE GOT THE CATS, HUH?
NOT SO MUCH JEALOUSY AS SHEER TERROR.

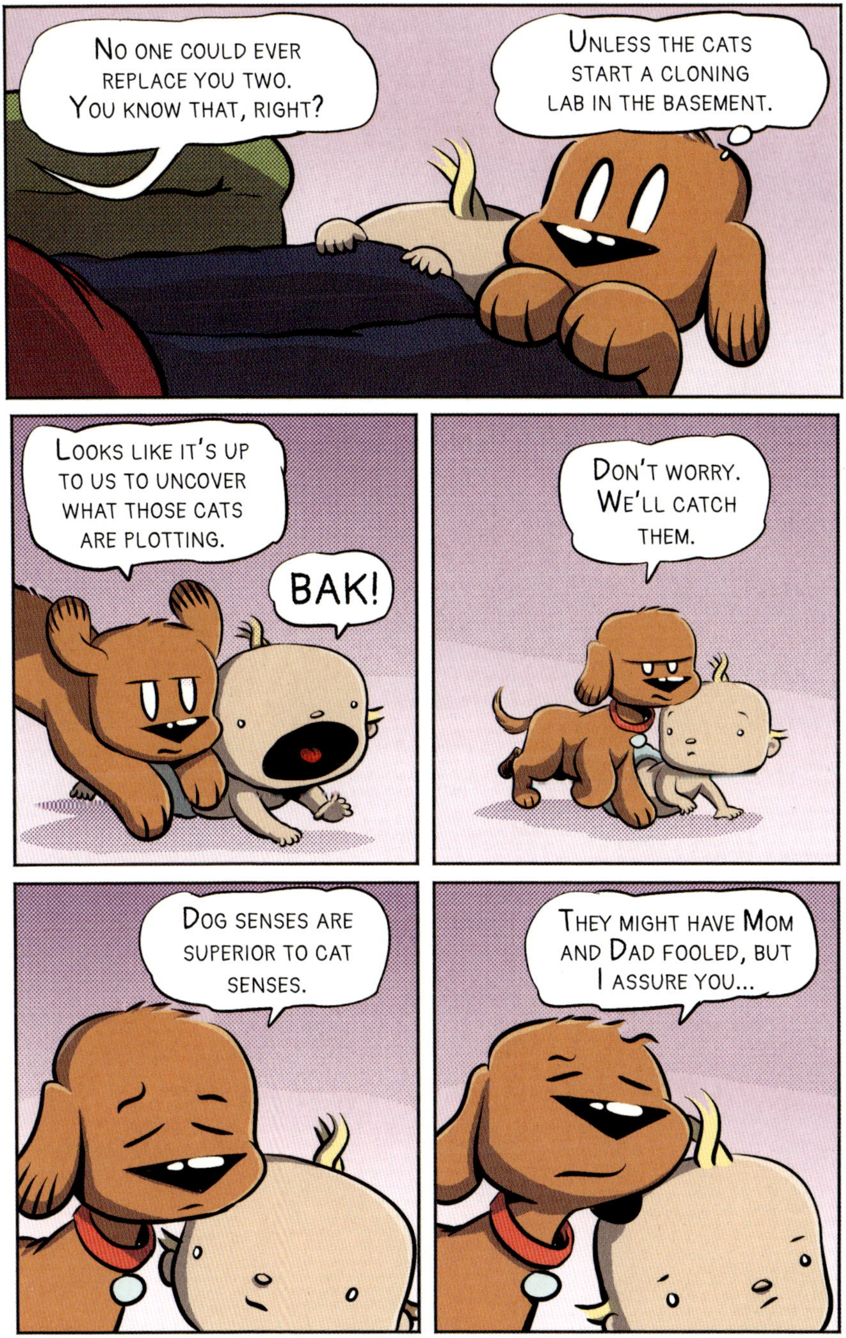
NO ONE COULD EVER REPLACE YOU TWO. YOU KNOW THAT, RIGHT?
UNLESS THE CATS START A CLONING LAB IN THE BASEMENT.
LOOKS LIKE IT'S UP TO US TO UNCOVER WHAT THOSE CATS ARE PLOTTING.
BAK!
DON'T WORRY. WE'LL CATCH THEM.
DOG SENSES ARE SUPERIOR TO CAT SENSES.
THEY MIGHT HAVE MOM AND DAD FOOLED, BUT I ASSURE YOU...

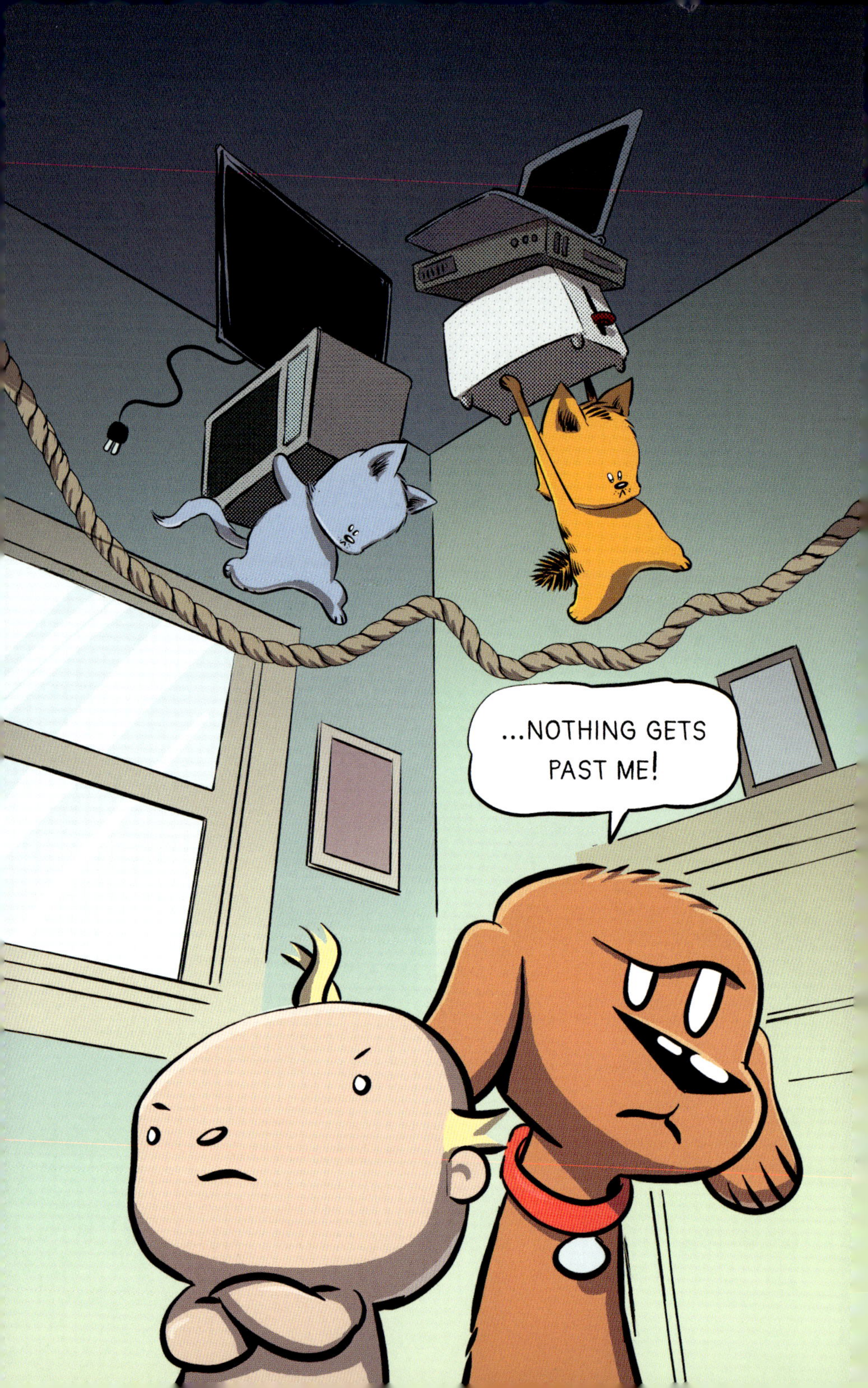
...NOTHING GETS PAST ME!

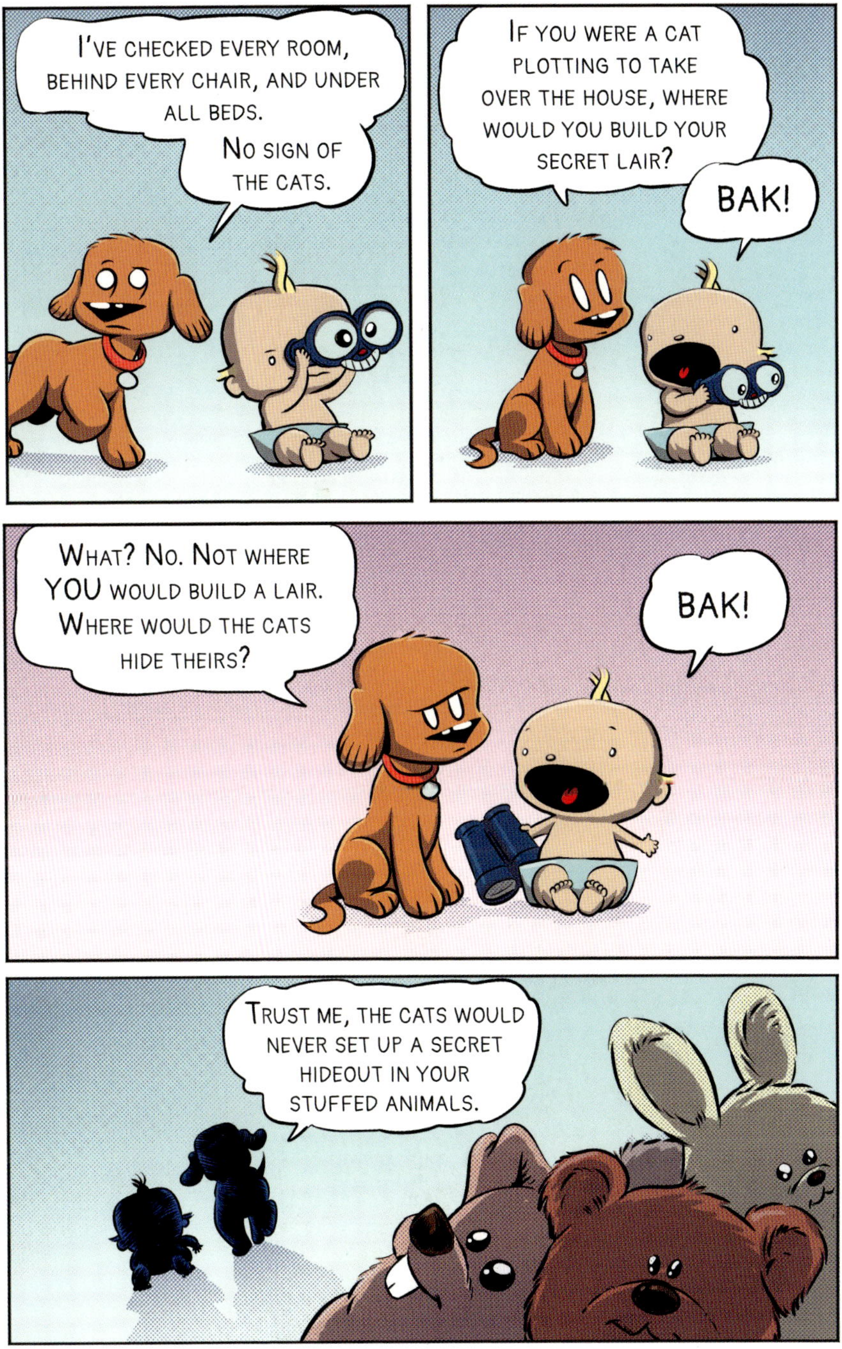
I'VE CHECKED EVERY ROOM, BEHIND EVERY CHAIR, AND UNDER ALL BEDS.
NO SIGN OF THE CATS.
IF YOU WERE A CAT PLOTTING TO TAKE OVER THE HOUSE, WHERE WOULD YOU BUILD YOUR SECRET LAIR?
BAK!
WHAT? NO. NOT WHERE YOU WOULD BUILD A LAIR. WHERE WOULD THE CATS HIDE THEIRS?
BAK!
TRUST ME, THE CATS WOULD NEVER SET UP A SECRET HIDEOUT IN YOUR STUFFED ANIMALS.

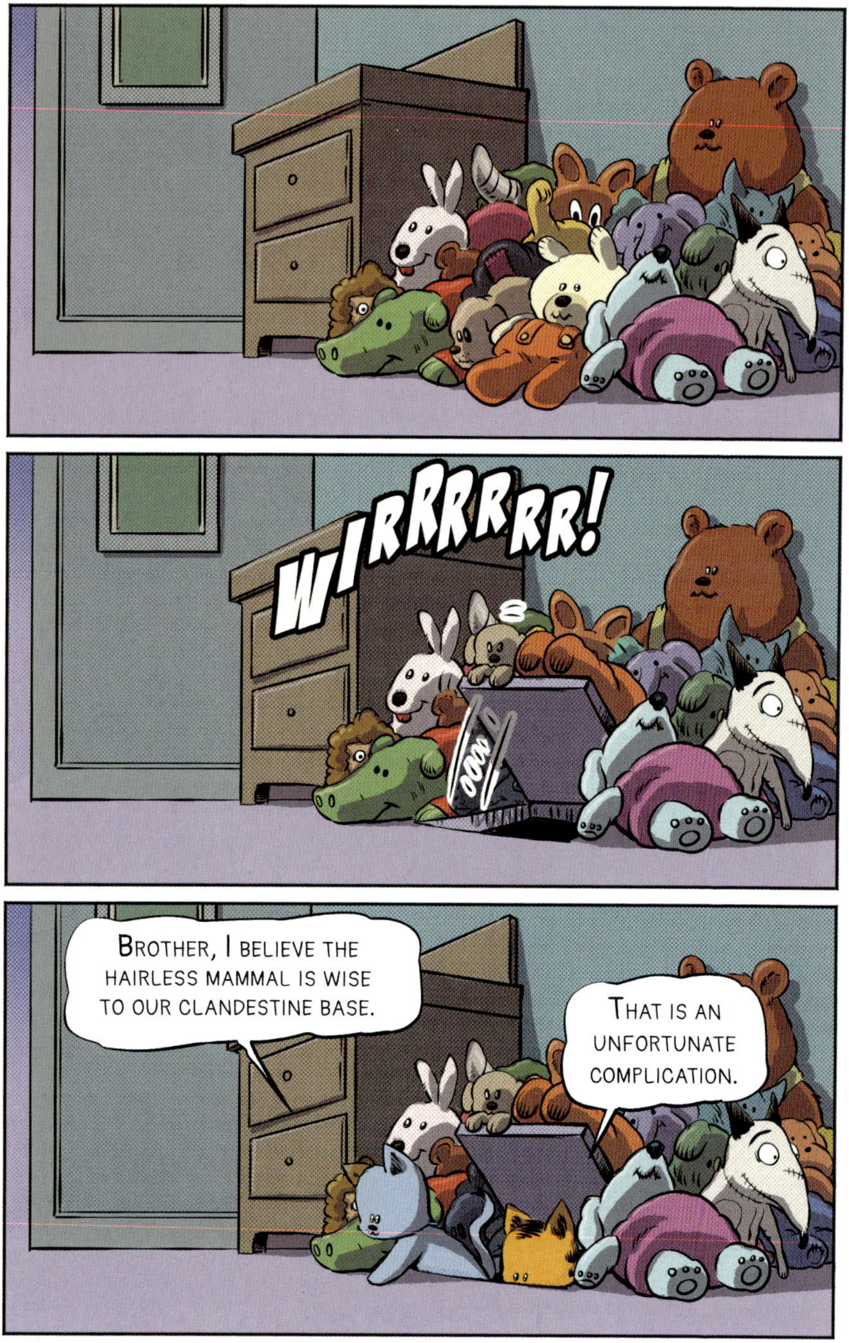
WIRRRRRRR!
BROTHER, I BELIEVE THE HAIRLESS MAMMAL IS WISE TO OUR CLANDESTINE BASE.
THAT IS AN UNFORTUNATE COMPLICATION.

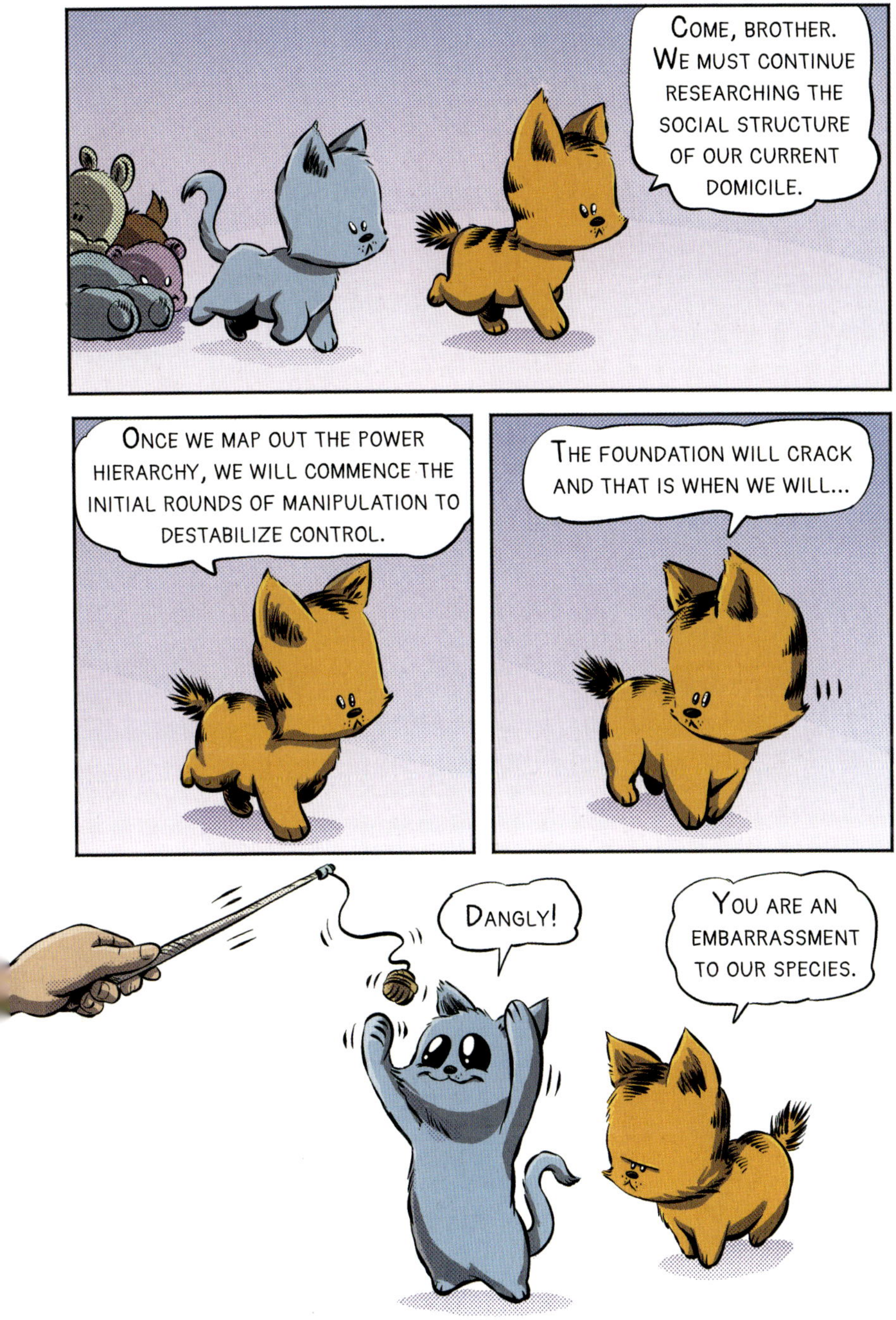
COME, BROTHER. WE MUST CONTINUE RESEARCHING THE SOCIAL STRUCTURE OF OUR CURRENT DOMICILE.
ONCE WE MAP OUT THE POWER HIERARCHY, WE WILL COMMENCE THE INITIAL ROUNDS OF MANIPULATION TO DESTABILIZE CONTROL.
THE FOUNDATION WILL CRACK AND THAT IS WHEN WE WILL...
DANGLY!
YOU ARE AN EMBARRASSMENT TO OUR SPECIES.

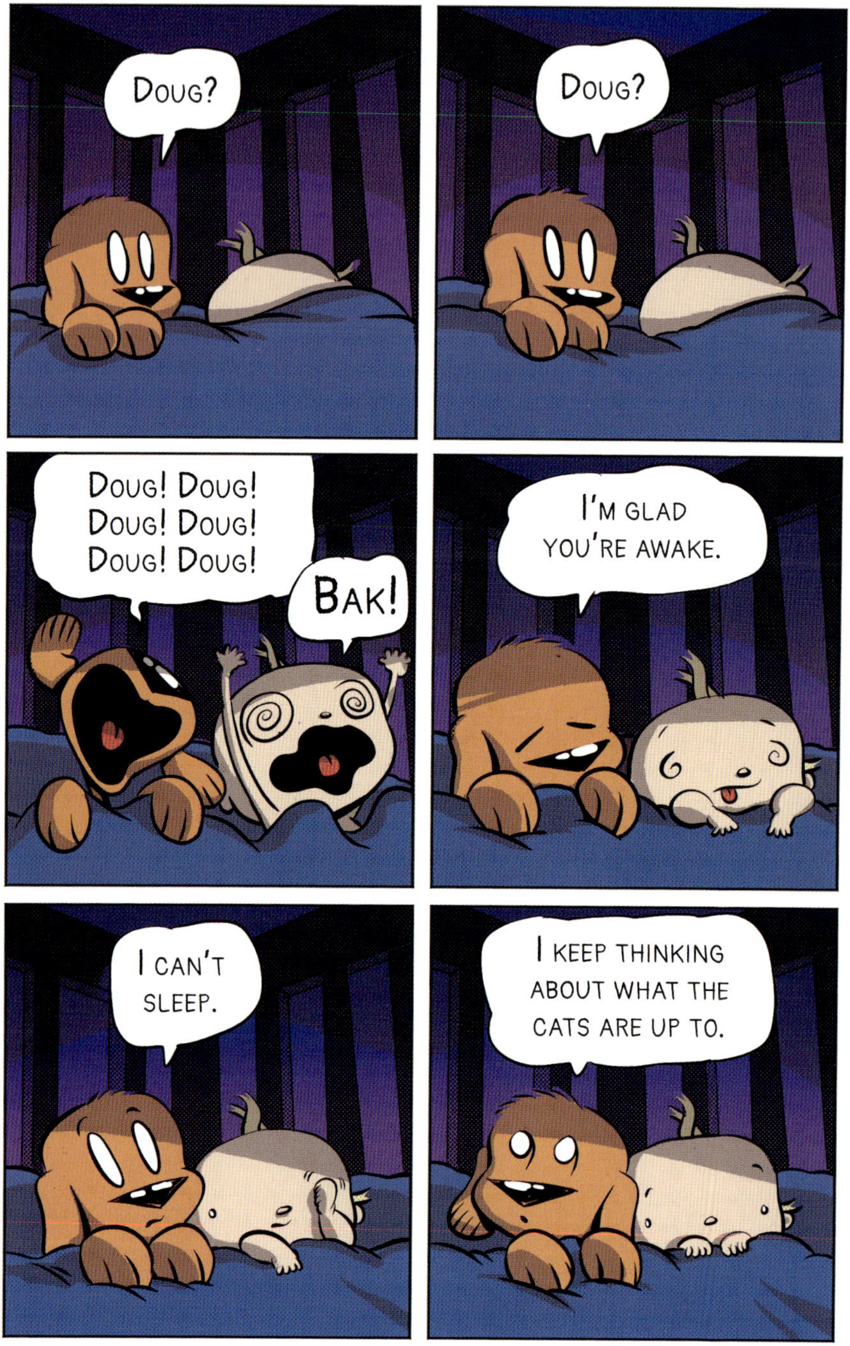
Doug?
Doug?
Doug! Doug! Doug! Doug! Doug! Doug!
Bak!
I'm glad you're awake.
I can't sleep.
I keep thinking about what the cats are up to.

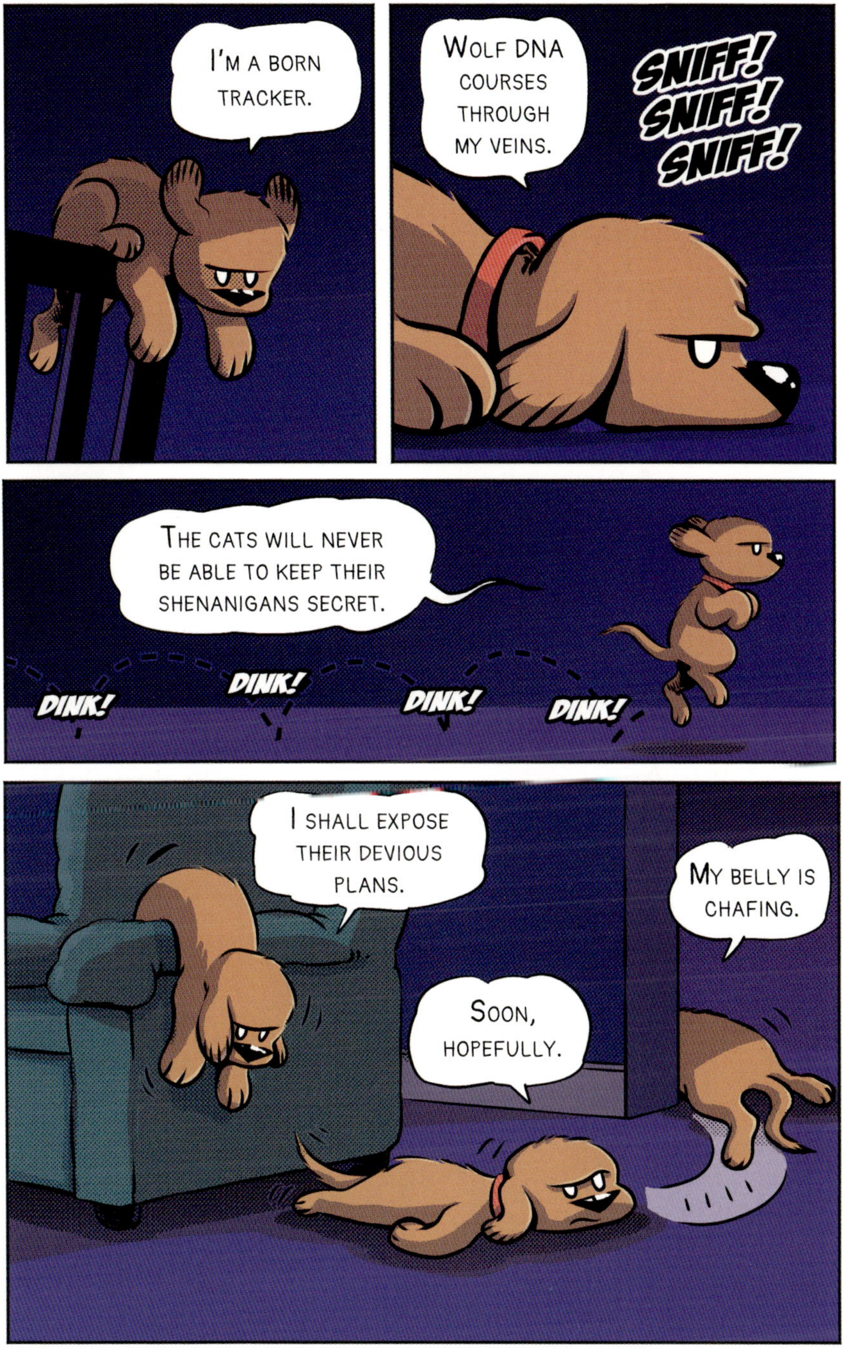

I'M A BORN TRACKER.
WOLF DNA COURSES THROUGH MY VEINS.
SNIFF! SNIFF! SNIFF!
THE CATS WILL NEVER BE ABLE TO KEEP THEIR SHENANIGANS SECRET.
DINK!
DINK!
DINK!
DINK!
I SHALL EXPOSE THEIR DEVIOUS PLANS.
MY BELLY IS CHAFING.
SOON, HOPEFULLY.

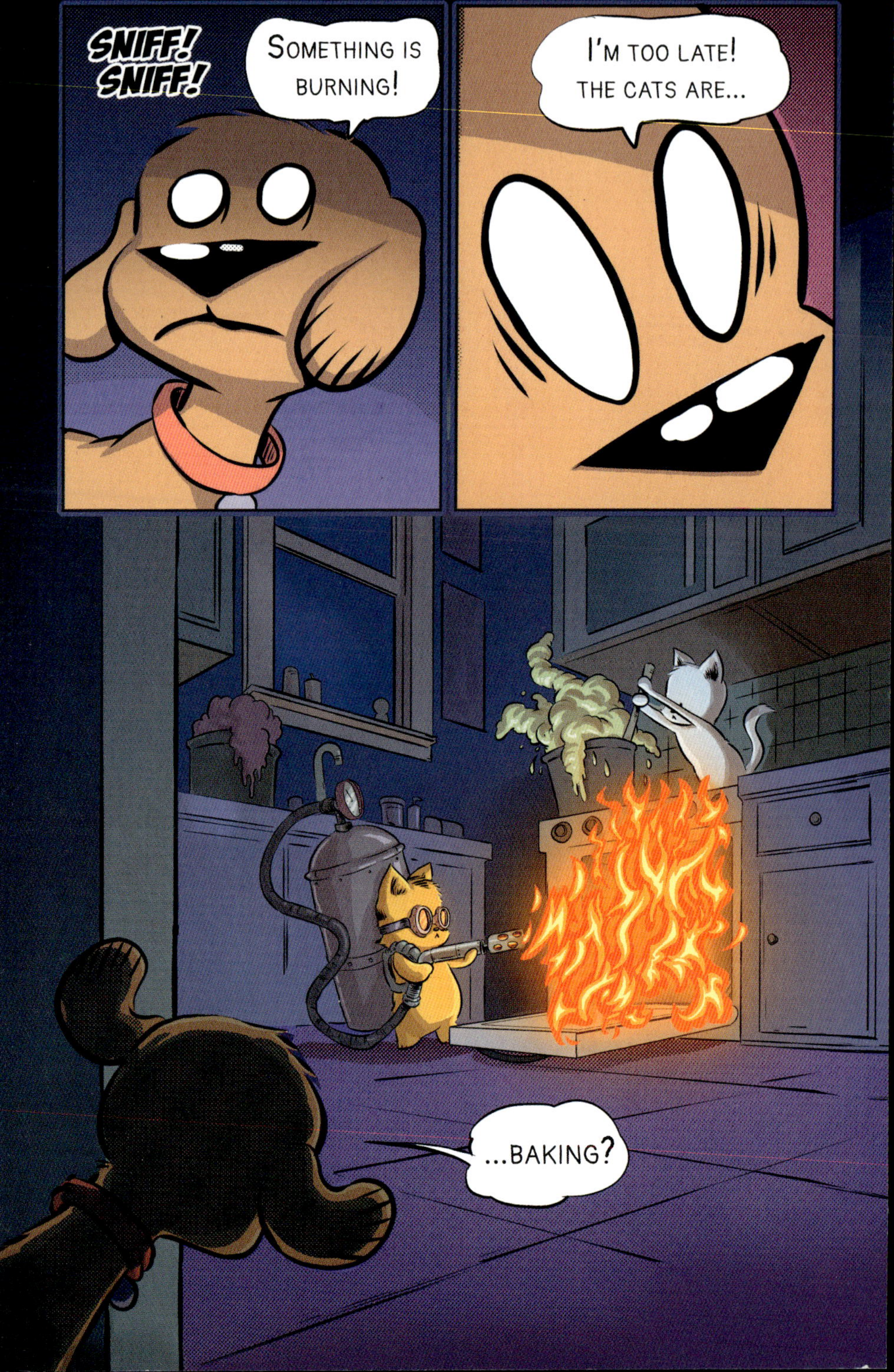
SNIFF! SNIFF!
SOMETHING IS BURNING!
I'M TOO LATE! THE CATS ARE...
...BAKING?

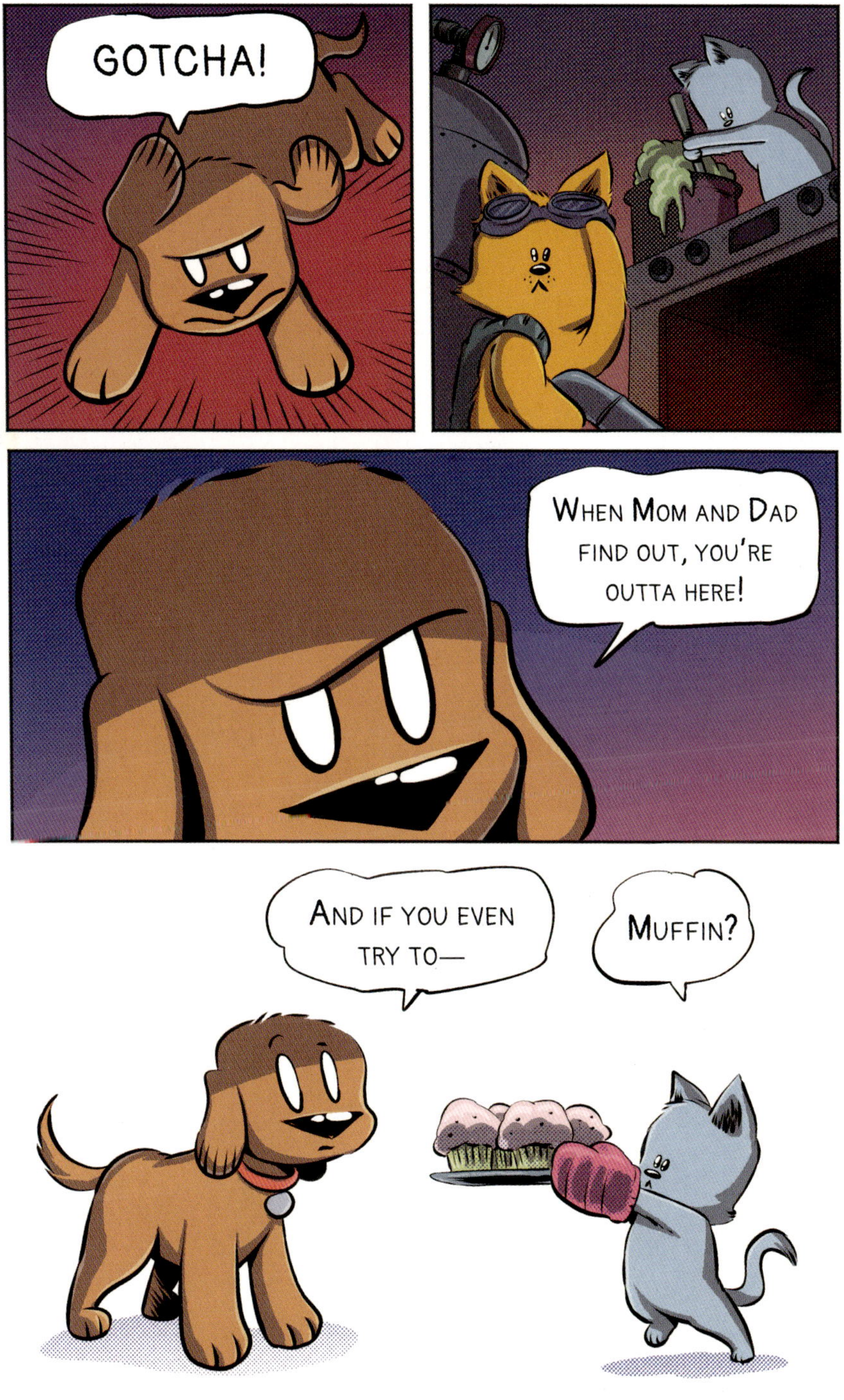
GOTCHA!
WHEN MOM AND DAD FIND OUT, YOU'RE OUTTA HERE!
AND IF YOU EVEN TRY TO—
MUFFIN?

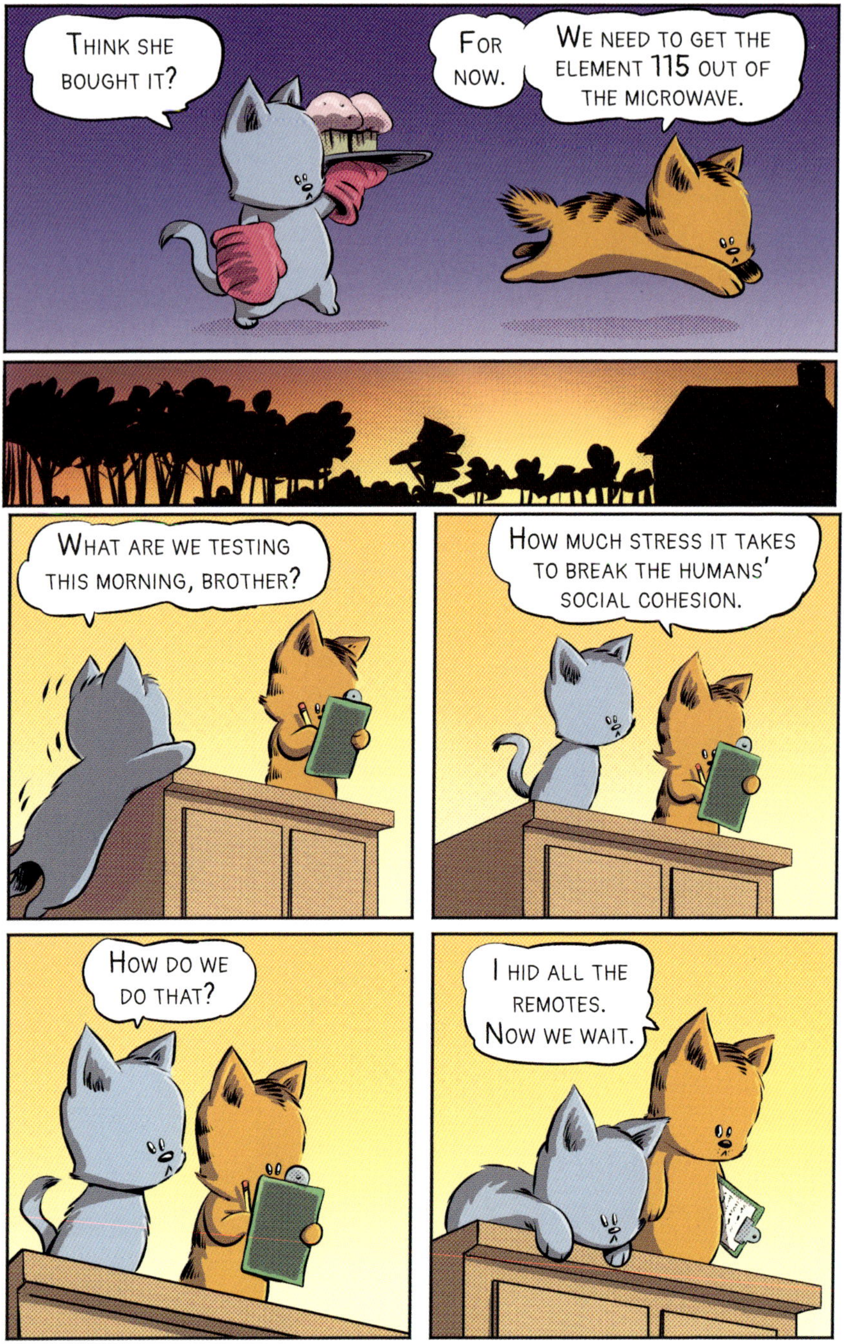

THINK SHE BOUGHT IT?
FOR NOW.
WE NEED TO GET THE ELEMENT 115 OUT OF THE MICROWAVE.
WHAT ARE WE TESTING THIS MORNING, BROTHER?
HOW MUCH STRESS IT TAKES TO BREAK THE HUMANS' SOCIAL COHESION.
HOW DO WE DO THAT?
I HID ALL THE REMOTES. NOW WE WAIT.

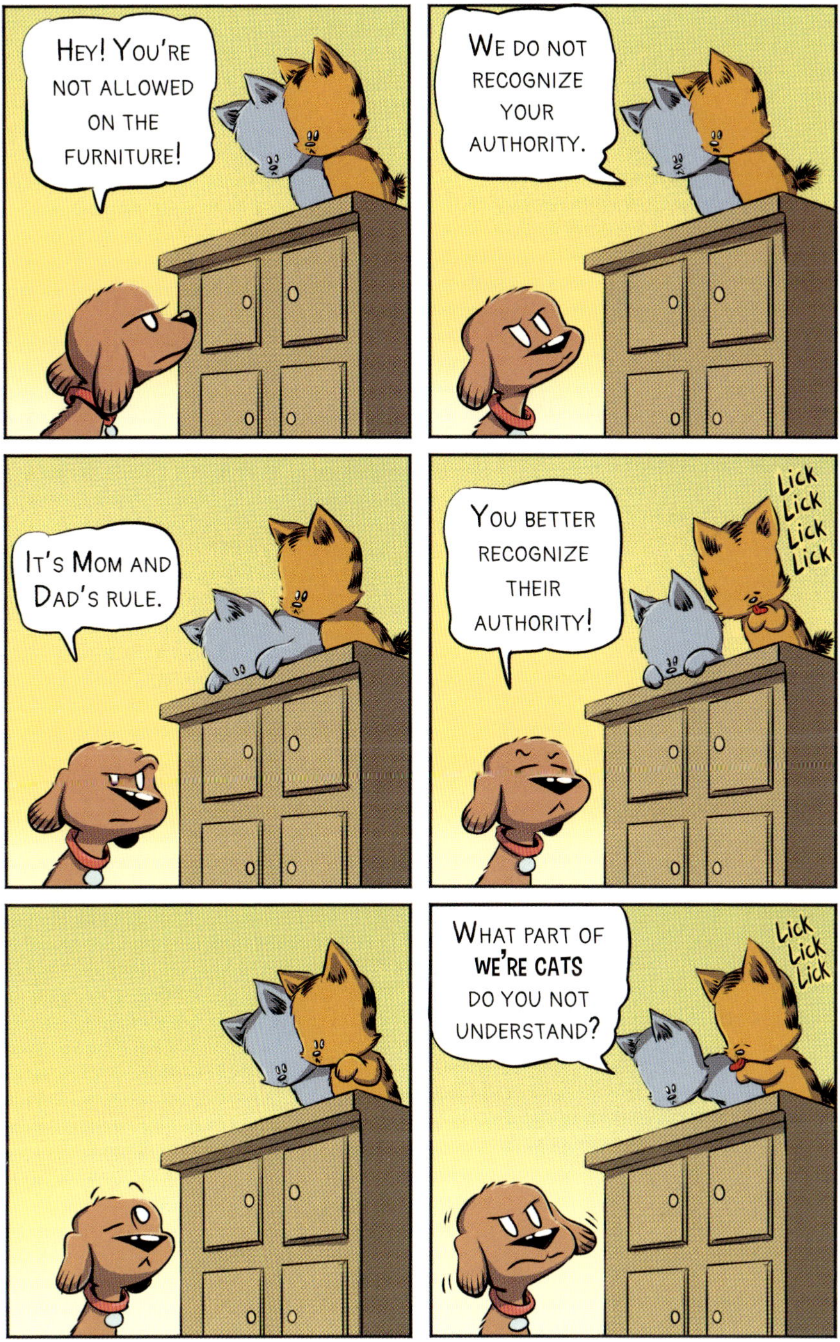
HEY! YOU'RE NOT ALLOWED ON THE FURNITURE!
WE DO NOT RECOGNIZE YOUR AUTHORITY.
IT'S MOM AND DAD'S RULE.
YOU BETTER RECOGNIZE THEIR AUTHORITY!
Lick Lick Lick Lick
WHAT PART OF **WE'RE CATS** DO YOU NOT UNDERSTAND?
Lick Lick Lick

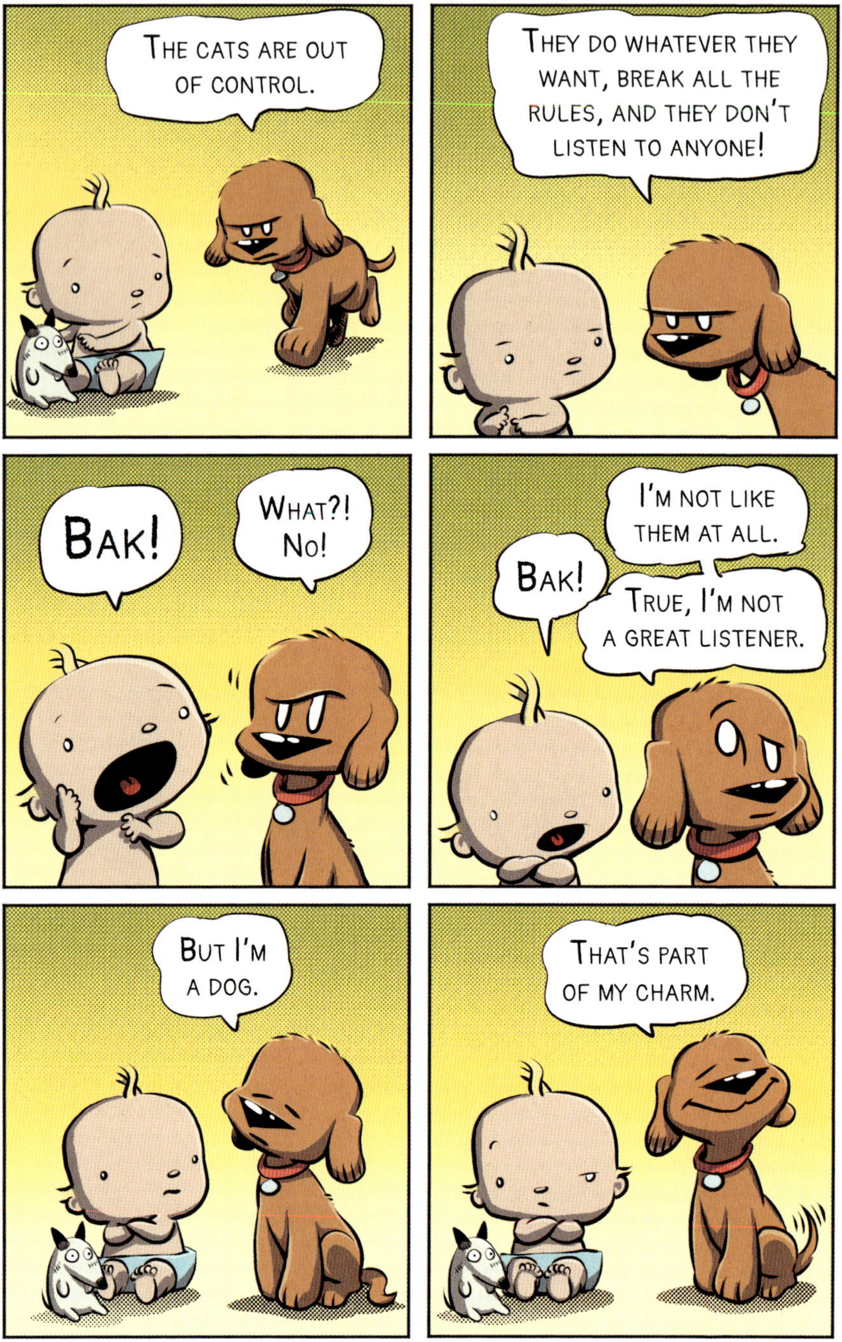
THE CATS ARE OUT OF CONTROL.
THEY DO WHATEVER THEY WANT, BREAK ALL THE RULES, AND THEY DON'T LISTEN TO ANYONE!
BAK!
WHAT?! NO!
I'M NOT LIKE THEM AT ALL.
BAK!
TRUE, I'M NOT A GREAT LISTENER.
BUT I'M A DOG.
THAT'S PART OF MY CHARM.

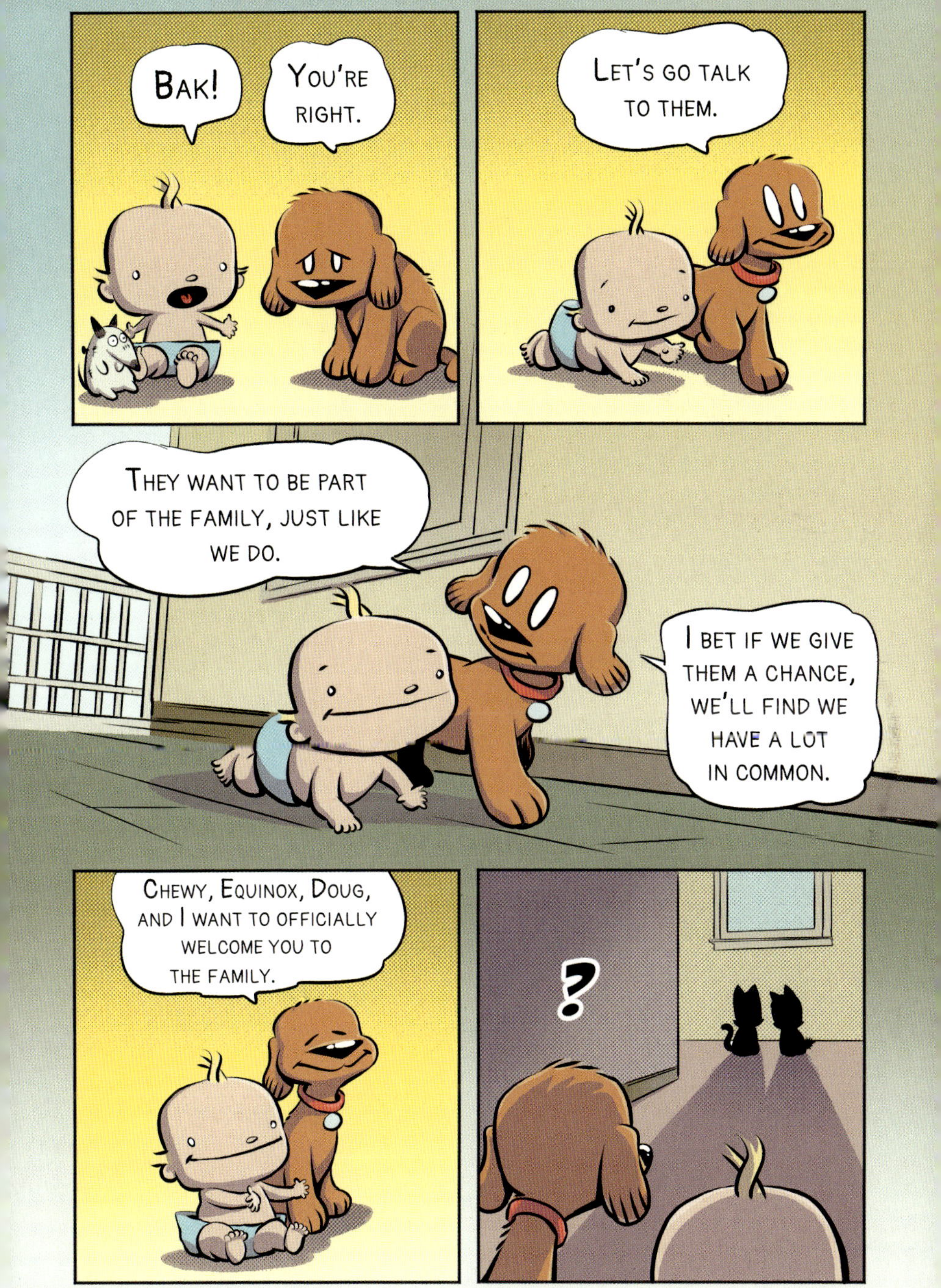
BAK!
YOU'RE RIGHT.
LET'S GO TALK TO THEM.
THEY WANT TO BE PART OF THE FAMILY, JUST LIKE WE DO.
I BET IF WE GIVE THEM A CHANCE, WE'LL FIND WE HAVE A LOT IN COMMON.
CHEWY, EQUINOX, DOUG, AND I WANT TO OFFICIALLY WELCOME YOU TO THE FAMILY.
?

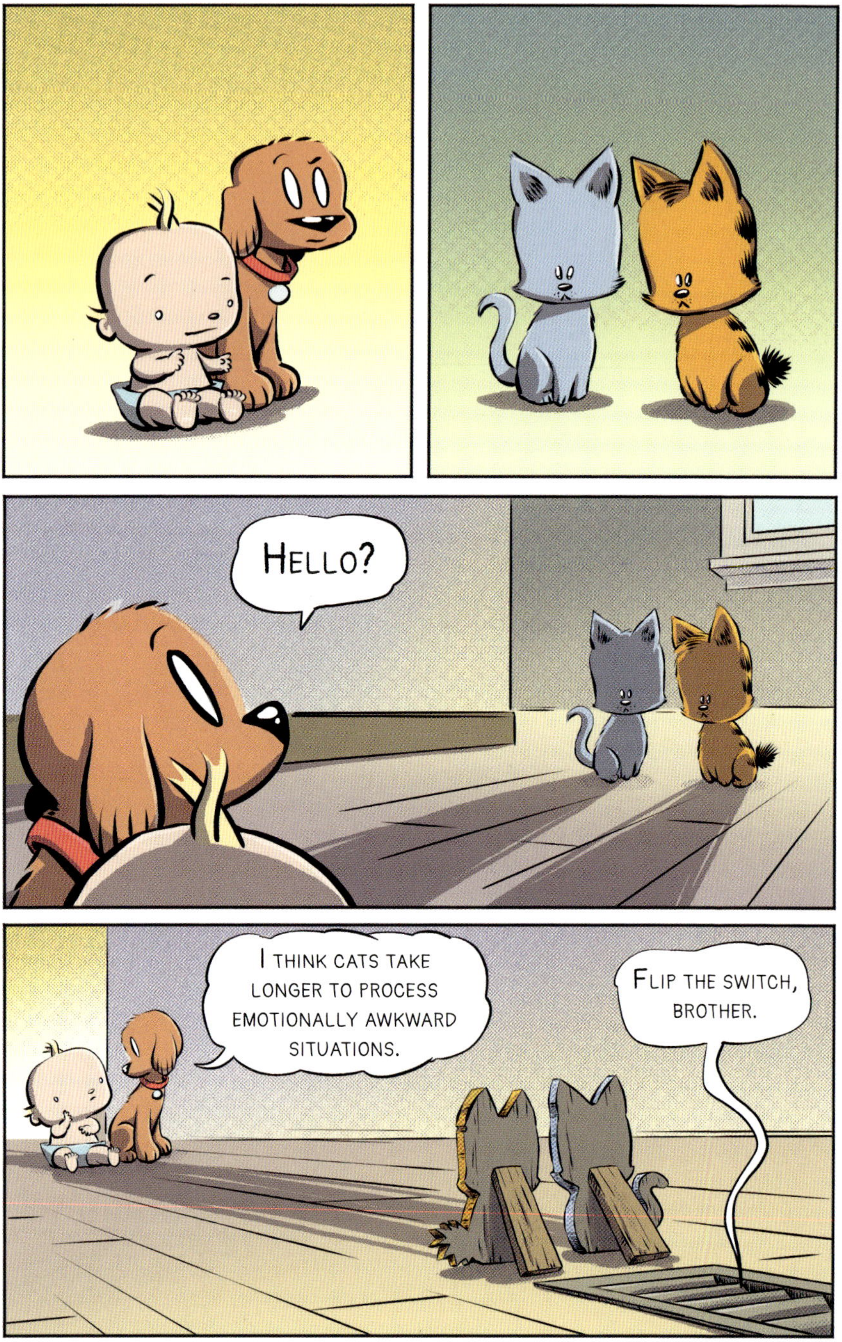
HELLO?
I THINK CATS TAKE LONGER TO PROCESS EMOTIONALLY AWKWARD SITUATIONS.
FLIP THE SWITCH, BROTHER.

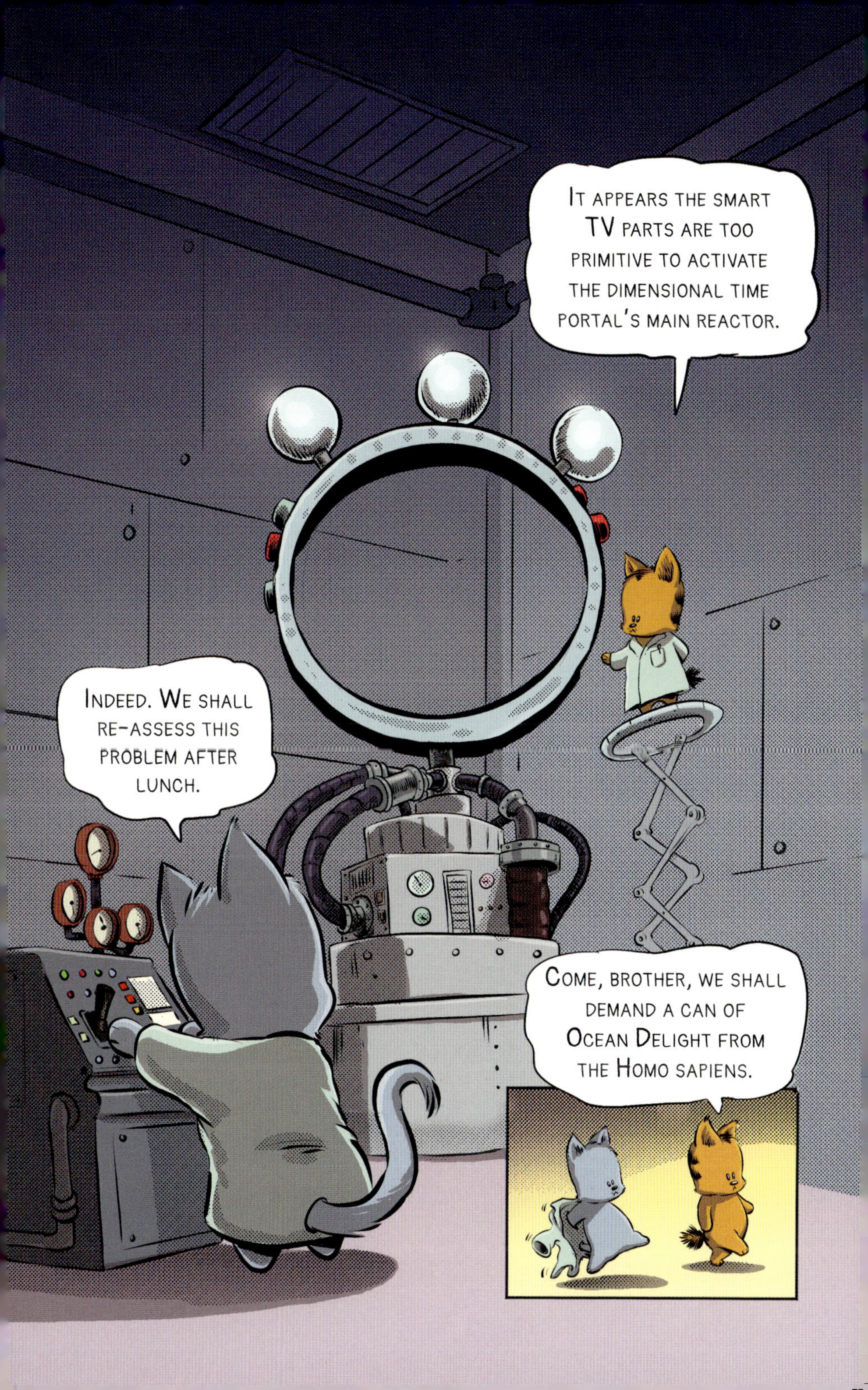
IT APPEARS THE SMART TV PARTS ARE TOO PRIMITIVE TO ACTIVATE THE DIMENSIONAL TIME PORTAL'S MAIN REACTOR.
INDEED. WE SHALL RE-ASSESS THIS PROBLEM AFTER LUNCH.
COME, BROTHER, WE SHALL DEMAND A CAN OF OCEAN DELIGHT FROM THE HOMO SAPIENS.

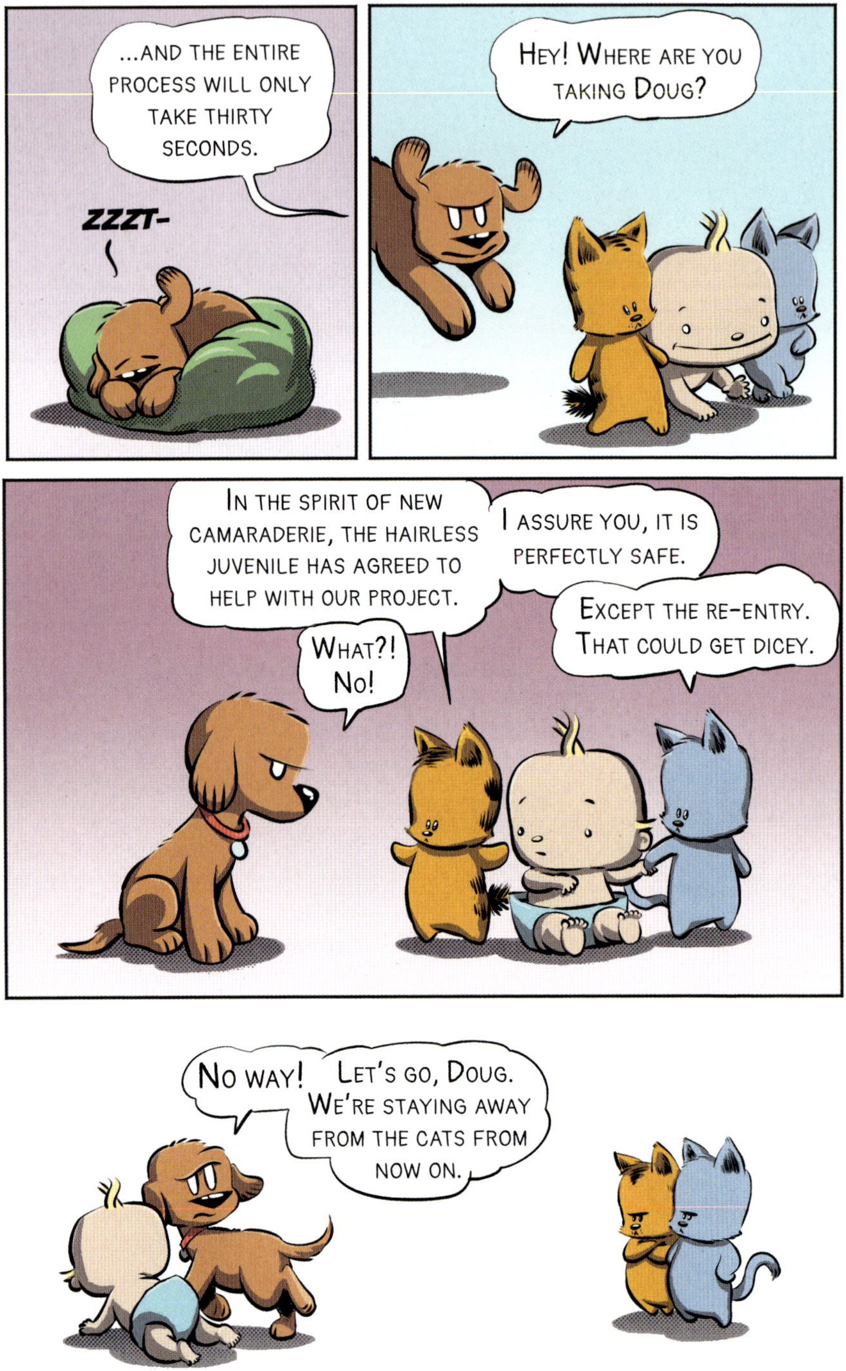
...AND THE ENTIRE PROCESS WILL ONLY TAKE THIRTY SECONDS.
ZZZT-
HEY! WHERE ARE YOU TAKING DOUG?
IN THE SPIRIT OF NEW CAMARADERIE, THE HAIRLESS JUVENILE HAS AGREED TO HELP WITH OUR PROJECT.
I ASSURE YOU, IT IS PERFECTLY SAFE.
EXCEPT THE RE-ENTRY. THAT COULD GET DICEY.
WHAT?! NO!
NO WAY!
LET'S GO, DOUG. WE'RE STAYING AWAY FROM THE CATS FROM NOW ON.

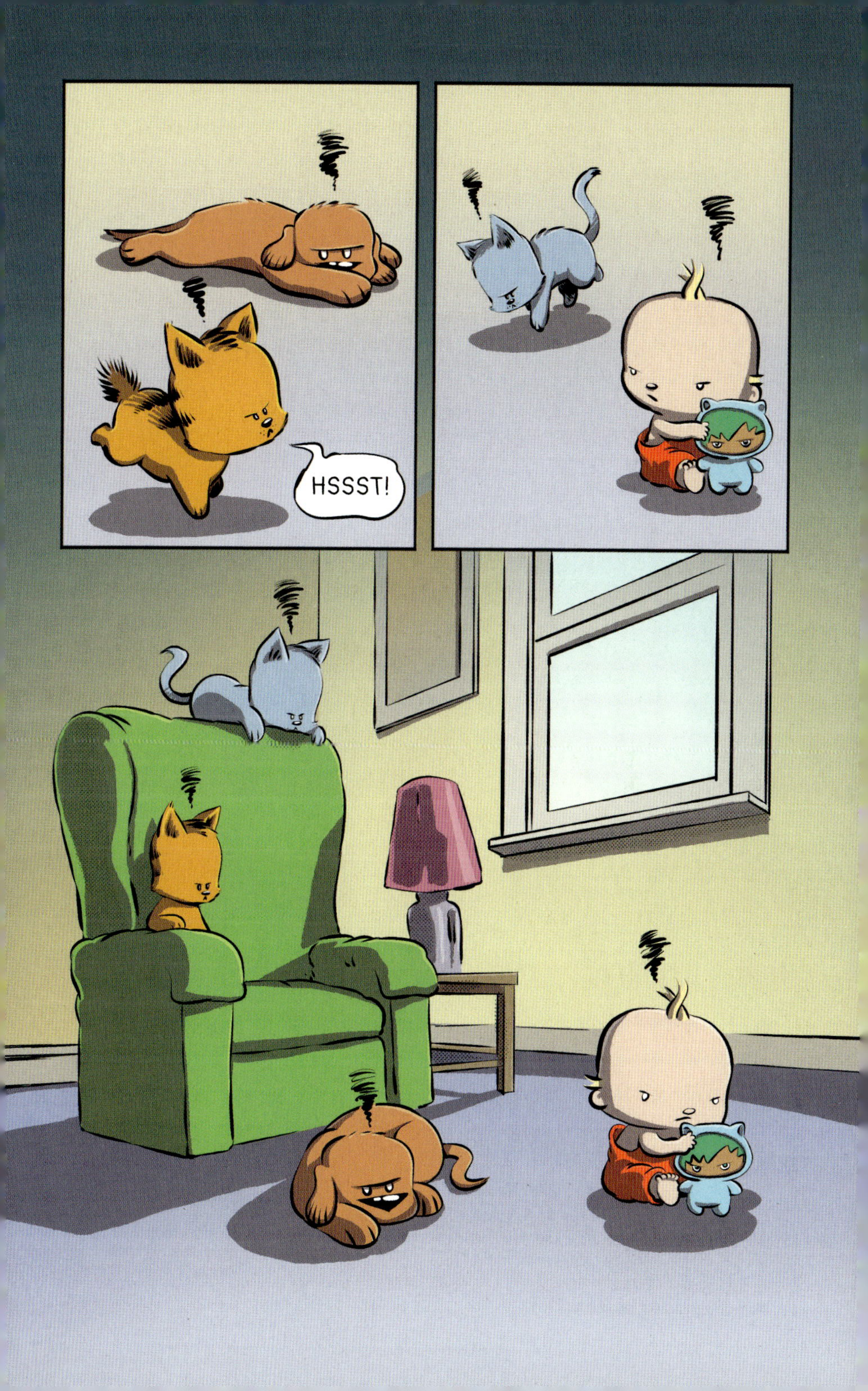
HSSST!

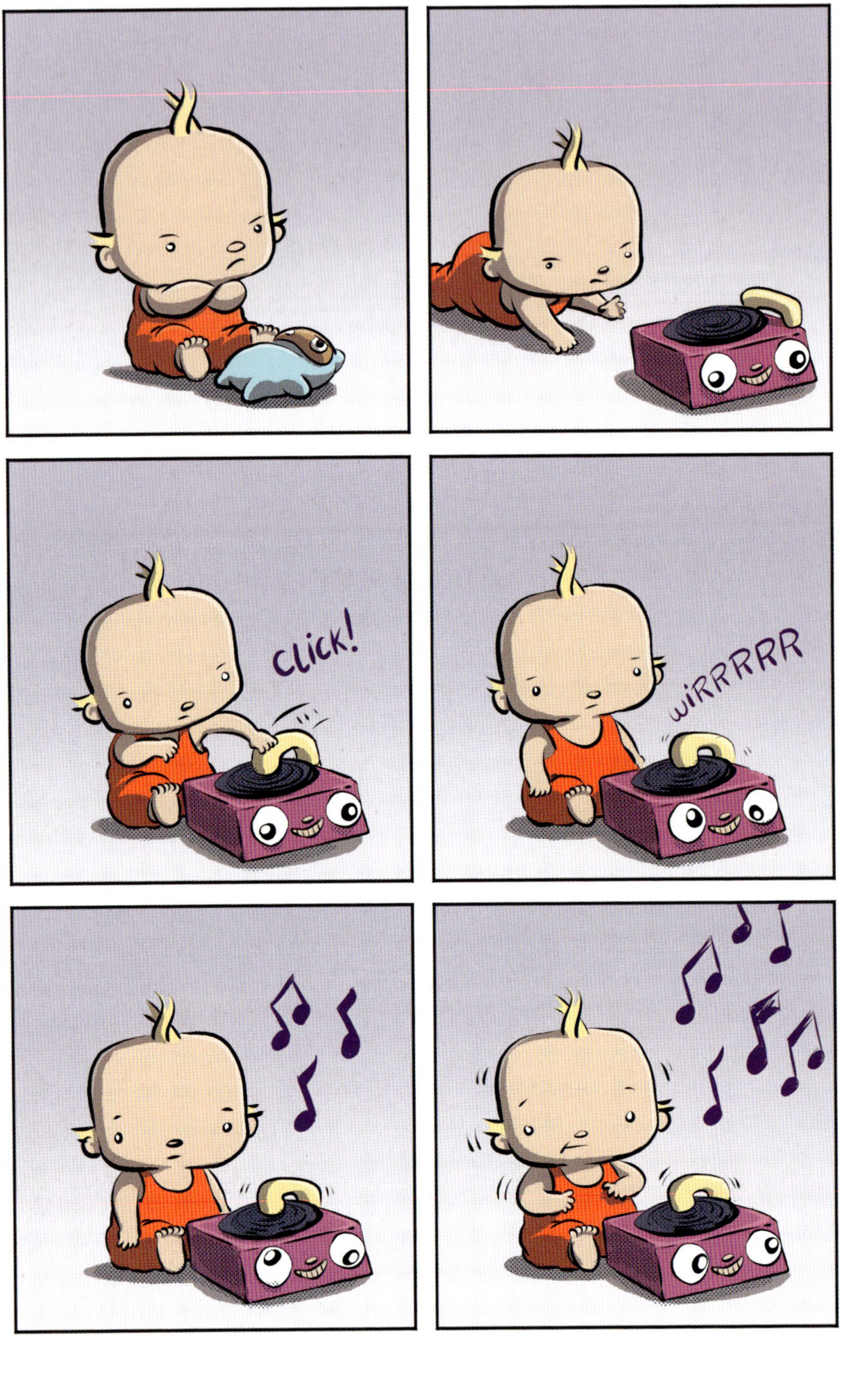
CLICK!
WIRRRRR

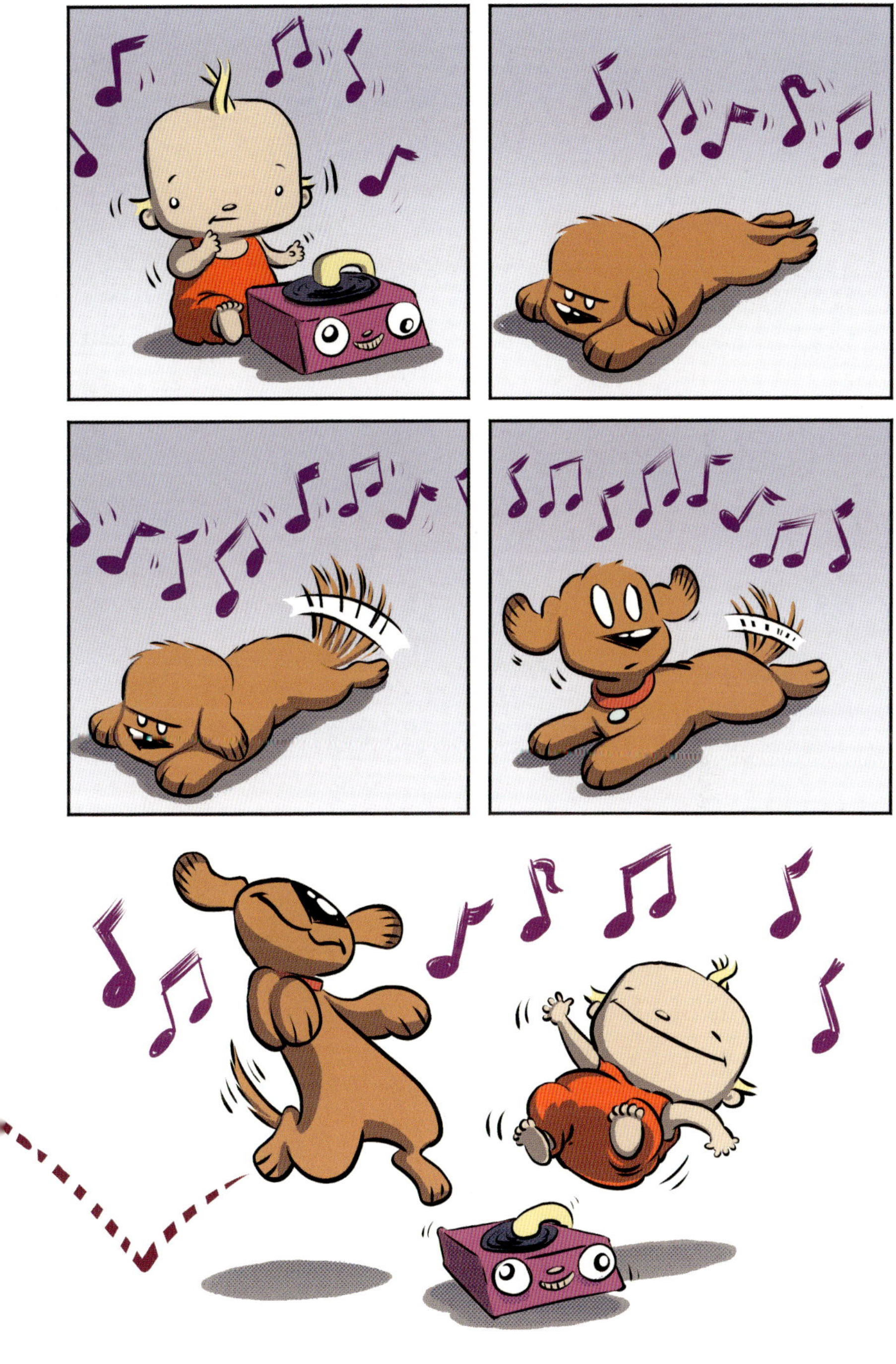

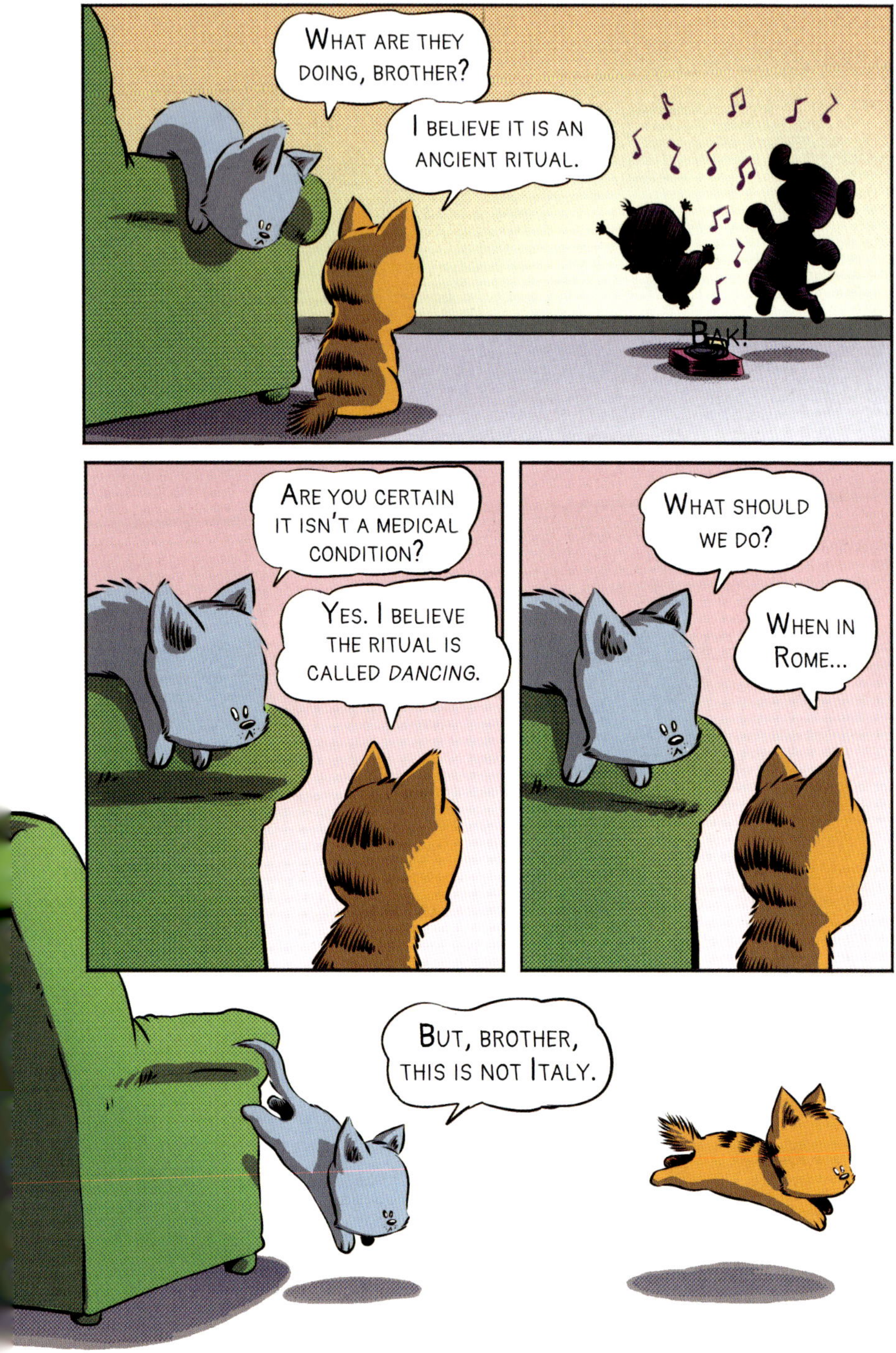
WHAT ARE THEY DOING, BROTHER?
I BELIEVE IT IS AN ANCIENT RITUAL.
BAK!
ARE YOU CERTAIN IT ISN'T A MEDICAL CONDITION?
YES. I BELIEVE THE RITUAL IS CALLED *DANCING*.
WHAT SHOULD WE DO?
WHEN IN ROME...
BUT, BROTHER, THIS IS NOT ITALY.

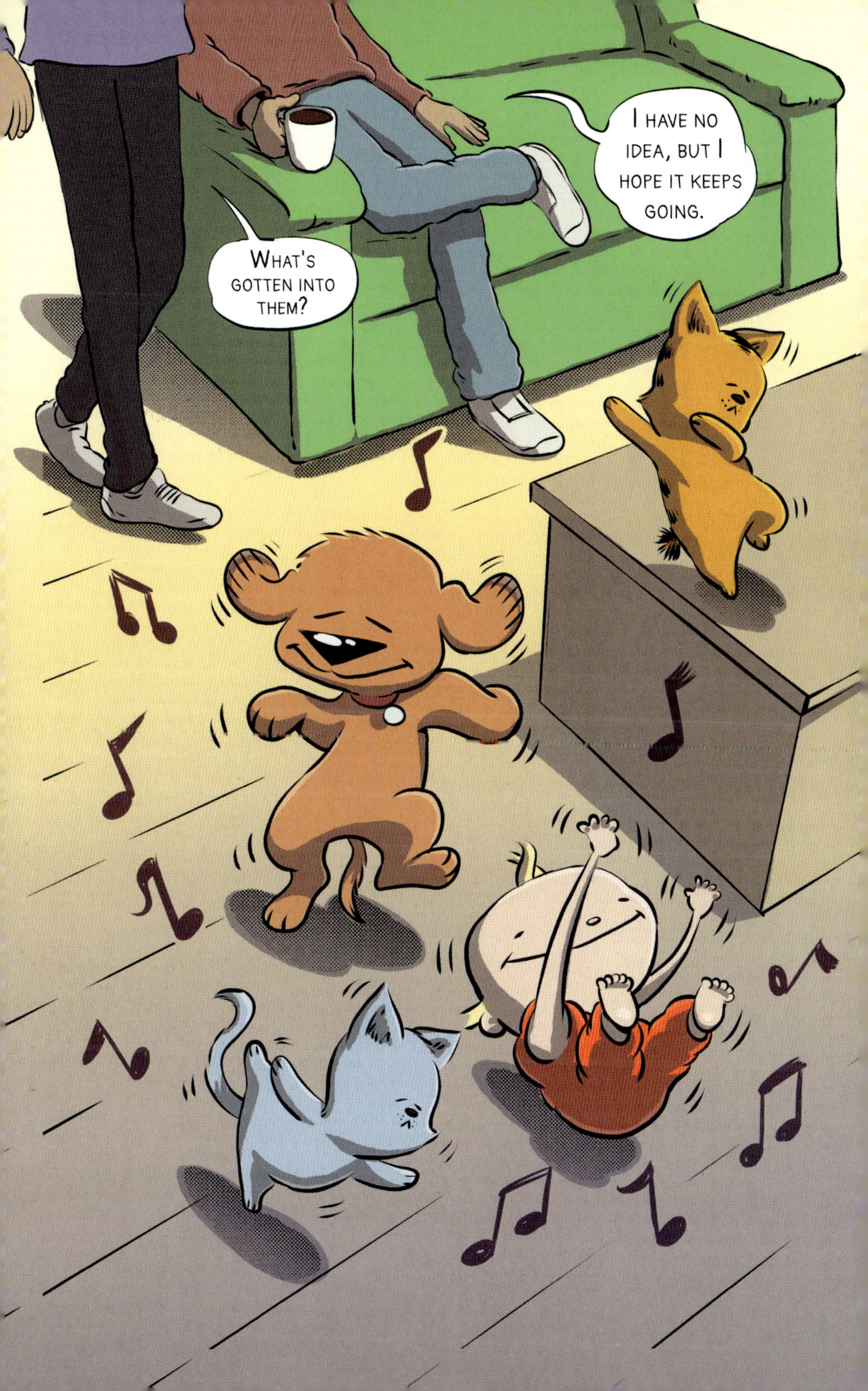
WHAT'S GOTTEN INTO THEM?
I HAVE NO IDEA, BUT I HOPE IT KEEPS GOING.

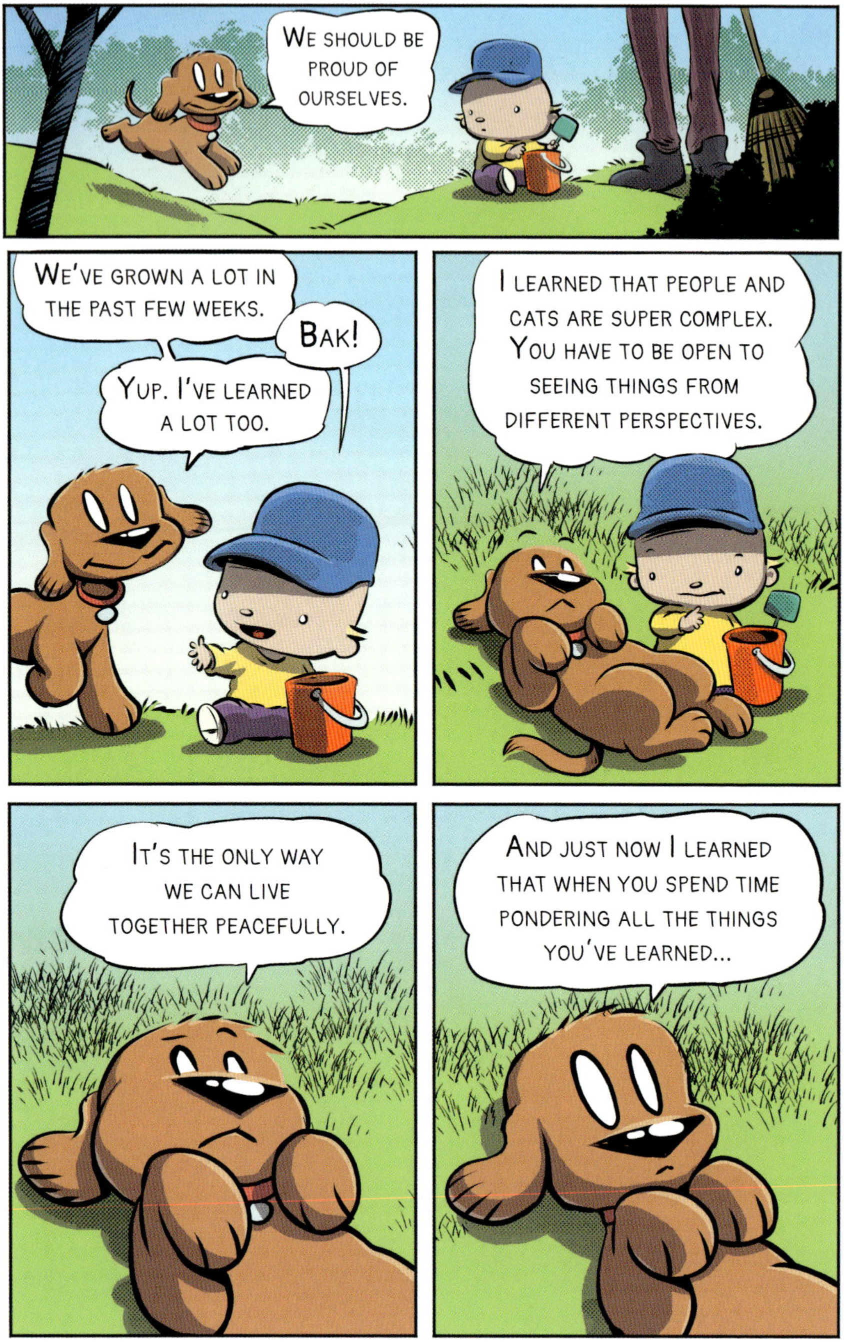
WE SHOULD BE PROUD OF OURSELVES.
WE'VE GROWN A LOT IN THE PAST FEW WEEKS.
BAK!
YUP. I'VE LEARNED A LOT TOO.
I LEARNED THAT PEOPLE AND CATS ARE SUPER COMPLEX. YOU HAVE TO BE OPEN TO SEEING THINGS FROM DIFFERENT PERSPECTIVES.
IT'S THE ONLY WAY WE CAN LIVE TOGETHER PEACEFULLY.
AND JUST NOW I LEARNED THAT WHEN YOU SPEND TIME PONDERING ALL THE THINGS YOU'VE LEARNED...

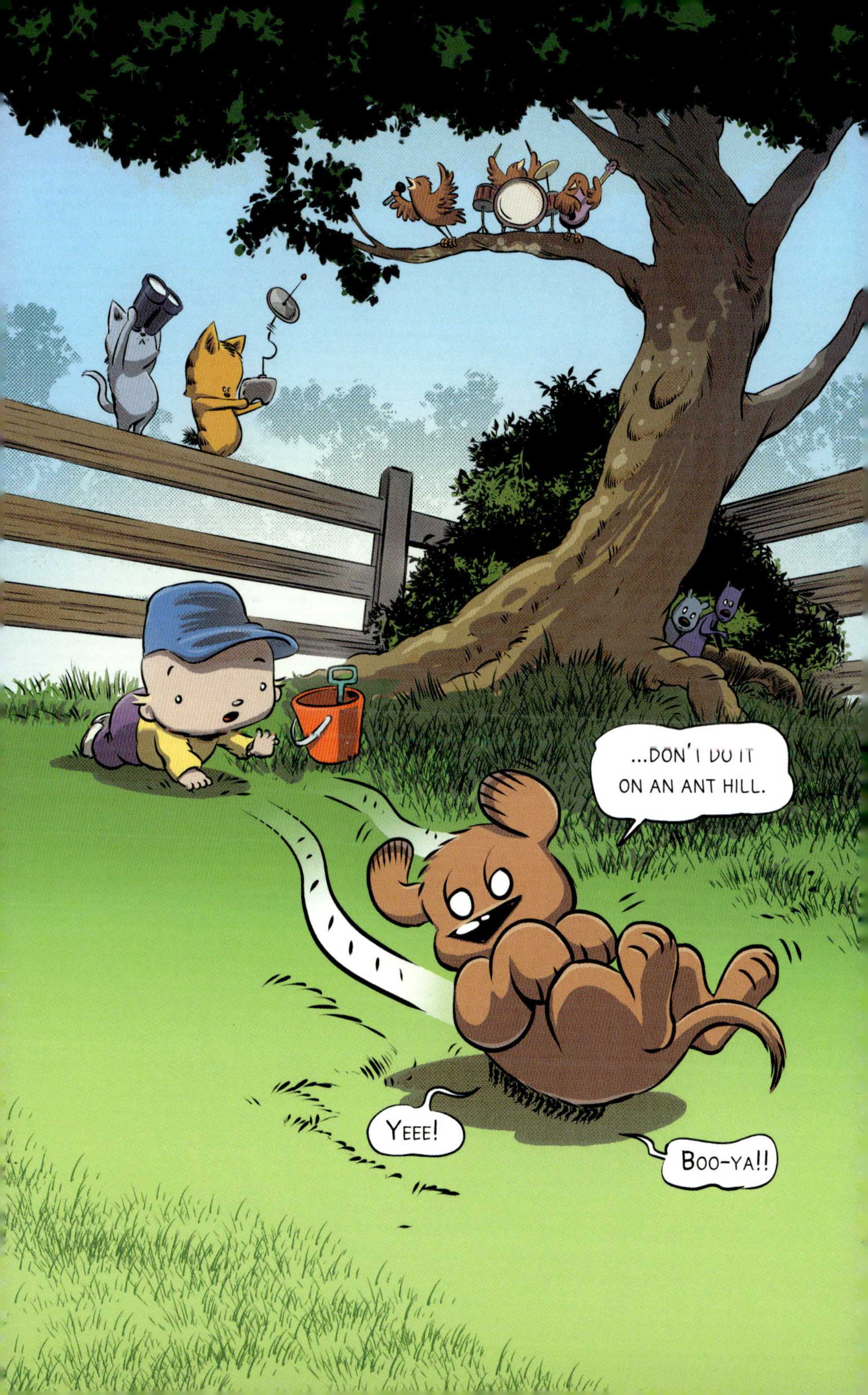
...DON'T DO IT ON AN ANT HILL.
YEEE!
BOO-YA!!

IT'S SOPHIE'S WORLD

MEET THE CREW

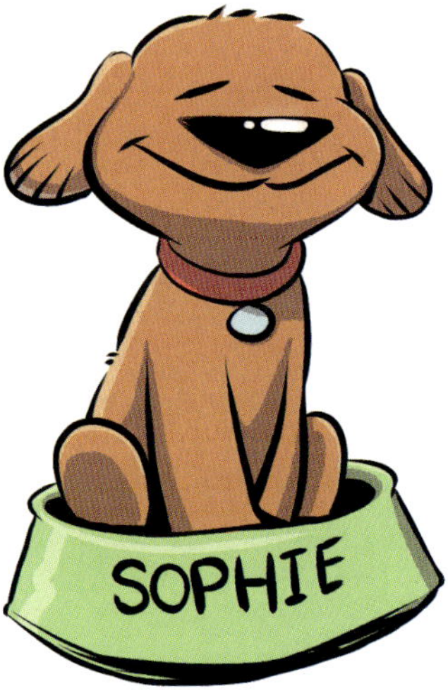
SOPHIE

SOPHIE

A lovable Chocolate Lab with an insatiable curiosity of the world around her that gets her into all sorts of trouble. She has a boundless imagination and often fantasizes herself as a great explorer, questing for cookies and cheese.

DOUG

The only thing bigger than his almost hairless head is his heart. Despite having a one-word vocabulary, he finds endless creative ways to communicate. He naps hard and dreams big.

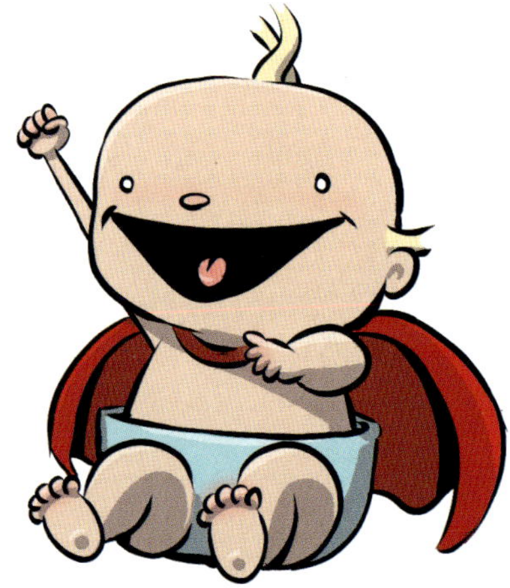

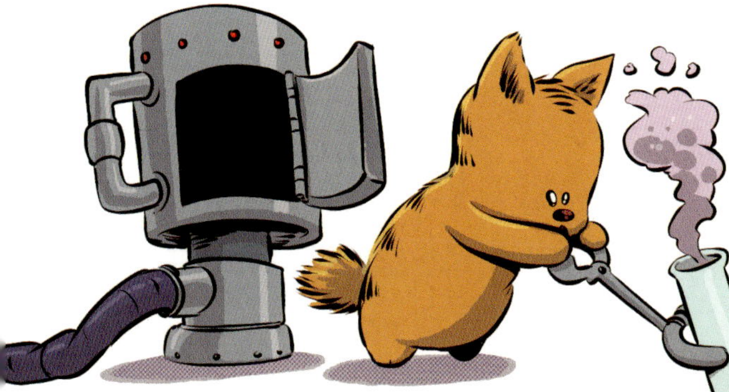

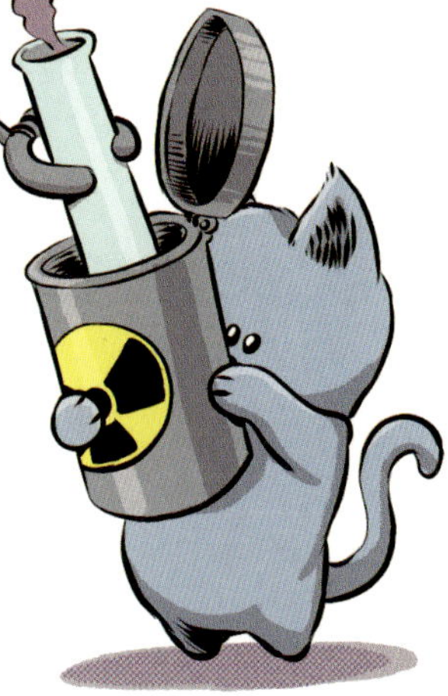

CHEWY AND EQUINOX

The fan-favorite cats are always up to something weird like quantum physics experiments, steampunk contraptions, or opening portals to other dimensions. Readers never know what's coming next.

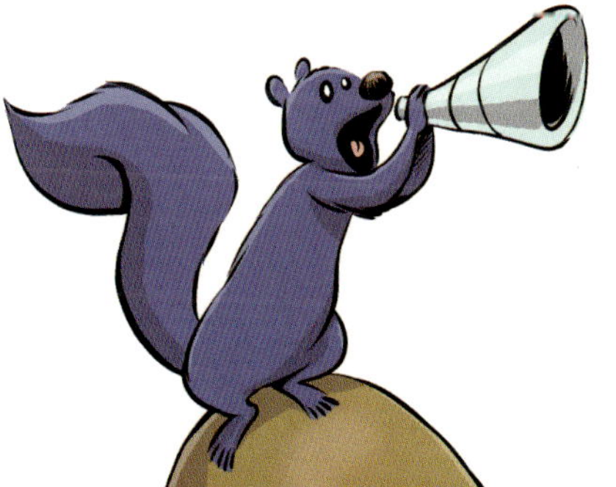

THE SQUIRRELS

They might be twitchy, but the squirrels love sharing their exuberantly odd perspective on the world.

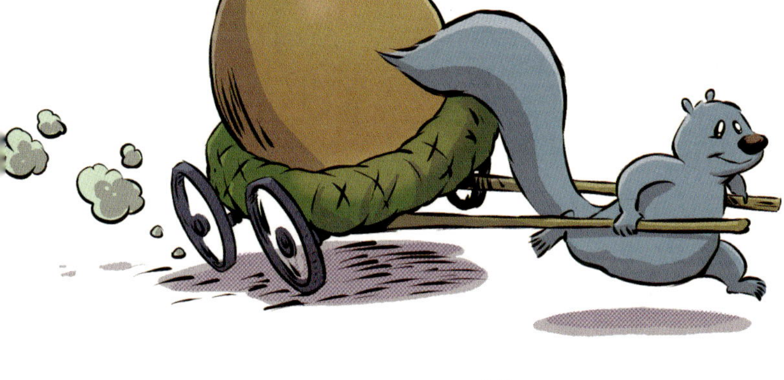

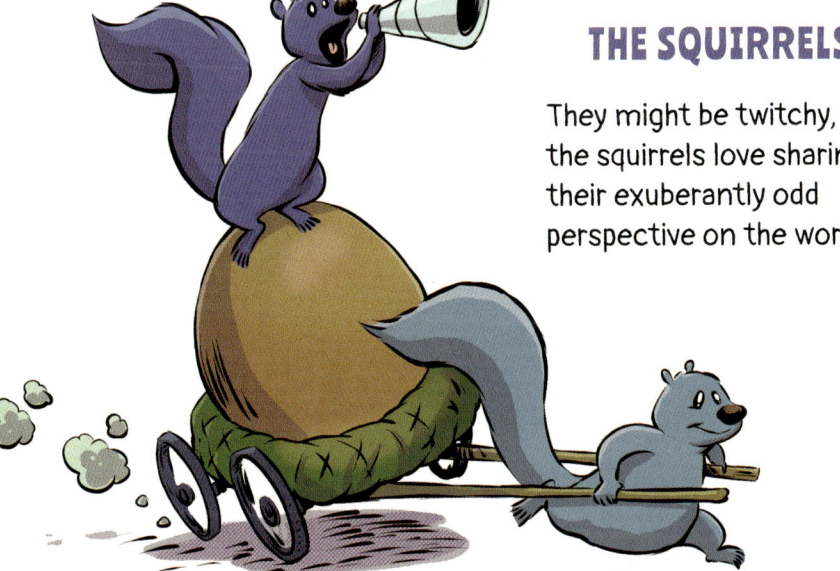

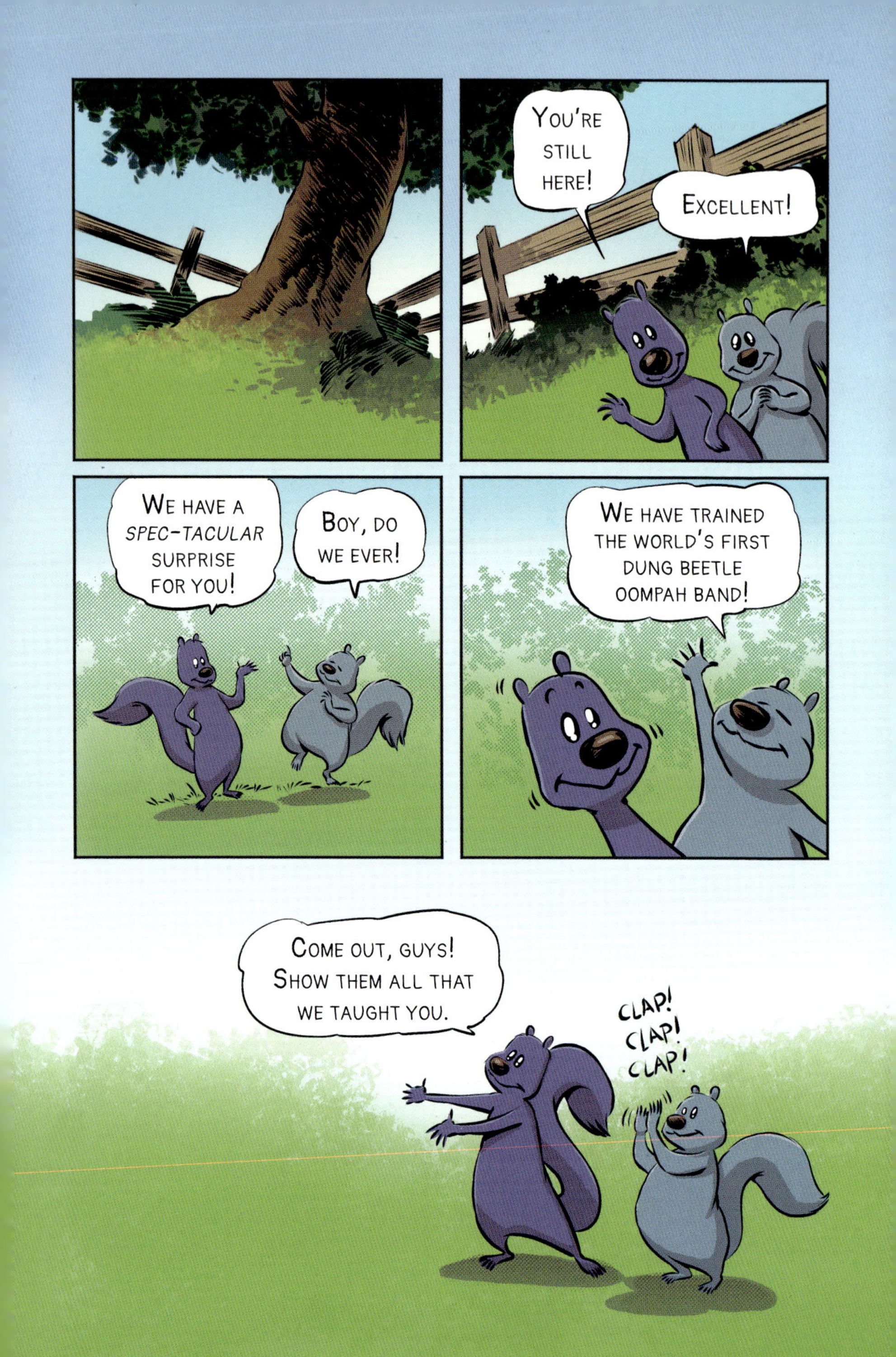
YOU'RE STILL HERE!
EXCELLENT!
WE HAVE A *SPEC-TACULAR* SURPRISE FOR YOU!
BOY, DO WE EVER!
WE HAVE TRAINED THE WORLD'S FIRST DUNG BEETLE OOMPAH BAND!
COME OUT, GUYS! SHOW THEM ALL THAT WE TAUGHT YOU.
CLAP! CLAP! CLAP!

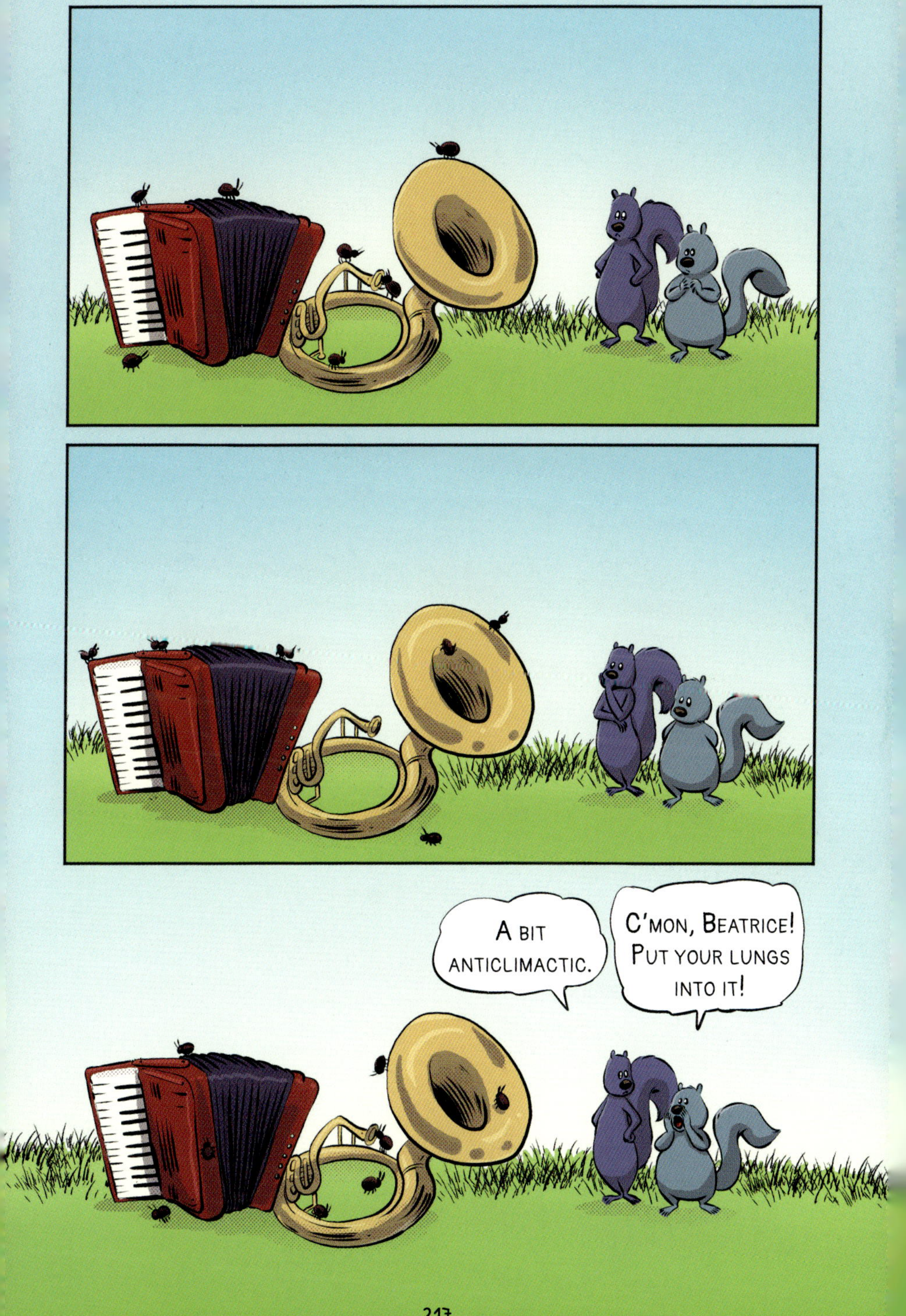

A BIT ANTICLIMACTIC.
C'MON, BEATRICE! PUT YOUR LUNGS INTO IT!

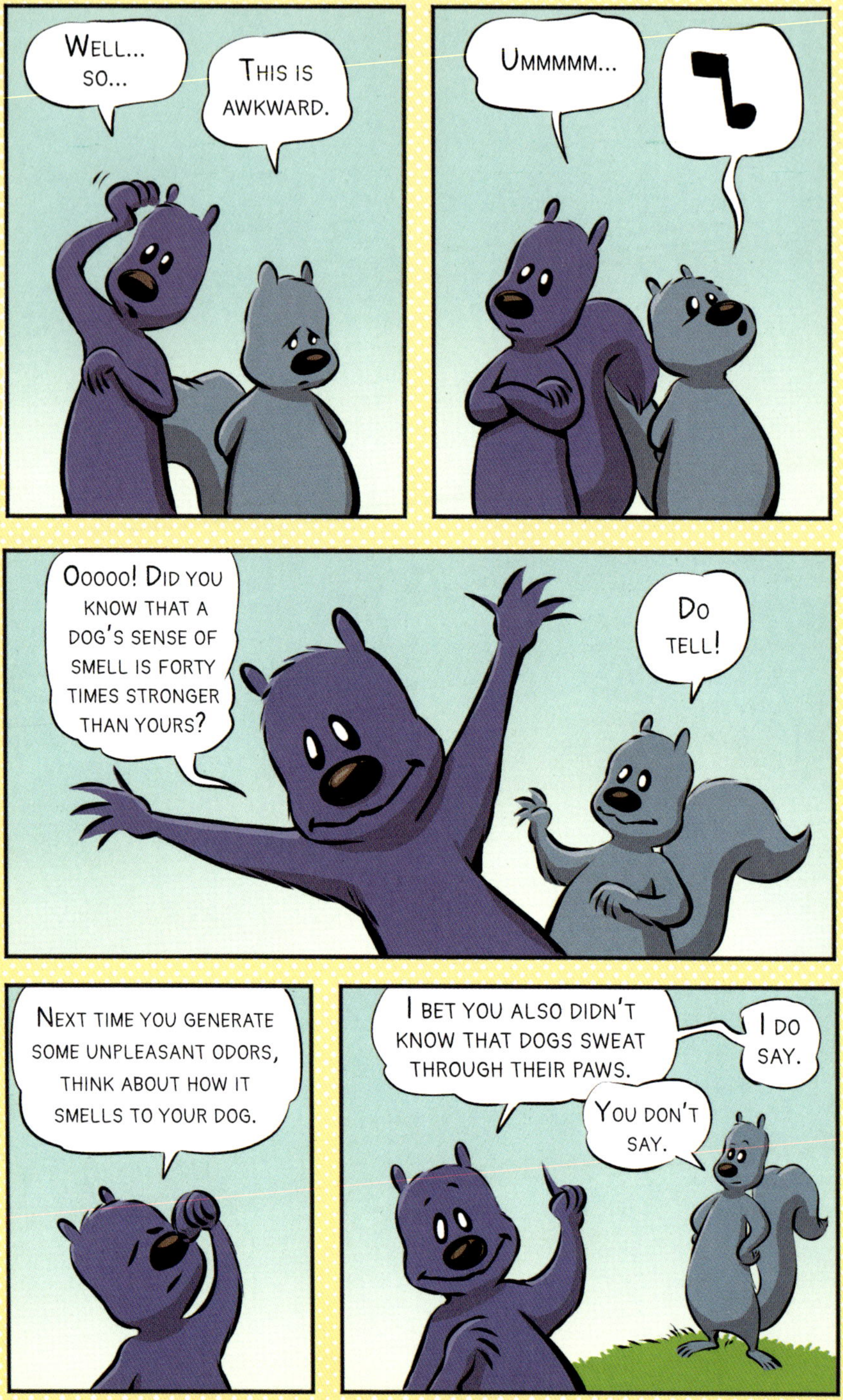
WELL... SO...
THIS IS AWKWARD.
UMMMMM...
OOOOO! DID YOU KNOW THAT A DOG'S SENSE OF SMELL IS FORTY TIMES STRONGER THAN YOURS?
DO TELL!
NEXT TIME YOU GENERATE SOME UNPLEASANT ODORS, THINK ABOUT HOW IT SMELLS TO YOUR DOG.
I BET YOU ALSO DIDN'T KNOW THAT DOGS SWEAT THROUGH THEIR PAWS.
YOU DON'T SAY.
I DO SAY.

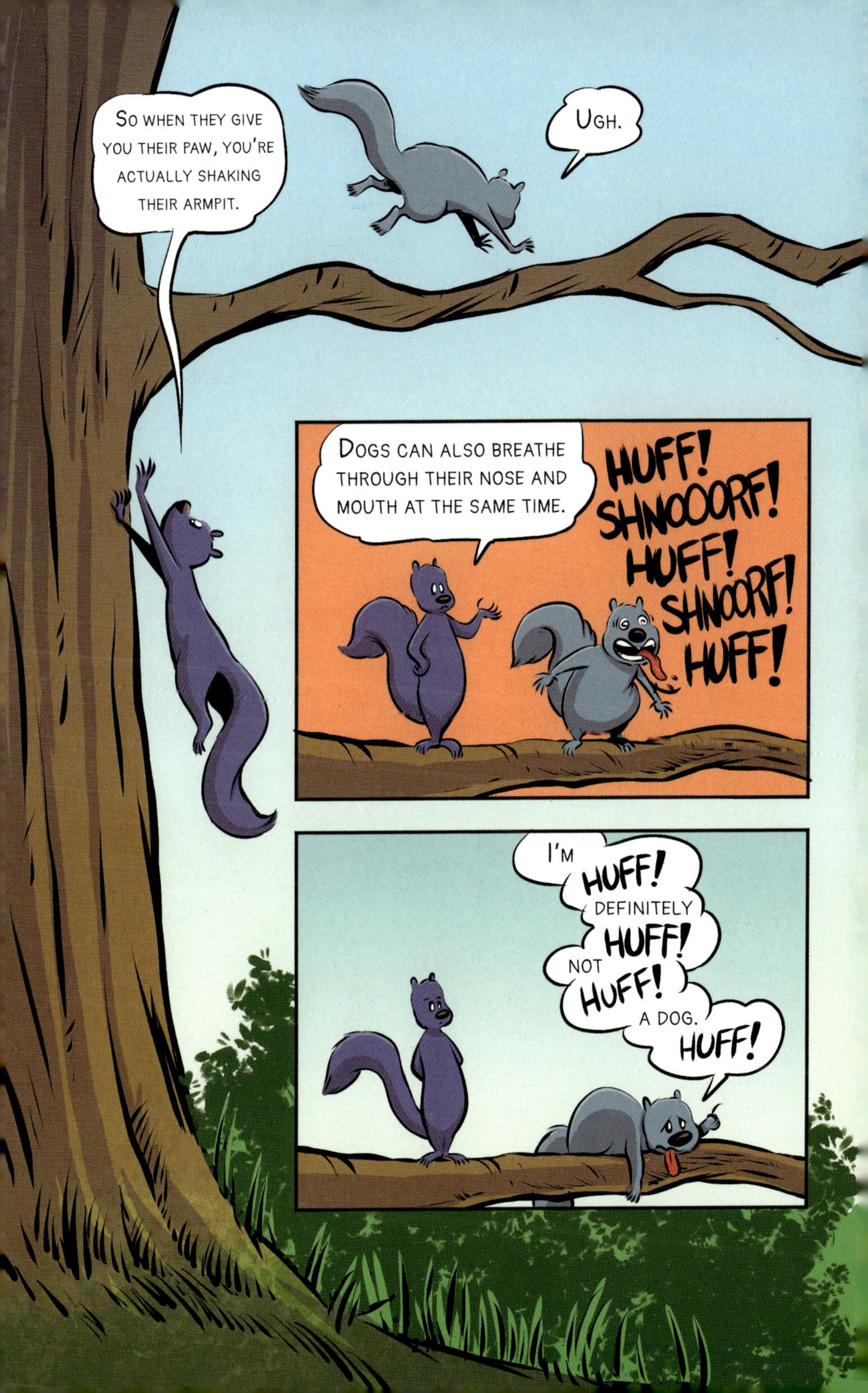

So when they give you their paw, you're actually shaking their armpit.
Ugh.
Dogs can also breathe through their nose and mouth at the same time.
HUFF! SHNOOORF! HUFF! SHNOORF! HUFF!
I'm HUFF! definitely HUFF! not HUFF! a dog. HUFF!

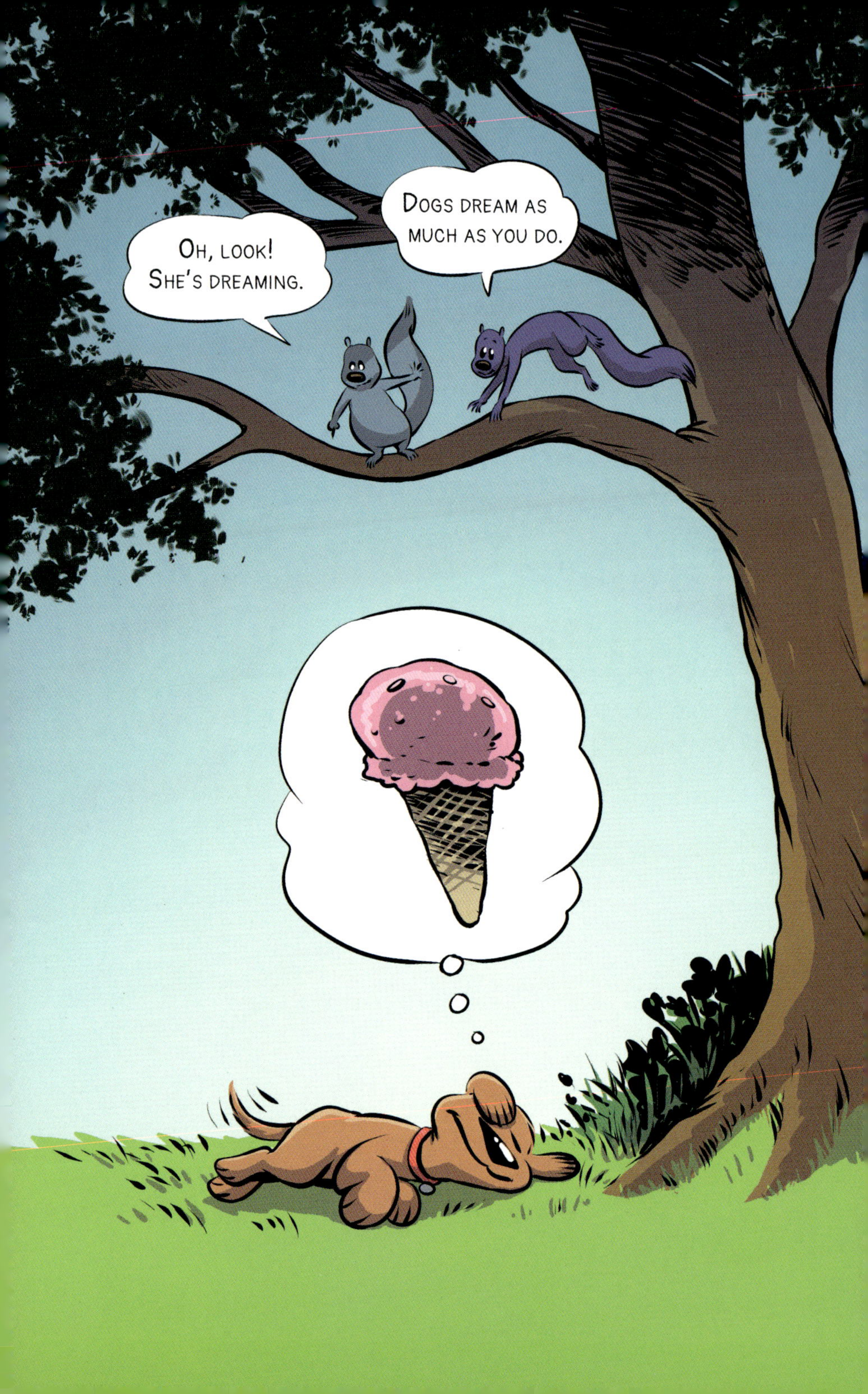
OH, LOOK! SHE'S DREAMING.
DOGS DREAM AS MUCH AS YOU DO.

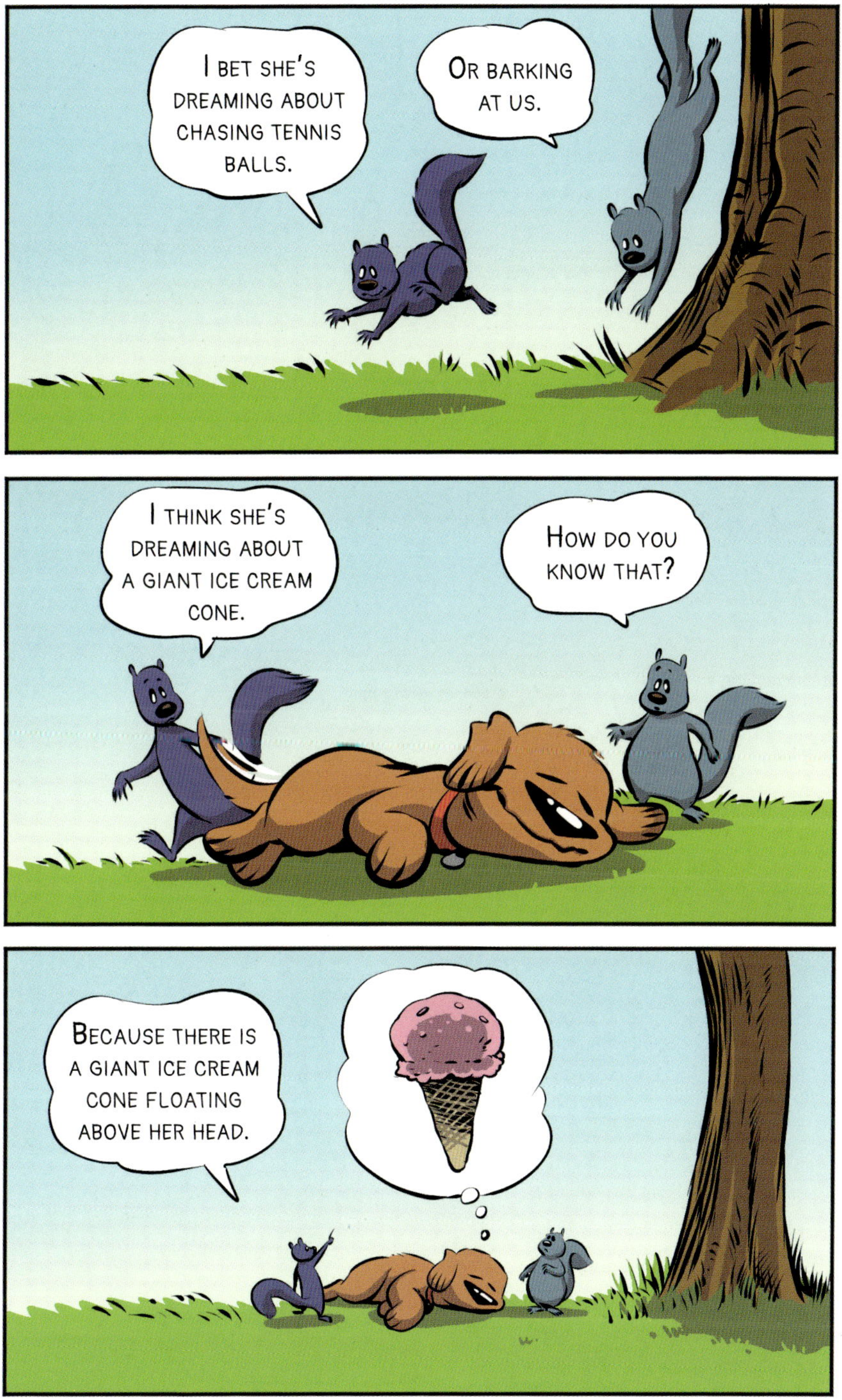
I BET SHE'S DREAMING ABOUT CHASING TENNIS BALLS.
OR BARKING AT US.
I THINK SHE'S DREAMING ABOUT A GIANT ICE CREAM CONE.
HOW DO YOU KNOW THAT?
BECAUSE THERE IS A GIANT ICE CREAM CONE FLOATING ABOVE HER HEAD.

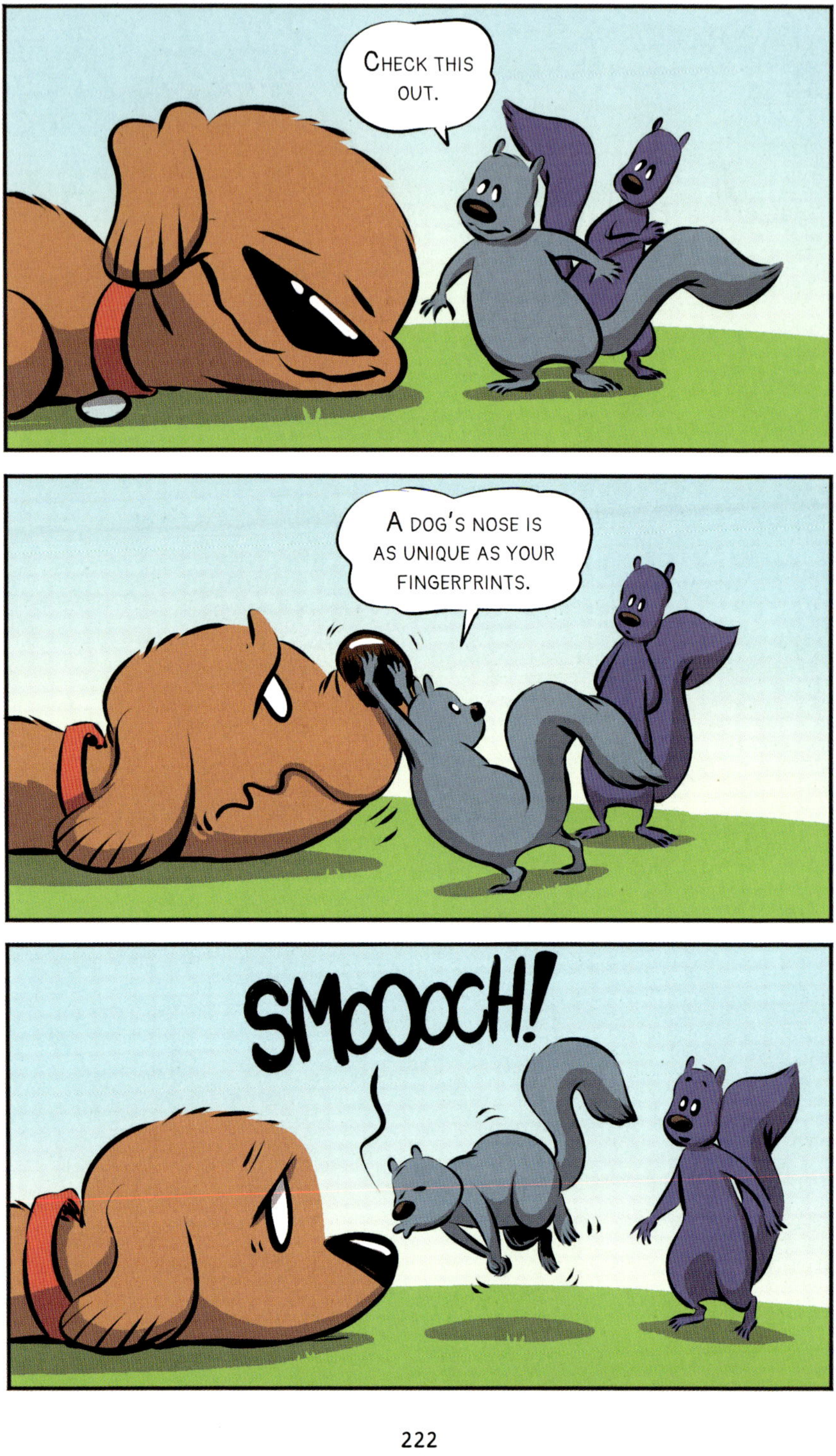
CHECK THIS OUT.
A DOG'S NOSE IS AS UNIQUE AS YOUR FINGERPRINTS.
SMOOOCH!

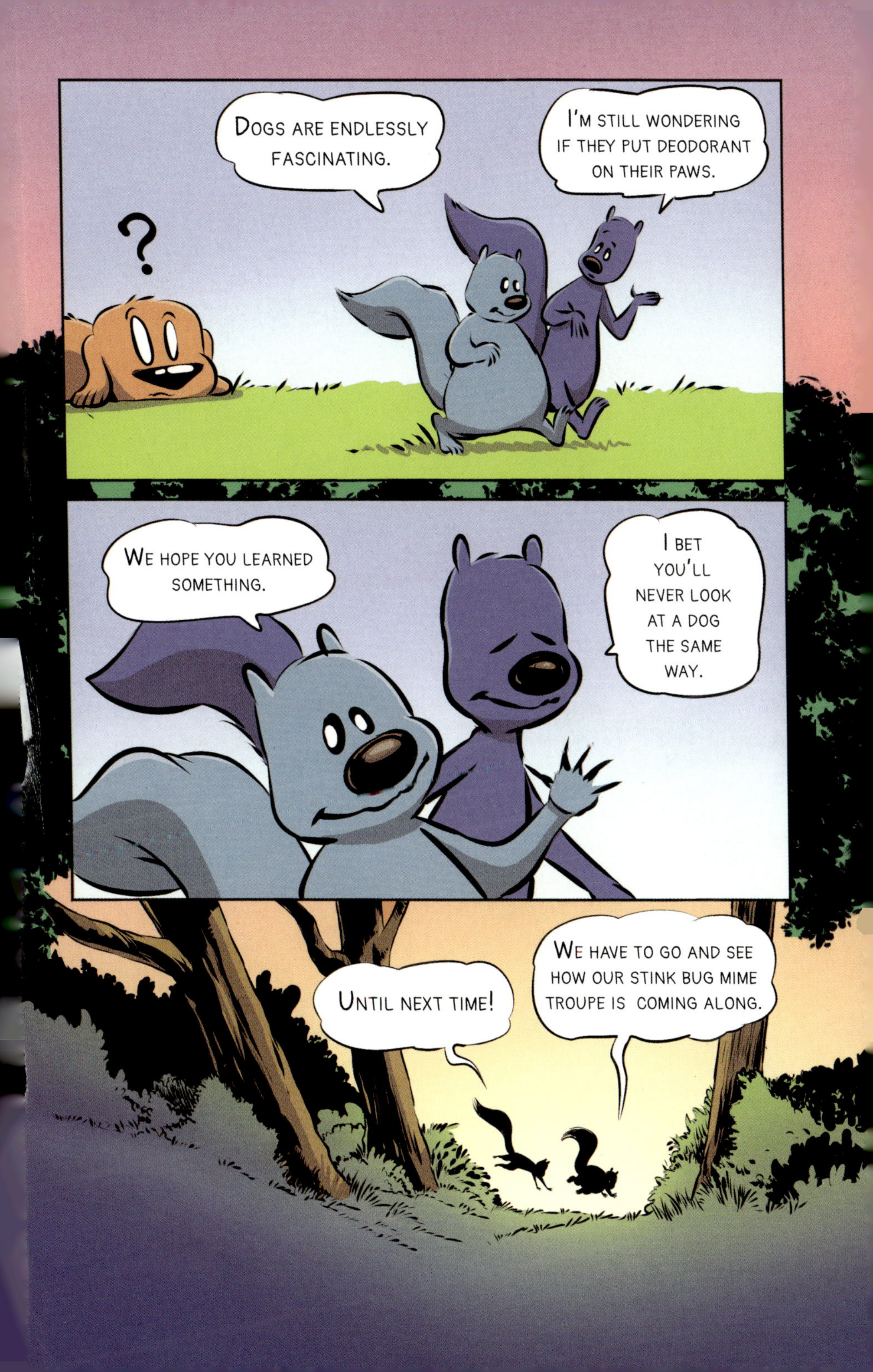

DOGS ARE ENDLESSLY FASCINATING.
I'M STILL WONDERING IF THEY PUT DEODORANT ON THEIR PAWS.
?
WE HOPE YOU LEARNED SOMETHING.
I BET YOU'LL NEVER LOOK AT A DOG THE SAME WAY.
UNTIL NEXT TIME!
WE HAVE TO GO AND SEE HOW OUR STINK BUG MIME TROUPE IS COMING ALONG.

ABOUT THE AUTHOR-ILLUSTRATOR

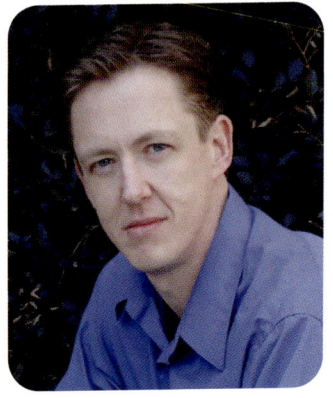

BRIAN ANDERSON

(www.briandersonwriter.com) Brian Anderson is the author of *The Conjurers* trilogy (*Rise of the Shadow, Hunt for the Lost,* and *Fight of the Fallen*) as well as the picture books *Nighty Night, Sleepy Sleeps, The Prince's New Pet,* and *Monster Chefs*. He is also an optioned screenwriter and the creator of the syndicated popular comic strip *Dog Eat Doug*. He lives in North Carolina with his family, which includes a herd of rescued dogs and cats.

READ THEM ALL: SOPHIE 2 FRANKENSTEIN'S HOUND

"SOPHIE IS THE PERFECT MIX OF HEART, HUMOR, AND HILARITY!"
- LINCOLN PEIRCE, CREATOR OF BIG NATE
SOPHIE
FRANKENSTEIN'S HOUND
Brian Anderson

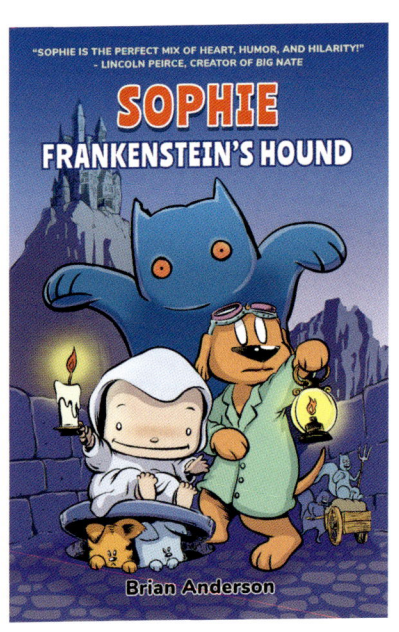

Get ready for double the fun with the Sophie series, launching two awesome books in 2024! In *Frankenstein's Hound* (Book 2), join a gang of foster puppies on a dragon hunt, witness Sophie and Jack's epic battle against the Ninja Socks, and brace yourself for the mischievous duo Chewy and Equi, who create a Cat-ificial Intelligence robot that thinks just like them. Ever wondered what the Yeti of Enlightenment has to spill about the secret of happiness? Dive into the book and unravel the excitement yourself!

YAY!
Sophie 3 is coming in 2025!

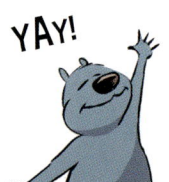

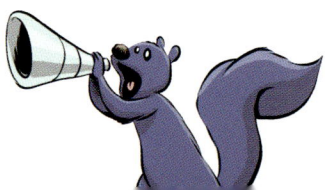